LEOPARD'S FURY

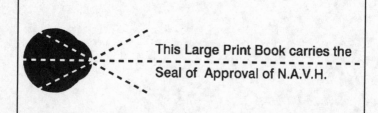

This Large Print Book carries the
Seal of Approval of N.A.V.H.

LEOPARD'S FURY

CHRISTINE FEEHAN

THORNDIKE PRESS
A part of Gale, Cengage Learning

GALE
CENGAGE Learning®

Farmington Hills, Mich • San Francisco • New York • Waterville, Maine
Meriden, Conn • Mason, Ohio • Chicago

GALE
CENGAGE Learning·

Thorndike Press® Large Print Romance.
The text of this Large Print edition is unabridged.
Other aspects of the book may vary from the original edition.
Set in 16 pt. Plantin.

LIBRARY OF CONGRESS CATALOGING-IN-PUBLICATION DATA

Names: Feehan, Christine, author.
Title: Leopard's fury / by Christine Feehan.
Description: Waterville, Maine : Thorndike Press, 2016. | Series: A Leopard novel | Series: Thorndike Press large print romance
Identifiers: LCCN 2016042667| ISBN 9781410496676 (hardcover) | ISBN 1410496678 (hardcover)
Subjects: LCSH: Leopard men—Fiction. | Shapeshifting—Fiction. | Large type books. | GSAFD: Love stories. | Fantasy fiction.
Classification: LCC PS3606.E36 L455 2016 | DDC 813/.6—dc23
LC record available at https://lccn.loc.gov/2016042667

Published in 2017 by arrangement with The Berkley Publishing Group, an imprint of Penguin Publishing Group, a division of Penguin Random House LLC

Printed in Mexico
1 2 3 4 5 6 7 21 20 19 18 17

For my beautiful, courageous granddaughter Shylah. You face every situation with courage and grace, and I'm always so very proud of you! This one's for you.

FOR MY READERS

Be sure to go to christinefeehan.com/ members/ to sign up for my private book announcement list and download the free ebook of *Dark Desserts.* Join my community and get firsthand news, enter the book discussions, ask your questions and chat with me. Please feel free to email me at Christine@christinefeehan.com. I would love to hear from you.

ACKNOWLEDGMENTS

With any book there are many people to thank. In this case, the usual suspects: Domini, for her research and help; my power hours group, who always make certain I'm up at the crack of dawn working; and of course Brian Feehan, who I can call anytime and brainstorm with so I don't lose a single hour. Thank you to Denise Tucker for all her hours of hard work researching and putting my website together. You're much appreciated.

1

"Damn it, Evangeline, you need to come back home."

Evangeline Tregre shook her head and took a slow look around the bakery. It wasn't exactly thriving, but it was still afloat and becoming more popular every day. The walls were painted a soft blue. She'd done that herself. Every cupboard, every placement of the display cases, every single thing from the lettering to the floor — she'd done it. The dusty old, torn-up space had been renovated by her. It was now cozy and inviting with the tables and chairs. She loved the way the bakery smelled. Every single morning when she got up to bake, she looked forward to the day. Back "home" she detested her very existence.

"*This* is home, Robert. I love it here and I'm stayin'. It's more home to me than that place ever was." She kept her voice quiet. Low. She was used to being silent. She didn't argue, nor did she like arguments. She especially didn't like Robert Lenoux coming to her hard-won business and insisting she return. "In any case, I thought you were travelin', going to the Borneo rain forest."

She knew all about Robert, although she'd never actually met him until he'd walked into her bake shop. He had been sent away in disgrace, had served a brief jail stint, but got out of a real sentence from the law by turning evidence against his friends. Murderers. He'd participated in beating and robbing the elderly in their homes, in raping exotic dancers. He had committed countless crimes against his lair, and looking at him, she knew he didn't care about anyone but himself. Especially women.

"Fuck that," Robert spat. "I'm not goin' to be sent away from my home by some outsider who thinks he can order me around. The entire point of goin' to Borneo is to bring home a woman. You'll do just fine. I don' care that you aren' a shifter."

Her stomach lurched and then tied into knots. She took a deep calming breath. She'd left that world behind. She wasn't about to allow a bad-tempered, evil male leopard, one who no doubt didn't mind hitting a woman, into her life.

"The answer is no. I am never goin' back there."

"You have a duty to the rest of us." Robert reached out, settled hard fingers around her upper arm and yanked her close to him.

Alarm skittered down her spine. She took a step back but his fingers only tightened into an iron band. "Let go of me, Robert. *Now.*" She hissed the word, letting him see she wouldn't stand for being pushed around by him. By anyone. Not ever again. "I want you to leave. This is my shop and I'm askin' you politely to leave."

The bell over the bakery door tinkled merrily, at odds with the tension in the room. Both turned their heads toward the sound. Evangeline's breath caught in her throat. She'd grown up around dangerous men. Criminals. Horrible, cunning, viciously cruel men. She knew criminals. She had a radar for them. No one needed radar to know without a single doubt that the man walking through the door of her bakery was dangerous. Terrifyingly so.

He glanced around her beautiful little shop and saw every single detail, yet he didn't *see* it because there could be no appreciation. None. There was no emotion on his face or in his flat, cold, *dead* eyes. Beautiful eyes. *Gorgeous* eyes. A shocking blue. Like the blue ice of a glacier. His lashes were long and as black as night, framing those icy blue eyes. But there was not a single hint of emotion, not even when his gaze settled on Robert's hand on her arm. Absolutely nothing. He walked. He breathed. He probably killed people. But if he did, he did it with absolutely no emotion. And he'd heard them arguing. She could tell by the way he looked at Robert's fingers wrapped around her.

He was very tall, ruggedly built, all roped muscle, and he looked absolutely invincible. She was used to men with muscle, but he was a fighter, through and through. The way he moved — the control, the containment, smooth, fluid, easy, as if he glided or flowed across the floor rather than walked. He did that in absolute silence too, as if his very expensive Italian leather shoes didn't actually touch the floor.

His suit looked as if it had cost as much as the renovations on the bakery space and been custom made for him — which it probably had been. His icy gaze remained on Robert's fingers digging into her bicep. She'd all but forgotten he was gripping her so hard until fear sent a chill arrowing through her.

Robert must have felt it too. He was

leopard. A shifter. She knew from gossip he had a nasty temper and was as strong as an ox. Like most shifters, he didn't fear much. His leopard would shred an enemy in seconds if he were threatened. Still, he let her go and stepped back away from her. Away from the newcomer. Subtly putting her between them.

"Can I help you?" Evangeline asked. Her voice sounded different, even to her. Her accent was deeper, a soft sultry lure she hadn't meant to throw, but really? Every single cell in her body was aware of him. The bayou came out in her voice more than it ever had before, and it sounded like an invitation to spend the night floating down a lazy canal together under a starlit night.

She wasn't the type of woman to flirt with a man, let alone speak to him in a voice like that. She knew better. She knew danger when she saw it, but she came alive the moment he entered her bakery. Her body had been asleep but now it was wide awake and very aware of every inch of the Iceman. She'd already nicknamed him and thought of him as *her* Iceman, even if it was just in her fantasies.

His eyes focused on her. He looked at her through a blue glacier without once blinking. "Coffee. Black. A piece of your cinnamon cake."

His voice was deep. Dark. As cold as his eyes. As cold as Siberia — the dead of winter in Siberia. At the same time, it was low and sensual. She couldn't stop the little shiver that ran through her body at the sound of it. Heat pooled low and wicked, and something wild and feral deep inside her stirred. She had an unexpected urge to take all of that molten heat spreading through her and see if she could unthaw the Iceman's cold.

He spoke with a heavy Italian accent. For some reason that shocked her. She didn't expect Italian. More . . . Russian. Maybe because she associated him with Siberia. She couldn't get that out of her mind. To her, he would always be her Russian Iceman.

Evangeline nodded and turned away from his male potency. He was definitely out of her league. Out of her world. Her universe. This was not a man any sane person would want in their life. Her hands trembled as she poured the coffee — her special all-natural brew customers raved about. The pieces of the cinnamon cake were generous and she arranged one on one of the oblong-shaped plates with her fancy gold logo on it. The *E* for Evangeline running through

16

the center of it.

He took it without a word. He simply nodded at her, those icy blue eyes never lighting up, never registering life in them at all. No emotion. No nothing. He certainly wasn't feeling the electrical attraction she was. He turned away and moved across the room. He pulled a chair around so that his back would be to the wall facing the plate-glass entry. He dragged a small table in front of him, put the coffee and the plate on the table and then went to the small stand where the napkins and silverware were.

Evangeline took a deep breath and let it out. She couldn't — *wouldn't* — stare at him. Robert stepped close again, leaning into her, so that his breath puffed into her ear, an intrusion that annoyed her. She'd been so aware of the Iceman that she'd all but forgotten Robert.

"We aren' finished, Evangeline. I'm takin' you back with me."

"I asked you to leave," she said equally as quiet. "And please don' come back."

Robert hissed at her, his eyes going sheer cat, his temper rising at her defiance. She stood her ground, her heart suddenly pounding. She didn't want to be afraid of him, but it was impossible with him standing so close, scowling fiercely at her. He was

17

deliberately trying to intimidate her. She barely knew him, only what her friend Saria Boudreux — now Donovan — had told her about him, and none of it was good. Saria knew everyone, and Robert Lenoux was from one of the seven shifter families leasing thousands of acres in the swamp.

Robert stepped even closer, deliberately towering over her smaller figure. Once again his fingers bit into her arm, this time hard enough to leave bruises. There was the softest of rustlings and they both turned to see the Iceman standing a few feet from them, one great big fist encased in a very expensive leather glove, shoving a napkin into the trash can. His eyes were on Robert's face and they were colder than ever. The blue in them appeared to be glowing, a flame beneath all that ice.

Evangeline's breath caught in her lungs and everything in her stilled. He was leopard. A shifter. It seemed impossible there in San Antonio, a place far from where she grew up. Shifters were rare and to find one in a city . . . Impossible, but there was no mistaking those eyes. Exotic. Terrifying. Totally focused on Robert.

"Let. Her. Go." Each word was soft. Spoken in a low tone. Ice dripped from the voice. The Iceman didn't look at Evangeline, his entire focus on the man hurting her.

Robert couldn't fail to see those eyes, read death in them and know what the Iceman was. He hissed a curse word, let go of Evangeline, turned and stormed out, slamming the door. The Iceman turned back toward his table.

"Thank you," Evangeline said softly. Meaning it. She'd left all that behind her and she never wanted to go back. It didn't matter that this man clearly was a criminal. Or far more dangerous than Robert could ever be. Or that Robert ran like a rabbit from him when his leopard had to have been raking and clawing for a fight. He'd stepped in when he didn't have to, and she was grateful. He deserved to know it.

The Iceman turned slightly, looking at her over one broad shoulder. His glacier-blue eyes swept over her and then he nodded slightly before turning away.

Evangeline let out her breath slowly and turned back to straightening the baked goods in the case. She got up at three A.M. every morning and baked the day's goods so they were fresh. She couldn't afford to hire anyone else to work in her shop, so she did it all. The baking, the coffee, the dishes, the cleaning of the shop, *all* of it, and she took pride in her work. She was getting by, managing to pay the bills each month, and that meant she could keep her independence. She was determined to make it on her own.

She snuck another quick look at her Iceman. He wasn't paying her the slightest bit of attention. Not. At. All. She knew she was easy on the eyes. Since coming to San Antonio, men had flirted outrageously with her. She had no idea what to do with their attention, nor did she want it, but she'd come to realize all the things Saria had tried to convince her about her looks might actually be true.

She wasn't quite five foot four, so she didn't have those long legs that attracted men, but she had generous curves and a small waist to emphasize them. Her hair was long and very dark, her eyes a true green, like emeralds, a startling color surrounded by long, thick, black lashes. She had great skin, a luscious mouth and a small, straight nose. All in all, she wasn't hard to look at. But he wasn't looking.

Fortunately, so she didn't make a complete fool of herself, customers began to trickle in. She knew when he got up and left that he didn't look back.

Over the next week, her Iceman came in three more times. He tried something different each time by pointing or jerking his chin, not speaking. She noticed he preferred things with cinnamon and he liked apples. He always took his coffee black and all three times he indicated he wanted a refill. Each time he came in he rearranged her tables so he could sit with his back against the wall. After the third time, she moved the table herself and left it there permanently for him. He didn't acknowledge that she'd done it, and in a way she was glad. She needed the business, but she didn't want a relationship with him.

She'd thought with time he would become less scary, less intimidating, but she was wrong. He was more so. An aura of danger clung to him like a second skin. He never laughed. He never smiled. He barely acknowledged her, yet he was aware of everything, every movement, in her shop and on the street. She was certain he was armed to the teeth and sometimes she was afraid the few cops who frequented her shop would come in at the same time and there would be a shoot-out or something equally as awful.

Two months passed and he came in three times a week, sometimes four, but he never spoke beyond placing his order. She found herself watching for him. Smiling at him when he came in. He never smiled back, but he did stay longer. At least a half an hour longer than he had before.

A few others dressed in Italian suits came in over the third month, never at the same time as her Iceman, but she knew he'd sent them her way. Business seemed to pick up even more after that, as if seeing people in her shop brought in even more customers. That meant she had to work harder, baking more goods, but she didn't mind; she was finally making it.

She'd all but forgotten Robert. He was waiting for her to open on a Thursday morning, a day her Iceman rarely came in. That told her Robert had been watching the store, probably looking for a pattern. Her heart stuttered when she saw him come through the door. He casually reached over and turned her sign from *open* to *closed.*

She reached for her cell phone. He leapt across the room the way leopards could do, jerking it from her hand and flinging it onto the floor a distance away. It shattered, pieces scattering. Evangeline took a deep breath and moved out from behind the counter, not wanting anything to get broken.

"You bitch," Robert bit out. "You aren' gettin' away with this."

"What are you talkin' about? I'm not

tryin' to get away with anythin'."

"You told Saria I wasn't in the rain forest. You couldn't just let it go."

She frowned, shaking her head. "I haven't spoken to Saria in months. I've been too busy." She should have. Her friend would be worried about her.

Robert stalked her across the room, and she couldn't help herself. In spite of her determination not to give ground, she did, backing up almost to the door.

"Fuckin' liar. Tryin' to get me in trouble. I was goin' to let it go. The last thing I want is a woman who can't shift, but now you're goin' to pay for tryin' to get Drake and the others to come lookin' for me. This is the way it's goin' to be. I've been stayin' in a room in town but now I'm goin' to be stayin' with you. Hand over the keys to your house. And I need money. I know you got it, and you can give it to me."

"You're out of your mind if you think I'm goin' to let you move in with me. I earned any money I have and it goes to payin' bills."

He backhanded her. Hard. Her cheek felt as if it had exploded. Her eyes teared up and she found herself on the floor. He was strong, incredibly strong, and his leopard was close. She could see it in his eyes, those

23

yellowish-green eyes glowing with menace at her.

Deep inside her, wildness woke a feral, dark creature; furious, raging even. The skin raised along her arms and legs, an itch heralding the arrival of her other.

No, Bebe, she said sharply. *He can't know about you.* She'd take a beating before she'd ever expose her best friend to such an abomination of a shifter.

Robert came at her again, deliberately using the stalking motion of the leopard. When she tried to get up off the floor, he hit her again, striking the same side of her face. The pain made her feel sick to her stomach.

She heard the bell over the door as if in the distance, and then, blinking to clear the tears from her eyes, she saw Robert doubling over, grunting, his breath a sob. Her Iceman was standing over him, his big, gloved fist hitting hard, over and over. She heard ribs crack. *Heard* them. A short uppercut to the chin staggered Robert and he went to his knees. The Iceman caught him around the waist and half walked, half dragged him out the door.

Evangeline tried to pull herself up by using the wall, all the while staring out the window. There was a black town car with darkened windows parked in front of her bakery. A man in a suit held the door open while the Iceman thrust Robert inside and then climbed in after him. It wasn't more than thirty seconds at most before he emerged, looking exactly the same.

Through the open door of the car she caught a glimpse of Robert slumped on the seat, his neck at an odd angle. She shivered as her Iceman spoke briefly to the driver and then slammed the door. He waited until the car drove off, spoke briefly into his phone and then returned to the shop.

He hadn't changed expression. Not once. Not when he'd been beating the crap out of Robert and not when he'd gotten out of the car. She was almost certain Robert was dead. Her Iceman hadn't bothered to call his leopard to fight Robert's. She knew that would have been a sign of respect and clearly the Iceman didn't feel any at all for Robert.

"Are you all right?" He crouched beside her.

Up close he smelled as good as he looked. A little wild. But like a cool forest, one covered in snow in the winter. His eyes were even more beautiful than she'd first thought. So cold they made her shiver. So blue she thought she could drown.

"Evangeline." She needed him to know

her name. "I'm Evangeline."

"I know." He touched her cheek with gentle fingers. He wore gloves, so it wasn't skin-to-skin contact, but it didn't matter, her body still reacted with heat.

How could he know her name? It wasn't like it was on the bakery anywhere. Just an *E.* She'd used calligraphy and the letter came out elegant, just what she was going for in her shop. *Small Sweet Shoppe.* She'd loved that for some odd reason and she still did.

"This is where you tell me your name."

He wrapped his arm around her waist and lifted her to her feet, retaining his hold so that she didn't fall. That something wild in her unfurled. Stretched. Reached toward her Iceman until her skin felt tight, itched like crazy and then receded.

Don't you dare, she cautioned.

She had the impression of amusement and then she was alone again.

"You don' want me to keep callin' you my Iceman. That's what I do in my head. Better to have a name, don' you think?"

Her cheek throbbed and burned like hell and she knew it was swelling. So was her eye. *Great.* She'd have to go all day answering questions when customers started coming in. If they came in. She'd forgotten the

26

sign was turned to *closed.*

His glacier-blue eyes moved over her face. No change in expression. So much for being alluring with her sense of humor and her really nicely swollen face. She had to look awful. This was what came from being vain about her skin.

"Alonzo."

A word. His name. Elation swept through her even as she knew, deep down, he was lying to her. His name was *not* Alonzo. She heard the lie. Still, she let him get away with it because he'd just saved her from a savage beating. Robert would have robbed her as well.

"Is he alive?" She knew he wasn't. She *knew* it with the same certainty that she knew Alonzo wasn't her Iceman's real name.

"Does it matter?" He began walking her toward the back room, going around the counter space over her beautiful display cases.

Did it? It was wrong to kill someone by civilized law. The law of the shifters was different, and rogues received a death sentence if they endangered others of the lair. She'd left the lair and that life behind.

She glanced up at him to see him looking down at her with a leopard's focus. No change in expression. He was as cold as ice.

"He mean something to you?"

She shook her head and immediately wished she hadn't. A small sound escaped before she could stop it. He instantly lifted her into his arms, clearly done with their slow progress. In his arms, held tightly against his chest, she could feel those heavy muscles rippling as he glided across the floor. There was no jarring of her body, not the way he moved, so fluid, and not the way he held her, nearly crushing her against his chest.

He swept into her kitchen, placed her into a chair and went to the refrigerator. She wished she'd worn something nice. She didn't have a lot in the way of nice. She'd used her money for a down payment on a small house, and the rest of it went to the bakery. Every cent she had was tied up in her business, so no nice clothes. She didn't date so she didn't need them — until now.

He pressed a bag of ice into her hand. "Hold that against your cheek and answer me. When I ask a question I expect an answer."

"Does that go both ways?"

Her eyes met his and she shivered again. The glacier had just gotten colder if that was possible. "I barely knew him. He was a troublemaker back home. I'd never met him until he came to the bakery. He wanted money."

"And you. He wanted you."

She didn't think so, but she wasn't going to argue with him.

"Does it matter if he's dead?"

She took a deep breath. Really, she didn't want to answer because it wasn't going to show her in a good light, but Robert wouldn't have stopped at a beating. She knew his reputation.

Evangeline lifted her chin, looked him straight in the eye and shook her head. "Only if it meant you would get into trouble for savin' me."

"He won't bother you again." He didn't take his gaze from hers, watching carefully for her reaction.

She felt relief more than anything else. And guilt that she felt relief. The ice burned on her cheek but felt good. "Thank you. It seems I owe you again. I guess I'll have to give you free cinnamon cake for the rest of your life."

He didn't respond. Nor did he smile. She sighed and looked down at her lap. She shouldn't want his attention. He'd just killed a man. She couldn't be certain, but if he had, he'd done so casually and without emotion. She would be insane to be attracted to him and yet . . . she was. *Attracted* wasn't even a word she would use for what she was around him.

"Why are you here? You never come on Thursday, that's why he chose today."

"His bad luck. I wanted to get a few dozen of your cinnamon-apple cookies for my boss. I came in early so you would have plenty."

She started to put the ice pack down but he pushed her hand back, covering it with his own. He always wore those butter-soft gloves. Under them she could see the bulges of several rings. Big square, thick ones. She noticed them every single time he reached for his coffee mug. They intrigued her, just as the tattoos she could see drifting up his neck from under that perfect suit. For some reason those tattoos made him all the hotter to her. She'd awakened twice now from a dream of peeling that suit from him to uncover all the treasures underneath.

She felt the color rising, and there was no way to stop it. "I have to open the store."

"You have to sit for a full fifteen minutes with that ice pack on. Then you open the store. Your customers will wait."

Even his voice affected her body, bringing all her nerve endings alive as if he had created an electrical charge between them.

30

Again, the female inside her moved toward the surface, toward him. Lazily, really. As if she couldn't quite be bothered. She subsided quickly as she'd done before, leaving behind an unsettling itch that settled between her legs. Deep. She was going to *kill* her leopard.

Stop, you little hussy. You don' want him takin' an interest in us.

Again there was that impression of amusement before Bebe settled completely.

Evangeline had been born into a family of shifters. Her brothers had leopards. Her father and uncle did. It stood to reason she might as well. Saria had talked to her about the feeling when a leopard began to surface. She knew she was one. She'd always known. Her female, Bebe, was as much a part of her as her own skin. As breathing. She had hidden the fact that she had a leopard from her friends, from her family. They would insist she return to the lair and she was *never* going back there.

"Evangeline?"

Her name rolled off Alonzo's tongue with that accent that sent another shiver of awareness down her spine. Heat curled but Bebe stayed still. Hidden. She breathed a sigh of relief and looked up at him.

"Did he get you anywhere else?"

31

She shook her head and again wished she hadn't moved so fast. Her cheek pounded and her eye hurt. *Oh no.* That was swelling too. Of course — she just had to look the absolute worst when he came in.

He glanced at his watch, took the ice pack from her, threw it into the sink and tipped her head back, using one finger under her chin. "You're going to bruise, bad enough that makeup won't hide it, but you can make up some story for your customers. I noticed there are a lot of men. They'll believe anything you have to say."

Her gaze jumped to his face. His voice was exactly the same. His face could have been carved from the glacier in his eyes. Remote. Uncaring. Dead. With all that, she felt like there was just a little bite in his remark, as if maybe the thought of those male customers didn't sit well with him.

He looked at her for a long time, wholly focused on her, his gaze drifting over her body and then moving back up to her face. He nodded and turned away from her. Instinctively she knew that was the most she was going to get out of him. He bought three dozen of her cinnamon-apple cookies and didn't stay to drink coffee. Another car, this one also a town car, but with red trim through the black, was waiting at the curb for him.

He came back on his usual days, Monday, Wednesday and Friday, sat in his seat with his back to the wall and drank his coffee and ate his baked goods. They had progressed to smiles and greeting him by name on her part and a nod with one single word, "Evangeline," on his. She looked forward to him coming in. She tried to give him his cinnamon-apple cake free, but he merely looked at her and pushed money across the counter at her. At least he said her name. That was progress, even if it took six months for him to do it.

Several customers, male, noticed him, but left him strictly alone. When he wasn't there, they came back and warned her that he was dangerous. She shrugged and said he was a good customer and never caused any problems.

One of the many times her Iceman sat at the table drinking his coffee, he suddenly looked up, his gaze going straight to the walkway outside her shop. Evangeline followed his gaze and immediately stiffened. This could be bad. Quickly, she reached inside her cash register and grabbed the envelope stuffed there and hurried toward the front door. Alonzo was there before her. One arm circled her waist and he gently but very firmly put her behind him as he opened the door for the two men coming in. Only he blocked the entrance, preventing them from coming inside.

"Alonzo." One of the men smiled hesitantly at him. "We're here on business."

Alonzo shook his head. Evangeline curled her fingers into the back of his suit jacket and held on, her heart pounding. If she didn't pay these men off, like everyone on the street did, she would find herself without a shop. They'd come in when she was renovating and explained they would never take more than necessary to keep her shop safe. She knew that meant pay up or they'd burn her out or something equally as horrible. She'd talked with other shop owners and all of them paid protection money. She figured the price into her monthly budget.

"They have guns," she whispered against his back. "I've got their money."

"The boss won't like this," one said, but he took a step back.

"You let me worry about that. This shop is mine to take care of. He has a problem with that, I'll settle it myself."

She was fairly certain he was talking about the mafia. Was he involved? The men shaking her down knew him by name, but they appeared to be afraid of him. She didn't want him in trouble with a mafia boss.

"I've got the money," she reiterated, trying to reach around him to hand the envelope to the two men.

Both men nearly fell backward, stumbling away from her hand. Her Iceman caught her wrist with a gentleness that shocked her and brought her hand down to his thigh. Alonzo didn't look at her, but continued staring at the two men who turned and walked very briskly away.

"If I don' pay, they'll ruin my business," she said, taking a step around him toward the door.

"They won't." He tugged on her hand and led her back to the counter. "In the six months I've been coming here, your male customers have quadrupled and they hit on you continually. You never date. Why?"

It was the last thing Evangeline expected him to ask. She still clutched the envelope in her hand, holding it tight against his rock-hard thigh. "Why do you ask?"

"A woman like you has no business being alone."

"Like me?" She echoed it, trying to figure out where he was going with his questions and that statement that she found alternatingly annoying and alarming. Did he know she was leopard? Just what did "like you" mean?

Subtly she twisted her hand, expecting him to release her. She couldn't keep her palm pressed against the heat of his thigh with his muscles moving deliciously beneath it and not react. Heat spread through her like molten lava, a slow fire building in her veins and pooling low.

He didn't release her hand. He didn't even seem to notice her small movement of retreat, but she knew he had. He noticed everything. His gaze remained on her face. All ice. So cold she thought she might freeze. There was no hint of his leopard. There never was. She could almost forget he was a shifter, but she could never forget the danger that clung to him like a second skin.

"Yes, Evangeline, like you. I've never seen a more beautiful woman in my life. This isn't a bad part of town, but it's near enough. You come here at three in the morning and work alone until you close. You need a man."

He wasn't volunteering, that was for certain. But he'd said she was the most beautiful woman he'd ever seen. That was something. Of course he'd said it in his cold, devoid-of-all-feeling voice, but he had at least thought it to say it. Again, even though there was no emotion in his voice, she still felt that little bite, as if he were annoyed beyond all endurance that she was single.

She lifted her chin at him. "Some women prefer to be single."

He was silent, studying her face. Slowly he shook his head. "Some women shouldn't ever be single." He let go of her hand. "They won't come back. They know they will answer to me if they do."

She dared to lay her hand on his arm as he turned away from her. "Alonzo, I don' mind payin' the money. I don' want you to get in trouble with anyone. Those men made it sound like someone was goin' to be upset with you for interferin'. I'd rather pay the money than have you get into trouble."

He halted and looked down at her hand. Her fingers didn't even curl halfway around his forearm. As a deterrent her hand seemed rather absurd to try to stop him. Still, he remained there, towering over her. "Don't worry about me, Evangeline."

"I think when you said if there was a problem, you'd take care of it yourself, you meant you'd pay the money. I'm not going to let you do that."

He removed her hand very gently and

stepped away, toward the door. "You don't really have a choice one way or the other." He walked out like he always did — without looking back.

Evangeline waited for him for the next two weeks. She had the envelope filled with cash waiting for him or for the two men who came to collect each week. Neither showed up and that worried her. Had something happened to him because he'd stood up for her? There was no way to get in touch with him. She didn't know his last name or where he worked.

The other customers, the ones in their suits that she was certain Alonzo had sent, suddenly stopped coming in as well. She'd heard on the news that Antonio Arnotto, famous for his wines, had been murdered. It was rumored he was actually a crime boss, and his territory was wide open for takeover. Speculation of a war began with various faces being flashed on the television screen. She watched carefully, but none of those faces belonged to Alonzo.

Another week went by and still he didn't come. She was fairly certain he wouldn't now, and she went over every single thing she'd said and done. She'd touched him. She knew better. He was a man alone. He was frozen. Dead inside. Without emotion

— and she'd crossed a line.

She wasn't able to sleep very well, dreaming he'd been shot and killed. Beaten and stabbed. Buried alive in cement. She was afraid to close her eyes. The shop was thriving, but it didn't seem the same, not without him in it. She kept the news playing at home and work. On week five, she saw a picture of him on the television. He was standing beside another known crime boss, Elijah Lospostos, and his wife, Siena. Siena was the granddaughter of Antonio Arnotto. Alonzo Massi had been a soldier for her grandfather and was now her soldier. The news anchor asked if Alonzo Massi was the new crime boss rising out of the ranks to become the newest don, taking over Arnotto territory.

At least she knew he was alive. Still, she knew he wouldn't be coming back. And Siena Arnotto Lospostos was gorgeous. She couldn't hope to hold a candle to her, whether or not her Iceman had declared Evangeline the most beautiful woman he'd ever seen. Siena might be married, but how could Alonzo possibly think Evangeline was beautiful next to Siena? Was he taking care of Siena? *Her soldier.* What did that mean? That he wasn't coming back. That was what it meant.

2

"Not a good idea, Fyodor. This is the kind of thing that will get you killed."

Fyodor Amurov stopped abruptly on the sidewalk in front of the bakery, his long coat swirling around his ankles. Glaring at his brother, he shook his head. "*Never* use that name. I am Italian. I was born Italian. My name is Alonzo Massi. You have to remember that at all times, Timur. It was foolish of you to keep your name." His gaze swept the other man flanking him. "Both of you should have known better."

"I'm tired of hiding, *Alonzo.*" Timur emphasized the name, disgust in his tone. "But I'm not the point. We take great care with your route, never going the same way twice. We change vehicles. We watch over you and yet you insist on coming back to this place. The other men said you used to come here all the time. I'm beginning to think your sweet tooth has nothing to do with the goods in the cases and more to do with the goods behind the counter."

Alonzo didn't smile. He rarely, if ever, smiled. His gaze was restless, scanning the streets, the sidewalks, and most of all, looking through the plate-glass windows of the Small Sweet Shoppe. She was there, just as she always was. Working. Beautiful. Breathtaking. He shouldn't be there. He was the last man that should ever go into that bakery and put his gaze on that woman, but he couldn't stop himself. Timur was right. She was his Achilles' heel.

He sighed and put his hand to the door, shoving it open because he couldn't stop himself. He was a disciplined man in every area of his life, he *had* to be, yet for eight months he'd come to the bakery at least three times a week. That was him being disciplined. He'd wanted to go every damn day. He'd stayed away over a month, nearly two. He could count the weeks, days, hours and minutes since he'd last seen her.

"Bad idea, boss," Timur muttered. He was deadly serious and when he pushed past Alonzo to take a sweep of the small interior, his body in front of his brother's, he scowled at the woman behind the counter — the one who eventually was going to be the death of his brother if Fyodor kept this madness up.

41

Alonzo paused inside the door, taking a moment to drink her in. Savor her. Just for that moment before she looked up. He found he was holding his breath. A part of him almost wished she had a man. That she wouldn't look up, see him and smile that innocent, shy smile that told him she was interested in a monster. On the other hand, if she didn't smile at him that way, he'd be crushed. Shattered. It had been so damned long since he'd laid eyes on her, and he couldn't take it one more minute. More, if she was smiling that way for another man, he might commit murder and it would have nothing to do with his leopard.

Her name was Evangeline Bouvier. She was small and curvy with beautiful breasts that called to him. Her hair was a thick, dark silky mass that cascaded over her shoulders nearly to her waist. She wore it pulled back from her face in a thick, intricate braid that always made him want to run his hand down it to the very end, where it rested in the sweet curve of her ass. And she had a very nice ass. He spent far too much time thinking about it, just as he did every single part of her.

Evangeline glanced up, and instantly it was there. That smile she reserved solely for him. He'd seen countless customers come in over the last few months. She always smiled at them, but not like that. That smile was reserved for him alone and that told him she didn't have a man. No one had come in and tried to steal her out from under him.

She had a fantasy mouth — one he'd dreamt of many times. He'd woken up every one of those times with his fist on his cock and the dream of her mouth tight around him. Her eyes were a true emerald, startling green, rich and warm, and he wanted her looking up at him when he fucked her mouth. He always dreamt of her that way. If she had any idea of the dirty things he wanted to do to her, she'd order him out and lock the door behind him. Yeah, and if any other man ever had the same thoughts about her and he knew it, that man would be dead within the hour.

"Alonzo, I haven't seen you in a while."

Even her voice got to him. Low. Sexy. So damned sweet he wanted to take a bite out of her. He stepped up to the counter. Behind him, Timur prowled to the restroom, yanked open the door and looked inside and then moved back to the storefront windows to peer out. Alonzo thought about pulling out a gun and shooting him. He didn't need Timur acting like his bodyguard, even though that was what he was.

Gorya was worse. His cousin was a ladies' man. Handsome. Charming. He had that lean, lithe build women seemed to go for. He was everything Alonzo wasn't. Alonzo was all corded muscle. Ropes of it. Rugged. He always looked like he had a two-day growth on his jaw, no matter how many times he shaved. He was tall, towering over Evangeline and probably intimidating the hell out of her. If he didn't, he should. He had scars on his face and neck. More on his body. He didn't smile, nor did he know how to make clever conversation. He was rough-looking by any standard, and next to his cousin, he would come up short every time.

Evangeline's gaze left his face and moved to Gorya's. She flashed a smile at him and for a moment Alonzo stiffened, his fingers curling into a tight fist inside his thin leather gloves. He had the fists of a fighter and he'd never lost a fight yet. He hoped like hell Gorya remembered that fact. He hoped he was aware of just what the tattoos covering his body meant as well.

He realized she had given his cousin her low-watt smile. Polite. Sweet, but impersonal. She still reserved the real one for him. His gut, tied up in knots, relaxed a little.

"Good morning. Can I get something for

44

you?" That was directed at Gorya.

Her voice stroked caresses over Alonzo's skin. Men like Alonzo didn't have a woman of their own. Not ever. It was far too dangerous. He didn't live in Evangeline's world. He stayed in the underbelly, where it was dark and ugly and everyone existing there was dark and ugly as well. He knew the business inside and out, smuggling, gunrunning, prostitutes, gambling, money laundering, the list went on and on. He knew them all. He'd been born into that ugly world — on the other side of the world in Russia, but still the same everywhere. He'd never left it. Never gotten out of it. Not even when he'd come to the States.

Gorya winked at Evangeline. "I had no idea the women were so beautiful in this city or I would have come sooner."

"Gorya." It was a warning. No one could mistake it for anything else. Alonzo wasn't about to have his cousin flirt with his woman. Okay. She wasn't his. Not yet. She never would be, because along with taking over the Arnotto territory when Antonio Arnotto had been murdered, Alonzo was a shifter with the worst leopard imaginable.

His leopard, an Amur leopard, was a killer. Vicious. Cunning. Fast as hell. Ready to fight at the drop of a hat. Prodding, raking and clawing Alonzo every moment of every day. The cat hated everyone equally. Women were in danger. Alonzo could fuck them but then he had to get them the hell out of his sight because his leopard was so savage after, he was never certain he could control the beast. There were no cozy dates and romantic interludes. He'd never had that. The only place his cat subsided and gave him a respite was here, in this bakery. Even at night, when he slept, his cat wanted to hunt and often challenged him. He'd had to put up metal bars on the windows and steel plating on the doors to ensure his cat remained indoors while he slept. What man could ask a woman to share that kind of life?

Evangeline was a woman a man kept. He wanted her in his bed. He wanted to wake up to her, go to sleep with her. Have those fucking romantic dates with her. He didn't realize he was scowling at Gorya until his cousin moved nervously away from the counter.

"I'll have a cup of coffee and one of your famous cinnamon cakes Alonzo is always going on about," Gorya said as he backed away. He glanced at Timur, who was talking into his cell phone, still staring out the window. No help there.

Satisfied, Alonzo watched patiently as Evangeline got the coffee and cake for Gorya. Alonzo enjoyed watching her work. She was very efficient, her movements mesmerizing. He'd spent countless hours watching her, just enjoying the way her breasts swayed temptingly and her hips had a sexy little swing to them. He had memorized her body and knew he would know her blindfolded, and he hadn't even touched her yet.

Her gaze jumped to his and she blushed. That was the other thing he loved about her. She didn't look at other men. Only him. He knew better. It wasn't safe. She would never have the things she deserved if she was with him. Things like neighbors who came over to borrow sugar and leaned over a fence to talk. She would never be able to be alone in her bakery. Hell, if she would even have her bakery, and he could tell it meant the world to her. He didn't look away, holding her gaze deliberately. He should have looked away, made it clear it was never going to happen between them. He was the last man on earth she should ever be with, but it didn't matter how many times, how many ways, he told himself that, he kept coming back.

"I missed you, Alonzo." She whispered her

confession for him alone.

He knew his brother and cousin would hear. They were leopard. Of course they'd hear, and he hated that too. That should have been for him alone. Intimate. Just between the two of them. Deep inside, his leopard snarled, catching his mood, and he realized the beast didn't like the other males close to Evangeline any more than he did.

She might have said such a thing to any customer returning after a lengthy disappearance, but he was not just any customer and they both knew it. His body stirred in spite of every effort not to allow it. Worse, she got to him somewhere deeper. He'd lost everything. His family. His home. His self-respect. Everything important. He'd lost so much he'd placed himself in an untenable position, setting himself up as a target for police and criminals alike.

He knew better. He knew better than to risk her. An innocent. Sweet. Beautiful. He nearly groaned with his need of her, but someone had to protect her. She'd be a weakness his enemies could exploit. He wasn't a gentle man. He was a killer, born and bred. Worse, he had a leopard . . .

"You shouldn't." His warning dripped with ice. He wasn't strong enough to stay away from her, but he could make it so she wouldn't want to have anything to do with him.

Evangeline didn't flinch. She nodded, her gaze never wavering from his. "I know."

She did know. He saw knowledge in her eyes. Of who he was. What he was. And now it was worse. Back home, he'd been a ruthless enforcer. Here, when he'd first met her, he'd become a bodyguard, a soldier, nothing else. Now, he was the boss. A target. A man who was forced to make ugly decisions.

"And still you missed me."

"Yes. Coffee? Cinnamon-apple cookies?"

He should turn his back on her, walk right out, but he wasn't that strong. He almost did. He turned away from her, looking toward the door, wishing he were a better man. When he turned, his fierce cat leapt toward the surface, raking and clawing in protest. Everything in him stilled. He turned slowly back toward Evangeline and his cat settled instantly. Nearly purred. Stretched leisurely.

"Coffee and a piece of the cinnamon cake."

He had always known his cat calmed when he went to the bakery, but he hadn't realized his leopard was as enamored with Evangeline as he was. His leopard had settled down in the bakery, but his reaction wasn't just about the place, the scent of baked goods, the peaceful atmosphere; this was about the woman. He studied her carefully as she poured his coffee and arranged the cake on the plate.

What did he really know about her? Deliberately, he hadn't investigated her. He didn't want to know more than he already did about her. She worked hard. She loved what she did and it showed. Her bakery was immaculate, the baked goods superb. She was beautiful, far beyond his imagination. He liked the way she dealt with problem customers. He'd seen her hang on to her smile when a customer had raged at her about something minor. She easily defused the situation, speaking in her warm, low tone. He loved her voice. She always spoke softly, giving him the impression of an intimacy they didn't have.

He couldn't deny the connection between them. He took the coffee from her in the way he always did, one gloved finger brushing along the back of her hand. He didn't dare allow himself the pleasure of skin to skin. He took the plate as well and went to his table to contemplate the situation.

He hadn't been able to be with a woman without that woman being in extreme danger. Not once. Not ever. His leopard's fierce, killing nature had gotten so bad he hadn't bothered to try in a very long time. Controlling his cat was difficult enough on a day-to-day basis, without tempting the beast. His leopard raged at him, and he'd seen the result of his kind of animal and never wanted to witness it again. He stayed disciplined. He didn't tempt fate.

He glanced at her. She wasn't looking at him, but he'd already seen the hurt in her eyes. She'd tried to mask it, but it had been there. He'd done that. Acting as if she didn't matter when she did. Acting cold because that was the only way to save both of them. He had been secretly happy that she'd left his table in place, as if waiting for him. She'd admitted she'd missed him.

But . . . He risked another glance at her. If she soothed his leopard and the hideous man who had confronted her months earlier had been leopard — could she be one? He needed to find out.

Gorya seated himself across the room where he could easily defend both men if trouble came in, but Timur dragged a chair to the left side of the table so he could scowl at Evangeline. "She's gorgeous. What the hell's wrong with the men around here?"

Alonzo's gut knotted and his leopard roared, leaping to the surface so fast he

51

could barely contain the beast. His knuckles ached. His skull felt too tight. The itch of fur rushed over his body beneath his immaculate suit. *"Vai a fan culo,"* he swore, remembering at the last minute to use Italian and not Russian.

Timur leaned back in his chair. "Oh, yeah. You aren't going to walk away from her. You're well and truly caught and you'd better get to a point where you acknowledge it, before something bad happens." The taunting smile faded and Timur leaned close. "She's beautiful, *Alonzo.*" He clearly hated calling his brother by that name. "Some man is going to come in eventually or follow her home or steal her away from you . . ."

"Get the fuck away from me before something bad happens right here," Alonzo snapped, meaning it. "You know what I have to put up with day and night. Why the hell are you making it more difficult? I can barely contain him and the more you stir him up, the worse it gets."

Genuine shock crossed Timur's face. "Your leopard is reacting to what I'm saying? About . . ." He turned his head and looked at Evangeline as she served two women who had come in. *"Her?"*

Alonzo nodded. "This is the only place

he's quiet. He's gotten crazy lately. I let him out every night and run him until we're both exhausted, but it doesn't seem to get any better. I figured, sooner or later, I was going to have to . . ." He trailed off, shaking his head. He would rather be dead than to fulfill the legacy of his father.

"You're certain it's her? *She* soothes him?"

"It's Evangeline. She does the same thing for me. She's quiet. Calm. Watch how she is with everyone, it's genuine, that peace she has. She knows who she is and what she wants. She doesn't get ruffled over anything. I've seen her handle difficult customers. They end up smiling and go away happy. She's just peaceful to be around and for someone like me, someone living in hell, that's a gift."

Timur got up, shoving his chair back, and stalked over to the counter without a word. He stood waiting for his turn, his entire focus on the woman behind the counter. Alonzo didn't like it, but not only was Timur his brother, he was his bodyguard. Anything unusual in Alonzo's world had to be checked out. He understood that, but he didn't have to like it.

Evangeline looked up, saw the look on Timur's face and glanced at Alonzo. His eyes met hers. He stared at her, trying to feel nothing. Knowing she thought he didn't feel a single emotion, and he hadn't — until he'd walked into the bakery all those months ago and met her. Hurt flashed in her eyes for a brief moment and then she turned her entire attention on Timur.

Her smile. The way she tipped her head slightly to the side and tendrils of her thick, glossy hair curled around her face giving her a sexy, take-me-to-bed kind of look. Alonzo wanted to pound his brother into the ground.

"What can I get for you?"

Her voice. Sin and sex. Alonzo tried not to listen. Tried not to hear or look as his brother ordered and she moved from the counter to the espresso machine to get Timur's drink for him. He couldn't help but watch the sway of her hips. She was wearing soft blue jeans. Nothing special, but they cupped her ass in a way that made his palms itch. He needed to run his hands possessively over her curves. Claim them. She belonged to him, not his brother and not any other male walking into the bakery. She half turned toward Timur when he told her what he wanted from the display case. The movement pulled the thin material of her black-and-white sweater across her full breasts. There was no hiding the fact that she had curves, the kind a man wanted to feel when he took her to bed. Soft. Inviting. All the fuck his.

It took every ounce of discipline he possessed to stay in his seat and watch his brother engage her in conversation when she handed him his coffee and reached into the case for his macaroons.

"I'm Timur, Timur Amurov. And you are?" Timur lifted the drink to his mouth and sipped cautiously.

Alonzo watched him take that first drink and get the look on his face that most of her customers did. The woman knew how to make coffee and drinks. On the other hand, she knew his brother's real name, and his was a fake. When she talked to him, she thought of him as Alonzo, an Italian. He was Fyodor Amurov, from Russia. He was an Amur leopard shifter, and that made him a rarity even among rare shifters. It also made him a member of the *bratya.* In fact, he was from one of the most lucrative and cruel families involved. His legacy was one of blood and death. Of patricide. Of mass murder.

"I'm Evangeline. It's nice to meet you."

Her voice went right through him. Wrapped around his heart. Fisted his fucking cock until he thought he might scream with need. All the while his leopard purred. Rubbed. Needed like he needed. Alonzo's breath stilled in his body. His leopard only needed one thing — to hunt. He lived for the hunt. He loved the freedom, and he saw everything and everyone as prey. Not Evangeline. He looked at her amorously. That was new.

"Your last name?" Timur pushed as he took the plate of macaroons.

Alonzo heard her heart accelerate. He caught the jerk of Gorya's body as he heard it as well. Timur was relentless, standing still with no intention of moving.

Evangeline turned her head toward Alonzo. "Don't," she said softly.

She knew Timur worked for him. She thought, correctly, Timur was getting information for an investigation, but, incorrectly, that Alonzo had ordered him to do so. His woman had secrets.

"Don't what?" Timur pushed. "Look at me, not him," he ordered. His voice gentled. "I'm just asking for your last name."

She didn't obey him. She kept looking at Alonzo. "I haven't pried. I haven't done one thing to give you cause to do this."

The bell over the door tinkled and Timur instantly spun around, his hand going inside his coat. Three men entered. They were in their thirties and all three looked carefully around, noting Alonzo first, then Gorya and Timur. Right away Alonzo pegged them as undercover cops. They were dressed in casual clothes, jeans and tees stretched tight over muscles. Tattoos down their arms. One had a short beard and mustache. One just the mustache. The third man hadn't shaved in a couple of days.

Timur thanked Evangeline and took his coffee and the plate of cookies in one hand, keeping his other hand free. Of course they had concealed weapon permits. Alonzo had made certain everything was aboveboard should they ever be stopped for any reason. He didn't want that reason to happen there in the bakery. Not with his woman watching.

Timur sank into the chair and grinned at him over his coffee. "That woman is breathtaking. My leopard definitely was soothed, but not interested. There's a difference. Clearly she's a leopard whisperer. When you're close to her, you feel peace. Sounds crazy, but I felt it too." He kept his eyes on the cops without appearing to do so.

"Don't get too used to being close to her," Alonzo warned. Icicles dripped from his voice.

Timur, damn him, grinned wider. "It's not me you have to worry about, *moy brat,* those three didn't come in here expecting us. And she clearly knows them. They're regulars, and I'm guessing it isn't all about her bad-ass coffee."

"Brice, good to see you. Your usual?"

She sounded like sex and sin to Alonzo every time she opened her mouth. His body was as hard as a rock. His mind was filled with a million ways to kill the newcomers, and his leopard raked at him in a rage at the idea of the three men so close to what was so clearly theirs.

"You bet, sweetheart."

"Sweetheart"? What the fuck was that? It was all Alonzo could do not to leap up and kill the son of a bitch.

"Reeve, Crispin? The usual?"

Both undercover cops nodded, smiling at her, but looking at Alonzo. They turned their bodies slightly, just enough to be able to watch Alonzo, Gorya and Timur yet still flirt with Evangeline.

"You ever going to go out with me?" the one she'd called Brice asked, leaning one elbow on the counter to put his chin in his palm so he could stare at her very enticing ass.

Alonzo's leopard lifted its head and

snarled. Alonzo wanted to do the same but he kept his expressionless mask on. The last thing he wanted was for anyone — let alone the cops — to know he was interested in Evangeline. On the other hand, if she said yes, he was going to follow the fucker right out of the bakery and make certain he wouldn't be asking Alonzo's woman out again.

Evangeline's gaze shifted to his for just a moment, to read his reaction no doubt. He should have stayed frozen. He should have kept all emotion out of it. That was what kept him alive and her safe. He gave the slightest shake of his head. He had to warn her. He had to keep as much honesty between them as possible. She had to know dating Brice wasn't in the cards for her. Six months ago. Even two days ago. But he'd walked back into the bakery and she didn't have a man. She'd said she missed him. She'd chosen him. She might not realize that was what she'd done, but she belonged to him and Brice had lost his shot.

Evangeline shook her head, her smile sweet and teasing over her shoulder as she made a drink at the machine for him. "One of these days, you keep asking, Brice, and I might scare you to death and say yes. I'd turn into a clingy, nagging witch and drive you nuts."

"It would be worth it, sweetheart," Brice said, his eyes on her butt, lovingly encased in those tight jeans.

Alonzo wanted to take out his gun and shoot the bastard. The man had no business ogling what belonged to him.

She laughed and set their coffees on the bar in to-go cups. Their pastries went into small paper bags. At least they weren't staying. They'd probably wait around to follow Alonzo and his bodyguards later, but it wouldn't get them anything. They wouldn't want to blow their covers and in a way, that protected Alonzo.

"Throw me a crumb of hope," Brice encouraged. "These two are going to be giving me hell for even trying again." He jerked his thumb at his two companions, who both grinned like idiots.

Alonzo wasn't deceived. Neither were his two bodyguards. They watched without looking, something they'd perfected from the time they were infants and had had to keep an eye on their fathers and older brothers. Their leopards never failed them.

"A crumb? Saying that to a baker is dangerous," she teased.

Her voice didn't have to be so damned soft. Or intimate. Alonzo imagined that alone was enough of a crumb for the cop to return. He consoled himself that he wasn't the only one lying about his identity to her.

Brice reached across the counter and caught her by the nape of the neck, drawing her close. Everything in Alonzo went still. Ice flowed through his veins. The brutal, vicious killer in him merged with the man trained from birth to take out enemies. He flowed to his feet, too graceful to knock over the table. Timur put a hand on his arm to try to stop him but it was impossible. Both knew it. He was too far gone. Heat banded across his eyes, showing him his three targets in colors rather than images. He could kill all three in seconds. One leap and he'd be on them.

As all three cops turned at his movement, Evangeline took the opportunity to free herself. Immediately she smiled at Alonzo. "You need a refill? No need to get up, I can bring it to you."

That sense of peace she created with her voice, with her calm, instantly overrode the roar of his leopard, the thunder of his blood pounding with the need to remove every threat to his claim on his woman. His leopard backed off as she reached casually for the coffeepot, already out of reach of the three cops. He didn't ever ask for fancy coffee. He liked her natural brew and he took it black. In that moment he was very grateful he did. He forced his body back into the chair, sinking down, breathing deeply, watching her the entire time so his cat could see that no one else touched her.

The bell sounded as the three undercover cops slipped out of the shop. He was aware of them looking over their shoulders at him, but he ignored them now that they weren't close to Evangeline. She came across the room with her coffeepot, not looking at his face now that the threat was gone. Not smiling. Damn it, he'd done that. He deserved that. She poured his coffee without a word, and when she turned to go, he shackled her wrist, at the same time jerking his chin at his brother to indicate he wanted to be alone with her.

Timur immediately rose and wandered to the other side of the room, pretending great interest in the baked goods in the display cases, but all the while watching the streets.

Evangeline looked down at his fingers wrapped around her wrist. She had a small wrist and his hands were large, nearly swallowing not only her wrist but a good part of her forearm. She sighed and put the coffeepot on the table.

"I can't do this with you," she said softly.

"You're not bein' fair."

Her accent got to him every time. "Sit down for a minute, Evangeline. You have a few minutes with no customers. The big crowd will be coming in soon."

She hesitated, but he didn't release her. He couldn't have even if he wanted to. Once he had her close to him, he didn't want to give that up. Such close proximity had his leopard rolling around amorously. The crazy cat stretched and unsheathed claws but only to try to push Alonzo to stake his claim legitimately. Impossible in her shop, but he knew soon he would have no choice, not the way his leopard was acting and not the way his body, heart and soul responded to her.

Evangeline slipped into the chair beside him. "I thought we'd agreed this was a bad idea. Was I reading you wrong?"

He kept possession of her wrist, looking down at her hands. She didn't wear paint on her nails. They were cut short and very clean, but completely bare. Her hands were small, but they'd seen work. His heart tripped a little looking at them. No rings. No sign there had ever been a ring, but then she was young. No more than twenty or twenty-one. Young to own a shop.

"You weren't wrong." It came out clipped.

Frozen. He didn't know how to be any different than he was so he didn't try to be.

She tried to get her hand back, tugging. He didn't have to tighten his hold, she wasn't going anywhere.

"I'm not a good man." Hell. He wasn't even a man. How did he say that to her? *My life is killing. It doesn't matter what form I take, human or leopard; that's who I am.* Not what; who. He'd been born into a lair of killers. Of vicious, cruel, cunning killers. He'd been bred for that purpose deliberately. Raised to be what his father and the lair needed. Even in the brotherhood, his family was feared above all others.

"I get that."

He didn't want her to get it or agree with him. He wanted a protest. She didn't give him one, but she didn't stare at the table like most women would have. She didn't cry or look sad. She looked him right in the eye. His Evangeline. His woman. She was quiet and accepting. She didn't even look as if she blamed him.

"I'm protecting you from my life. From me." He tried again. Maybe he needed her to continue looking at him the way she did. He needed her to see him as noble when he was anything but. This wasn't going to end well for her. He tried, for her sake, but he was so far gone. So empty. So alone. So fucking tired of killing. He couldn't fight his leopard forever. He realized that without her, his leopard was going to go insane. He could try to protect her from who and what he was, but if he wanted to survive with his soul intact, he needed her. Sooner or later he'd get too tired, he'd slip up and his leopard would slip his leash.

"I get that." No judgment. Just acceptance.

"You don't," he said, bringing her hand to his mouth. "You don't get it and I don't know how to tell you." He couldn't help himself. His teeth scraped over the pads of her fingers and then he sucked one into his mouth.

"Zashchitit' yeye."

That was the only warning Alonzo got, but it was all he needed. He surged to his feet, jerking her up with him and turned, pushing her face and the front of her body into the wall, covering her with his own. He was big, surrounding her, his arms protecting her head while his body sheltered the rest of her.

There was the sound of brakes locking up. The terrible smash of glass as a truck jumped the sidewalk and hit the front of the store. It came to a shuddering halt with just the bumper and a small part of the hood inside the store. Glass rained down. The truck had taken out the glass door and both picture windows. The aim couldn't have been better. Timur was already striding through the glass to berate the driver.

Very slowly, Alonzo released Evangeline. She turned reluctantly to survey the damage. All color leeched from her face, leaving her shockingly pale, so much so that he locked his arm around her belly and pulled her back against him for support.

"It is only glass, *amore.* No one was hurt. Timur will get the necessary information and I'll make certain this is repaired today."

People were crowding in, gawking. The driver shook his head, apologizing over and over, handing over his license and insurance and showing Timur the gas pedal had stuck. Timur glanced back at Alonzo. Alonzo scowled at his brother. Of course his brother had arranged the accident. His fault for insisting on frequenting the bakery. He'd made it clear he would continue to go there on a regular basis, even though it wasn't safe. He knew exactly what Timur was up to, and his brother would get the lecture of a lifetime — not that it would do any good.

A little shudder ran through Evangeline's body. She breathed deep and pressed her fingers to her eyes for a moment before her chin went up. "No one can get glass installed that fast. It has to be special ordered and . . ."

"Evangeline." Just her name. A reprimand. He didn't need to say anything else. No matter what, if he said he'd take care of it, he would. She should at least know who she was dealing with. In any case, Timur would have made the order already for bulletproof glass. The workmen would show up very soon. She would lose business today, but he would find a way to make that up to her.

"You can't take care of this for me," she said decisively.

She hadn't made a move to pull out of his arms yet, still so shocked he doubted she was aware that she leaned heavily into him. His leopard was happy, his body, not so much.

"It is done. Timur is already arranging it."

"I don' have the money," she admitted. "The insurance has to be called, and they'll come out and determine what they can do and —"

"It is done." He made that decisive. "Come sit down." He steered her toward the small table again, the one far from the mess.

She glanced at Gorya as she allowed

Alonzo to seat her. He calmly finished his coffee, saluting her with the mug. "Nothing seems to throw your friend."

"He likes to eat and drink, that one," Alonzo agreed.

"I at least should be sweeping up the glass," she protested.

"It will be taken care of." He didn't want her anywhere near the glass. If she cut herself, he'd have to give Timur a beating and Timur wasn't all that easy to put the smackdown on.

3

Everything had changed — yet nothing had changed. Evangeline wasn't certain exactly what to do about Alonzo. He came to the bakery on average about four days a week now. Two months had gone by since the accident with the truck. He'd had her bakery cleaned up and new glass in by ten that evening, refusing to even consider allowing her to pay him back — and then they were back to normal — except — he talked to her now. Not much, because he still seemed a man of few words, but at least he spoke to her.

Timur and Gorya, his two bodyguards, always accompanied him. They teased her a little bit, at least Gorya did. Timur was very much like Alonzo, quieter and not quick to smile. She'd never actually seen Alonzo smile and he'd been coming to her shop for a year now.

She had to bake far more than when she'd

first started because the demand was so high. Her little shop had caught on and soon she would have to hire someone to help her. If business continued to increase, she'd be able to hire help in the next couple of months. She was fairly certain her business had picked up because of Alonzo. She had a couple of celebrities come in a few times. Jake Bannaconni, a local billionaire, had come in saying Alonzo raved about her baked goods and he was taking some home to his wife and children. That was huge. After that, some of his employees began to come.

Timur came into the shop as she opened it. Clearly he'd been waiting for the door to be unlocked. He strode in as she flipped her sign to *open* and then made her way back to the counter. He had never come in so early before and he seemed much more tense than usual — which meant he was definitely scaring her.

Inwardly she sighed. She had no idea how her little shop had become the hangout for the local mafia, but she couldn't very well ask them to stop coming. Maybe Alonzo would listen to her but she didn't want to go through another couple of months wondering where he was, if he was all right and whom he was with.

"What's wrong?" Timur demanded, leaning on the counter. "You're frowning. I've never seen you frown before. Not even when you're dealing with a crazy customer. Sometimes I want to take my gun out and shoot them for you."

Evangeline supposed she should be grateful he wanted to shoot someone for her, but it only confirmed she'd managed to get in over her head with the criminal element in her beloved new home.

"I appreciate that you don't," she said softly and then found herself laughing. What else could she do? She was *never* going to ask Alonzo to stay away. "What brings you in so early? Can't live without your macaroons?"

"Alonzo wanted me to come in and talk to you." His eyes were hard. Flat and cold, very similar to Alonzo's. Too similar. Even the color was the same, that piercing, beautiful glacier blue. As if deep inside both men were mountains of ice that could never be thawed. That was how she thought of Alonzo. Timur was . . . difficult. He didn't like her. He especially didn't like Alonzo anywhere near her.

"Talk to me about what?" She fixed a latte for him without him asking for it, glancing over her shoulder as she asked the question.

"He wants me to explain things to you before he comes in."

There was a definite warning in his voice. She turned back to him and set the latte on the counter, reaching for a pair of gloves in order to pick up the cookies he preferred. "Why would he have to explain anything to me?"

"Exactly." His voice was clipped. His eyes bored into her. Not like Alonzo, not with interest, more with annoyance and speculation. "Why the hell can't I find out any information about you? You don't exist. You have this bakery and a driver's license, but that's it. I can't even find a birth certificate for you."

Her stomach muscles knotted hard, so much so that she pressed her hand tightly against her belly in an effort to ease the ache. She'd known Timur would investigate her. He didn't want anyone near his boss, not unless he knew everything about them.

The bell over the door rang and that started the steady stream of her usual early morning customers. Businessmen and women, rushing to work, grabbing pastries, tea and coffee, smiling without really noticing anything but the time. Timur seemed to fade into the background, drinking his coffee and eating his cookies while reading.

Not one person so much as glanced at him, as he sat so quietly, seemingly absorbed in his book. Evangeline knew better. He saw every single person and probably could tell her all sorts of things about them.

It took a good hour and forty-five minutes of hard work to get through the first wave of customers before the shop was empty and she could begin to restock the cases with her baked pastries. Her ham-and-cheese pastries were very popular, along with her mushroom-spinach quiche. She'd learned that most of the early risers didn't eat breakfast at home so when she'd introduced those fluffy pastries, they'd been a big early morning hit.

The moment the door had closed on the last customer, Timur materialized in front of her. "You didn't answer me."

"Why would Alonzo have you investigate me?" She couldn't keep the hurt out of her voice, and that bothered her. It was giving too much away to this man. She shouldn't care about Alonzo. They didn't have any kind of a relationship, nor could they. She had left that world behind and she didn't want to go back to it. Still, Alonzo was the only man she ever thought about. Ever dreamed about. Fantasized over.

"He gave me strict instructions not to

investigate you."

Her gaze jumped to his face at the same time her heart clenched tightly in her chest. "Then why are you askin' me?"

"Because I don't like anything out of the ordinary, and you're out of the ordinary."

There was no apology in his voice. None whatsoever. His gaze was so hard and cold she shivered as she filled the last spot in the case and glanced at the time. Another five minutes and the second wave would start. That was far too long to be alone with Timur. She didn't trust him or herself. She didn't want to blurt out her own questions in retaliation. Questions such as why Alonzo was pretending to be Italian when it was so clear he was Russian and Timur's brother. That kind of question was the kind that might get her killed.

"I'm no threat to your boss," she said.

"Don't kid yourself, honey," he snapped, all but slamming his empty mug on the counter and leaning close to glare at her. "You're the biggest threat to him there is."

She didn't know what to say to that. To do with it. "Just tell me whatever it is he sent you to say." *And get out.* She was beginning to shake. She wasn't going to let Timur intimidate her.

"There's a big meeting today and it is to

take place here. We didn't call it. Alonzo couldn't protest, not without putting you in jeopardy. When we come in, he won't talk to you. He wants you to know it isn't personal."

She fought the inclination to roll her eyes and shrugged instead. "He never talks to me. How is this any different? I don't take it personal."

He sighed. "It's more about the way you look at him."

Her breath caught in her lungs. "Oh. My. God. I'm not supposed to even look at him? Why are you holdin' your meetin' in my bakery? Pick somewhere else." Was it so obvious to everyone that she was attracted to Alonzo? She didn't even know his real name.

"The meeting's set. Just don't look at him the way you do."

She could feel her color rising. How totally embarrassing. "You know what, just tell him not to come back here. Seriously. I don' want him in here if it's such a big deal." Her accent was thicker than ever and she didn't care. Didn't care if he knew she was from the swamp and her grandfather was a horrible man, feared by everyone around him, so much so that her own family had hidden her away. "I want you all gone. I mean it. Just tell him to stay away, and then no one will have to worry about how I look at him or don' look at him." Tears burned behind her eyes, and that was even more humiliating.

"Stop." He said the word softly. A command nevertheless. "You and I both know he isn't going to stop coming here. And don't you fucking cry. He'll put a bullet in my head."

"He won't know. I'm not about to tell him and neither are you."

"He'll know." He pushed his latte mug at her. "Make me another one."

"What part of 'I want you out' didn' you understand?"

"The part where you're acting crazy. Just make me a latte and do what I tell you to do and don't cry. Don't even look like you're about to cry."

That stopped her. She turned back to him when she'd nearly walked into her kitchen to avoid talking to him. Why shouldn't she look as if she were about to cry? There was an undertone to Timur's voice, as if he were just a little nervous. Very slowly she lifted her gaze to the higher walls of her bakery and took a long look around. She couldn't see anything but the smooth walls. Still . . .

"Did you put cameras in here?"

He tapped the latte mug on the counter. "Seriously, Evangeline."

"Seriously, Timur." She couldn't believe she was challenging him. He was mafia. A mafia bodyguard. Maybe even a hit man.

She was crazy to challenge him. She should just shut up and do what he said. That wasn't exactly in her nature. She didn't want to ever do what anyone said again. She'd made herself that promise, but then she'd promised she'd never be around criminals. She'd work hard and find a really nice man who had a boring job and he'd come home to their little house every night. She wouldn't have to worry about him cheating on her because he'd be so crazy about her . . .

"Evangeline." Timur's voice was sharp.

She didn't care if he was angry with her. She was done. Done pining away for a man who was absolutely, completely inappropriate and wrong. What had gotten into her? Alonzo Massi — and that wasn't even his real name — was as cold as ice. His emotions were frozen, if he had any, and she doubted he did. She didn't think he could feel at all. He was a walking, talking robot and she had built too many fantasies around him. Stupid, but then she didn't have a lot of experience. She should have gone to bed with him, it would have been awful. She wouldn't know what she was doing, and he would hate that. He'd be an icicle and she would hate that. Perfect.

The bell sounded and for the first time she whipped her head up, glaring. Instead of Alonzo, it was her second wave of customers pushing through the door. She plastered on her smile, ignored Timur's empty latte mug and went on full automatic. *Screw Timur and screw Alonzo as well.*

Evangeline was so upset with her decision to end it with Alonzo, and that told her more than anything else that she'd gone way too far in her fantasies. There never was an Alonzo and Evangeline. Not. Ever. Yet she was on the verge of tears most of the day as if she'd really broken up with her boyfriend. It was ludicrous. Ridiculous. It just showed her how naïve and strange she was still. A mythical boyfriend. A criminal one at that. What was wrong with her? She lived in her head too much. She always had.

Alonzo had been coming into her shop for a year. He barely spoke to her. Even when she had admitted she missed him, nothing had changed. Did she even want it to? He was everything she despised, and yet her made-up world had been completely formed around him. And they all knew it. *Everyone* knew it. She hadn't even been under the radar about her interest in Alonzo, and that was mortifying. Absolutely mortifying.

Timur was still in the shop. He'd made no more attempts to talk to her with all the customers and she was grateful but wished he'd leave. He hadn't made the mistake of coming back up to the counter for another latte either.

She worked hard, but time went by fast because she was so angry over her own stupidity. She spent the hours chastising herself while she worked. That took her past noon and into her lightest period. Customers tapered off around one thirty, and by two the store was in what she always referred to as "the dead zone." She welcomed that period because it gave her a chance to restock, get off her feet and take a short break.

When the last customer left the shop, Evangeline heaved a sigh of relief and took a much-needed bathroom break. When she returned, Timur was at the door. He casually turned the sign from *open* to *closed* and he locked the door. With a key. His own key. She knew it was his because her key was safely in the coat pocket of her jacket in the kitchen closet. Without a word to her, he moved behind the counter and into her kitchen.

"What are you doin'?"

"They'll be coming in through the back door." He spoke tersely.

"You aren't takin' over my shop, Timur." She lifted her chin. This would really get her into trouble, but she didn't care. She marched over to her phone.

Before she could lift it, Timur's hand clamped down on hers, preventing movement. "Don't be ridiculous. I get that this isn't a good thing and you're probably scared, but nothing will happen to you. You'll have customers in the store and we'll compensate you for the use of the bakery. We'll be out by four. You have light or no business during this time, so it will be good for you financially."

His fingers were surprisingly gentle as he pried her hand from the phone, while his eyes were as cold as ice and his face was hard and scary. She glared at him and then her gaze swept the room. "Is he goin' to be angry about this too? Will he know about this? Me tryin' to call the cops and you stoppin' me?" It was a challenge. She forced him to answer, even though she already knew the answer.

He nodded slowly. "Yes."

She jerked her hand away from his as if

he'd burned her. "I'm doin' this today because I have no choice, but tonight I'll be sweepin' this store for cameras. I want all of you gone, out of my life. Do you understand me?"

He sighed. "*Miadshaya sestra,* you understand me. You no longer have a choice. Just do your job and you'll get through this. Don't look at Alonzo as if he is anything at all to you. Don't look too closely at the others here."

She turned away from him, her stomach churning. How the hell had this happened? After making certain the display cases were full, she went into the restroom, away from Timur's all-seeing eyes, and stared at herself in the mirror. She wasn't that girl alone in the swamp. She wasn't abandoned. She wasn't helpless. She wasn't even what her last name represented. She was Evangeline Bouvier-Tregre. She mostly went by her mother's name Bouvier. It was on her license and her business license. Bouvier-Tregre was on her birth certificate. She was whatever she made herself to be.

Very carefully she applied her lip stain and went over it with a gloss. She took her time brushing out her hair and restyling it. She wanted to look and feel her best to get through this. She had no idea what she was going to do once they were gone, but she wasn't going to think about that until she had to. For now, she was the owner of the bakery and the men coming in were nothing more than customers.

She slid her hands down her hips, smoothing the material of her soft vintage blue jeans, a pair that were very comfortable because she'd had them for years. Since they were worn and ripped in places, she rarely wore them to work, wanting to appear a little dressier, but she'd woken up from one of her bad dreams with a headache because her skull felt too tight, her body ached, joints painful, and the familiar clothes always comforted her. Her jeans. The emerald green camisole that matched her eyes and had been a gift from her friend Saria back when things weren't so good.

She had nice eyes. Her mouth was too . . . big. Pouty. She practiced smiling to relieve the pout that was there when she wasn't thinking about it. But her eyes . . . She must have gotten them from her mother. They were large and shaped exotically, like a cat's eyes. Most of the time they were pure, startling emerald, the color emphasized by her thick, dark lashes. Lately she'd noticed little gold flecks at times. She wasn't certain what to think about that gold, but at least she liked her eyes.

The problem with her jeans and camisole was, they were old and she'd put on a little weight growing up. The denim clung to her hips and thighs, and the camisole emphasized her small waist and generous breasts. She couldn't loosen the laces in the front because the camisole zipped and the lacing was for show. She sighed.

A fist banging on the door made her jump and her heart stuttered. "Get out of there, Evangeline." There was pure steel in that voice. Timur was every bit as commanding as Alonzo. "I didn't think you were the type of woman to hide."

She threw the door open, hoping to hit him right in the face with it, but of course he wasn't there. She sent him one look from under her long lashes. "Like I would *ever* hide from you or your brother." She was terrified now and humiliated, but she'd spent her entire life hiding and she wasn't doing it again. Not. *Ever.*

She positioned herself behind the counter as Timur went to the back door and let someone in. She stayed locked against the counter close to the espresso machine, and pasted a smile on her face when the first few men came through the kitchen. She recognized Elijah Lospostos. He was notorious. His family had been in the crime business for generations. He was a good-looking but very dangerous man, and she knew he'd recently married Siena Arnotto. That bit of information was in every single tabloid and magazine. Alonzo had taken over the Arnotto estate. For *her.* Siena.

She realized that while she'd been in the bathroom, Timur had rearranged her tables to make one big one down the center of the room and several smaller ones surrounding it. There appeared to be a sign on her door. She didn't bother to go look and see what it said. What did it matter? She was stuck with this mess. She had to get through it and make certain it never happened again.

Elijah went straight up to her. "Thank you for being so generous with your bakery. We really appreciate it." He gave his order and she made his cappuccino while he surveyed the display for pastries. Her smile was practiced and didn't let her down. She made coffee for him and the four men with him. She assumed they were his bodyguards. *All* of them were leopard. That was easy enough for her to see.

She hung on to her smile a little grimly when Patrizio Amodeo walked in. He was tall and rather good-looking by most standards. He had two gold teeth that flashed

84

when he smiled — and he smiled *a lot*. He was oily smooth, leered at her from the moment he set eyes on her, changed his coffee order three times, waiting each time until she'd begun to make it. He also had four bodyguards with him, big hulks, definitely carrying guns and very nervous. She didn't think they were leopard, but they looked scary.

She'd seen Amodeo on the news. He'd been arrested several times but was never actually convicted. Witnesses disappeared or insisted they'd lied. He walked out of the courthouse with a huge, mocking smile and cameras on him. Twice he'd given the cops the finger as he'd gotten into his very expensive car and been driven away from the frenzy of the media. Her skin crawled a little bit every time he looked at her.

His men were equally as bad, ogling her and making little comments to each other like high school boys. She wanted to roll her eyes at them but thought it best to just get them their drinks and pastries and hope they would stare at their boss instead of her.

Alonzo arrived next. Instantly she was angry. He'd done this, brought her right into the middle of his criminal world. She looked right through him as she gave him her fake smile and made his familiar drink, not that it mattered. At. All. Alonzo didn't notice her hostility. His eyes were so iced she thought she might freeze when he looked at her. There was no emotion. He looked more dangerous than ever. Scary. Lethal.

Alonzo Massi was a man no woman should ever want to be with. So why did her heart beat faster when he was close to her? Why did her breasts tingle and damp heat gather between her legs? It made no sense at all, but no matter how angry she was, or how determined not to react to him, her body seemed to have a mind of its own. Her freakin' female leopard unfurled and stretched languidly. Sensuously. She hissed her displeasure at the cat. The last thing she wanted was for any of the male leopards to catch a glimpse of Bebe.

Alonzo took his coffee from her, shifting on his feet to angle his body so that her smaller body couldn't be seen by the others. "Cover up," he hissed.

She frowned at him. He didn't have the right to tell her what to do in her own bakery. But then he didn't have the right to have his private meetings there or his cameras either.

"Do. It. *Now.*" He bit out each word.

A shiver went down her spine. He meant

it. It didn't matter that his voice was low; she had the feeling that force would come next. She stuck her chin out, scowled at him and turned to head to the kitchen, where her cardigan hung over the chair. Gorya came through the door, the sweater bunched in his hand. He carried it down low, so the others couldn't see him hand it off to her. She took it without a word and went back to the espresso machine in order to make Gorya's favorite drink.

Alonzo was already seated at the table. Emotionless. Pure ice. He didn't glance her way, but she knew he saw her. She shrugged into the sweater and kept working. Alonzo had brought two other men besides Timur and Gorya with him, both leopards. She gave them their drinks and pastries just as more men came through her back door.

Evangeline didn't know what to think of this new development. Her bakery was a hangout for criminals. It was just a little ironic when she'd left her home in the swamps near New Orleans, traveled to Texas and set up her bakery thinking she'd left all that behind. She couldn't help wanting to laugh. The old adage "out of the frying pan and into the fire" certainly applied. At least business was brisk. Apparently men with guns and criminal activities on their minds were hungry.

The fourth crime boss entering had been in her bakery a few times. He was older, with silver streaks in his dark hair, a kind face, rather like a grandfather might have. A face others would trust. He smiled at her as she greeted him.

"Evangeline." The first time he'd come into the bakery, he'd made it a point to know her name and he'd never seemed to forget it. He was charming and sweet, always polite, as were his men.

"Emilio," she said, giving him her first genuine smile. She'd tried calling him a respectful "Mr. Bassini," but he had insisted on Emilio.

"How have you been, *mia cara*?" he asked.

She glanced at him over her shoulder as she prepared to make his caffe macchiato. "Good, and you?"

His smile was warm. "Perfect. I need to visit more often. No one does *sfogliatelle* like you do. As good as when I'm in Naples."

"Thank you, Emilio. That's the highest compliment anyone could give me."

She didn't know much about him. She knew if she looked him up on the Internet she'd probably find all sorts of horrible things about him that she didn't want to know. He was a good customer and he brought his men with him. They had also turned into good customers and usually bought out all her cannolis. Now she was fairly certain Alonzo had mentioned her bakery to him. She should be grateful, but right now she didn't want to credit Alonzo for anything.

There was another group coming in behind her, from her kitchen. Timur led them. The first two men entering were clearly bodyguards and they were all business, their gazes sweeping the room, seeing everything including her. Behind them came their boss, and her breath caught in her throat. She knew all the color leeched from her face.

Joshua Tregre. Her first cousin. He was the last person she ever thought would walk through her door, and for a moment, the room actually tilted and she thought she might go down. Instead, she caught the counter edge and held on, praying he wouldn't notice any resemblance. He'd never met her. He'd most likely never heard of her. He had been taken away from the bayou when he was a toddler. His mother had run with him back to the Borneo rain forest. His father, her Uncle Renard, had been murdered by their grandfather, Buford Tregre. She had been a well-kept secret from everyone, and she left the moment she was old enough.

Of course he would be a criminal. Her entire family seemed to be criminals. What difference did it make if Joshua had been raised in Borneo? She supposed it was in their blood. That was why every time she looked at Alonzo that wild part of her reacted.

She was careful to keep her eyes on her work, not meeting his gaze directly as he placed his order. She didn't want to see recognition there. She was very aware of Timur watching her curiously. She was acting out of character and that wasn't good. Of course he would notice. Alonzo had most likely noticed as well. It didn't matter, she couldn't control her fear so she dealt with it the way she did best. She stayed very calm, kept her voice soft and low, and worked fast and efficiently to get Joshua Tregre and his men to their seats as quickly as possible.

Evangeline needed to restock and when she started into the kitchen, it seemed as though every bodyguard went on alert. Alonzo nodded at Timur, and Elijah did the same to one of his guards. Both men followed her.

She began to put various pastries on a tray. "I keep the machine guns in the refrigerator," she sniped, without looking at either man.

Neither answered her and she didn't care. She walked straight toward the back door. She knew Timur had locked it, but there was no logical reason for her not to step outside into the cooler air. Since she had to wear a cardigan as Alonzo commanded, and it had been a clear order, she was hot. The shop was warm for her customers and working by herself behind the counter made for very hot work.

"Don't." Timur's warning stopped her in her tracks as she reached for the doorknob.

She halted, facing away from him, feeling a little sick. "I'm not your prisoner," she snapped. "It's hot workin' back here and I need to cool off."

"Don't," he repeated.

One simple word, but his tone made her shiver. He was fast curing her from her apparent — and unfortunate — attraction to criminals. She took a deep breath to keep from doing something stupid, reminding herself that they would leave soon and she could refuse them service. In fact, she was going to put up a sign refusing service to any criminals.

She couldn't just fling open the door and run for it. That would mean abandoning her business. She'd sunk every penny of the money she'd inherited from her mother into the shop and her house. If she couldn't work, she couldn't pay her mortgage and she'd lose everything.

She shrugged out of her sweater and turned back toward the two men. Both were watching her warily, as if they expected her to do something crazy and were ready to pounce. The instant she saw them looking at her, she felt Bebe rising.

Don't. They're leopard. Too close.
You're upset.

I can handle it. She breathed away the desire to claw and rake at both men like her female wanted. They had no right to come into her beloved sanctuary, her haven, and order her around.

She took a quick bathroom break and then hurried to restock. There were so many men eating her inventory, she knew she wouldn't have any left even if the meeting broke up before closing time. She was aware of that hideous man Patrizio Amodeo staring at her, and she wished she'd put her sweater back on. She served a few of the bodyguards, noting only one guard from each crime boss came up at a time, leaving three to watch over their man.

The phone rang as she turned to go into

the back to get her sweater. She couldn't stand being ogled. Not like that. "Small Sweet Shoppe."

"Hey, beautiful, I'm standing outside and there's a sign saying you've got a private party going on. I need some of your famous cannolis. Just sneak me in."

Brice. A friendly voice. She glanced through the enormous window and smiled at him. "I can't do that. I do have a private party going on. You'll live without them." She kept her voice low. Whispering almost, trying to create an intimacy between them so she could forget for a moment she was surrounded by criminals.

"Come on, babe. I won't be able to live without seeing you today. You're my fix. You know that. Meet me at the back door with a box of cannolis then. At least I'll get a chance to ask you out."

Alonzo's tall, very large body suddenly blocked her view of Brice. He stood solidly in front of her, his back to the others. "Coffee," he snapped.

She glared at him. That didn't faze him in the least. He stared down at her with dead eyes, pushing the mug across the counter at her. Something in his frozen stare was very, very scary.

"I've got to get back to work, Brice. See

you tomorrow."

She put the phone down on his protest, filled Alonzo's coffee mug and watched him walk back to the table. God, he was perfection sitting with his back to the wall, totally ignoring her as if she didn't exist while he conducted business. She could look at him all day. The first time she ever saw him, he'd scared the daylights out of her. She knew dangerous. She knew criminal. He was both, but far, far scarier and much more dangerous than anything she'd ever known. Worse, she was certain he was a shifter. Almost certain. His eyes — those beautiful, cold eyes — had given him away. But maybe not. She'd watched him closely and she still couldn't say with certainty — not like she could about his name, which she was very sure wasn't Alonzo Massi.

She knew certain things about Alonzo, things she was afraid he'd be very upset that she'd learned. He appeared to be Italian. He spoke Italian with a perfect accent, but more and more she was certain he was Russian, not Italian. She still privately thought of him as her Russian Iceman. She also believed Timur was related to him in some way, most likely his brother. Possibly Gorya as well, although he had a different build.

"Hey! You! Little sexpot," Patrizio yelled.

"Come on over here and bring the coffee."

"I'll be right with you," she said softly, trying not to wince. She'd never been called *sexpot* before. She supposed, if she tried very hard, she could think of it as a compliment — not that it sounded that way. He made it sound dirty.

Patrizio Amodeo was in his fifties and clearly thought he was entitled to say or do whatever he wanted. She didn't know if most people were intimidated by him because of what he was, or whether it was simply his arrogance and no one challenged him. He'd been rude when he'd come in, staring at her breasts and licking his lips. He'd said something to his companions who had stared at her as well. She was certain whatever he'd said about her wasn't good.

"Now, not later. You can't rely on displaying the goods, honey, if you want your little bakery to be successful. You actually have to give it up." He threw back his head and laughed, winking at Elijah.

Instantly all conversation at the table ceased. The atmosphere in the bakery went from tense to downright frightening. She glanced at Alonzo as she picked up the coffeepot. His face was a mask that could have been carved from a block of ice. His eyes were twin glaciers. Pure blue ice. Not good.

He might not want her, but he was protective of her. She had the feeling that he would reach across the table any moment and kill Amodeo.

Emilio Bassini frowned and looked around the table as if he didn't quite know what to do with the situation. Both Joshua and Elijah appeared as if they were locked in place, unable to move for fear of shattering. She couldn't tell if that was bad for her or good for her, but she didn't want bloodshed in her shop. More, she didn't want Alonzo vulnerable, not for her, and that alarmed her more than the bloodshed. That told her she still wasn't quite over her crush and she needed to be.

"Evangeline isn't a waitress, Patrizio." Elijah's voice was very soft. "She owns this establishment. When you want a refill you go up to the counter."

Patrizio leaned back in his seat. His face flushed a dark red and his white teeth disappeared as he glared at Elijah. "We're in the middle of an important discussion here. I'm not going to interrupt everyone when she's just standing there doing nothing."

Gritting her teeth, Evangeline grabbed the coffeepot and came out from around the counter. She needed to defuse the situation before there was a shoot-out in her bakery.

"I don' mind. Does anyone else want a refill?"

She detested the way Patrizio stared at her breasts as she walked across the room. She'd forgotten she'd removed her cardigan and only wore the camisole. It covered everything, but still emphasized her waist and breasts, not good when she had a jerk for a customer. Alonzo was seated where he always sat, his back to the wall at the end of the table. Patrizio was on his left with Joshua next to him. Elijah sat at the head of the table with Emilio on Alonzo's right.

All the bodyguards shifted position, spreading out, facing one another. There didn't seem to be a lot of trust, which made her uneasy. The tension was so thick in the bakery one could cut it with a knife. She kept her eyes down as she stepped between Patrizio and Alonzo, looking at the empty coffee mugs, not at any of the men.

4

Alonzo's leopard snarled, raging at the idea of Evangeline in such close proximity to Patrizio. The beast had been prowling close to the surface from the moment Patrizio and his guards had entered the bakery and they both had smelled deceit, cruelty and perversion on him. Talk had flowed around him and of course he'd taken in every word because he'd been trained from birth to pay attention to everything around him, but most of his attention was on Evangeline.

She was miserable. Angry. Hurt. Everything in him wanted to go to her, wrap her up and shelter her from all of this — from him. From what he was and would always be. He'd noticed the sweep of her lashes covering her beautiful eyes when Patrizio or one of his men spoke to her. He'd noted the color in her face when Brice had called her, flirting with Alonzo's woman. He'd wanted to rip the phone from her hand and throw it across the room. He'd seen the small bead of sweat glistening for a moment on her perfect skin and then sliding down to disappear between her breasts encased in that sweet camisole he wanted to unlace slowly.

Now she was without her sweater and Patrizio couldn't stop staring at her breasts. His gaze continually went to her, his mouth open, leering. He'd used the excuse of coffee to call her to him. Like a servant. Disrespectful. It would take Alonzo approximately three seconds to kill him. He mapped it out in his mind. He'd move with his leopard's speed, snapping the man's neck and then drawing his weapon as he let go of the dead body. He'd kill all four guards and immediately turn and put a bullet in Emilio's head. He'd have to. Emilio had arranged this meeting, insisting it be held at the bakery. There was a reason for that and it left Evangeline in danger.

Emilio's guards would retaliate. Alonzo would have to get Evangeline out of the line of fire fast, which meant forcing her to the ground. Timur would take Emilio's guards, and Gorya would head out to the parking lot to do the drivers of both crime bosses. Then there would be the cleanup . . .

Evangeline moved toward them, her hips

swaying in invitation, something she couldn't help. She looked sexy, alluring, her skin almost glowing. Alonzo imagined he could see her nipples pushing against the soft material of her camisole. She was covered, but it didn't matter. There was no missing the fact that she had high, firm breasts, soft and sensual, a constant temptation to a man — and Patrizio was tempted.

She stepped in between Alonzo and Patrizio to pour the coffee. At once his leopard purred, moving toward the surface to get close to her. Her scent enveloped him. She always smelled of cinnamon and spice. The combination was heady. Irresistible. It was both sensual and soothing to Alonzo and he found himself leaning toward her — close enough — so that the heat of her body touched the frozen ice inside of him.

Patrizio shifted, a slight, furtive movement that was barely perceptible, but Alonzo's leopard roared and he reached out just as the crime boss tried to slap Evangeline's round ass, cupped so lovingly in her soft jeans. The sound of Patrizio's hand hitting Alonzo's arm was loud in the silence of the room. Alonzo was already on his feet, moving with blurring speed, yanking Evangeline behind him, coffeepot and all. He let go of her to reach for Patrizio, counting the seconds in his head, his movements already practiced and smooth.

The instant Patrizio tried to touch Evangeline, Alonzo's leopard roared for blood. Alonzo was already on the move, even before his leopard had time to react, something that had never happened before in his life. His beast rose to the surface, fury driving it, even as he started toward the crime boss with his blurring speed.

"Patrizio." Elijah spoke, holding up his hand to stop the others. His voice was quiet. A whip lashing at the other man. "I asked Evangeline to do me a personal favor and close her shop during business hours because Emilio suggested we use her bakery as neutral territory. She did me that favor, and you've insulted her. In doing so, you've insulted me."

Alonzo breathed through the heat and fire, the cracking of joints. His jaw ached. His skull felt too tight. His ribs felt as if they would break with the leopard pushing and demanding the kill. Red heat fueled his vision so that he saw in colored bands, heat imagery, and all he saw was targets. He didn't want the leopard to kill the crime boss. He wanted to do it as a man, feeling his head between his hands as he snapped the neck.

Patrizio looked at the giant of a man standing in front of him. He had no idea how Alonzo had gotten there. No sound, but so fast the man was a blur. He had four guards, all armed, but they would be up against sixteen guards. Worse, he needed the alliance with these men. He was going to start being picked apart. He'd blown it for a *puttana.* A whore. He didn't know whom she belonged to, but she caused this, walking the way she did, showing him her breasts.

"I meant no harm. She's a beautiful woman. It was a compliment to give her attention. I was teasing her a little. No harm done, Elijah." Patrizio sounded appeasing. Just knowing he had to backpedal in order to keep in their good graces infuriated him, but he had no choice. The *puttana* would pay, just not today. He forced a smile at Elijah, not daring to look into those cold dead eyes of Alonzo's. The man was the walking dead. He lived and breathed but he didn't feel any emotion.

Alonzo could hear the lies in his enemy's voice. It mattered little that Joshua and Elijah heard them too. Evangeline was *his.* She was under his protection. He'd brought this down on her, by allowing Joshua and Elijah to override him when Emilio had first come up with the idea of the bakery as a neutral meeting place. He knew Emilio frequented the bakery, but he still questioned the motive for using Evangeline's shop. Was it so obvious to everyone that Evangeline was the draw, not the pastries and coffee?

Three seconds was all he needed and he would kill the man and his bodyguards and end the threat to Evangeline.

"Don't." Elijah's voice was a whip of authority.

The sound of it snaked through the ice in Alonzo's mind like the hot lash. He actually saw the snakelike whip sizzling through the glacier that kept his emotions from playing a part in his life. It took every ounce of discipline he possessed to stay still.

Elijah and Joshua were also on their feet. Bodyguards instantly squared off with the others in the room. Emilio sat quietly looking around at the men standing as if he were a bit puzzled by everything. Amodeo's bodyguards rushed to get to him, one knocking into Evangeline's arm as he swept in close to his boss. The coffeepot fell from her hand to the floor, shattering. A dark stain, much like a puddle of blood, spread across her tiled floor.

"Joaquin," Elijah addressed his personal

bodyguard. "Please escort Evangeline to the kitchen and stay there with her. She's under my protection. Patrizio, tell your bodyguards to stand down immediately. Everyone sit down and take a breath."

There was no mistaking the complete authority in that voice, and immediately Patrizio took the "out" Elijah offered and sent his bodyguards back to their original stations, leaving Alonzo his opportunity to kill the man. Three seconds to kill five men. Maybe six. That was all he needed once the bodyguards obeyed and settled into their previous positions.

Evangeline's fingers found the back of his shirt, beneath his suit jacket, and bunched the material into her palm. She leaned into him. Close. Her front to his back. She was trembling. "Don't." She whispered the word against his back. Lips against the material of his suit jacket while her fist held his shirt captive.

She knew. She knew things about him she shouldn't know. She should be terrified of him. Running. But instead she stood behind him knowing he would give his life for her. Knowing she was under his protection. She stood close. Her body was so close he felt her breasts and hips. One arm. That single word spoken so low was far more of a com-

104

mand to him than Elijah's had been. He drew air into his lungs and breathed away the need to kill.

Reaching behind him, he caught Evangeline's wrist and slowly drew her around him. Elijah nodded toward the kitchen. She shook her head, just once, but Alonzo saw her chin lift as she glanced down at the broken glass and pool of coffee. She didn't understand that Elijah was trying to save Alonzo from killing. Alonzo could have told him there was no saving him from anything, but he didn't want to terrify Evangeline.

"Go with him," he said, his hand on her arm all but forcing her toward Elijah's guard. "Timur will go with you as well."

"And Jeremiah," Joshua said.

Emilio stood slowly, and instantly there was silence. "I apologize for the behavior of my friends, Evangeline. Please accept the protection we're offering you. Martino will also accompany you." He looked around the table and shook his head. "I apologize to you, Elijah and Alonzo and Joshua as well. Patrizio, sit down and think with your head, not your dick for a change. What we do here is important."

Alonzo kept his gaze fixed on Patrizio even as his hand continued to urge Evangeline toward safety. Timur took her wrist and pulled gently. To Alonzo's relief, she went with his brother and the other bodyguards. He didn't look away from Patrizio, but he saw everything as a man rather than a leopard. Mostly he saw Evangeline's body, the way her shoulders were slumped as if in defeat. He hated that. And he knew she was going to send him away from her. That gutted him. He deserved it, but it gutted him all the same because in the end, he was already lost. His leopard would grow in power and cruelty until Alonzo wouldn't be able to control him and they'd both go the way of his family unless he killed himself or made someone else do it.

Patrizio sank into his chair, shaking his head. "There is no excuse so I make none, only offer my apologies."

He looked around the table with his lying smile and his hate-filled eyes — eyes that settled on Evangeline with a dark, ugly promise. He must have felt Alonzo's steady stare, the focused stare of the leopard that was unsettling and terrifying. Alonzo didn't take his gaze from the man, not once during all the negotiations. Not when he smiled or tried to fawn, not when he practically gave up everything to be a part of the alliance they were forming. Especially not when Elijah pushed back his chair and stood, silently declaring the meeting over.

"We'll get back to you soon," he promised both Emilio and Patrizio.

Alonzo stood as well, hating to let the man go. His leopard was watchful, angry that the enemy was walking out unscathed, raking and clawing with the need to end the man. He felt as his leopard did, a terrible need consuming every part of him to feel Patrizio Amodeo's life fade in his hands.

We'll get him, he promised. *Think of him as a walking dead man. We'll get him.*

Patrizio was no fool. He knew he'd made enemies in that room and that Alonzo was one of them. Joshua was a puzzle to the crime boss, as he would be to Emilio. Alonzo knew Joshua and had fought enemies beside him. Joshua was fast and his leopard was fierce. He was also cool under fire. Alonzo liked him, but he hadn't liked the way Joshua was watching Evangeline — almost as if he had some proprietary relationship over her. His gaze had followed her speculatively.

Joshua was single, but his gaze, as focused as it was on Evangeline, hadn't held heat exactly. Interest, yes, but heat, no. Alonzo didn't like anything touching Evangeline he didn't understand. He had done everything in his power to make her safe, but people were always unpredictable, leopards even more so.

"I'm sorry about Amodeo," Emilio said as Elijah sat back down into his seat. He looked down at the coffee spill still on the floor. "I know you took it as an insult, and I don't blame you. You haven't had much contact with Patrizio. I knew his father. Same problem. They traffic in women and they have no respect for them. Not even their own wives." He shook his head. "Otherwise, they are good businessmen and they have excellent laundries."

"It's a weakness." Joshua spoke for nearly the first time. "A man thinks with his dick during a business meeting to the point of disrupting it, he's a question mark any time we're doing business if there's a woman in the room."

"You knew that he'd react that way to Evangeline," Elijah accused, sounding almost bored. "Why?"

Emilio shrugged. "I wanted to see everyone's reaction to her. She's stunning. She's intelligent. I am thinking of taking her for my wife."

The shock wave went around the table. Truth was in every word. Alonzo's leopard roared with fury and leapt for the surface, shoving himself into his shifter's throat, pushing into his jaw and down into his hands and feet, determined to take over, to rip apart his opponent.

"There's a bit of an age difference," Elijah pointed out politely. "She's barely legal."

Emilio nodded. "Young enough to give me children. I wanted to see how she did with a meeting of my friends held here and how she would handle Patrizio pawing at her."

Alonzo fought back the change. His skull hurt. His jaw ached. Teeth were too big for his mouth. Every joint flared with pain, and his hands, curled into fists, were excruciatingly painful. *We'll get him when the time is right.* So many lives his leopard demanded, but Alonzo had always refused the bloodthirsty creature.

He'd spent a lifetime killing already. First the training, killing at six under his father's watchful eye. The emotions he had to lock up in a block of ice. The terrible things demanded of him. Demanded of his brother and cousin. The things his father and other brothers and cousins had done in front of him. The cruelty. The cunning. The viciousness.

He'd turned his back on that life, no longer the enforcer. No longer Fyodor Amurov. No longer Russian. He had been a bodyguard. He'd come to Antonio Arnotto at a young age, made the man believe he was Italian, and he'd hired on as a soldier. None of them saw the killer in him. None of them saw what he was or what he was capable of. He'd been simply a bodyguard to Antonio's beloved granddaughter, Siena. Now she was married to Elijah and Antonio was dead. Elijah had convinced him to step into Antonio's shoes for Siena and he'd done it, never once thinking he would find a woman like Evangeline. Never once thinking that his leopard would give him a chance with her.

"No." Joshua said the word softly. "I respect you, Emilio, more than I can say, but Evangeline cannot marry you. I can't give you reasons, other than she has obligations."

Heat had banded across Alonzo's eyes and he saw the flare of anger as a sharp red burst from Emilio, but the man's anger quickly cooled and he shifted forward in his chair to pin Joshua with his hard gaze. "You cannot speak for her. You have no right."

"I have every right. She is under my protection and the protection of my family. She is my first cousin." Joshua made the announcement in his low tone, never realizing he was sealing Evangeline's fate to Alonzo.

There was no turning away from her. No walking away. She was a Tregre. She was leopard. Whether or not her leopard ever showed didn't matter, nor would it ever matter to him. Alonzo didn't know how it happened that he'd ever walked into her bakery by chance and found he couldn't walk away. Fate maybe. Destiny. What were the odds of meeting a woman in San Antonio who was from a lair of leopards from Louisiana?

His leopard settled. Knew for certain Alonzo would never give Evangeline up. Not. Ever. Alonzo sighed inwardly. He would have to come to terms with the fact that he was a complete bastard. There would be no redemption for him. If he had a shred of decency in him he would walk out of the bakery and never go back, but the belief that someday he'd be strong enough to do that was in tatters with Joshua's declaration.

In the world of shifters, a man and a woman could come together in more than one lifetime. His family refused to find their true mates. They wanted sons for their work, a daughter if they could use her to barter an alliance with another lair, but rarely did they keep a female alive. In their lair only males were trusted into the brotherhood, the sacred shifter *bratya*. When a wife had done her duty and given her husband as many sons as he demanded, she met with a cruel and very untimely death. He'd been born into that. He'd failed to save his mother, but he'd managed to save Timur and Gorya from his father's wrath.

Both had been there that day. Gorya had been given to Ogfia, Alonzo's mother, when Gorya's mother had died. Alonzo now knew her own husband had murdered her. It was a sign of loyalty to their lair, to the brotherhood. Gorya and Timur had been home the day Alonzo and Timur's father had chosen to murder his wife. Both tried to fight him, but Alonzo's father, like Alonzo, was a giant of a man and incredibly strong and fast. He'd killed his wife and then begun to beat both boys to death. Alonzo had come in.

Around him the meeting was breaking up, Emilio seemingly accepting Joshua's verdict and leaving with his bodyguards, stopping to kiss Evangeline's hand as he swept through the bakery to the back entrance. She gave Emilio a genuine smile and a little wave as he left via the kitchen.

Once again his leopard protested another man touching her. *It won't be long. Once we claim her, no other man will put his hands on her . . . and live.* He closed his eyes briefly on that thought. That made him far too much like his father. The opposite, but still willing to kill. He would keep her any way he had to.

Evangeline returned from the kitchen and stood just behind the counter, frowning a little as she stared at the coffee stain. She didn't have a poker face at all. Every expression gave away her thoughts, and without a doubt she thought to send all of them away.

Joshua and Elijah left next, both stopping to thank her. She avoided Joshua's gaze, which told Alonzo she refused to acknowledge the family connection between them. He needed to find out why. She had been using another name. Bouvier, not Tregre. Timur would find out everything there was to know about her. He needed to know. He couldn't walk into the relationship and be blindsided now that he'd made up his mind.

Eventually there was only Alonzo and his four bodyguards left in the store. Evangeline took towels to soak up the coffee and dropped them on the wide stain. She bent to pick up the glass. Alonzo caught her arm, preventing her from dropping to the floor. "We're going into the kitchen to talk."

"No, we're not," she protested even as he

began to propel her across the room. He had a big stride and he used it, taking her with him. "I mean it, Alonzo. You and your men are leavin' and you're never comin' back. Tell me where the cameras are so I can get rid of them."

His gaze jumped to Timur, letting him know silently that as soon as they were home, at the Arnotto estate, he was going to get pounded into the ground.

"We'll discuss that in the kitchen," he said softly. Not in front of his soldiers. He had things to make clear to her and she wasn't going to like anything he had to say. He wanted her to be able to be as angry as she needed to be, and having a woman yell at him in front of his soldiers wasn't a good idea. In his business, respect was everything. To protect her and give her the privacy to do what she needed to do, they had to be in the kitchen. He kept walking her right around the counter, even when she turned as if she'd go back.

"Stop it, Alonzo," she hissed. "I mean it. You don' have the right to tell me —"

He cut off her protests by simply lifting her into his arms. Cradling her close. Taking the chance she'd rake his face with her nails. He knew her leopard was close because his leopard was purring and strutting, and her eyes were glowing. She looked more exotic than ever and thoroughly pissed.

"Clean that mess up and make certain you get every single splinter of glass." He gave the command over his shoulder and kicked the door shut behind him.

He set her carefully on her feet and she backed away from him, putting a short distance between them as if that would make her safe.

"I want you gone, Alonzo. I mean it. Leave and don' come back. I don' want your friends in my bakery either, so make that happen. I want to know where every single camera is and quit havin' Timur or Gorya follow me home every night."

She looked . . . beautiful. Gorgeous. She took his breath away. Her skin was flushed, her eyes so bright they were two emeralds shaped like a cat's eye with many fascinating facets. A gold ring had formed as flecks merged, telling him that when she was all cat — if that ever happened — her eyes would be molten gold. Lashes were as dark as the long thick hair he wanted to sink his fingers into.

"That isn't going to happen." He said it quietly with a heavy note of finality.

She heard the note. Processed it instantly. He saw knowledge on her face. Wariness crept into her eyes, into her expression. Her tongue touched her bottom lip, that full bottom lip he wanted to bite. He dreamt of biting it. Now it was going to happen.

She shook her head and took another step back, throwing up her hand, palm out facing him, warding him off. So fragile. So little. Such a small thing to think she could hold back the force of an Amurov. "I'll admit I flirted with the idea. I had a hard time with the idea of givin' anyone else a chance because I was so attracted to you, but it isn't right. What's between us isn't right. You clearly didn't want it when I was dancin' around the idea and now I *know* I don't want it."

"You do."

Faint color crept up her body, flushed the curves of her breasts, her neck and face. Her chin lifted. "Maybe I am *physically* attracted to you, Alonzo, but I don' have to act on it. You put cameras in my place of business like a stalker. You have me followed home every night. You brought horrible people into my bakery, men with guns, and there was nearly a shoot-out. Don' pretend that didn't happen because it did."

He liked that even angry and afraid — and she was both — her voice was pitched low. She always talked softly, and that soothed him just as it did his leopard. "I put cameras in your business to protect you, so someone I trusted had eyes on you when I wasn't here. I put you in danger by coming here, I know that, but I couldn't stop myself. I have you escorted home. They're visible to protect you from any enemy I have that might think to strike at me through you. You're my one vulnerability. The only one I have. I can't stay away so I have to protect you."

She opened her mouth twice to protest what he said. He knew she could throw attitude and sass at him, but she wouldn't do it just for the sake of throwing it. She was a reasonable woman and she would hear the ring of truth in his voice because her leopard would hear it.

"I didn't want to keep coming here and putting you in jeopardy. Believe me, Evangeline, I know how selfish it was, but when I'm here, you make my world okay for just a little bit. I don't know if I would have survived it intact had I managed to find the strength to leave you alone. And I tried. Five weeks, four days, three hours and twenty-seven minutes I made it. Each one of those days was agony."

"Alonzo . . ."

"You know that's not my name." He said

it quietly.

Her small white teeth sank into her lower lip. *Yeah. She knew.* She was very observant. Her gaze shifted from his.

"Evangeline." Just her name. A command. He waited. She took a breath. A second one and then her eyes lifted to his. His woman had the courage of a leopard. "I'm not going anywhere. It's not possible, so you're going to have to get over being angry about the cameras and the protection. You'll have to get used to that." He said it as gently as possible, but he meant every word. There was a slight shake to her head that told him she was still going to try to fight the inevitable.

"Leave the cameras for the time bein' if they make you feel better, but this . . ." She swept her hand between them. "This isn't goin' to happen. Yes, I'm not goin' to lie, because clearly you know I'm attracted to you. *Very* attracted."

That honest admission cost her and he wanted to reach out and pull her into his arms to comfort her.

"But it can't happen. Not for all the reasons you think either. It has nothin' to do with you and what you've chosen to do with your life. It's about me and what I can't go back to. I won't go back."

Her voice trembled a little and that cost him. He didn't like her scared, or hurt or embarrassed. Still, she was cute as all hell standing up to him.

"Back to what?" he prompted.

Her chin lifted. That little defiant gesture drove him wild — sent his leopard into a fury of need to claim her. To show her just whom she belonged to.

For one moment she struggled with her decision to admit she knew he was leopard. Or that she was. He saw it on her face, but then she shrugged and just committed.

"A lair. Never again. I don' care what Joshua said, I have no responsibilities to any lair or any leader of a lair."

He opened his mouth to deny she would be in a lair of any kind, but then realized that wasn't true. His brother and cousin were leopards. He'd already acquired two more men from the Borneo rain forest, both leopards, men he could trust. Timur had sent for Amur leopards that had left the lairs right after they had. Technically, he was the head of the lair. The leader. She said she had no responsibilities to a lair.

"You didn't ask for Joshua's protection, or for anyone's protection for that matter. Why not?"

She looked confused. Puzzled. "Why

would I? I don' want anything from them."

"It wouldn't have mattered," he said truthfully. "But it would have caused complications. Come here."

She heard the note of finality in his voice and she knew she was in danger. His woman. Smart. She stepped back. He stepped forward, maneuvering her toward the wall. He stalked her like the leopard he was, gaze focused on her, his mouth set in grim, determined lines. Deep inside, his beast surged toward the surface over and over in elation. So close. They were so close.

Her back hit the wall and she held up her hand as if that would ward him off. Stop a leopard. Stop an enforcer. Stop a man like him. He was a big man. He towered over her, his shoulders wide, his chest broad. He dwarfed her in size. One of his hands easily spanned her throat, his thumb tipping her head up. He stood close, so close he could feel the brush of her soft breasts against his ribs. So close he felt every breath she took.

"You. Are. *Mine.*" He enunciated each word carefully so there was no misunderstanding. He knew she would protest, but he didn't want to argue. There was no arguing with fate.

He bent his head and took her mouth. Her lips were soft and trembled beneath his. She didn't part her lips for him so he coaxed. Gently. Rubbing his lips over hers. Tiny kisses when no part of him had ever been gentle. He caught her lower lip between his teeth, that bitable lip he fixated on often, and he did exactly what he'd been fantasizing about for months. He bit down and tugged. She gasped. He took instant advantage, both hands cupping her face, fingers sliding around to find her thick hair while he kissed her. Deep. Hard. Passionately. Sparing neither of them. It was a claiming and they both knew it.

She wasn't very experienced, but that made it all the sweeter for him. Her untutored mouth, the taste of cinnamon and spice, did something to him — something extraordinary. He came from a family of users. The men used women to get what they wanted. He'd been no different. He'd fucked women to get off and he'd made certain they were women who were willing but knew he'd walk away immediately after. And he had — to save their lives. He'd done that. Got up. Got dressed. Left without a word. Fast.

He'd never enjoyed kissing. It was too — intimate. He took a woman from behind so he didn't have to look into her eyes. So he didn't have to pretend to smile. To pretend he felt anything at all but his body's re-action. He took her hard and fast. He was every bit as savage as his leopard, and he found women who enjoyed that sort of thing. Getting off as he got off and just walking away.

He hadn't touched a woman for a long while before meeting Evangeline and he certainly hadn't wanted to touch one since. First, it was because his leopard *hated* the women, and Alonzo had begun to fear that in that moment of climax, his leopard would leap, shredding his tattered control and kill-ing the woman. Then it was because neither man nor leopard wanted any woman near but Evangeline.

Kissing Evangeline opened up an entire world to him. He had felt protective of her. He wanted her body with every cell in his. She brought him to life. He hadn't known she would give him gifts. Of tenderness. Gentleness. Of slow, leisurely exploration. Coaxing her response. Reveling in it. Feel-ing that first glide of her tongue along his. Savoring it. In a way kissing was a first for him as well, and she gave that to him.

The fire started with a slow burn and spread like molasses through his veins. Blood pooled. Low. Wicked. He had never been so hard or so in need. He pressed close, snug, wanting to lift her up, but he didn't. He was careful of her. Found a gentleness he didn't know he had. Had never seen before. Never felt before.

She moaned into his mouth and the fire went from molasses to molten lava. Still burning slow, but hotter than hell. Every nerve ending came alive until not only his mind and body knew she was his — he knew it deep down in his soul. She was the woman who would center him. Be the center of his world. Hell. Who was he kidding? She already was.

He didn't know the first thing about relationships. He'd been born into a family of killers. Men. Women. Children. None of those lives mattered. Only wealth. Power. Only the male members of the lair. He had no idea what he was doing, but he knew he wouldn't survive without her. She was the one. The only one.

He kissed her over and over. Exchanged breath. Took the kiss from gentle to passionate but was careful to keep his wild nature in check. For her. He could do that for her. The fire began to rage. Her breasts pushed against him. Her hands slipped up his ribs, fingers digging in.

Alonzo forced himself to lift his head, lips inches from hers. He stared down. Waiting.

Her lashes lifted and he saw heat and something far stronger than mere affection in her eyes. For him. There was passion to match his. Need. Hunger. That changed to confusion. Wariness. Not quite a protest but building. It was too late. She'd already shown him those gorgeous green eyes and all the emotion any man could want to see for a lifetime. He couldn't wait to look into her eyes when he claimed her body.

He kept possession of her, refusing to allow her to move or look away. "When we're alone together, you call me Fyodor." He was so close his mouth was a whisper from hers. His voice so low that she had to use her leopard senses to hear him. "That's my name. Fyodor. Only for you. Just you. When I make love to you, that's the name you call me."

Before she could answer, before she could protest or say a single word, he spun her around, her front to the wall, holding her there, his body pressed tightly against hers. He kept his face close to hers. "I'm giving that to you and it's my life in your hands. Do you understand, *solnyshko moyo*?"

One hand stayed on the nape of her neck, pressing her face forward while the other unzipped her camisole and opened it slowly. Her breath hitched and she tried to pull away from him, but his body was too big, too strong, and she couldn't move.

"Trust me, *devochka moya,* I am only going to claim you. Do you feel her inside of you? Right now, is she pushing to rise?" He whispered each word into her ear.

She tensed even more as his hand pushed the material of her camisole up her back until he gathered it into the fingers at her nape, leaving her back exposed.

"What are you doing?" she whispered, matching his tone.

"Answer me. Do you feel her?" He bent his head, holding her in place as he kissed his way from the little indentation at the base of her spine all the way up to her shoulder.

"Yes." Her voice trembled. Her body did as well.

"Trust me. This is for them. For us." He felt the joy in his leopard. He'd never felt that before. He didn't know his leopard could feel anything other than sheer savagery. The beast leapt for the surface.

For just a moment Alonzo hesitated. What if he was wrong and the leopard killed her? Could he take that chance? He bent his head to her shoulder and kissed her. Once. Twice. His leopard was so close he felt the ache in his bones. In his jaw. In his mouth.

So close.

Evangeline moaned and suddenly cinnamon and spice were wild. Female. Wanton. Her cat was close and throwing off enough pheromones that his leopard feared the other male leopards would scent her and come bursting in. At once he raked and clawed for freedom and Alonzo partially shifted. Fur slid along Evangeline's bare back and his cat rubbed up her spine and over both shoulders, scent marking, and then he sank his teeth into her shoulder, pinning her in the way of their kind.

Evangeline cried out, a soft plea of shock and pain. His leopard was being gentle. Like he'd been. Unnatural for his beast, but Alonzo felt him, was monitoring closely just to be safe, but he shouldn't have worried. The leopard held her with care, waiting for her female to rise. To accept him.

5

The leopard's teeth hurt, but not nearly as bad as Evangeline had expected. She couldn't move, not with Alonzo's big body pressing against her, holding her pinned to the wall. She couldn't scream for help. The only ones that would hear her were Alonzo's men. Other leopards. Tears burned in her eyes. He was claiming her. His leopard was claiming her female. That meant her female would be bonded to his male. There was no going back from that.

Bebe, I'm sorry, I couldn't protect you.

She held herself very still, pressed her forehead into the wall and closed her eyes tightly against the memories flooding her. Sounds of the swamp. Her heart pounding. The slide of fur against the walls of the tiny building she was huddled in. She had only her blanket to cover her small little body. She wasn't yet four, her mass of hair in tangles around her face. She remembered putting her hand over her mouth to keep from crying out. She didn't have that luxury now. Her hands were trapped against the wall.

Her heartbeat was a drum of fear as the leopard rubbed his face so gently against her, his fur almost comforting. But the teeth were steady. Unrelenting. The sounds of her screams deep in her head filled her ears. She remembered those same screams in her head when the large cat had pushed against the flimsy door of the tiny structure her father locked her in at night — a structure deep in the swamp. He locked her in and left her. She begged and cried but he told her to be quiet. To not make a sound or the bad leopard would come for her. And it had come. Night after night.

Way back then that wild thing inside of her had unfurled and reached out to comfort her — to try to keep her from going insane with fear. Even then, at the age of four, she knew that hideous cat pawing around the building was looking for her — for what was inside of her — and she had to protect it. They had to protect each other. She stayed very still, that little child, her fist jammed in her mouth, eyes closed, and waited for the thing to go away.

There was no waiting now. It was too late.

She had never told anyone about her leopard. No one. Not even Saria, her best friend. Not Pauline, the woman who had taught her to bake. No one. Saria and Pauline had both explained that women didn't know if they had a leopard or not until it began to emerge, but she knew. She just didn't say a word to them. Still, this man had known. His leopard had known.

Her legs trembled until she knew she would have fallen to the floor had Alonzo not been holding her up with his body. The moment the leopard sank his teeth into her, pinning her in the way of the shifter so the male could bond with her female, Evangeline felt the extreme power and danger in the animal. It was savage and feral. The leopard was a brutal, relentless killer. Bad-tempered, jealous, a brute of an animal in its prime, and nothing, no one but his human partner, no one but Alonzo, was strong enough to stop its formidable nature. What did that say about Alonzo?

A shudder went through her. A small sound escaped her throat when she'd been so certain she was too scared to make any noise. Despair. Pain. Anger. This leopard was far worse than any of the leopards she'd ever encountered. She'd wanted Alonzo, but all along she'd known she couldn't have him. She'd longed for him, fantasized over him, dreamt of him — but she knew there was this. The leopard. The worst of the worst. A killer. Another sob welled up and escaped before she could stop it.

The leopard pinning her with his teeth did a very strange thing. She felt her female rise to accept him, sealing the bond and then he slowly opened his mouth, his tongue lapping gently over the bite mark in her shoulder. He rubbed his face along the bite, the fur soft and warm. He purred. It was soft and gentle sounding. Strange. Unexpected. From such a savage animal, the soothing touch seemed totally against his nature.

She felt the slide of fur as it disappeared and then Alonzo's mouth was moving over her shoulder, taking away the last of the sting. Very slowly, keeping her in place so she wouldn't fall, he pulled down the camisole and zipped it back into place. Because she was shaking so much, he slipped his arm around her body, right below her breasts, and locked her body to his as he stepped back.

"It's done, *solnyshko moyo*. It's over. Come over here to the table and sit down for a moment."

His voice. She hated that she reacted to

his voice. So low and mesmerizing. Commanding. Yet careful of her. She didn't want him to be careful or sweet. She wanted him to be what she knew he was — savage and cruel.

"Let go of me." She kept her voice low, her back to his front, head down, not wanting him to see her face. She'd learned to pitch her voice very low from the time she was just a child. *Don't ever let anyone hear you talking or laughing. Stay secret. Stay quiet. If you don't, the leopard will come.* Her Bebe had taught her that.

"*Malyutka,* if I let you go, you'll fall down."

"I'd rather fall down than have you touch me," she sniped.

She meant it too. He'd found her leopard and he'd captured her. No one, not her family, not her friends, *no one* had ever known about her leopard. She had sworn to protect her and she'd failed. All because she was weak whenever she looked at Alonzo. So weak. Even now, being so close to him all she could do was smell his scent, the one that took her away from everything and sent her head spinning and set her body on fire. She couldn't look at his mouth without remembering how he'd kissed her.

"Go away and do whatever it is you do and leave me alone. I don't care what your leopard did to me. Or that mine accepted yours. I refuse to accept you. Or it. I mean it, Alonzo, just go. What you did was wrong. So wrong."

She detested that she had tears on her face and he would see them the moment he turned her around. She couldn't wipe at them either, not without him seeing. It was humiliating. She didn't cry. She'd learned not to cry a long, long time ago in that tiny shack out in the middle of the swamp when she was a toddler. Alone. In the dark, afraid the leopard would come for her.

"What I did was necessary and you know it. There was no choice. They . . . belong."

His arm unlocked around her, setting her free for a moment to turn her around to face him, but when she swayed unsteadily, his hand immediately went to her arm and then slid down to her wrist.

She jerked at her arm, intending to get away, but his fingers wrapped around her entire wrist shackling her to him. Gently. But there was no escape.

"I don't care if they belong. She'll do as I wish. She always has. If I say no, she won't accept him, bond or no bond, and I say no. You had no right."

He didn't respond to her threat, but led her to a kitchen chair. "Where's your first aid kit?" His voice was pitched low. So soft. So without emotion when she was all about emotion.

"I don't want your help. Just go away."

He was as gentle as ever, but he forced her into the chair and leaned down to wipe at a tear on her face with his thumb. "Don't cry, Evangeline. I can take a lot of things, but I don't have the first clue what to do when you cry. It tears me up inside. Let me take care of this bite for you and then we'll talk."

She hated that he sounded so reasonable. Almost sweet. The ring of truth was in his statement and that made her want to cry more. She took a deep breath and forced her emotions under a semblance of control — another thing she'd learned as a child in the dark.

"The kit is in the bathroom under the sink. Just see to the bite and go. I don' want you here ever again." She sounded like a broken record and she didn't know if she was trying to convince him or her. The thought of what he would lure her into was horrendous to her. Impossible to even contemplate. A lair of vicious leopards. Cruelty. Depravity. He was a criminal and that just made it more certain. And yet . . . she couldn't imagine never seeing him again. That was equally or even more terrifying.

She watched him go into her bathroom and crouch beside the sink. She should have run for the back door and made a break for it. Brice was most likely somewhere outside. He or one of the other two cops were usually around if Alonzo was in the bakery.

"Don't try it, *malyutka.* You won't make it and then you'll be even more upset than you already are."

He didn't even turn around and he'd known what she was thinking. She didn't bother to confirm or deny that he was right. Instead, she admired the silent, fluid way he moved. She saw the leopard in him, the way his roped muscles rippled beneath his immaculate suit as he returned to her and opened the first aid kit.

"If you can't stop lying to me, don't speak, Evangeline," he said, sweeping the hair from her shoulder to expose the bite. "I hear the truth, the same as you."

"I don' understand. You were determined to leave me alone. All those months you kept comin' into the bakery. You barely spoke to me." That had hurt. Really hurt. She had convinced herself the interest was all one-sided. And then he'd been gone for those weeks. Endless weeks. She counted the days. The hours. Even the minutes at times. She worried about him. Couldn't sleep at night. Wondered if he was with another woman. Afraid he'd been killed.

"You know why." His voice was a thread of sound. "This may sting."

After the claiming bite of his leopard she doubted it would register. That brought her up short. She *knew* Alonzo was a scary, dangerous man. He was fast. He was some kind of crime lord leading other leopards, all scary, dangerous men. She knew his leopard was the same, even worse, driving him all the time, yet when the cat had claimed its mate, it had been weirdly gentle. Everything it had done had been done to soothe her while it held her pinned. It didn't rake her or claw. It gave her a low purr that was strange in a leopard.

"You were goin' to let me go."

"I *wanted* to let you go. You deserve a white knight, Evangeline. I'm a dark knight, not like you deserve. I'll never be that man. I can't give you the life you crave. You made up your mind to live among humans and stay away from shifters. More, you were so determined to live clean you turned your back on your family name. I wanted that for you. I tried to give it to you, but I couldn't stay away. When I'm close to you, my leopard is calm. In all the years of my life, he's never been that way. I've never been that way. When I'm with you, there's peace. I need that and crave it the way my body craves you."

He couldn't say those things to her. She didn't want to hear them. She couldn't hear them, not if she was going to stay strong. She knew what a vicious leopard could do to its human counterpart. Alonzo was a violent man. He just was. There was no getting around that. His leopard drove him, and once unleashed, the savagery of a leopard had few comparisons. It wouldn't matter how calm she made him, he would go his own way. She could see that in him just like now, when she told him to leave and he didn't.

She shook her head as he applied a triple antibiotic cream and then put a large round Band-Aid over the bite.

"You kissed me back."

Her heart jerked hard in her chest. A thousand butterflies took wing in her stomach. She'd done that. She had. "I didn't mean to." She knew how absurd that sounded, but it was all she had. She truly hadn't thought she would kiss him back. There'd been nothing else to do. Her mind had melted and there'd been only her body responding.

"I know that, Evangeline, but you did. If you hadn't I might have found the strength to walk away, but it's too late and we both know it. My male rose and so did your female. He'd never stand for it, even if she would. There's no going back from that. We'll take it slow. One day at a time. I'm not going to throw you over my shoulder and carry you off into a cave. We'll go on as we have been but spend more time together, get to know each other."

That was so reasonable. She didn't want him to be reasonable. She wanted him gone because if he didn't go, she would succumb. She wasn't that strong around him. "You don' know me at all."

"Malyutka." One word. A reprimand. She didn't speak Russian and she had no idea what he was calling her, but she suspected it was an endearment of some kind. "I have been around you nearly a year. You're soft inside. Sweet. Strong and independent. You can handle the worst customer with grace, defusing any situation."

"I could have ignored your friend."

"Patrizio Amodeo is not my friend. That was my first meeting with him. No man puts his hand on you. No man but me. His intentions weren't good and you know it. He all but insinuated you were a whore out for money."

She touched her tongue to her bottom lip. Just that small action made it tingle, remembering the taste of Alonzo, the way his mouth moved over hers. In hers. Branding her. "Elijah left a fat envelope on the counter. I imagine he paid me a great deal of money I didn't earn in the small amount of time you were all here."

His eyebrow shot up. "I hope you're not implying taking his money means you're a whore. You lost business. We rented out your establishment. It is fair to pay you. That is not the same thing as Amodeo attempting to touch you inappropriately."

"True, but I could have handled it. He pretended to be sorry, Alonzo, but he wasn't. He was angry. Not just with all of you, but with me. I made an enemy there. I think all of you did, especially you."

She didn't like that. She could have prevented it if he'd just let the man grab her butt. She would have protested, let him smirk thinking he was all that and walked away. Alonzo would have been safe. He wasn't safe now.

"Amodeo is my problem. Elijah's reputation will most likely keep him contained. He wants an alliance with us all."

"Is he going to get it?" She knew the answer. None of those men would form an alliance with a man with so little control. Alonzo and Elijah were the epitome of control. She suspected Joshua was as well. Emilio was just a nice older gentleman surrounded by sharks, at least he seemed that way. So far, the times she'd been around him, she hadn't seen evidence of his criminal activities, but if he was with them, he had to be dirty as well. She sighed. So much for a nice older gentleman.

He remained silent, and it occurred to her that he'd said more to her in the last few minutes than he had in the nearly entire year he'd been coming to her bakery.

She covered her face with her hands for a moment and then scrubbed them down her cheeks hard as if she could wipe away every evidence of tears from him. "*Bondye*, Alonzo, do you not see that he's goin' to come after you? Because of me? You stopped him from touchin' me, somethin', I might add, that happens more often than you might care to know about. I could have handled it. Now that odious man is goin' to try to kill you. Because of me."

He shook his head and crouched down, so that his head was level with hers. "Not because of you, Evangeline. I *chose* to stop

139

him. I had a choice. I know what kind of man he is. Do I look like a man who needs my woman's protection? *I* protect *you.* You should never have to put up with a man touching you inappropriately. No woman should. Never think for one moment that I didn't know exactly what I was doing."

"You still shouldn't have. You put yourself in danger unnecessarily."

He reached out, his hand cupping her jaw so gently it took her breath. His thumb traced her lower lip, sending little wicked spirals of desire threading through her veins. "I'm coming home with you, *malysh.*"

He shook his head when she attempted to pull back, a little forbidden thrill making its way down her spine. How perverse of her that she *wanted* him to come home with her, even when she knew they couldn't have a relationship. If he was willing to just have sex, she was all over that, but a relationship with a man like Fyodor/Alonzo was something else altogether. Throw in the fact that he was leopard — a vicious, killing leopard — that sealed the deal as far as she was concerned. Yet every cell in her body was aware of him. More, she wanted his mouth on hers again. It was all she could do not to stare at it or lean forward and kiss him.

"Just to spend time. I promised we'd take

this slow, and we will."

She knew she should protest. She should. She should find her anger again, but she couldn't. He was too close, and for the first time in her life she realized just how powerful a connection between two shifters could be once their leopards were mated. A sudden thought occurred to her.

"Oh. My. God. Tell me you didn't put cameras in my house." Of course he knew where she lived, he had her followed home every night. Twice she was certain a car sat outside all night with a couple of sentries in it. From him. Alonzo had done that to keep her safe. She didn't even know what she was supposed to be kept safe from. His enemies? Patrizio Amodeo had wanted an alliance with him.

There was a small, telling silence.

"You did not."

He didn't say anything, just looked at her with his glacier-cold eyes. She shoved at his chest, angry all over again when it didn't even rock him.

"What would you have done if I'd brought a man home and had wild sex in my livin' room or wherever you put the cameras? For all you knew I paraded around naked the moment I got home. How many people have been watchin' me?"

He straightened slowly, with the fluid grace of a cat, looking menacing and intimidating all at once. His blue eyes went from ice to blue flame, a scary focused blue that seemed to spread out from the iris, slowly turning the white to a frozen flame of blue. The cat was there, easy to see, and it wasn't a happy animal. A chill went down her spine and she tried to shift back in her chair. He was standing right in front of her, blocking her every escape, so she didn't have any option but to sit there, staring up at him.

"You were raised in a lair, Evangeline. You know you don't put the idea of you with another man in front of a shifter after your female has been claimed."

"I wasn't raised in a lair." Contempt crept into her voice. Disgust even. "My father and brothers were in a lair. My uncle and my grandfather. Not that it did any of them any good. I don' know the first thing about lairs, other than they are corrupt and I want no part of them."

She couldn't help the fact that her voice was almost a hiss of anger. She meant it and he needed to know that. To hear it. To understand that she wouldn't be intimidated into living under lair rule. She was independent. Had she dreamt of having her own family? A man she could love? Of course.

But she was born a shifter. Whether or not her female would ever emerge remained to be seen, but even if she did, no way in hell was Evangeline going to be part of a lair.

His eyebrow went up, and she realized she'd revealed too much information to him. She shoved again and this time he stepped back enough to allow her up out of her chair. It didn't seem to matter. He had a good thirteen inches at least on her, maybe more. She still had to look up at him and that just fueled her anger.

"Alonzo, I'm askin' you to leave and never come back. I mean it. I want you gone and I'm tryin' to be nice about this. I'll have the cameras removed and you stop comin' here." She tipped her head up further, narrowing her eyes, wanting him to see she meant business and she refused to be intimidated by him or his leopard. "If you don', you'll give me no other recourse than to call the police."

He didn't blink. His body was completely still. Impossibly still, as if coiled and ready to spring — and leopards could leap great distances. His eyes had gone glacier blue, so cold she shivered. There was no expression on his face, but for the very first time she was afraid of him. Really afraid.

There was nothing to hold on to. No way

to protect herself. She'd threatened him with the police. A man like Alonzo Massi wouldn't take something like that lightly. And she'd meant it. Self-preservation had finally kicked in and she'd made her last-ditch effort to save herself. Now she was in *so* much trouble. She had learned from birth that no one was safe from a vicious, angry leopard, not even family or mates.

"Don't."

He hissed the word at her. Low. Furious. The whites were gone completely from his eyes and she found herself mesmerized by the pure blue flames staring down at her, licking over her skin so that she shuddered, whether from fear or arousal she wasn't sure.

"You are the only person in this world truly safe from me and from my leopard. Never look at me with fear on your face." It was a decree, nothing less. A command. He seemed to do that a lot and expect obedience. She'd been her own person since birth, responsible for her safety and even, most times, food. She lived an isolated life, but one she was used to, one she'd learned to enjoy. The swamp had been her home and she'd learned its secrets through trial and error. It had been a miracle a child could survive the dangers, but she'd done it and she'd become all the stronger for it. She had done it by recognizing when she was in danger. Like precisely this moment.

"You can't say that, Alonzo." She whispered it to him, knowing it was the truth. Knowing he knew it too. "I'm probably the person most in danger."

"Not from harm, Evangeline. Pleasure until you're screaming, but not from harm."

He couldn't say things like that so casually with his eyes so focused on her and his mouth so close. Her nipples hardened and instantly her panties were damp. She felt hot and needy. That wild thing inside of her stretched again. This time, her female gave her a little rake with her claws and then settled.

"And if she never emerges? He won't be content forever. He'll lose his mind and then you will."

"He's at peace, *malyutka,* but he'll lure her out. He's big and he's powerful and when he gets amorous, he'll bring her out. It will get rough, I won't lie to you about that. Leopard sex is rough, but I'll take care of you. You have to trust me to do that."

She pressed her fingers to her eyes, taking a deep breath. There was no getting out of this. No running away. He'd claimed her in the way of the shifters. She knew what that meant. She knew her female would always crave his male. And she . . . It was Alonzo. She'd only ever responded physically to him. She had no idea what to do. Her brain seemed to have shut down.

"Don't threaten me with the police, Evangeline," he warned softly. "No one will come between us. No one. We can fight things out between us. Talk to me. Yell at me. Be angry with me, but don't involve anyone else. What we have is between us alone."

She shook her head. "Comin' up against you is like comin' up against a brick wall. I don' have any recourse. You leave me none." She knew her tone gave away the desperate despair she was feeling, but it didn't matter. He was adept at reading people and he'd had a year to study her. She knew he could read her emotions.

His hand curved around the nape of her neck, his thumb sliding along her jaw. "Give us a chance, Evangeline. You're scared, and I get that. I understand you being afraid of us. Of me. Of my leopard. But give us a chance."

"You don' know anythin' at all about me. Not one single thin'. What you're askin' of me is nearly impossible. I can't breathe." She couldn't. "Just the thought of it makes me feel as if I can't breathe." It did. It was that bad.

Living in a lair. Living with a leopard that was beyond wild. Her children were never going to live as she had. Never. She wouldn't bring children into the world if the only way to save them was to force them to live alone in a terrifying place, never to know family or friends. Never to be able to go to a school. She'd missed so much in her life. No child of hers would ever live that way. Not. Ever. Not if it meant she had to take a life, even the life of the man she loved.

"You're askin' me, Alonzo, but you aren' really goin' to give me a choice, are you? Your leopard claimed mine."

"And I claimed you. You say you don't have a lair, but I'll go to your cousin and make it official through him."

She stuck her chin out. "I don' answer to him, or to my father or uncle. Not to my brothers and yes, I have them and yet I don'. I came here to start a new life. I sank every single penny I have into my bakery and my home. It isn't right that you can come in and just take it all away from me."

The pad of his thumb rubbed back and forth along her jaw in a caress, one she felt all the way to her toes. She couldn't spend time with him, not close like this, because if she did, she'd lose herself in him. The chemistry was too fiery. He knew it too. He was too experienced for a woman like her. She couldn't escape him. It was stupid to try, a waste of her time. She could see the implacable look on his face. Frozen stone. A mountain of a man who moved with blurring speed and had a vicious, killing weapon inside of him.

Again he didn't answer her. That was her answer. He was taking her choice. There was no turning back as far as he was concerned, so she had to play along for just the rest of the evening and then she could plan her escape. It would suck to leave her bakery and her home, but she wasn't going to be forced into anything, especially a relationship with a dangerous, lethal being.

She took a breath. "All right, Alonzo, I'll show you my home. I need to close up the bakery. And I want you out of my house early. I get up at three to start work."

He nodded but didn't move away from her. His eyes drifted possessively over her. Brooding. A little moody, yet she couldn't see what was behind his gaze.

"Were you aware that Emilio Bassini was planning to marry you?"

Her eyebrows shot up and she smiled before she could stop herself because Emilio had to be sixty if he was a day and very sweet. "No way. Why did you think that?"

"He told us so. Joshua shut that shit down. But he would have asked you."

"He's a dear, sweet man, at least I thought he was. I didn't know he was into whatever it is you're into. I would have said no very gently."

"You do not say no to a man like Bassini, Evangeline. He wouldn't have taken no for an answer."

She threw her arms into the air, pushing at him as if she could shove him and his honesty away from her. "What is wrong with me that I attract criminal types?"

"The cop isn't a criminal." It came out an accusation. "I had to watch that idiot undercover cop flirt with you and then insist on dating you for far too many weeks. Every time he came into the bakery, my leopard went insane, and each time he touched you, which he did every time you handed him his coffee, I wanted to rip his head off. I showed admirable restraint."

That made her want to smile at him again, but she didn't. "He's probably a dirty cop," she groused.

That made him smile for one tiny, brief second and then it was gone. He didn't smile ever. Not ever, and that smile changed his face. It didn't warm the cold of his eyes, but the hard lines carved so deep softened, just for a moment. She liked that more than she wanted to admit. The moment he gave her that ghost of a smile she was lost. She was very grateful he didn't try another kiss right then because she would have been all over him just for that smile.

"Probably not, but he's looking to take me down now." All warmth disappeared, leaving him as cold as ice again. "He follows me all the time. Like I'm not going to notice him or his clown friends."

He was probably right about Brice. He wanted to find a way to get to Alonzo and probably planned to do it through her. Still, it was cheating just a little bit that Alonzo's leopard could scent Brice at a great distance away. He could track him as well. He could track her . . .

She lifted her chin — she couldn't think about that. She was intelligent. If she could stay alive in the swamp as a little child, she could certainly maneuver her way around the situation. She just had to stay calm.

"Do you know why you waited, Evangeline? Why you didn't date? Why once you laid eyes on me there was never going to be anyone else?"

She shook her head. "That's not true." It was a lie and they both knew it.

"You. Are. Mine."

Her heart pounded in fear, but her panties were suddenly damp and those butterflies in her stomach continued to flutter their wings. She detested that he could do that to her with his voice. With his frozen eyes. With the thumb sliding along her jaw, mesmerizing her with his slow caresses.

"Don't try to run from me. I won't like it."

"Has it occurred to you that I don' much care what you like?" She wanted to snap her teeth at him. Maybe her leopard was closer than she thought because raking him down his arrogant expressionless face and kicking him in the shins seemed a very good idea. "You're turnin' my life upside down and you don' care about that. Why should it matter to me what you like?"

His lips twitched. Not that smile she'd gotten out of him before, but definitely he was on the verge. This time she didn't melt. He was being a superior, amused male, looking down at the little female while she defied him. His expression hadn't changed, other than that twitch, but she knew. She couldn't stop herself. She kicked him in the shins. Hard.

He still didn't change expression. His hand tightened around the nape of her neck. "A man like me likes his woman to put up a fight. This is not discouragement, Evangeline. It shows me you have fire in you. Enough that you can match me when I want to get rough."

Her breath hissed out. She didn't want that to make her hot, but it did. Everything about him made her hot. She was in so far over her head she didn't know what to do. All the while his thumb kept sliding back and forth in that slow, burning caress that was driving her insane. She didn't want to pull away. That would give him far too much satisfaction, and everything seemed to be going his way. She certainly wasn't going to give him the satisfaction of knowing he was getting to her.

"I have to close the shop."

"Tell us what to do."

She glared at him. "Whoever you have starin' at me through your cameras ought to be able to tell you what to do. You've evidently been watchin' me."

"You work too hard. You need help during the day. You don't take breaks. You rarely eat your lunch. You get up at three and start baking. You stay here until seven cleaning. That is going to stop. Timur is making arrangements to have cleaners come in starting tonight."

She gasped. "You are not just goin' to take over my life. I mean it, Alonzo. This is my bakery. I've worked hard for it. You're not takin' over. Not my life, and certainly not my bakery."

"Is it so wrong to want to keep you from killing yourself with work? I've never seen a woman work so fucking hard." There was admiration in his voice. Respect.

That brought her up short. It was genuine. She was a shifter whether or not her leopard had emerged. From a very young age, her female had made her presence known to help her. One of the very first things she'd done was to aid her in hearing truth or lies. He definitely respected her. He meant every word he said.

She pushed a hand through her hair in agitation. He didn't seem to think there was anything wrong with taking over her life. Dictating to her. She knew it was the shifter in him. The leopard. She couldn't live with his dominance, and that was one thing she wasn't going to kid herself about — Alonzo Massi, or Fyodor, was an extremely dominant male.

"It isn't wrong to want to see that I don' work so hard, Alonzo," she said patiently, her voice low and soothing. She couldn't help that either. It was ingrained in her.

153

That soft tone. Defusing every situation. Self-preservation. "If you're concerned, you should talk to me about how to solve the situation, not just take over."

"You would argue with me."

She might just kick him in the shin again. "I'd give you my point of view."

"It is the same thing. Arguing when there is no need. I don't do that, woman. I make the best decision and I carry it out. In this case, calling in a cleaning crew and hiring you help alleviates the problem. You go home earlier and have less work. How is that not a good solution?"

"Oh. My. God." She actually fisted both hands in her hair and pulled. "You're makin' me crazy. Fine. Let's just go before I do somethin' drastic. And keep your hands to yourself. I mean it. I have no intention of having a physical relationship with you."

Again his mouth hinted at a smile and for just one brief second, the hard lines in his face softened. "Because you know you can't resist me. That once I take you, there will be no other man to satisfy you."

She deliberately rolled her eyes, but she didn't answer him. He was leopard and he could hear lies.

6

"In this house you will always call me Fyodor when we are alone," Alonzo decreed. He had to give that much of himself to her. His real name. The fact that he was Russian and proud of it. He would give her as much of himself as he possibly could.

Evangeline didn't respond. Dropping her car keys on the counter she immediately took off her shoes and put them on a small shelf built into the wall near the door. He walked right into the center of the room. It was wide and spacious with a high ceiling. He needed room, lots of it. The Arnotto mansion had room, but without Siena, Antonio Arnotto's granddaughter, there, it was cold and hollow — like him. Siena was safe now, with Elijah, and he'd keep her that way, but Alonzo would always watch over her.

He liked Evangeline's home. It was . . . her. Sweet. Homey. All the little touches that said Evangeline. It was neat, with gleaming, polished wood floors in rich, warm tones. Her sofa was small, like her. Suited to her. But it was inviting and very comfortable-looking in tan and brown tones. There were two smaller chairs positioned in front of a fireplace. A sheepskin rug gave him far too many ideas.

He kept moving, wandering through her private space, guessing he was the first to ever be there — man or woman. She was private, his woman. She seemed friendly and approachable, but even here in her private sanctuary, there were no pictures of family, nothing to give her past away.

The living room gave way to a nice-sized dining room. A cherrywood table that seated six with a chandelier hanging over it. The chandelier appeared to be branches dripping with leaves, small lights on them. Classy. Beautiful. Like Evangeline.

She was going to run from him. He was certain of that. She was intelligent and she knew what he was. What his leopard was. She saw the killer in both of them. She didn't accept that it was too late for her, but he knew it was. He'd spent every damned day of his life in brutal, relentless hell. His childhood had been hell. His young adult life.

His leopard had grown vicious with the childhood abuse heaped on him, the violence and the cruelty of his life. The leopard had raged to protect him and in raging, had grown more and more dangerous until, as controlled, as disciplined and as powerfully dangerous as Fyodor was, his leopard was nearly his equal match. The beast raged for blood. A fury of need. Of demand. Every second, sleeping or waking. Until he walked into that bakery. Until Evangeline.

He ran his hand along the granite counter in her kitchen. Clearly she'd bought this house for the kitchen. It was easily the largest room in the house. The most modern. It smelled like her. Cinnamon and spice. Like Evangeline. His woman. He never thought he'd ever have that. Have someone of his own. For himself.

"Sit down, Alonzo, tell me about yourself. About your leopard." She came up behind him and extended her arm toward the inviting living space that opened through the archway of the dining room and kitchen so that the house seemed to be much larger than it really was.

He took two steps toward the room with its comfortable chairs and then turned so that he was towering over her. His hand curled around her throat, tipping her head up because if he was going to give her this, he damned well was going to look into her eyes. "Be very sure you want the truth about me, *malyutka,* because it will scare you to death and I'm still not going to let you go. And when we're together like this, I am Fyodor. Give me that." Because he was giving himself to her whether she liked it or not.

She took a breath. He felt it in his lungs. The way they'd shared breath when he'd kissed her. He tasted her in his mouth. His cock jerked, already hard and hurting. Already making demands.

"Then tell me the worst so I know what I'm facing."

"You hear this, there is no turning back. The things I tell you can get you killed. Not by me, Evangeline, so don't think I'm threatening you. You just have to be certain you really want to know the real me."

"What's the point of this if you aren't sharing who you really are?"

He could hear that she genuinely wanted to know him, but not for the reasons he wanted to know her. She was looking for affirmation that he was a bad bet — and he was. Still, in her home, when he was alone with her, he would give her truth.

"I'm a shifter. Shifters need sex. A lot of

sex. My body is as hard as a rock most of the time, a painful ache that refuses to leave me seemingly ever. Night and day, that need never changes other than to get worse sometimes. It doesn't matter how many times I jerk off, it doesn't help. My leopard makes fucking a woman a nightmare."

He saw the trepidation in her eyes, but also the arousal. His thumb moved over her skin because he couldn't help himself. There was no way *not* to touch her. It was a compulsion. A need far stronger than he was. He was scaring her, yes, but she was also feeling the beginnings of hunger for him just at the thought of his need.

"I was always careful. I never took a woman to my home. Not. Ever. That was his territory. My leopard's territory. I went to her apartment, kept her turned away from me so she wasn't looking into my eyes and I wasn't looking into hers." He rubbed his thumb over her lips. That full bottom lip that he loved and wanted to take a bite out of.

She swallowed hard. He felt the movement of her throat in the palm of his hand and that was intimate and sexy. Her breath was against the pad of his thumb. Her tongue tasted, just for a moment, and the soft brush of moist velvet sent heat shimmering through his veins.

"I like rough sex. I need it. I like a lot of things I couldn't have, things I fantasized about, but knew were impossible because of my leopard." He bent his head until his forehead touched hers. Rested there. "Until you. Until you, Evangeline. There was no having anything for myself until you."

His gaze never left hers. He held her captive, refusing to look away, letting his leopard focus completely on her. Their miracle. Their savior. The woman who would give them everything they needed and hungered for. Evangeline.

His leopard stretched. Stroked. Purred. Rubbed amorously along the surface. Not clawing. No raking. No snarling for the kill. After years of fighting for supremacy, he seemed content to allow Alonzo to seduce their mate.

"There was no taking my time with a woman. I did the minimum of what it took to get her ready, did my thing, got off and got the hell out fast before my leopard could hurt her. Every moment I was with a woman, her life was in danger. Every second. The worst was when I climaxed. At that moment, any man, me included, no matter how strong, is on the very edge of his control. My cat would always push closer, wanting revenge."

She frowned. An adorable little frown that told him in that moment she wasn't thinking about running like she should have been — the way she would later. She was thinking about what it was like to *be* him. He resisted kissing her because he knew he might not stop once he started and she deserved better than the life he was going to give her. She needed care. Patience. Gentleness if he could manage it.

"I don' understand, Alon—" At his narrowed gaze she shrugged. "Fyodor." His name rolled off her tongue with her Louisiana accent. A Russian name pronounced with a Southern accent. He loved how hot that sounded. "Why would he want revenge on the woman, and what did he intend to do?"

"He would have killed her. He needed to kill her."

She gasped and the sympathy in her eyes overwhelmed him. No one had sympathy for him. No one worried about him or thought about what his life was like. He couldn't remember anyone asking. Compassion and sympathy were two emotions to beat out of children, to never give them. He found her reaction disconcerting.

Abruptly he lifted his head and made to

move away from her. Her hands slid up his chest to curl into his shirt. She held him there, not by her strength or even her will, but by something he'd never had before. He didn't know what to do with it and like his leopard, when he was threatened, he stood very still, something lethal unfolding in him. Simultaneously, emotion spread like a wildfire. Need. Hunger. Something bigger. Much bigger. Looking down into her face, his heart contracted and he knew she was in there. Wrapped there, never to get out, and he didn't even know how or when it had happened.

"Sit down, Fyodor. I'll fix us something to eat. You can talk while you eat."

That was a first as well. He barely recalled his mother making them food. She had, now that he thought about it, but it had been a rare occasion, not normal. His mother had hidden herself from her husband as much as possible. Alonzo had learned to cook at a very early age. To rummage for food. His brothers had done the same.

Evangeline slowly eased her fists from his shirt and rubbed her palms down his chest, smoothing the material. "Go sit." She indicated a kitchen chair.

The small breakfast nook was cozy, unlike the more formal dining room. Even the nook opened up to the kitchen and other rooms. The thing about it was . . . He hesitated. The area was a wide, round, low tower built with windows curving around to serve as walls. It was beautiful, open, and during the day would invite in the sun, but not made for a man like him — a man belonging to the dark. He didn't sit with his back to the world. He didn't sit in front of windows — exposed.

He took a barstool instead at the counter and watched as she pulled down a couple of pans and skillets. She smiled at him, her first genuine smile in what seemed a long while. It was the one she reserved for him alone.

"Stir-fry with chicken? It's the fastest."

"You don't have to cook for me, Evangeline."

"I know that. I hadn't planned to, but you're here and we both have to eat."

That wasn't the reason and he knew it. Instead of running away at the truth he gave her, she was reaching out to him. He could feel the threads binding them together tighter and tighter. Could she feel it as well? He studied her face as she chopped vegetables. And she was fast with the knife. He'd have to remember that.

"Keep talkin'. You were sayin' your leopard wanted to kill any woman you were with." Her exotic green eyes were suddenly on him, just for a moment, looking at him from under her thick, black lashes. She looked as if she might have sympathy for his leopard as well.

"He wanted to kill. He needed it then." He sighed and ran one hand through his hair. He had scars on his body. Scars on his face. Several on his hands and arms. He looked what he was, a savage, violent man matching the nature of his animal. "I knew it was only a matter of time before my leopard escaped while I was fucking some woman and then he'd kill. I had to stop giving in to my own needs to consider those of my cat."

"No sex?" She didn't sound in the least sympathetic; more amused.

There was a small smile playing with the curve of her bottom lip and he couldn't help himself. He stood up abruptly, leaned over the counter, one large fist closing over her hand holding the knife because he didn't trust that she wouldn't stab him. His mouth found hers, lips brushing gently. So gently. He heard her gasp. Her lips parted. That soft rush of air against his mouth. His teeth found her lower lip and he tugged. Then bit down.

She gave a small shocked cry and his tongue slid along her lip, easing the ache he'd caused. He should have backed off, but he couldn't. Almost of its own volition, his other hand slid beneath the heavy fall of hair to curl around her nape, bringing her closer. His mouth came down on hers, taking control. Losing himself in all that cinnamon and spice. She looked sweet. Maybe she was, but she had a definite kick to her. She wasn't going to let him take her over, not without a fight. He tasted that in her mouth. That kick. That spice. It fed his hunger like a drug.

He couldn't stop. There were no brakes and she didn't help, her mouth moving under his, her tongue dancing and stroking, feeding the fire that began to flicker hot and bright through his body. Wanting a woman had never been like this. Feeling. So strong. So much. He could kiss her forever when he never gave that intimacy to other women. He hadn't known kissing could be an obsession with a woman.

She gave a soft little moan that inflamed him more. He not only heard it, but he felt it right through his cock, just as he did his hammering heartbeat. Everything seemed to center there in his groin, hot blood filling him so full he thought he might burst. The drumming of his heart pulsing right through his heavy shaft. The feel of her soft mouth, a kind of paradise he was lost in.

She started to pull back, looking for air. Looking for space. Looking for sanity. His hand moved, fisted in her hair, holding her still while he took what he needed from her. Everything. He wouldn't settle for less. She had to give herself to him, right there in her kitchen, her mouth moving under his. And she did. No hesitation. Her lips melted under his. Her mouth grew hotter. The kiss grew wild and maybe edged on brutal. She didn't pull away. She didn't hesitate. She was his. He knew that with more certainty than ever. She belonged to him.

He forced himself to lift his head just enough to rest his forehead against hers. "Woman, you could drive a man to his knees."

Her eyes searched his. At first she looked dazed, as if she were coming out of a dream. Then she looked shocked and her free hand went to her mouth. He loved that her lips looked thoroughly kissed. Red. Swollen. Inviting. Wariness crept into the green of her gaze and he saw her leopard staring at him. Focused. Her leopard was no shy, retiring female. She sized him up, looking to protect her human counterpart should she need to do so. That shocked him. *Shocked* him. Female leopards were always quiet until they emerged. They didn't show themselves, and they definitely didn't threaten anyone. Her leopard was looking at him as if she might rip him to shreds.

"I scared you," he acknowledged, reluctantly releasing her and stepping back. That step cost him. His cock hurt like a son of a bitch, but he gripped the counter instead of sliding the zipper down and wrapping his fist around the heavy throbbing shaft.

"You can be . . . intense." Her tongue came out and she touched the little bite mark with the tip. Her hands were shaking and for a moment she rested them on the counter, the knife still in her fist as if she'd forgotten it.

He reached out and gently took it from her. "I like kissing you." It was the understatement of the year. "You taste so good, *malyutka,* I could kiss you for a very long time and never get tired of it."

He forced himself back onto the stool, hoping with him seated and the counter between them she would feel safer. Her leopard was too close. The gold flecks in her green eyes began to glow. His big male reacted, but not in the way he expected. He thought the female's obvious aggression would trigger the dominant in the male, but like Alonzo, the cat wanted only to soothe her. To reassure her that she was safe with him.

He studied Evangeline as she began once more to prepare the food for dinner. She didn't look at him, instead paying strict attention to chopping the chicken into very small pieces.

She hadn't reacted when her female rose. Not in the least. She hadn't looked frightened or alarmed. There was only one conclusion he could come up with — her female had risen often enough that she was used to her. Comfortable with her. Even partners with her.

A shifter had to come to terms with his or her leopard. The leopard might be separate, but they were also the same. Emotions and characteristics were so intertwined it was impossible to tell sometimes who was driving whom.

"I never blame my leopard for its dangerous nature. I'm every bit as savage. I need violence. I crave it."

Her gaze jumped to his face, and there it was. The fear he knew was under all that calm. All that sympathy. It was her fear of him that had brought her leopard close.

She deserved truth and he was determined

to give it to her no matter the cost. She should be afraid — he was a man to fear. But he'd never hurt her. He meant it when he said she was the only one truly safe from him. "I was conditioned for violence from almost the moment of my birth. The fists. The kicks. The learning to inflict as much damage as possible without a single visible mark or ensuring every bit of damage showed. My body was turned into a weapon and once I mastered that, I learned to use objects as weapons. Guns, knives. Hell, *malyutka,* something so ordinary as a pen."

Her gaze flicked over him again. He loved the way she looked at him sometimes. He could see the hunger in her which she couldn't quite control. The compassion was back.

"Who did that to you? Who beat you, Fyodor? Who forced you into hurtin' others?"

Very slowly he drew the thin gloves he always wore from his hands. He never forgot to wear them. "I have a death sentence hanging over my head. You should know that up front. More danger surrounds me than you can imagine." He closed his fists and rested them on the counter so she could see the tattoos there. He had tattoos everywhere, all over his body just as he had the scars.

"These tell the world what I am. I am in the brotherhood, the *bratya*. Our lair was among the oldest and the most feared. Of course no one knew we were leopard, only that our family was considered the bloodiest and cruelest of all territories. No one ever messed with us and lived. We had riches and power, and that wasn't enough. It was the blood that my family craved. The depravity. The violence. Their leopards were bathed in it."

He kept his gaze fixed on her face. Watching her as he confessed. As he told her the truth of his life. Of who and what he was and would always be because they'd shaped him that way. They'd made him into a killer. It mattered little that he hadn't wanted it, they'd carved that into him so deep there was no getting it out. He was intelligent and cunning. He moved with blurring speed. Sadly, when it came to enemies, his first thought was to end them. Always.

She was silent for so long he didn't think she would speak. She added ingredients to the stir-fry and the air in the room began to smell homey and comforting. He hadn't known he was hungry. He certainly hadn't known he wanted a woman to care enough to cook for him.

"Do you suppose those men before you

drove their leopards to be killers or was it the leopard that drove them?"

Again she shocked him. It was an intelligent and legitimate question. He kept his gaze on her face because he'd thought of just such a question a thousand times. "I believe it was the men driving the leopards. I look back to when I was a child and he always wanted to protect me from the beatings. I knew they would kill him, let their leopards loose on him, so I refused to let him out even when I needed him."

She was silent again for a long while and then she turned toward him, taking a deep breath. He knew why. He knew she was going to ask him and that would make her sad for him. Compassionate. Understanding. She didn't want to be any of those things. Still, his woman had courage.

"Tell me when he needed to protect you."

"Evangeline. My life was a living hell as a child. Are you certain? Be certain. Once you hear. Once you know, there is no going back from this."

"Eventually, if we were together, I would have to know."

They were already together, she just didn't know it. Didn't want to believe it. She began to tear lettuce for a salad while he watched her, fascinated by the sure way she moved her hands. A born leopard with her female solidly behind her every move.

"I was six years old the first time I killed a man," he confessed.

Evangeline gasped and spun toward him, the color draining from her face. "Fyodor. No." She said it softly. Fiercely. She wouldn't have cowered in her room, hiding from her abusive husband while her husband forced terrible things on their child. She would have fought him to the death for their son or daughter. He saw that. He knew what was inside his woman and he needed that more than anything else in her. She would fight for their children. She would stand for them.

"The man pleaded for his life. *Begged.* He had tears in his eyes. My father forced me to hold a gun to the man's head in front of his wife and children. They were all crying. Looking at me like I was the same as my father. A monster. I hesitated, looking into the man's eyes, hating myself. Hating my father."

"Honey, I'm so sorry. That must have been so terrible for a child."

"We hadn't gone there alone. Both my uncles were there. They held neighboring territories and they were cruel and vicious as well. But my Uncle Lazar, the eldest, was the worst, his cruelties legendary. They wanted to be there for my first kill."

She shook her head, glanced at the table beside the bank of windows and then set two plates on the counter.

"I was afraid of what my father would do to the wife and children. When I hesitated, my father went mad, kicking me in the stomach repeatedly while my uncles laughed at him. He yanked me up by my shirt, forced the gun back into my hand, closed his fist over it and snarled at me to pull the trigger."

He tried not to feel anything as he told her. He recited the incident as if it happened to someone else, or as if it were an article he'd read. He'd learned not to feel. Feeling made one vulnerable and he could never be that.

"My leopard rose in a rush of anger and determination, of sheer courage, knowing it would have to face the demon leopards of my father and uncles." He'd been proud of his leopard then and was proud of it now. No, the vicious need for blood and the kill had been taught first by the man. Now it drove the leopard, but he hadn't started out that way.

"I was afraid for my leopard. I knew their leopards would really hurt him, so I fought him back — and pulled the trigger. It was . . . the worst moment of my life. The absolute worst, taking that man's life in front of his wife and children. All for what? Money? So little they owed and we had so much. Blood and brains splattered over me, I was that close. I stood there horrified, unable to move or speak, tears running down my face while my father and uncles did unspeakable, vicious things to the wife and daughters and then allowed their leopards to kill them. They flung the bodies aside as if they were so much garbage."

He no longer had bile rising even when he had nightmares thinking of his first kill. "I was traumatized. Sick. My father and uncles beat me for hesitating and then for crying and finally because I threw up. They called me names and forced me to crawl, covered in blood, back home. My father kicked me every inch of the way while my uncles taunted and made fun of me."

She had laid out the silverware and napkins and put the food on the counter in front of them. A meal, shared with a woman. A first for him. As she slipped up onto the barstool beside his, her hand trailed across his back, a gesture, he knew, that was sympathy, but he found it oddly compelling. Disturbing. Sensual. His cock, already raging, refused to stand down.

"I think the men in your family corrupted their leopards, not the other way around. I believe that happened in my family as well." The admission was soft. A thread of sound, but she'd given something of herself back.

His heart contracted and he picked up the fork, his gaze fixed on her face. She looked so beautiful to him. So fragile. He was a big man. He had more than a foot on her, and his shoulders were twice as wide as her body. There was no back up in her though. She would stand for their children — and she would stand for him.

"I'm a man who needs control, Evangeline. In all things. My childhood was a training ground for control and power. I crave the feeling of my fists striking flesh, of having fists hit me."

"Fyodor." Just his name. A reprimand.

"I'm trying to give you truth."

"That's the truth as they made you see yourself. The truth is far more than that."

"I don't want to be that man. I don't want my leopard to be a killer, but I didn't get what I wanted, not from birth, Evangeline. I was born into a fucked-up family. A fucked-up lair. The worst of the worst. No loving mother. No loving father. Just fists and kicks and blood."

"Your mother didn't protect you? I don't get that."

She really didn't, he could hear it in her voice. She would never leave her children to fend for themselves. Not ever. There was even repressed fury in her voice, as if she would like to talk to his mother.

"She wasn't his real mate." He'd come to know that long before his father disposed of her. "The theory was, they wouldn't look for their real mates. They wanted nothing that might make them vulnerable. Generations of that made for vicious brutes and equally cruel leopards."

"So who was she? Where did she come from?"

"Each lair bred women so other lairs could take them as wives to produce sons. I lived in Primorye, in southeastern Russia. We are Amur leopards. A rare breed, now dying out and with good reason."

He took a bite of the stir-fry, and it was really good. Far better than he'd expected and from Evangeline, he expected a lot. "This is great."

"If they weren't meant to be mates, did their leopards mate?"

Very slowly Alonzo shook his head, watching her the entire time. Waiting for her to get it — what his father and uncles had done to their leopards. What he had tried so hard to keep from happening. "Never. They never let them mate. They wanted them vicious. They wanted them mad with hunger and need. When they took a woman they wanted their leopards to roar with rage."

"That's just sick."

"That's what's in my blood."

Her eyes flashed at him, twin emerald stones, glittering in fury. "That's bullshit, Fyodor, and you know it, or by now, you should know it. They were vicious men because they chose to be, not because it was in their blood. They had the choice to find their real mate and they didn't do it. For their leopard, they should have."

She was fierce about it and he could see she didn't relate what she was saying to their situation. He needed to bring her back to that. "My leopard has had to live with no mate and no hope of one. There was no allowing him freedom to retaliate against what my own family did to me, and it has driven my leopard nearly insane. The constant scent of blood has made him irrevocably mad."

She held the fork to her lips, chicken on the end of it. He took her wrist, turned the fork around and deliberately ate the bite of food.

"Your leopard has been through a lot, honey," she said.

"The first time I entered the bakery I didn't even realize my leopard had settled — that I'd been given a respite. It was only when I walked out that I knew. He went crazy. Clawing, raking, demanding he shift. He vied for supremacy. He'd never been that wild before and I had to fight to control him. I used every ounce of discipline I'd developed over the years. At first I thought maybe he was reacting to someone, but then, I turned and went back into the bakery."

"I remember that," she said, again revealing quite a bit to him without meaning to.

It had been the first time he'd entered her bakery and just seeing her, the impact of that on him had been tremendous. She'd stolen his breath. His hands had actually begun to shake. He knew. Not just for his leopard but for him. She was the one.

"You walked back into the bakery and looked at me. You looked very intimidatin' in that way you have and I remember thinkin' you were gorgeous but very cold and certainly dangerous. I asked you if you needed somethin' and you said . . ."

"Yes." He remembered. How could he ever forget? That moment had been etched into his brain for all time. He'd known she was the one, but more importantly, he realized that as long as she was around him, his leopard would be calm. He wouldn't have to fight night and day just to keep the animal from killing someone. It had been a revelation that changed his world.

She nodded. "But you walked out."

"The things I wanted from you were not fit for your ears."

She blushed. Color swept into her face and she ducked her head, as if that would stop him from seeing it. He loved that little air of innocence about her. He was bringing an inexperienced woman into a nightmare world. No decent man wanted to tie a woman to him when he knew the kind of life she would be facing — and he'd tried to stay away. He'd tried to be content with just keeping his cat sane. But she'd kissed him. He wasn't decent, and she kissed him. There was no getting rid of the taste of her in his mouth. The feel of her body against his. There was no stopping his cat from rising to claim what belonged to him — and Evangeline did belong to him. They both, man and leopard, recognized her. She was the real thing. Theirs. She belonged exclusively to them. And they were never giving her up.

"So even if your mother wasn't your father's real mate, she was your mother. That had to count for somethin'."

"She was trying to survive," Alonzo said, his voice cool. Dripping with ice even. As a child he hadn't understood that, only that she wasn't around and wouldn't protect the children. She was nice enough and very warm when her husband wasn't near, but she was only trying to survive.

"But she didn't," Evangeline said.

"No. She didn't." He fell silent eating the food. It was good food and deserved to be given some attention.

Evangeline got up and went to a small wine rack built in beneath the counter. "Is red all right?"

"Your leopard allows you to drink alcohol?"

"She's acquired a taste for red wine. She doesn't like white and no mixed drinks."

He shrugged. "It was important in our family that we drank. Every meeting, every dealing with other lairs or branches, we drank. It didn't matter what the leopards wanted and eventually they got used to it."

"You don' have to have a drink with me, Fyodor." She opened the wine. "This is all disturbin'. I thought my family's lair was bad; yours was far worse. I want to know what happened to your mother."

He couldn't sit there. Neither could his leopard. He pushed away from the counter and stalked across the room. Paced like the caged animal he was. "You can never tell anyone what you know. Not Timur. Not Gorya. If my uncle finds us he will try to kill us. I'm far stronger than he can possibly know, far faster. He remembers that boy, the one getting sick and crying over his first kill. He doesn't know the demon he'll be facing if he comes for me. For us."

He had to include her. She had to know no matter what, no matter how she took this next revelation, he was not giving her up. She would have to try to find a way to live with it — with him.

"I don' talk to people, Fyodor. I keep to myself and I keep my own counsel. My mother is dead and I don' remember her. I don' think I ever saw her outside the womb. My leopard remembers she wanted me but was afraid for me. I have no one to tell your secrets to, nor would I."

He heard the truth in her voice and knew what kind of a woman she was. He couldn't stop the restless pacing. No woman could accept what he was asking and even then he wouldn't be done. His world was one of danger and deceit. She would only have him to turn to. There would only be a handful of friends they could trust. Her children would live with that.

"He killed her," she stated softly.

He closed his eyes briefly. Of course she would know. "Yes. He killed her in front of Timur and Gorya. They tried to stop him, both with their leopards and as men. He ripped them apart and he was killing them systematically when I walked in. He was covered in the blood of my mother, my brother and my cousin. I went . . ." He trailed off. "Crazy. Insane. Mad with rage, grief and fear for my brother and cousin. I killed him. Not easily, and not cleanly. Not, Evangeline, because I couldn't, but I didn't want easy or clean. He died hard. Very hard. And then I killed every male in the lair. It was a cold, calculated choice. If I didn't, they would continue with their cruelties and they would kill their women and daughters. Or sell their daughters as they often did to other lairs to live the same fate as their mothers. I killed them all. Every. Single. One. Our lair was gone. I wiped it out."

He could have kept the satisfaction out of his voice, but he didn't try. She had to know him. Had to know what she would be living with. A ruthless man, cold as ice, as danger-ous as any predator she might run across.

He was a killer, and he'd taken down his entire lair.

7

It wasn't love yet, but it could be. Fast. She could fall fast. She might even be halfway there. Evangeline rolled over in her bed. She'd paid a fortune for the mattress, more than she had for just about any other piece of furniture because she was always so exhausted at night. There was no finding sleep and she knew there wouldn't be. Not with Alonzo's words drifting through her mind over and over.

"I went . . ." He'd trailed off. "Crazy. Insane. Mad with rage, grief and fear for my brother and cousin. I killed him. Not easily, and not cleanly. Not, Evangeline, because I couldn't, but I didn't want easy or clean. He died hard. Very hard. And then I killed every male in the lair. It was a cold, calculated choice. If I didn't, they would continue with their cruelties and they would kill their women and daughters. Or sell their daughters as they often did to other lairs to live the same fate as their mothers. I killed them all. Every. Single. One."

Evangeline sat up and pushed at the heavy fall of hair spilling around her face. She'd been so agitated she hadn't even put her hair in a braid, something she was always careful to do. He hadn't wanted to kill his father easy or clean. He'd said that. His father deserved to die. Had to die. What human or even shifter forced his child into being a killer?

Alonzo hadn't said anything about his life in the lair, in the *bratya,* as he'd called it, but she could imagine what he'd done. What was expected. If at six he was forced to kill, then that had been his way of life.

"All right, Bebe, we're in trouble. You get that, don' you?" she whispered aloud to her leopard, and her female rose immediately, rubbing fur along her insides to comfort her as she'd done since Evangeline was a toddler. "It isn't goin' to be just about sex for us, no matter how much that's what we want it to be. I'll fall for him. Not a little. A *lot.* I'll drown in him." She pressed her closed fist to her mouth and rocked gently back and forth.

He'd been *six.* She knew he hadn't told her so she would be sympathetic. He wanted her to know exactly who he was. What she would be living with. But she couldn't help but think of that little boy and what he'd been forced to do. Tears burned behind her eyes and clogged her throat — tears she hadn't shed when Alonzo was with her. She didn't dare. He would have tried to comfort her, and she couldn't get that close.

"What are we going to do?" she asked her leopard.

Alonzo might say she was the only one safe, but living with him would be difficult at best. He was as dominant as a man could get. She wasn't in the least submissive. She loved her bakery and she didn't want anyone telling her how to run it or interfering in any way. What if he suddenly decided she couldn't work?

Evangeline pressed her fingers to her eyes and shook her head, still rocking, trying to work out what she should do. If she stayed, she'd never get away from Alonzo. He'd made that clear, and she was too weak around him. Wanting him. Feeling for him. He hadn't just aroused her physically; what she felt was emotional as well. He was tying her to him in so many ways.

"We have to go, Bebe," she said reluctantly. "We have to walk away from all of this if we're going to survive. He'll eat us alive. I know he will."

Her leopard stretched and rubbed, still giving her comfort. Letting her know she wasn't alone. They were together. She would never be alone. Her leopard had given her that at an early age. Because Evangeline had had her all of her life, she hadn't realized what a rarity it was for a female leopard to reveal herself. No one ever knew whether or not a woman had her female until the time when she began to rise — when the cycle of the female leopard and her female human counterpart coincided. Evangeline's leopard had risen to provide her with comfort and security — with companionship and a fierce loyalty, that same fierce loyalty Evangeline felt for her leopard.

"We're a team," she whispered as she crushed the lace-trimmed sheet to her breasts. "I want him. I want to make certain someone loves him and watches out for him because he's never had that and he can be, with me, with us, so oddly gentle. But, Bebe, he will eat us alive. You know that, right? He'd take over our lives and I wouldn't be happy. Neither would you."

Evangeline didn't let too many people in. She didn't want or allow them close to her. Alonzo had crept inside when she wasn't really paying attention. All those months of him coming in and being so quiet. She liked quiet. She'd grown up in silence, listening to the breath of the swamp, and that was her safe place — silence. Away from people.

Confused and annoyed with herself, she hopped out of bed. Evangeline rarely used lights at night and she didn't now. Pacing, she thought about her options. If she stayed, she knew Alonzo Massi wouldn't go away. He'd made that very clear. "I wish you'd weigh in on this," she snapped, annoyed with her leopard.

She immediately got the impression of languid amusement. *We can handle them. Man and leopard. No problem.*

Evangeline clenched her teeth. "You just want that male."

The female moved restlessly for a moment and Evangeline instantly felt hunger rise. It was sharp and terrible, a burning need that subsided almost immediately but for that moment was intense and impossible to ignore. Evangeline went very still as fire raged through her. She swore softly in Cajun and then abruptly ripped a small bag from her closet.

"You freakin' hussy. You're goin' into heat, aren't you? Oh. My. God. I'm savin' us both. We'll go back to the swamp. Even if he tries to track us, no one is as good as we are there. I just have to hide you until it's over. You should have told me."

She threw jeans and shirts and underwear into the bag as fast as she could. She wouldn't need much else there. Hastily braiding her hair, she glared at herself in the mirror. "Don' tell me you didn' know, Bebe, because that's why you rose and accepted his claim. You were feelin' all amorous and you were willin' to throw me to that wolf just for sex."

Her cat was unrepentant. Even amused. *You want the man.*

She did. She *so* did, but that wasn't the point. "That male leopard is dangerous. You heard Alonzo or Fyodor or whoever he is. His cat wants to kill the women he sleeps with."

Not you. Again there was that impression of stretching. Unsheathing claws. *I would protect you.*

"He's a dangerous fighter. He's been fighting for years. He's experienced." Panic welled up, and for a moment she was that child in the swamp, listening to the alligators bellow and knowing the huge male leopard prowled outside, looking for her, wanting to kill her.

Evangeline drew in great gulps of air, trying to get her lungs to work properly again.

She couldn't think when she was panicked, she'd learned that early on as well. Alonzo could tie her to him in so many ways, but the worst would be sexually. She didn't want a man to be with her because she was leopard. Or because they had great sex. This was her worst nightmare. The very worst. A lair. A dangerous, killing leopard. Her female in heat causing her to be. She wouldn't be able to use her brain. Her body would be on fire and so hungry for him she wouldn't be able to think.

She swore even more as she snatched up her car keys and slipped out her back door. No way was she going to get caught up in Alonzo's world. She would be so vulnerable if her female went into heat. She would never be able to fight him or even stand up to him. He'd walk all over her. She'd be back in a world of deceit and violence. *No. No. No. Not happening.* She'd always decided her own fate. She wasn't about to let leopards or sex or the most gorgeous, irresistible man who *needed* her dictate her life.

She knew she was in a state of panic. The idea of her body betraying her. Her leopard betraying her. It was frightening. Terrifying. She was a woman always in control and if she was out of it . . . A small sob escaped. She couldn't let that happen. She wouldn't.

She backed the car out of the driveway without turning on lights. She didn't need them and wouldn't turn them on until she was in a high-traffic area. Her little tree-shaded road led to a cul-de-sac, so there were few cars. She'd chosen her house carefully for that reason. Few neighbors. Trees. The yard she had. The kitchen in her house. Damn Alonzo Massi for walking through the door of her bakery.

For a moment the windshield blurred and she nearly turned on her wipers before she realized the problem was her eyes and she dashed at the watery tears. She was *angry* that she had to leave, not upset for leaving Alonzo. She wasn't going to think about that six-year-old boy or what he had had to do to protect his brother and cousin. No wonder they were so loyal to him.

But to wipe out an entire lair. The *entire* thing. All those leopards. Fighting machines. Killing machines. What did that say about Alonzo or his leopard? To do that, he had to be insanely fast and ferocious. She stopped at the stop sign at the entrance to her street. Without warning, two large town cars converged on her, blocking her from moving forward. Another car fell in behind her. Dark. No lights. She knew *exactly* who that was.

Seriously, she was the most conflicted female on the planet. Every cell in her body told her to run, that she was in danger. Her head told her that. But her heart wavered. Stuttered a little. She sat quietly waiting, her breath in her throat rather than in her lungs.

Alonzo slid out of the backseat of the town car behind her and stalked to her car. He yanked open the door, his face an expressionless mask, his eyes all cat. Fierce. She'd aroused anger in both this time, leopard and man. She couldn't blame the leopard. He had claimed his mate. He'd waited a long time for her. Maybe it was the same for Alonzo. He'd said he'd had to stop having sex.

"Move over."

She did without a word, her heart hammering like mad. Loudly. So loudly she knew he heard. His eyes on her face, he moved the seat back so he could slide behind the wheel.

He gave some kind of signal through the window and all three town cars drove away, leaving them alone. Alonzo's presence took up the entire car. It wasn't just because he was a big man with all that muscle rippling beneath skin; it was him. He was truly larger than life. He poured into the air, taking it over. Tension rose and she found herself trembling, looking down at her hands, unable to think beyond the fact that she would be at the mercy of this man and the two leopards very soon.

"Evangeline."

Just her name. The way he said it was a command. She knew what he wanted, but it took her a few moments to find enough composure to lift her chin and give him her gaze.

Alonzo's glacier-blue eyes studied her for a long time. The cat was there, pinpoints of fury blazing with blue flame behind the frozen ice. "What's wrong, Evangeline? This isn't just a run so I'll give chase. You're scared out of your mind."

She touched the tip of her tongue to her lip. Her breath refused to come from her lungs, remaining stuck in her throat. She looked up at him with absolute despair. "She's risin'. My female. Tonight she . . ." She trailed off, seeing the dawning comprehension in his eyes. She couldn't tell him anything but the truth and in this case, he would find out soon enough.

Just saying the words aloud made the situation all too real. She wanted to run as fast as she could back to her beloved swamp and hide like that little child from the big bad leopard on the prowl to consume her. She hadn't realized her hand had dropped to the door handle until Alonzo very gently reached across her body and placed his hand over hers.

"Take a breath, *malyutka,* a nice deep one. I'm right here. I'm not going anywhere and neither are you. We'll handle this."

When he leaned across her in the small confines of the car, his body pushed against hers. Her breasts were soft against his back, pressed deep, an intimate connection she was instantly aware of. She had the mad desire to circle his waist with her arms and just hold on to all that solid muscle. He was a rock when her world felt built on sand.

His voice mesmerized her. She was so susceptible to the deep, low tones. His voice appealed to her in a way nothing else ever had. He was so calm. So quiet. So like the swamp. Danger swirled around him, but he could be counted on. He smelled wild and dangerous, a feral predator in the civilized trappings of a very expensive suit.

She instantly wanted him. Instantly. Her entire body felt hot and needy. Her breasts ached and pushed hard against the solid rock of his back. Her breath refused to come other than in short, ragged pants. She felt her female close, trying to comfort her when she was so out of control, something completely foreign to Evangeline's nature.

"Breathe, *devochka moya.*"

Evangeline did what he said, reaching for air, needing it. She drew him into her lungs, all that wild. All that danger. But she could breathe again. The panic was still there, but it receded enough that she could nod to him that she was all right. He lifted his hand from hers and took away the heat of his body as he straightened.

Evangeline shook her head. "I can't do this."

Alonzo didn't respond. He merely turned her car around and drove back to her house. She sat very still while he parked. It was impossible to judge his mood. She watched him catch her bag up with one hand and move around the hood of the car to come to the passenger side and open her door. She was fairly certain she was about to have a heart attack. The pounding hurt.

Alonzo reached into the car, shackled her wrist and pulled her out. It wasn't difficult for him to do. He was far stronger and when he wanted her to go with him, it didn't take much for him to get his way. She concentrated on her feet, walking beside him, admiring the fact that he moved in absolute silence.

"You didn't lock your door, Evangeline. You always have to remember to lock the door."

"I wasn't certain I'd be back." She didn't look at him as she admitted it. She hadn't known. She'd just run in a panic.

He closed and locked the door, stepped in front of her and took her hand. He was so gentle. His fingers closed around hers, but he didn't yank her or exert pressure of any kind. He walked and took her with him, but he was gentle about it. He went straight for the bedroom.

Her heart pounded harder than ever. She stopped when he did, right next to the bed. She could see her tank and boy shorts where she'd flung them. Neither turned on lights, but it wasn't necessary, not with both cats so close. He faced her, still retaining possession of her hand. Looking up at him was difficult. He looked invincible. An aura of danger surrounded him. Mystery. He was leopard, and there was a raw, erotic appeal to the roped muscles and sheer power he exuded.

His eyes, frozen ice, moved over her face. Seeing too much. Seeing everything there in the dark. He studied her face and she knew he saw the dark circles, the way her eyes looked like two dark bruises.

"You're wiped and you don't have the sense to know it."

She detested that he saw that in her. "I couldn't sleep," she defended. "The things you told me . . ." She trailed off, shaking her head, images of that little six-year-old boy so stark in her mind.

He sighed. "I should have taken into account how sensitive you are. Never should have told you."

"Don' say that." She narrowed her eyes at him. "I mean it, Fyodor. Don' you *ever* even think that. I'm not some plastic doll. I want to hear about your life. Yes, it's hard to hear, but you lived it, so I want to know everythin'." She stopped abruptly, one hand pressed to her mouth. She'd blurted out the truth. Told him too much. Told herself too much. She shouldn't want to know a single thing about him.

His expression hadn't changed in the least. She was a hot mess and he was — frozen. She was so tired she wanted to collapse into a little heap on the floor. What she didn't want to do was fall into bed with him. She was far too exhausted and upset to fight him. She'd lose control and have wild sex, and then she'd be tied to him in a way she'd never be able to get out of.

"Put your nightclothes on, *malyutka,* and

get in bed."

She shook her head. "I'm not ready for this." Her body said otherwise, but her mind was in complete chaos. She just couldn't. She was already so lost, so conflicted about him, and giving in to her body's demands would humiliate her. That loss of control. She wanted the decision to be hers. She *had* to make the decision. Not her leopard. Not Alonzo. Her.

He caught her chin between his finger and thumb. "Did I sound as if I were asking?"

She jerked away. Her entire body was trembling and she couldn't make it stop. She hated feeling so vulnerable. "You're such a jerk."

"Because I want you in bed? You're frightened and that, at least, is something I can help you with. Now please do as I ask so I am not forced to terrify you before I make it all better."

He strode out of the room and she heard him moving around to the doors. She listened so hard she even heard when he turned the dead bolt. Locking them both in. She closed her eyes briefly, trying to come to terms with her emotions that were clearly all over the place. She stood for a long time contemplating whether or not to try to make an escape through a window —

and she was fairly certain she wouldn't really get away with it. Mostly she didn't try that option because she was too darned tired.

He'd come back and take her clothes off. She knew enough of him now that she was certain he'd do that and he wouldn't say anything to her while he was stripping her. But he'd look and she'd get hotter than she already was. It just wasn't an option. Very slowly she stripped off her clothes and pulled on her boy shorts and tank.

Evangeline crawled onto the bed, wanting to just lie down, close her eyes and shut out her life for a while. Instead, she sat tailor-fashion in the middle of the bed, letting herself feel her absolute exhaustion. She'd gotten up at three and hadn't taken very many breaks. She'd only eaten when she'd fixed dinner for Alonzo, and then, not very much because she'd been so tired.

"In the bed."

"It's really annoying that you walk around and I can' hear you. Make some noise when you come into a room."

"Get. In. The. Bed." He bit the words out between clenched teeth.

She was grateful to know she was irritating him almost as much as he was her. She could hear the growl of warning from his leopard in his voice. They were both aggravated with her. Pleased, she made a face at him but obediently stretched out under the covers. "You're awfully bossy. Has anyone ever mentioned that to you?"

"Turn over, *devochka moya*. Lie on your stomach."

Evangeline had no idea why she obeyed him but she did, turning onto her front. Settling. She had full breasts. At the moment they felt achy and swollen, the tips burning. Lying on her stomach pressed her breasts into the cool sheets, immediately giving her some relief. Turning her head to the side, she peeked back at him over her shoulder. He was removing his trench coat. His jacket. Loosening his tie and then taking that off.

Alonzo was meticulous about folding his clothes. She imagined that had been beat into him as a child as well. He smoothed every line from his jacket with precise movements, and she could imagine him as a boy learning to be careful with everything he did. When he was satisfied his jacket and coat wouldn't wrinkle, he sat on the edge of the bed and removed his shoes. His back was to her as he bent to the task, leaving her free to admire the way his muscles played beneath the thin white of his very expensive shirt.

Again he placed his shoes and socks very carefully. Her heart fluttered and she had to bite down on her bottom lip to keep from saying anything. She let her lashes drift down for a moment in order to get that sight out of her mind. It was silly, really, to superimpose that little child on this huge giant of a man. He might have been innocent and sweet at six, but his father and uncles had done their best to shape him into a killer.

He padded barefoot into her bathroom. Opening her eyes when she felt him leave the bed, she saw him through the open door crouching low and looking under her sink. She had everything organized.

"What are you lookin' for?" He'd better not be looking for evidence that she was on birth control.

"Oil. Massage oil if you have it, anything oil if you don't."

Her heart jumped. Stuttered. Stammered. Began to accelerate. She was *so* not ready for this. "Um, Fyodor."

"Where?" His voice was clipped.

"It's in the third bin."

He found it, shut the doors on the cupboard carefully and returned to the bedroom. "I'm going to push your tank out of the way. Don't freak out on me. I'm just going to give you a massage to help you sleep."

She wasn't certain she could handle his hands on her body without going up in flames, but it was better than him insisting they have sex. A little of the tension eased in her as he sat on the bed beside her. Close. Very close. She pulled him into her lungs with every breath she took. Her lips tingled and she wanted to touch them, remembering the feel of his mouth on hers. That brought the memory of his taste. So good. So wild. He was addicting. She knew for certain she wanted him to kiss her again and that was dangerous and perverse when she was telling him absolutely no to sex. *All right, so it wasn't absolute.*

"Stop thinking about sex. You're making me hard."

"You're always hard. That isn't me." She said it without thinking and then bit her lip. Why in the world did she have to have a sassy mouth? She usually just thought her sass and smiled sweetly. He seemed to like her sass, and right now, in the bedroom, it was far too intimate between them.

"It's you."

Just the way he said it, his voice decisive. Low. Seductive. She didn't need him to seduce her with his voice — she was already there.

He pushed her tank up slowly. Not fast. Slowly. She felt his breath on her bare skin. Warm. Soothing. The pads of his fingers brushed lightly. Seductively. Every nerve ending in her body awakened. She felt the pulse of her heart hammering secretly between her legs. His breath was closer. Closer still. Her lashes drifted down and there was one fleeting thought of self-preservation, but then his lips touched her. Barely there. A brush.

Electricity arched through her. Bright. Hot. A sizzling fire that sank into her veins and seemed to settle there. His gentleness was so unexpected, so unlike his dangerous demeanor, it disarmed her every time. There was no thought of running, only of lying there, drifting into a world of pure feeling, her body not her own.

His mouth moved up her spine, his lips claiming every inch of her backbone. She felt the nip of his teeth and the soothing lap of his tongue, but mostly, the whisper-soft touch of his lips on her skin. The blood in her veins turned to molten lava, a slow spread of heat that turned her body to liquid pleasure.

No one in her entire life had touched her

with such tenderness. Such exquisite gentleness. She'd never had care, and this felt like caring. There was no resisting Fyodor when he was like this. She could barely believe it was the same scary man with the violent leopard she knew him to be.

Fyodor pushed the thick braid of hair from her shoulder and poured oil into his hands, rubbed them together to warm the oil and then dropped them to her nape. His hands were large, his fingers strong as he began to massage her neck. "Tell me what you fear the most, Evangeline. The first thing that comes to mind."

She answered before she could think about it, her voice drowsy. Almost sensual. Not hers. "You'll take over and dictate. I'll have no choice in my life. No control."

There was a brief silence as he massaged the oil into the tense muscles of her neck and shoulders. "I won't pretend I'm an easy man. I'm not. Will I try to dictate to you? Of course. Do I think you'll allow it? No. You're a strong woman and I admire that in you. You'll know when I won't budge on something and I'll learn the same about you."

"You've already taken away choices." She didn't look at him, preferring to keep her eyes closed so she could absorb the feel of his hands moving over her tense, tight muscles. It was paradise, another pleasure she'd never experienced.

"Only one, *devochka moya*, you cannot run from me. There is no escape. You've been claimed. The rest of it is all choice. You can choose whether or not to love me. You can choose to keep your bakery. You have more choices than I do in this thing between us. I cannot be far from you or my leopard is mad with rage. With you, he is calm and I don't have him raking and clawing for blood."

"I don' want to be wanted because I calm a leopard." She murmured that truth as well. There was no lying to a leopard, and right then she didn't want to. He'd given her a glimpse into his childhood and that alone made her want honesty between them.

"Do you think that's even possible, *devochka moya*? Because I do not. I came to your bakery for you, not your leopard. I may have suspected you were a shifter eventually, because of the way my male reacted, but not at first. No, you are not wanted for your leopard alone, Evangeline."

Her breath hissed out of her lungs in a long, slow rush of confusion. There was no denying the honesty of his declaration, she could hear it in his voice. He wasn't saying he was in love, but he wanted her for Evangeline, not her leopard. That made it even harder to try to find resistance when she really needed to. His hands were a miracle. She never wanted him to stop. Never. She couldn't help but equate the massage with caring. He was so gentle. He paid attention to detail.

She hadn't known a man could touch her that way. His hands like magic, moving over her skin, finding every place that hurt, releasing the tension until she wanted to cry with relief. At the same time, his hands brought her something else, heat and liquid need. Hunger that was pleasant, not sharp and terrible. It built gradually, but wasn't so overwhelming that it scared her. The feeling only added to the pleasure.

"You want to keep your bakery. I want to lock you up somewhere safe. You get to keep your bakery because it means that much to you. Keeping you safe means that much to me, but making certain you're happy does as well." He rubbed more oil between his hands to heat it before rubbing down the center of her back and then flaring out to get every sore muscle. "So cameras, bulletproof glass, guards. We'll make it work."

"Bulletproof glass?" she echoed. She couldn't find the energy for anger, not when his hands were magic. But still, she couldn't let him get away with it. "The truck driving through my window."

"Timur is nothing if not thorough."

"I'll spit in his coffee tomorrow."

There was a small silence, and she opened her eyes just enough to look up at his face. There was that fleeting flash of amusement, as if every bit of humor had been stamped or beat out of him and he couldn't hold on to it. But he felt it. She gave him that and she liked giving it to him.

"Livin' with a violent man and an equally violent leopard." She blurted out the worst of her fears. He needed to know because there was nothing to be done about that. Nothing. That was the deal breaker. He could compromise or she could on almost everything else, but how did one fix that?

"Are you afraid of me, Evangeline? Afraid that I'll hurt you?"

How could she answer when his hands were so gentle? Gave her so much care when no other hands ever had? But she was afraid. Of him. Mostly of his leopard. "You said yourself that your cat hated every woman you've been with and wanted to kill them. Even if he doesn't want to kill me, he's so scary. He is. You know he is. Whatever made him like that doesn't matter. It's what I would have to deal with all the time. And now, with her risin', I don' have any choice. I don' want this relationship. I don' know the first thin' about bein' in a relationship. Or bein' with a man."

"That's your worry? That you won't know what to do?"

She bit down on her lower lip hard to keep from blurting out anything else. She sounded like an idiot. She just had to stop talking to him.

His thumbs dug into her lower back, easing the tension there in spite of the fact that she was already stiffening beneath his hands again. "Relax, *malyutka,* I'm going to try something. Just stay still, keep your eyes closed and trust me."

Evangeline didn't like him telling her to keep her eyes closed. She'd been doing it most of the time, but the minute he told her to, she wanted to see what was coming. He kept massaging the oil into her back and she couldn't help but relax beneath his magic hands. With a little sigh she let her lashes drift down.

Immediately she felt the slide of fur along her bare skin. A blast of hot breath signaled the leopard was lying beside her, his face pressed against her shoulder. The Amur leopard's fur was thick and long. It felt a little like heaven sliding over her skin, but at the same time, she knew how close those teeth were. The claws. The male could kill her in less than a second.

She held her breath. Waiting for death. Her female didn't react, didn't rise to protect her. She felt the cat stretch languidly, a long slow rub and then she settled. When her cat came close to the surface, the male made that strange purring noise. It was odd, not like a domestic cat's purr, but distinct and definitely a sound of pleasure.

Her leopard communicated with him. Evangeline felt her movement, felt that moment of connection between the two cats. It hit her hard on several levels. She felt betrayed. Her leopard had been her only companion since birth. Her only real family. No one else had ever shared her, nor had the cat felt inclined to allow anyone to know she existed. She'd been exclusively Evangeline's.

Tears burned behind her eyes and she jerked her body, trying to get out from under the heavy cat. He was big. Really, really big. Like Alonzo was big. All roped muscle, heavy bone and thick fur. He didn't budge and instantly she felt the change. Skin to skin. Bare skin. Hot. Arms around her.

"Ssh, Evangeline. Don't fight me. Just lie still and listen to me." It was Alonzo's breath in her ear, not the leopard's. One hand bunched in her hair, the other massaged the nape of her neck. His heavy weight didn't move off of her, pinning her to the bed. One thigh lay over hers, holding her down.

"He says she isn't quite ready to rise, but she's going into her heat. We have time and that's a good thing."

"I don' want this. I don' want either of you. Not you, not your leopard." She pressed her body against the sheets trying to make herself smaller. "Please just go, Alonzo, and don' come back."

He rolled, caught the sheet and pulled it up over the two of them. "I'm not going anywhere, Evangeline. You want me and I want you. Your leopard has been claimed by mine. We'll work this out. Right now, you're very tired and you need to sleep."

She squeezed her eyes shut even tighter, trying to make him go away. She couldn't deny she wanted him. Her body did, not the rest of her, although she was a little worried her heart was becoming involved. That was the last thing she wanted. She kept her head turned away from him.

You talked to him. That was an accusation.

He is my mate. He wanted to reassure you.

Evangeline's breath caught in her throat. The leopard had been trying to reassure *her,* not her female.

He was worried about you. I am worried. Why are you so upset?

That vicious killing machine had been concerned about her. Evangeline didn't know what to think about that.

I'm afraid.

They would never hurt us. Can't you feel their caring? In any case — the leopard yawned and curled up — *I would kill them both if they tried to harm you.*

Her leopard gave the impression as she always did of them — the two of them united. One. Evangeline was certain the leopard couldn't actually fight and win with the male leopard, but it was nice that she thought she could. That she thought she would.

Taking a deep breath, pulling Alonzo's wild scent into her lungs, she forced her body to relax. The instant she did, he wrapped his arm around her waist and pulled her tightly against him so that his body curved protectively around hers. She held her breath, held him there inside of her, but all he did was bury his face in her hair for a moment.

211

"Go to sleep, woman. This isn't the easiest thing I've ever done."

Why that made her smile, she didn't know, but she fell asleep with the scent of him surrounding her, his body close, his arm possessive and a smile on her face.

8

"I've claimed her," Alonzo announced, looking around the table, his gaze resting on Joshua Tregre, Evangeline's self-proclaimed cousin. They were all there. His allies. The men he knew he could count on. There were few of them and all of them lived a precarious existence, a double life.

Joshua scowled. "When the hell did that happen?"

"She's mine. She was always mine."

Joshua had been set up in Bayou country, taking over the territory of a very ruthless crime boss. Evangeline's home turf. He was younger than some of the others, but no less battle scarred. He'd been raised in Borneo and had worked for Drake Donovan's team there, rescuing kidnap victims. His leopard was fast and an experienced fighter.

"You'd better be good to her, Alonzo, she had a shit childhood and she wanted out,"

Joshua said. "All the way out."

Alonzo didn't respond, but he was going to grab Joshua after the meeting and find out what "shit childhood" meant.

"Was it wise to claim her now?" Drake Donovan asked. Drake was the man they all looked up to. He was the force behind what they all did. Taking down crime lords, setting up their own people to fill the void so someone worse wouldn't take over. They cut back in the areas they could and ruled with an iron hand where they needed.

Drake was interesting to Alonzo because he was married to Saria Boudreux. Saria had been a friend to Evangeline and probably knew more about her than anyone else. Alonzo had gone through Evangeline's phone. She had two numbers she called, not frequently, but more than any other — Saria, and a woman named Pauline Lafont Jeanmard. Saria, she texted occasionally. Never about Alonzo. As far as he could see, she'd never mentioned him to anyone, at least through text. He'd like to talk to Saria.

Alonzo looked at him without expression. "She's mine." That said it all. He didn't need to defend his actions, nor would he. Evangeline was his woman. Her leopard was his male's mate. That was enough for any lair, and he'd challenge anyone trying to deny him. He'd win. He was fast and he only knew all or nothing. He didn't fight for fun. He didn't fight for glory. He fought to kill.

Drake sighed. "Bad timing, but I guess finding one's mate takes precedent over everything else. We got word that Emilio is shipping a load of weapons to Indonesia. We all know what that means. He's using his furniture business as his cover. The weapons are built into the furniture. We don't yet know when he's going to actually send them out using his trucking company. My man will let us know when that is happening. We can't allow that shipment to make it to Indonesia."

"How reliable is that information?" Elijah asked.

Elijah Lospostos, the man with the largest territory, an international monster that he was slowly taking apart, piece by piece, was a man they all listened to. He was considered the most dangerous of the men at the table. He had married Siena Arnotto, and that made him family. Alonzo was all about loyalty, and he'd given his to Siena when she was just fifteen. Now that loyalty extended to her husband. She was in the early stages of pregnancy but she was carrying triplets, so all of them were watching over her — something she didn't like. He'd like Evangeline to meet her.

"His word is gold," Drake stated.

"Is Emilio going to lose his mind when he finds out that Alonzo has claimed Evangeline? He wanted her. He made that clear at the table," Joshua said. "We've got an enemy in Patrizio Amodeo. If Bassini loses it over Evangeline, we'll be fighting on two fronts."

"It's bad timing," Elijah agreed. "Emilio is hard to predict. If his pride is hurt because Joshua stepped in to stop his claim on her then he'll go after Joshua. He could be upset at Alonzo and go after him."

"Will he hurt a woman?" Alonzo asked.

Elijah shook his head. "It isn't his style. He's protective of women as a rule. I was surprised he didn't come across the table and slap Patrizio when the man insulted Evangeline. We've weakened him as a boss. If he doesn't throw in with us, Patrizio will swallow him up and he knows that."

"If we take this shipment, that could tip the scales," Drake said, reaching across the table for the coffeepot. It was Cajun coffee, black and strong, something they all needed. "We don't want Emilio taken out as a boss. He's one of the better ones."

Jake Bannaconni let out a sigh. "I'll have to agree with that. We don't have anyone ready to take his place yet." He glanced at Timur.

Timur lounged against the wall looking for all the world as if he was bored, but Alonzo knew better. His brother was aware of everything and everyone. He was ready to spring into action the moment there was need. He'd been raised the same as Alonzo, and his leopard was equally as vicious and cruel. Alonzo also knew Timur would kill anyone to protect his brother.

"I'm not going to ask you two why you aren't admitting to the relationship," Jake said, looking from Alonzo to Timur. "But if there's a problem that could jeopardize what we're doing, we need to know."

Alonzo didn't look at his brother. There was nothing to say. Sooner or later their uncles might find out they were still alive and come after them, but that time wasn't now. He shrugged. "You wanted me in the position of the king. I told all of you it wasn't for me, but you insisted. You want someone else, I'll stand down." That would make it so much easier with Evangeline. She didn't want a criminal for a husband. He was all that word implied and more.

"Sorry, Alonzo," Elijah said, not sounding it. "You're a natural and we need you. Patrizio will go to Custer Carlson next. Custer will demand too much from him, and he knows that, but he'll have no choice. I sent the message to him this morning that there would be no alliance between us. I told him we like to fly under the radar and his need for the spotlight didn't fit with us, but we held no animosity and would certainly do business with him any time."

"Alonzo." Drake sent him a small grin. "You managed to piss off just about everyone with your defense of your woman."

He didn't respond. There was no response to make. He wouldn't apologize for keeping Patrizio in line. He resisted looking at his brother. They'd discussed killing the bastard, the pros and cons. Both were for it, believing that he'd come after them eventually, but they'd decided to bide their time. They didn't want anything coming back on them, and the "undercover" cops had been all over that meeting in the bakery. There was no doubt that they had pictures of every single person attending. Multiple pictures. When they killed Patrizio, they wouldn't want anyone to know they were involved, not even the men sitting at the table — the men they trusted most.

"Watch your back," Elijah advised.

Timur stirred, but didn't speak. The atmosphere in the room grew tense for a moment. Every leopard could feel the rage of the male lounging against the wall, looking on the outside as cool as ever. Inside, his leopard raked and clawed for freedom and the other leopards in the room reacted. Alonzo shot his brother a quick, quelling look. Timur shrugged.

"So what do we do about this shipment?" Jake brought the conversation back to the present problem. "We don't want Emilio to lose his trucks. That would cripple him beyond recovery. If he loses the weapons, he'll lose a lot of money. He's already in a bit of trouble. I took apart three of his most lucrative companies and that's hurt him."

"No cops, he'd lose his trucks and end up facing a trial. The cops would love to nail Emilio to the wall," Elijah said.

"So we take the weapons when the trucks are heading down the highway in the early morning hours. He'll send them out around two or three A.M. We'll hit them hard, put the drivers on the ground and hope the guards aren't stupid. There's a strip of access road we can use, right off the freeway. Flatten a tire or two and they'll pull off. We transfer the furniture to smaller vans and get out of there," Alonzo said.

"Why there?" Joshua asked.

"No homes in that area. No lights. It's

rural and dark," Alonzo pointed out. "I scouted that area a long time ago. It was a place I worried Arnotto would get hit."

"Sounds like you've done this before," Joshua said.

Alonzo knew that challenge was all about Evangeline and nothing to do with the hit on the weapons. Joshua didn't like his cousin anywhere near the business and Alonzo couldn't blame him. He didn't like her near it either. Evangeline was the one woman his leopard would accept. She could soothe that brutal need for bloodshed in both man and beast. More importantly, he was already gone on her. Completely. No half measures. There was no going back from his decision, no matter how tough it got for the both of them.

"Yeah," he conceded. "I have."

No one touched that and it was just as well. He wasn't about to explain himself. They didn't like it, he could walk. They all knew it too. They knew he wouldn't mind pushing them in that direction.

"Okay, once we have the weapons, where do we want to stash them?"

"We aren't stashing them," Drake said. "I'll take them with Joshua back to the bayou and they'll disappear into the sea."

"It's too far. The risk is too great," Jake

objected.

"We'll use trucks no one can identify. The furniture is built around the weapons. Emilio's people will be on the lookout for a couple of large trucks traveling together or the vans Alonzo uses. We're going to use several smaller ones. A leopard driving each with one guard inside the cab with the driver. There won't be anything suspicious in that at all," Drake insisted. "Saria's pregnant and I don't like being away from her right now. She understands what we're doing and she's okay with it, but I don't like leaving her all the time and I don't want her traveling. So I'll head back with the trucks."

Alonzo wondered if Evangeline knew Saria was pregnant. If she did, it wasn't in the text messages. Siena was pregnant and so was Jake Bannaconni's wife, Emma, who was due soon. In a few months there were going to be more babies. He hoped Evangeline would get pregnant as well. Not only would that tie her to him even more, but she would have friends and so would their child. It would be nice to allow his son or daughter to grow up with people he could trust and count on.

"You'll handle the hit, Alonzo?" Elijah asked. "Then Joshua and Drake will be responsible for the weapons."

"Sounds good to me," Alonzo agreed. He was desperate for action. It had been too long. He let his leopard out to run every night, but it wasn't the same as a fight. As that adrenaline rush.

"The next order of business is Patrizio Amodeo," Elijah said. "He's a pain and we can't afford him."

"You have to give me more time," Jake said. "I've gotten access to his computers and even some of his books, but he's got a human trafficking ring. Even if you take him out, one of his lieutenants will take his place and that ring will still be there. The word is, he's taking women from Mexico, the United States and Canada and selling them in Russia, Europe and the Middle East. We have to shut that shit down first."

Alonzo stiffened. His gaze slid to Timur's. His eldest uncle, Lazar Amurov, was one of the main suppliers of women and children throughout Europe, the Middle East and the United States. He had to be in league with Patrizio. No one could possibly traffic women and not deal with Lazar. Patrizio would know him. Do business with him. That hit very close to home.

"We can take him. I'll make him talk," Alonzo said, confidence in his voice. He'd learned interrogation at an early age. He knew more ways to hurt a man than most knew existed.

"I want to make certain we get the entire ring and know where it leads and to whom. He'll have tentacles everywhere. I want it all," Jake said. "Give me just a couple more weeks. Don't move on Patrizio until it's absolutely necessary."

Alonzo waited, his body still, feeling his leopard waiting too. They both knew what was at stake. Timur and Gorya did as well. Lazar couldn't be allowed to get too cozy with Patrizio. Alonzo wouldn't put it past Patrizio to go to Lazar and ask for a favor, never realizing he'd be selling whatever was left of his soul to the devil. But that favor would be a hit from the Russian mob on Alonzo. As soon as his picture was distributed, Lazar would know right where to find him.

"We'll wait," Elijah decided. "That's too important, but you'll have to hurry, Jake. Patrizio will make a move soon against Alonzo." He glanced at him. "Watch your back."

That was the second warning. That meant Elijah was really concerned about an attack. Alonzo simply nodded and glanced at his brother. Their eyes met. Patrizio was going to die very soon, much sooner than Jake might want. He'd track down the trafficking ring himself if he had to.

They went on to the next order of business. Alonzo allowed the talk to swirl around him but he pulled out his phone and brought up the live feed at the bakery. There were seven cameras and he cued up each one.

His woman was laughing, leaning one hand on the counter, her manner open and friendly, not at all guarded as she'd been the day before. He liked seeing her that way as she talked with a customer. The customer shifted just a little, and he instantly recognized Brice Addler. The man was dressed in the clothes he often wore, making himself out to be a carpenter.

Alonzo imagined his leopard chasing the bastard down and ripping him apart before ending him. Evangeline shook her head and gestured toward the door, still laughing. Brice and his two fellow cops obediently sauntered out, but not before Brice put his fingers to his ear mimicking a phone. She shook her head again, and smiling, went to help the next customer in line.

She was beautiful. He swept his finger over the screen, touching her face, that flawless skin, her gorgeous, exotic eyes, the long hair she liked to tame by weaving it into some intricate classy braid, and the curves that filled out her luscious figure. She was his. All his. Brice could go fuck himself because he was never going to have Evangeline.

Without warning he smelled blood. Water. Fear. Every leopard in the room went still, and Jake froze. The door opened and Emma was standing there, looking very pale and clearly scared.

"Jake. My water broke. The contractions are very strong."

Jake was up so fast he knocked over the chair he'd been in. Drake was moving as well, calling into a radio for a helicopter as he rushed around the table toward Emma. Jake got there first, sweeping her up into his arms, barking orders to someone Alonzo couldn't see, presumably someone to watch his other children as he raced his wife to the hospital.

Alonzo hadn't known Jake Bannaconni long, but he knew his wife had nearly died in childbirth. He couldn't imagine how the man had to feel. There was blood on the floor, more than seemed likely for a birth. Elijah and Joshua had gotten to their feet instantly, both looking grim, and he remembered that both men had worked on Jake's ranch for a long time.

Alonzo signaled to Timur and Gorya. There wasn't anything he could do there. Elijah would talk with Siena, probably order her on bed rest and lock her down for the duration of her pregnancy. Alonzo couldn't blame him if he did. He had business of his own to take care of at the Arnotto estates before he made it to the bakery to escort Evangeline home. He hoped he'd have good news on Emma by that time.

He rethought the pregnancy idea half a dozen times while he planned with Timur, Gorya and two more of his cousins Timur had brought in. Alonzo hadn't been thrilled when two Amur shifters had shown up, but Timur vouched for them and admitted the two men had been with him for the last few years and he trusted them.

The oldest, Mitya Amurov, was his uncle Lazar's eldest son. Like Alonzo, Mitya had been subjected to unspeakable brutality from the moment of his birth. As Lazar had been even crueler than Alonzo's father, Alonzo didn't want to think too much about Mitya's life or his leopard. On the other hand, if his loyalty was truly to Timur, Gorya and Alonzo, they would have a fierce, unbeatable fighting team.

Sevastyan Amurov was his uncle Rolan's oldest son. He was cool under fire, said little and saw everything. Like Alonzo and Mitya, he didn't like his mother being brutalized and then murdered. The moment his cousins, Fyodor, Timur and Gorya had disappeared, he and Mitya had done the same. Alonzo hadn't known that the cousins had been in touch. He would have put a stop to it for safety reasons. Now, they were here and he was glad.

They had managed to complete their plans for intercepting Emilio's weapons when Drake called. Emma had delivered a healthy baby boy. She had lost a great deal of blood and it was touch-and-go for a short while, but the doctor had pulled both through.

Timur opened the car door for Alonzo after sweeping it carefully for bombs. It helped that leopards had a good sense of smell. Timur settled into the seat beside him. "I don't like this, Alonzo."

"What? I thought you were fine with the plan to stop the trucks. We've done it hundreds of times back home. What don't you like?"

"The bakery. You're exposed there. *She's* exposed there. I'll be the first to admit I don't know shit about a relationship, but aren't you supposed to protect her?"

There was a soft gasp of protest from

Gorya, but then silence. Alonzo allowed it to stretch out. He loved his brother, but Timur didn't ever respect boundaries. Evangeline was a boundary he didn't want his brother crossing.

Timur shook his head. "I get the fact that she's your woman and you're willing to risk your life for her. That alone makes her different, something I've never seen in our family. So, Alonzo, I'm telling you, and I hope you can hear me, I'm willing to risk my life for her too. I want this for you. Hell, for all of us. But we can't protect her adequately there. You know that."

Alonzo could hear the genuine concern. He sighed. "I'm fully aware of that. I put the two leopards Drake gave us on her. They're fast and they know how to fight. She'll never be happy if I try to take her bakery away from her. I'd lose her as surely as if someone put a bullet in her head."

Timur swore in Russian. "I was afraid you'd say that. She has too much sass, you know that don't you?"

"Yes." What else was there to say? She did. He liked it.

"She's going to lead you around by your cock."

They wished it were just his cock. She had his heart, and that was the problem. If it

228

was just his cock he could say no to her when it was necessary, but she had his heart all the way. There was no way for Timur or his cousins to understand because they'd never seen a true leopard's mate. They had no idea their leopards would give them peace when the right woman was around — they had to know for themselves.

"When I'm in the room with her, my male is calm."

There was silence while the others gaped at him. Mitya, driving, actually turned and looked over his shoulder for a moment, clearly shocked.

"He's absolutely quiet. He was before we knew she was leopard."

"That's why you kept going back there all those months, before they named you *vor*," Gorya said.

"Not *vor*. Don. And yes, I hadn't known there could be a respite. He had gotten so bad I had to put steel bars on my door and windows to keep him in if I slept, and I didn't dare fuck a woman. He would have killed her."

Mitya and Sevastyan exchanged a long, knowing look.

"He's quiet?" Gorya asked, unbelieving.

"He must have recognized Evangeline even before her female began to show signs of emerging."

"Does she want you?" Timur asked. "Evangeline. Is she on board?"

"No. She wants me, but she doesn't want the life, and I can't blame her. She doesn't want to live under lair rule. She doesn't want a man like me, a criminal with violent tendencies, and a leopard that is a true killing machine."

Mitya took the car around to the back of the shop and parked in the little alley beside Evangeline's car. That was another thing he would have to do. Her car wasn't safe. His men would have to make certain every day no one tried to strike at him through her.

"What are you going to do?" Timur asked.

Alonzo shrugged. "What I've already done. My leopard claimed her female and I claimed her as my woman. There's no going back from that for either of us. When there isn't a choice one accepts fate."

But she had a choice. She could choose not to love him. She wouldn't be able to get away from him or his leopard, but she could always choose not to love him. He didn't voice that. He waited for the others to get out of the car, look carefully on the rooftops and every place where a gunman could hide before they walked into the kitchen of the bakery.

He'd made keys for himself of course. He'd done that very early on when he knew he wasn't going to be able to leave her alone. Long before he'd taken over Antonio Arnotto's position as don. He'd spent more and more time in the bakery and sent others there to ensure its success. As don, he had no business bringing danger to her, but then, when word got out that she was his woman — and he planned to put a ring on her finger as soon as possible — she'd be in danger anyway.

He'd already been looking over jewelry for her. She didn't wear much, but he wanted to see her in diamonds and sapphires, his personal favorite. Emeralds would go with her eyes and probably suit her more, but she was his and he was all about ice.

The scent of the bakery hit him even before he stepped through the door. All Evangeline. Cinnamon. Spice. Sugar.

"I fucking love how this place smells," Gorya said, voicing his own thoughts.

The others nodded, inhaling. Alonzo stopped just inside the door and allowed himself to feel. For so long there had been . . . nothing. He didn't feel emotion. He didn't want to feel. Until Evangeline. She'd changed his world with her sweetness and sass. With her bakery. That smile she reserved only for him. He didn't know if she was aware she had that smile — the real thing — and she gave it to him.

Her smile was like the sun coming out on a frozen day in Russia. Beautiful. He hadn't believed anything could melt the iceberg, but she'd done it. Evangeline. When he inhaled, he took in the scent of the bakery, but more importantly, her. And she was home to him.

He'd never had a home. He hadn't known the meaning of the word. Not even all those years ago when his mother hid in her room to keep from getting beaten. He'd foraged for food and dodged his father's fists and boots. Nothing had ever smelled like the bakery. Or her house. Or car. Or just plain Evangeline.

He was pretty damn certain that his feeling emotion for Evangeline didn't bode well for her, but for him it was a kind of rebirth. He thought about her every minute of every day. He couldn't wait to see her. He spent more time than he would ever admit looking at his phone, at the camera feed, just to see her.

"She has several customers in the store," Timur reported. "Including the cops."

Again? How many times a day did Brice

come in to see her? If he didn't have ice in his veins, Alonzo would have felt a rush of adrenaline. His leopard didn't have ice. He raged and prowled and raked, furious that the three men were haunting the bakery. That was their territory. Evangeline was theirs. No matter how much Alonzo tried to reassure the cat that Brice was only after Evangeline to get to him, neither believed it. The man was too persistent. A cop. A good guy. Everything that Alonzo wasn't and would never be. Everything Evangeline deserved and would never get.

Alonzo deliberately walked out of the kitchen as if he owned the place, as if he did it every fucking day, ignoring Timur and Gorya as they scowled at him. He was very aware of the three cops at the door, on their way out, turning to face him. He could have waited for them to leave but he didn't. It was a dick thing to do but then, along with being a criminal, and a killer, he was discovering he could be a dick too.

He went right up behind Evangeline, circled her waist with his arm and pulled her back into his front. At the same time, he caught her chin with his free hand and turned her head so she was forced to look at him. He took her mouth.

He might have kissed her for all the wrong

reasons, but the moment his lips touched hers, those reasons became all about Evangeline. Tasting her. Losing himself in her taste. In that fire that rose so fast he didn't know when the ice melted and the burn started. Only that it was there. That her mouth was fucking paradise and he never wanted to leave.

He kissed her like he owned her. He kissed her like he was in mad, passionate lust with her. He kissed her like he loved her. Because he felt all those things at once. She should have pushed him away, but she didn't. She opened her mouth under his and gave herself to him. Evangeline didn't do anything in half measures. She gave herself completely to him, handing herself into his keeping without hesitation.

Her brain, that intelligent, logical part of her, might feel conflicted, but her body was all his. She reached one arm back to circle his neck and she kissed him just as thoroughly, just as intimately and as possessively as he kissed her.

Alonzo lifted his lips just a whisper from hers. "I missed you, woman, far too much." He meant it. Every damn word. He had missed her. "I'm considering moving my office into the bakery."

"I missed you too," she admitted. "Now

234

sit down out of the way so I can close. You're a distraction."

He liked that he was a distraction. "Am I too late for my coffee?" He kept his eye on the door. Brice was scowling, and he was just dick enough that he took far too much pleasure in that.

"I haven't cleaned the machines. I'll get all of you coffee and then I'll close."

"What are you going to do with the left-over pastries?" Sevastyan asked, a hopeful note in his voice.

She laughed. Alonzo loved that sound. It was the sweetest music he'd ever heard. "I bag them up and take them to a shelter." Of course she did. What else would she do with them?

"Then can I just . . ."

"You want pastries, Sevastyan, you buy them," Alonzo growled.

Sevastyan and Gorya both made for the counter, pointing out their favorites. There wasn't much left. Evangeline had it down to a science and when she ran out of each type of pastry that was all there was for the day. Today there wasn't going to be much to bag and give away, and it looked as if Timur and Mitya were going to grab whatever was left. They were just going to be casual about it.

Alonzo moved out from behind the counter and instantly both Timur and Mitya stepped between him and the door. Alonzo didn't look at the undercover cops, but he saw them, saw Brice's exchange with the other two, and knew at some point they would be trying to talk to his woman and dissuade her from seeing him. He was going to have to shut that shit down fast.

He took his table, drank his coffee and ate the cinnamon apple pastry she'd made for him. It was light and flaky and warm. It smelled like her. The last of the work crowd came in, hastily trying to get coffee for their trip home. Her smile never wavered, although he knew she had to be exhausted. She knew most of her customers by name and genuinely seemed to want to know about them. That, he decided, was her gift. She was interested in the people coming to her bakery. She always asked about loved ones. She laughed a lot, but he noticed that the affectionate, loving smile she gave only to him was never in evidence.

He loved her for that. Loved that something in the world was his alone. His woman. Her kisses. That smile. When the last customer was gone, she flipped the sign to *closed* and then went back behind the counter. He sipped coffee that was ambrosia for the gods and watched her clean the machines. She was fast and efficient. He loved watching her work. He didn't even pretend he wasn't watching.

She glanced up, color swept up her face and she shook her head, a small smile curving her bottom lip. He was going to spend time biting that bottom lip.

"Stop lookin' at me."

"I like looking at you."

"Well, stop it. It's distractin'."

Timur snickered, a sound Alonzo found annoying. Timur had made it clear over and over that Evangeline was a danger to his brother. He'd been raised the same as Alonzo and didn't get what a relationship with the right woman could be. All he saw was that every enemy Alonzo had would know to go to the bakery if they wanted a shot at killing him. She was a vulnerability he couldn't afford. Worse, Timur knew Alonzo would do anything he could to keep her safe.

He shot his brother a look that told him to back off. Timur raised an eyebrow but didn't look intimidated. That was the problem with brothers. And cousins. Mitya was giving him that same *are you nuts* look. It hadn't occurred to either one of them that they could find a woman of their own.

"There's a storage room."

Evangeline's voice was soft. Shy. An offering? He wasn't certain what she meant. He raised an eyebrow at her. She kept pulling the last of the pastries out of the display case and then began to wash it.

"In the back, off the kitchen."

"Your office, *kretin*," Timur translated.

That earned him a snicker from his cousins as well. Evangeline flushed more and turned away, clearly embarrassed. He considered leaping across the room and punching his brother in the face. That would be more than satisfactory. And then he'd do the same for Gorya, Mitya and Sevastyan. His leopard stretched, liking the idea. They hadn't seen action in a while. A good fight would take the edge off.

It would be pure sublimation, but he could live with that. He got up slowly, and instantly his brother and cousins knew his intent just by the way he moved. They spread out, Timur grinning a little bit.

"Not. In. Here." Evangeline enunciated each word carefully. "I mean it, Alonzo, you take it outside. I've had enough to last me a few weeks with your shenanigans. Don't make me angry."

Alonzo halted in the middle of the shop. Dead center. Right in the midst of his four bodyguards. His palms itched and his fingers curled into fists to relieve the ache in his joints. His leopard wanted a fight even more than he did, if that was possible. Still, he stopped moving. Forced his body to relax, to stand down. Timur, damn him, snickered again.

"My brother needs a little lesson in manners."

"I'm certain he does," Evangeline agreed. She sprayed the case with glass cleaner. "But not in here. You'll break something. Like my brand-new bulletproof-glass windows. Thank you very much, Timur."

"You're welcome," Timur murmured, unrepentant. Deliberately egging Alonzo on.

"We have a cleaning crew coming in to do that," Alonzo said. He put a hand to his neck and massaged at the tension coiled there. "Let's go home, *solnyshko moyo.* I'm tired tonight." He was tired. He hadn't slept all night and he wanted to go to that home where it smelled like paradise and lie beside her. Maybe, if he was really, really lucky, he could seduce her.

He'd made up his mind he wouldn't take advantage of the fact that he could seduce her with kisses. He wanted her to make the choice to give her body to his keeping. He knew she was nervous. She was inexperienced and she didn't give herself lightly, but he could have her. He just wanted to be her choice. He didn't blame her for being afraid. He wasn't a good man. He couldn't go back and change that. He could try to make up for it, but he couldn't change what he was at his core. What his father had shaped him to be.

Evangeline's eyes came to his. Rested there. Soft. That smile. All his. "Okay, honey," she said, surprising him. "We'll go home."

She hadn't gotten much sleep either. He wanted that for her, but more, he wanted to be inside of her where he belonged.

Her gaze suddenly jumped to something behind him, the smile fading, alarm taking its place. Simultaneously his leopard went crazy, raging a warning, all claws and fury, rising fast, pushing hard to emerge. Out of the corner of his eye he caught sight of Timur spinning, his hand going under his coat to pull his gun.

9

In that split second, Evangeline realized making a decision was not always rational or well thought out. She only knew that she made it decisively. Fyodor/Alonzo was her choice. Not her leopard's. Not his. He was *her* choice. He'd been her choice from the moment he'd sauntered into her bakery all those months ago.

These men were coming to kill him. In that instant, that split second, she knew they wanted his death. No one had ever stood for him, and she was going to do it. She didn't think about his bodyguards, only about making certain no one took him from her. No one got to shoot him or stab him or poison him. He belonged to her and she was going to take care of him.

She put one hand on the counter and launched herself, reaching for her female's speed and strength. Time slowed down. She saw every detail as she flung herself at

Alonzo. His bodyguards turning toward the door. Men filling the door, men with guns already spitting fire. Alonzo shouted at her, whipping a gun out, shaking his head, yelling to his guards to protect her.

She hit him hard — and he was a solid wall of muscle — taking him over face-first so that he staggered, but caught her in mid-flight. Still, her body covered his and she felt the burning kiss along the side of her head, up high near her temple and two more harder blasts that radiated throughout her body along her arm and thigh. Then Mitya hit them both, taking them to the ground. Alonzo's gun fired right next to her ear. She felt the heat of it, although mostly she felt pain. The agony spread through her fast.

She kept trying to cover Alonzo's body with her own, which now, thinking about it, was a little silly. He was twice her size, and Mitya had both of them locked to the ground. He was firing his weapon as well.

Alonzo's hand went to her hair. Stroked. Trembled. "*Solnyshko moyo,* don't move. Don't fucking move. Mitya, get off her."

She realized she couldn't hear the sound of guns anymore. It was quiet. Still. She kept her face buried in Alonzo's shirt, afraid if she moved her body would shatter.

"Talk to me, Evangeline. Let me know

you're still with me."

There was fear in his voice, but now that she had time to give it some thought and the shock was wearing off, she knew she couldn't be hurt too bad. She felt warm blood pouring down her head, lots of it, and more soaking her arm and thigh. The bullets had been sprayed across the room looking for any target. They'd hit her left side as she covered Alonzo before Mitya slammed into both of them, taking them to the ground.

"Are you hit?" She blurted out the question against his shirt.

His hands ran over her body. Mitya was doing the same. She tried not to cry. It hurt like a son of a bitch. Surely if it was really, really bad, she wouldn't be so aware of everything. Mostly she needed reassurance that Alonzo hadn't been shot.

Not too bad. Her female assured. *They weren't very good shots. Fyodor and his men were better at it.*

The animal didn't sound worried; in fact, she sounded almost complacent, but Evangeline *felt* her concern.

"Damn it, woman. What the fuck were you thinking?" Alonzo snarled.

"Are you hit?" she repeated, needing him to answer.

"He's not," Mitya said, his voice calm but strangely strained. "Stay still, I'm going to turn you over and lay you down. Sevastyan, Gorya, lock that door and turn off the lights. If we're lucky no one saw this mess. Call in help. We need someone to clean this up. Your first priority is Alonzo, no matter what the fuck he says."

"I've got her," Timur told Alonzo, his voice unexpectedly gentle. So were his hands. "Stop growling at her, *brat,* she protected you. We should have expected it."

Evangeline heard the wonder and a hint of respect. She managed to clench her teeth as both men very gently turned her over and laid her on the floor. Her breath hissed out of her lungs and then Alonzo was crouched beside her, his face set in grim lines. His eyes, always as cold as a glacier and just as beautifully blue, were all gold. Completely. His cat stared at her, assessing the damage along with her man.

"Don't you *ever* do something like that again," Alonzo snarled, unable to get his leopard to stand down when he was raging as well. Worried out of his mind. She could see that and maybe another time might even appreciate it, but right now she hurt so bad she wanted to scream. She closed her eyes to block out the sight of leopard and man furious with her.

There was blood pooling under her and she thought that strange. She hadn't been shot in the back and yet when she'd been laid down, there was already a huge puddle of blood. She was lying in someone's blood. She was certain of it. She forced her eyes open and did an anxious scan of Alonzo again.

Mitya's large body trembled and then he sat abruptly. Her gaze jumped to his face and it was nearly gray.

"Oh, God," she whispered, "he's been shot."

Alonzo turned to look at his cousin. The others did the same. Timur immediately was at Mitya's side, carefully easing him down and finding the wound. He swore in Russian. Evangeline didn't like the look on his face, or the one he shot to his cousins. She especially didn't like the way they all looked at each other. Timur pressed his hands tightly to Mitya's thigh while Sevastyan gripped his hand.

"Not like this, Mitya," Alonzo whispered. "We survived all that shit. You can't go out like this."

"Don't you fuckin' die on us, Mitya. Not like this. Not with some lame-ass attempt that shouldn't have happened," Sevastyan added his demand.

Alonzo was calm again, his features frozen into their carved lines. His eyes were so gold she was afraid the leopard would break free, but his voice was absolutely under control, low and commanding as he spoke on the phone.

"A helicopter's in the air, both of you just hang on."

The bell hadn't worked when they'd opened the door. Evangeline relied on that bell. There was a motion detector over the door outside. That hadn't lit up either. She ran her hand along her hip and down her thigh until she found Mitya's arm and then she did the same to his arm until she found his hand. She gripped it tightly.

The world around her faded in and out, but she concentrated on feeling Mitya's hand in hers. "Hold on," she whispered softly. He had flung his body over hers. That was why she was hit on one side and not her back. He'd taken the bullet or bullets for her as well as Alonzo. He could have tackled Alonzo from the side and taken him down, leaving her to be shot, but he hadn't. "Just hold on."

She didn't know if he heard her, but Alonzo's hands moved on her body and it hurt. She would recognize his touch anywhere, but usually he was so gentle. "Hurts," she whispered, trying to move away from him.

"I know, *solnyshko moyo,* I'm sorry. Just hold still for me. We'll have help soon. Jake's sent a helicopter and the doctor is on standby. He's a friend of Jake's. He's leopard, one of us, and his team is as well."

A helicopter. That would be new. She'd never been in a helicopter before, but it was getting harder to stay focused, to even feel Mitya's hand in hers. His fingers sometimes gripped hers and other times went slack. That scared her, but Timur always seemed to rally him.

Sevastyan and Timur spoke to him in Russian, and twice Alonzo got down so his face was next to Mitya's, and he too spoke in Russian to his cousin. It sounded like affection and command mixed together. In spite of the fear and pain ripping through her, that moment would be forever etched on her mind. He looked so caring. It was beautiful to see him lying beside his cousin, whispering softly to him in their native language. Mitya tried to nod several times but then writhed in pain. Instantly Alonzo put a calming hand on him and the man shuddered and went still.

"Stay with us," she whispered, wishing she

knew Russian. But things were fading to black and she was afraid she wouldn't be able to hold on to anything, let alone a dying man.

"Evangeline. Open your eyes, *malyutka*. I need you to look at me," Alonzo insisted.

His voice shook her. Deep. Low. Commanding. He wasn't about to let her go. Either of them. Mitya or her. She counted on him. Counted on the fact that when he made up his mind on something, he meant it. She'd hated that trait in him. The one that had him arbitrarily claiming her. The one that had him putting bulletproof glass and cameras in her bakery. Now, she needed that stubborn, entitled, everyone-does-what-I-say trait desperately. She felt sick with pain. With fear. She couldn't imagine what Mitya felt like.

She knew she didn't make a sound because of her childhood. No matter how hurt she was, she knew not to give her position away. A wounded animal never allowed a predator to know it was wounded. That would be certain death.

"Evangeline. *Devochka moya*. Open your eyes. Look at me."

She'd gone still. Almost paralyzed with fear for Mitya. For herself. In spite of her leopard's reassurances, the worry in the animal and the pain she felt, along with the fact that she felt she couldn't move, were terrifying.

His voice gave her reassurance. She didn't like that he was anxious and she did her best to obey him. Her eyelids felt heavy, but she forced them up to look into his eyes. It was difficult and she wanted to sleep. That might take her away from the pain.

His hand went to her throat, wrapped around it so he could feel her heart beating into his palm. He leaned down until his lips were pressed against her ear. "*Ya tebya lyublyu.* I love you. *Ti nuzhna mne.* I need you, woman. Don't you leave me, Evangeline. I mean it. You stay with me."

It was a command. It was a plea. She heard both and she tried to stay focused on his eyes. She loved his eyes. Loved the way they were frozen, like she imagined Siberia to be, and yet, beneath those twin glaciers could burn a blue passionate flame. Right now they were all gold. Molten. Like his raging leopard. Why wasn't his leopard reassuring him? That was just a little scary. Was she really that bad?

They both refuse to listen. Her female sounded annoyed. *I'm supposed to take care of you. Not them.* Very snippy. *You're mine.*

Now Evangeline heard the worry just as

249

she'd felt it earlier. Her leopard had done exactly the same thing when she was a child and the vile, scary male leopard had prowled out in the swamp looking for her. He'd caught traces of her numerous times, but she was very good at hiding her trail, even her scent. She'd learned about mud and dirt and other plants that would mask any odor. Her leopard had reassured her in a casual, almost offhand way, as if there were no danger at all, but as she'd grown, she knew the leopard was trying to spare her.

You said it wasn't bad.

You hurt. He's bad. The other one with the bad-tempered male. His wound is very bad. Your man knows. He worries for both of you.

The male claiming you is bad tempered.

Not with me, her female pointed out.

Evangeline made an effort to squeeze Mitya's hand tightly, but the best she could do was a weak attempt. Her lashes drifted down several times. Each time, Alonzo tightened his hold on her throat as if by holding her like that, her pulse in his palm, he could keep her from stealing away.

"*Net, net,* Evangeline, don't you try to slip away from me." Alonzo pressed his mouth to hers. "Breathe, *devochka moya.*"

"They're here," Gorya announced. He stepped over two of the three dead bodies to unlock the door.

Two men swept in, one going to Mitya's side, the other to Evangeline's. They immediately began setting IVs.

"We'll give you morphine for the ride," the nurse said to Mitya. "You hold on, you hear me? We're transporting now. We don't have time to waste. Is she ready to travel?" he barked at his companion.

"Yes."

Evangeline had never had drugs of any kind before and her leopard didn't like it. At first the animal fought the sensations, but as her human companion's body accepted it and she was able to deal better with the pain as they were loading her onto a gurney, the cat settled, curling up and making herself small. Evangeline couldn't imagine what Mitya's male was doing. The danger was, while Mitya was unable to be in control, his male, every bit a killer like Alonzo's, would emerge and savage everyone in sight.

She felt Alonzo's hand in hers as he ran alongside the gurney to the helicopter the pilot had set down in the park just one block down from her shop. He couldn't ride with her, the space was cramped, and he bent to brush her lips with his.

"Stay, Evangeline. I'll meet you at the

hospital. You fight, you hear me? You fight."
Alonzo watched them get her inside and he
turned back toward his brother, his hand at
the nape of his neck, uncaring that he had
blood all over him. It was her blood. Mitya's
blood. "Let's go."

"We've got the cops and dead bodies,"
Timur ventured, reluctance in his voice.
"Thankfully we've got cameras. There is no
denying it was self-defense."

"I have to go to the hospital," Alonzo said.
"Send the cops there if they want to talk to
me. I can't be here when she's there. And
Mitya . . . . It doesn't look good."

"Go then. Sevastyan, go with Alonzo,"
Timur said decisively. "Don't let him out of
your sight, no matter what he says. Gorya
and I will stay and deal with the police and
their questions."

Alonzo went through the kitchen, out the
back. Timur had a driver waiting for them,
already called when Alonzo had called Jake
for the helicopter. *Stay alive for me. Want
me enough to live.* He slipped into the car,
Sevastyan slamming the door after him and
diving into the front passenger seat. The car
was in motion almost before Sevastyan got
the door closed.

Alonzo held himself very still. His leopard
was equally as still. For most of his life, he'd

been frozen inside. He needed it that way to survive. His leopard was all fiery passion, raging with fury and killing with ice-cold proficiency. He had lost so much in his life, lost it before it was ever that good.

Solnyshko moyo. Stay alive for me. Want me enough to live. He curled his fingers into a tight fist as if he could hold her in his palm. He brought his fist to his chest, rested it there against his heart. She was his sun. His heart. His everything.

He didn't know about families or relationships. He'd chosen loyalties. He'd been taught to be loyal at an early age. His father had beat it into him — he just hadn't told him he didn't have the freedom to choose who to be loyal to.

He'd chosen his mother. Timur, his brother. Gorya, his cousin. His loyalty had been to them. When his father made the decision to beat them to death, probably in one of his fits of rage, Alonzo had made the decision to protect them. That, more than any other time, was when he learned he had choices.

Evangeline was his choice. His loyalty was to her. *He* belonged to her. Everything good in him, everything bad that could protect her. All of him. Heart, mind, body and soul were hers. He'd never asked for anything in his life. Not once. He'd never had anything that belonged to him. Never.

"Evangeline." He whispered her name aloud. She had to be all right. She had to live. He'd make a bargain with the devil if he had to. He'd lived with demons, he knew them, was comfortable with them. He'd left that life to the best of his ability, only to fall into a dangerous life he thought might help make up for his past. Now he was afraid the price he would have to pay would be far, far worse than anything he'd ever expected. *Live for me. Don't leave me.*

The moment the car pulled up to the hospital, Alonzo and Sevastyan were out and striding through the doors. Jake and Elijah were there waiting. Alonzo couldn't help noting the number of bodyguards as they made their way toward the operating rooms. In the midst of all the leopards, the men there to support him, he felt alone. Isolated. She had to live because she was his entire world. Without her, he had nothing.

"They took Mitya in first. He's critical. Lost far too much blood. If he lives, it was Timur putting pressure on the wound, slowing the bleeding, he can thank."

"He stepped between the gunmen and

me," Alonzo said, his voice as dead as he felt.

Elijah nodded. "How did they get in without anyone knowing? I thought that place was buttoned down tight?"

Alonzo could barely hear the question. The roaring protest in his mind was so loud, so chaotic when he was always so focused, he couldn't think. His leopard was as out of control as he was, throwing itself at the surface, battering him for supremacy, needing to find his mate and assure himself she was fine. Desperate to remove all threats to her — and the one thing he knew for certain — she was in danger as long as Patrizio Amodeo walked the earth. It had to have been his gunmen sent to assassinate Alonzo.

Stay alive for me. Want me enough to live. He needed to see her. Feel her heart beating. He wanted her to know he was there. That he needed her when he'd never needed anyone.

He scrubbed his hand down his face as if he could wipe away his sins with that small gesture. Anything to deserve her. Anything. Anything to save her. His cousin, Mitya, he loved. Mitya had been born into the cruelest lair of all and like Alonzo and Sevastyan, he had chosen his mother. When his father had killed her, Mitya had bided his time, thinking he'd take his father's place as head of the lair and clean it up that way, but as time went on, he realized there was no taking back the legacy. Like Alonzo, he would have to kill every male and some female members of the lair. He had quietly disappeared and found Timur.

Mitya had known the life and what it entailed. Alonzo had brought that life to Evangeline when she'd gotten out.

"That isn't going to help," Elijah said softly.

Joshua came up behind him, matching his pace, pressing close. Alonzo realized the three leopards, Jake, Elijah and Joshua, were there not only because of Evangeline and Mitya, but to contain him if Evangeline didn't make it. He wasn't certain they could and that told him how far gone he was. That Evangeline was wrapped so tightly around his heart and woven so seamlessly into his soul that he wouldn't recover, he wouldn't even want to recover if he lost her.

He forced himself to stop the low growl and take a deep breath. Every joint ached. His skull felt too tight. His muscles hurt, and there wasn't a place on his body that didn't itch insanely. "She can't die." He made it a statement. "If she isn't in surgery, I want to be with her."

"They won't allow it," Elijah said. "You know that."

He looked at Jake. "Make it happen."

Jake didn't bother to argue. "I have to know you've got it under control."

"I do."

Jake assessed him for a long while. "Give me a minute." He strode away.

"We need to talk to your men, Alonzo," Joshua said. "We need to figure out how this happened."

Something in his voice brought Alonzo out of the haze of concentrating. *Stay alive for me. Want me enough to live.* He lifted his head alertly, swung around to face Joshua, although he still kept his eye on Jake, who was on his phone several feet away, his face carved in grim lines.

"There has to be a mole, Alonzo. Someone knew about the cameras outside the shop. They knew about the bell and the door and had access to them. They knew what time she locked up and when you'd be alone with her. They have an inside man." He kept his voice pitched low, a mere thread of sound. He clearly didn't want the other leopards in the room to hear.

Timur and Gorya had been with him since he'd taken over Antonio Arnotto's territory. He had new leopard recruits from

Borneo, friends of Drake Donovan's. Men proven in battle with no connections to Russia or to the mob in the United States. It was a long shot that one of them would be the mole. That left his cousins under suspicion. He took them with him to the bakery all the time. It was possible, but they'd had any number of chances to slip a knife into him. His leopard was always alert, but still, they got close.

Could he say he trusted them? He'd learned too early not to trust anyone. Timur had *earned* his trust. So had Gorya. Both had that same faith in Sevastyan and Mitya. Mitya had thrown his body over Evangeline's. Over his. That should buy him a little fucking trust.

He raked his fingers through his hair, something he never did in public. He was frozen — except deep inside he was screaming. He could hear himself, roaring like his leopard and then screaming his rage and fear to the demons below. "What the hell does it matter who the traitor is? My woman has been shot. When she lives, then I'll worry about traitors."

He turned his frozen stare on Joshua only to realize the man had deliberately distracted him. He shook his head and turned back to Jake. The man beckoned him and he stalked across the room and through the double doors to a small room. Jake stayed outside the doors, as did Sevastyan, who followed with a look on his face that dared anyone to stop him.

Alonzo stepped inside and inhaled the smell of blood and hospital. The combined scents bothered him and made his leopard leap and roar. Their mates were lying motionless, looking small and fragile beneath a single sheet. There were machines, bags of blood, morphine, lines running everywhere. At least she wasn't suffering. She hadn't made a sound after she'd been shot. Not of pain. No screaming. No thrashing. She'd been utterly still and quiet like a wounded animal. He had to find out more about her past. He'd told her about his; he needed her to confide in him about hers. What would make a woman react that way?

Taking another deep breath, he stepped up to the side of the bed and reached down to cup the uninjured side of her face. He could hear her heartbeat. The monitor showed her heart beating. Still, he needed to *feel* it. He wrapped his other hand around her throat and closed his eyes. His leopard settled. He settled. The wild, savage beast that was both leopard and man found strength to just breathe because her heart beat into his palm.

"*Ya tebya lyublyu,* Evangeline. I need you to open your eyes and look at me. Hear me. Do this for me."

Her pulse jumped beneath his palm. He could feel it. Hear it. A little faster. Maybe a little stronger. She heard him, and he felt the fight in her as her lashes fluttered and she managed to lift them. Her eyes were glazed from the drug, but she recognized him. He saw the relief in her eyes. She was too drugged to try to hide her feelings and it was there for him. Plain as day. He didn't deserve it, he never would deserve it, but he was taking it. That look that told him he was her man. Her choice. She'd made that choice when she'd leapt over the counter and tried to save his life.

"You fight your way through this, woman. You're tough. You're strong. Never in my life have I asked for anything. Never. Not once. But you, you're a fucking miracle and so much a part of me, I don't know how to survive without you. Not intact. Not with my soul, which is so far gone, shredded to pieces. You have to live. I can't make a deal with God, but I can with the devil. He'll recognize me."

She shook her head and that small smile came. When it did, he saw the instant bite of pain from the movement reflected in her eyes.

"Just listen, Evangeline." He bent closer, his lips moving against her ear. "Don't try to make me into a good man, because I'm not. There isn't much left in me at all. Until you. You're the good. Don't take that away from me. Not now. I could manage to get through life because I didn't feel. Anything. Nothing. I existed, and I did what I had to do to survive, but I didn't feel anything doing it. Until you. You're the feeling. Don't take it away from me. Don't take you away."

She turned her head toward him and again he felt and saw her wince. He shook his head and pressed his lips to her forehead. Both eyes. Her nose. The corners of her mouth. "Live for me, Evangeline. Do you understand what's at stake here? What's left of my soul? That's yours. That's your responsibility. Mine is to make you happy for the rest of your life. You keep my soul safe. Because if you're not in this world and I feel the hell every minute of every day, I'll break. You live."

He wasn't flowery. He wasn't a poet. He was raw and brutal and he was telling her the truth. He wasn't a good man. He'd never be a good man. He was shaped into something twisted and ugly. But she made him different. More, she made him want to be more than he was. She made him think about things, reach for things he had never felt were possible for him.

He loved her. He more than loved her. For a man who didn't feel a damned thing other than his leopard raging at him night and day, he was overwhelmed with the emotion he felt for Evangeline. He hadn't known one could feel such love. Even that with him was twisted and dark. His love damned her to the life he led. It wasn't a good one. It was dangerous and he shouldn't be selfish and insist on having her. But it all came back to the fact that he wasn't a good man and he could live with that as long as she could.

She managed another smile for him and this one lit her eyes under the haze of the drug. "No need to make a bargain with the devil, Alonzo, I'll live."

Her voice was a thread of sound, but there was a hint of amusement in it. He didn't find anything humorous in the situation. She just didn't understand what she was getting into with him. He was okay with that for now, as long as she held on for him. He found that his lungs had been squeezed for air. Now they were a little less restricted. He could take a breath and actually breathe.

"*Malyutka,* I am the devil."

Her smile faded slowly and she shook her head at him. Her lashes drifted down, and he knew she was going under the blanket of the morphine. He kept his hand on her throat. His other hand clasped hers in his. His hand engulfed hers, was so much bigger. He was a giant of a man in comparison to her. He was leopard, with a savage, cunning, fighter of a beast. He had fought countless battles and taken lives, yet his woman, small and fragile, lying there in the hospital bed, had leapt a counter in order to save his life.

He lifted his head to pin the nurse with his frozen stare. She shivered and swallowed, her face paling a little. Good. He wanted her scared. "Why isn't Evangeline in surgery?"

"The surgical team had to be called in. Doc is operating on the other one brought in with her. He called in a second team. They arrived a few minutes ago. The room is already set up so as soon as they're ready for her, I'll take her in."

The woman's voice shook enough that he was satisfied with the answer. She wasn't lying to him, trying to appease him because she thought he might take out his gun and shoot her.

263

He kept his hands on Evangeline, toed one of the rolling seats and sank onto it beside her bed. He murmured softly to her. Nonsense. Speaking in Italian to further the illusion for the nurse that he was from Italy. It occurred to him that even under the influence of morphine, hurting from several bullet wounds, Evangeline had called him Alonzo, not Fyodor. He might not want his life for her, but she was suited to it.

He pressed her fingers to his forehead, needing her touch. He'd held her all night, her soft body tight against his, and somehow he'd found the strength to keep from taking her. That had cost him, but it also had been important to her so it had been important to him. He had control to give her. He had discipline. He just didn't have the finer points of a relationship down, but he'd damn well learn. For her. He'd learn.

His leopard had gone quiet but now he stretched and pushed toward the surface, wanting to feel his female.

Is she hurt? Why isn't she responding? The anxiety was close, and with the cat's terror came the need for violence. Alonzo understood completely. They'd both been programed to respond that way.

The drug is keeping the pain at bay. She's sleeping, safe and secure inside of Evange-

line. Evangeline tried to protect her as well.

He realized that when he was on the floor of the bakery and she'd chosen the angle to hit him. It wasn't her most advantageous to get the job done, but if her leopard were stretched out from the leap and on her right side, or middle, she'd angled in so that the left side of her body was presented to the target, protecting both Alonzo and the cat.

She was brave.

She was foolish, he snapped back, although it was nice to hear the admiration in his leopard's purring voice. The big cat genuinely liked Evangeline and respected her.

Not foolish, his male insisted. *Brave. She is worthy of you.*

Alonzo felt like pounding his fist into something. Anything. The wall. The floor. A man. The man who had ordered the hit. He needed to find out just who had been that stupid. Evangeline was far too good for him. He wasn't worthy of her, but he was taking her. Keeping her. And this would never happen again.

Another nurse entered, this one dressed from head to toe in surgical garb. "We're ready for her now."

He stood immediately and bent to press his mouth against hers in a final kiss. "Live for me, Evangeline," he reminded.

Her lashes fluttered but didn't lift. Still, that beautiful lower lip of hers curved into a half smile. He stepped back and watched them take her away. His heart accelerated and for a moment his lungs went back to barely being able to breathe. Shaking his head, he stalked down the hall, Sevastyan falling in beside him.

"Jake said to meet him at Emma's room."

Alonzo strode through the hospital, Sevastyan prowling close but giving himself enough room to fight if he had to. His cousin wasn't taking any more chances with his life. Security would be tight for a while. Annoying, but necessary. No one stopped him as he approached Emma's room.

There was a security detail at the entrance and end of the hall as well as on her door, but he recognized the men and they recognized him. Trey Sinclair had worked with Drake Donovan in the rain forest rescuing kidnap victims, and he'd come to help Drake with Jake Bannaconni's security. Dash Boudreux was Drake's brother-in-law, from a lair in the bayou, and he had recently come back from a brief stint working in Borneo.

They nodded at Alonzo as he stepped inside the open doorway. Sevastyan remained outside with the other two guards. Jake sat on the bed with Emma and he didn't look in the least happy.

"You promise me you'll never bring this up again, Emma. I mean it. I won't have it. Not. Ever. Again. Am I making myself clear?"

"You haven't even gone to see our baby, Jake." Emma's voice was very quiet.

With Evangeline in surgery, Alonzo didn't blame Jake in the least for his fury. Terror did that to a man. Evangeline was going to survive because there was no other choice. None. And she was going to have to put up with his crazy protection for a while. At least until the terror faded a little.

"You promise me. We're done with you carrying kids. You were lucky this time. You heard Doc. Whatever the hell happened in that accident made it too dangerous for you to give birth. We're done."

She sighed and shook her head. "I wanted a big family, Jake. You wanted that. I hate that I can't give that to us."

"I want you more. Alive. With me. With Draya and Kyle and this one."

"I need you to go see him. They won't let me, Jake, and I need you to go and make certain he's all right. He'll know if you don't go. His leopard will know. He has to realize right away how important and wanted he is to us."

There were tears in Emma's voice. That was difficult. Having your woman cry was like shredding one's soul. Alonzo had learned that. Evangeline had taught him that lesson.

"Baby, listen to me." Jake's voice gentled. He leaned into his woman and cupped her chin, his thumb sliding gently along her cheek as if he could erase the tears. "I didn't say we wouldn't have more children. You want a dozen, we'll have them. You know I would love every one. We can adopt. We can have a surrogate. I don't care how it's done, only that you don't carry them. Promise me you won't even ask me."

"I heard Doc," Emma whispered. "I wouldn't risk leaving all of you. It's just hard when a doctor tells a woman she can't have any more children. For me, it makes me feel less."

"That's bullshit, Emma." Jake was back to snarling. "No woman is less because she can't have children. And for me, there is no other woman."

"I didn't say it was rational. I said it was how it made me feel. I just need a little time to process everything without you snarling at me."

Jake was silent for a moment and then he leaned closer to brush his mouth over the tears on her face. "Stop crying for me and I'll go see our boy. Give me a minute with Alonzo and I'll be right back."

Alonzo forced a frozen smile when Emma lifted her gaze to his. Clearly Jake hadn't said anything about Evangeline or the shooting because he straightened, turned slightly and shook his head.

"I'll come back later, Emma," Alonzo said. "Let you get some rest. I just wanted to make certain you were all right." His allowed his gaze to drift up toward the bags of blood they had obviously been used for transfusions.

"Just tired," she said.

"I'm glad you and the baby are all right." Alonzo backed out of the room and moved out of sight of the doorway, allowing Jake privacy to say good-bye to his woman.

He didn't understand certain things in relationships. Jake had allowed Emma to get pregnant and carry a child even though she'd nearly died and now he was angry — not, he knew, at her but at himself. He was taking it out on her. Making her miserable. Sad. Upset.

He'd snapped viciously at Evangeline as she'd lain in a pool of blood. He'd been so ridiculous, as if his anger would somehow make the terror go away. It was that feeling of helplessness. Feeling. Frozen sometimes was better. He knew he was never going to get the sight of her face covered in blood from his mind, not until the day he died. And it would never, *ever,* happen again.

10

Jake Bannaconni had a tremendous amount of pull at the hospital. The men came together around a large table in a conference room. They left guards at Emma's room and also the surgery entrance just in case a hit was planned against the women or Mitya. Timur and Gorya joined them, and they didn't look happy.

"The alarm above the door and over the sidewalk outside had been tampered with. The bell inside the shop had also been tampered with. The lock had been systematically shaved until it didn't work. That had to be done over a day or two or Evangeline would have noticed."

"The cleaning crew?" Alonzo asked.

Timur shook his head. "It's a crew the Arnotto family used for years. Same people. I doubt that it's any of them."

"Not my men from Borneo," Drake said. "I've known most of them since I was a child and they would have no reason to betray us. Nor would any of them have time to build a relationship with another crime family."

Alonzo sighed. "It isn't Mitya or Sevastyan. They've been with Timur and Gorya for the last few years. Had they wanted to kill me they certainly had many opportunities."

There was a small silence. Twice Elijah started to say something and then backed off. He ended by just shaking his head.

"Who put out the hit?" Joshua asked.

"The shooters are from out of town. They belong to a biker club from back East," Elijah said. "It's known the club has done hits for the Chicago mob."

Alonzo kept his face expressionless. He didn't make the mistake of glancing at Timur, even knowing his brother had to be as relieved as he was. In the back of his mind, he always had to remember that his uncles would someday track him down. If there had been a connection to the Russian mob, they would know that they'd been found. He wouldn't run, but he would have taken the fight to them in order to better protect Evangeline.

"Any one of the bosses could use the club to carry out the hit," Drake said.

"We need to look closely at Amodeo," Elijah said. "He has an inflated ego, demands respect when it isn't earned and has a huge sense of entitlement. Alonzo stepped all over his pride. I made him apologize and then we turned him down. I'd say he would believe he had every reason to order a hit."

"This soon? Doesn't that make it obvious?" Alonzo asked, playing devil's advocate. It did seem too soon to him. The shooters should have known Alonzo and his bodyguards would be there in full force. Armed. He had four bodyguards with him, not two. It didn't make sense to him. It was ill-conceived. Poorly carried out.

"Amodeo is a hothead," Joshua said, disgust in his voice.

"Emilio?" Drake asked. "You said he wanted Evangeline. He's certainly been around long enough to have affiliations with the biker club. He'd know whom to call on for a hit he didn't want traced back to him. Elijah? You would know that as well."

Elijah shrugged. "I prefer to do my own dirty work so there is no chance of it being traced back to me. Paying someone leaves a money trail. If they're caught, before I can have them killed, they might talk to the cops just for a plea bargain."

"Check into Emilio. And don't forget that

gun shipment. Alonzo, can your men still take care of that?" Jake asked. "If you can't . . ."

Timur stirred, irritated that their work integrity would be called into doubt. He didn't make the mistake of protesting, just looked as expressionless as Alonzo.

"We have it under control," Alonzo assured.

Eli Perez, a former DEA agent, hurried into the room. He was married to Catarina, the woman who had set so many things in motion. She'd run from Rafe Cordeau and when Rafe had disappeared, his territory had been left open. Joshua now ran it, but because the territory had been up for grabs, Siena's grandfather, Antonio Arnotto, had made his try for it. That had ended in his murder and forced Alonzo to fill the opening left by Antonio's death.

"Sorry I'm late. How's your woman? Have you heard anything? And the bodyguard?"

Alonzo had fought beside the man and knew him to be tough as nails. He hadn't expected the inquiry, especially about Mitya. He looked around the table at the men sitting there. Jake Bannaconni. Drake Donovan. Elijah Lospostos. Eli Perez. Joshua Tregre. The men guarding them. All leopards. All alpha. All in love with their women. So different than the way he was raised. The lair he'd been born into. They were genuine friends, watching one another's backs.

"They're both still in surgery," Alonzo said gruffly. "And Catarina?"

"She's good. She's visiting with Emma right now. I told her I'd drop her off to see Siena next."

"Thanks, Eli," Elijah said. "Triplets are tough to carry. She's exhausted a lot, although she pretends she's not." He turned toward Alonzo. "The women can't wait to meet Evangeline, Alonzo. She'll have plenty of friends."

He was grateful for that offer as well. As far as he could tell, Evangeline only had a couple of women she reached out to. "Drake, I know Saria is pregnant as well. You don't have to stay while we figure this out. I wouldn't want to be away from Evangeline if she was pregnant."

"I go home often. Jake lets me use his small jet. He's got a lot of toys, and someone has to use them."

"Can she fly?" Jake asked. "Emma would like to meet her. She talks to her on the phone, and they text, but mostly I think they laugh at the pair of us."

"When things settle down, I'll bring her

for a visit," Drake promised.

That told Alonzo Drake didn't want his woman anywhere near the explosive situation. He couldn't blame the man.

"We'll take care of the shipment," he said. "And we don't need help. I've given orders to put the house in order so I can bring Evangeline home with me to recover. I can protect her better there."

Joshua cleared his throat, bringing the attention to him. He was a man of few words, but he wasn't a man anyone ever wanted to go up against unless it was absolutely necessary. His fighting skills had been honed in the rain forest, both man and leopard, and he was fast and brutal when necessary. Alonzo knew he was like Drake in that he had patience and the kind of mind it took to run a lair. He was fair and just, and when he fought another leopard, he didn't automatically go for the kill. He wanted to force the other male to submit and, hopefully by winning the battle, keep a member of his lair in line.

Alonzo's leopard always went for the kill. It was difficult, once the big male cat was set free, to pull him back. Any lair he ruled, the members would have to know that up front before they challenged him, because the likelihood that a challenger would escape death was slim.

"I didn't grow up with my cousin. I never actually met her, not officially, but she's family and she had it far worse than I ever did. I grew up without a father, but I had the other leopards in the rain forest and I had my mother. Evangeline had no one. Not really. That bakery appears to mean everything to her. If she closes it for a few weeks, can she sustain that loss? I'm willing to back her financially. I'm also willing to find a baker and help for her, to step in while she's recouping, if you think that's the best idea, Alonzo."

He'd given Alonzo respect by asking his opinion instead of the opinion of the council or just arbitrarily deciding because Evangeline was his first cousin and he could make decisions for her.

"She wouldn't want anyone running her bakery, Joshua. She's very proprietorial over her business. I've tried to get her help and she didn't want anyone else in there yet. She said she wasn't ready. I did manage to get her to agree to a cleaning crew . . ."

Timur coughed. Alonzo sent him a "shut up or die" look. Timur coughed again and muttered something in Russian that sounded suspiciously like *bullshit.*

Sevastyan and Gorya turned their heads

to keep grins from showing. Alonzo didn't know whether to drag Timur to him in a bear hug that was a little too enthusiastic and maybe broke all his ribs and cut off his air or ignore him.

"The financial help will come from me. I plan to put a ring on her finger as soon as possible. My money will be her money."

"She might not go for that," Drake warned. "The money, not the ring. Saria tells me Evangeline is very independent."

Alonzo shrugged. Evangeline could be as independent as she wanted to believe she was, but she was going to be his wife. He took care of his wife. She wanted the bakery, then she would have the bakery, but he wouldn't argue about whose money paid for what.

He lifted his gaze to Timur, the one man in the room who knew him best, knew he would do what he deemed best for Evangeline. They'd talk it out because he knew he was supposed to do that. He saw Jake trying to do that with his woman. He'd seen Elijah doing the same with Siena. The thing was, neither seemed particularly successful at it. The more they talked, the more the woman won the argument. Emma got pregnant and nearly died. Siena was pregnant with triplets, and all of them knew that was risky. No, talking didn't do much for the man other than lose him the battle.

What was there to say? Evangeline didn't like his protection, too fucking bad, she was getting it. She wanted to keep the bakery and needed money, it was going to be *his* money, not her cousin's. He was compromising by letting her put herself in danger every damn day going to that bakery.

You like the bakery.

Shut the fuck up. You got us into this by being so bad tempered.

His male yawned. *I'm not the one with the bad temper now.*

Evangeline's female was having a bad effect on his male. Alonzo preferred the claws and teeth to his smart-ass comments. He was so over talking. He wanted to go back to the waiting room. He actually wanted to go into the operating room and stand guard over her. He stood abruptly.

"I'm done. Thanks for coming, all of you, but I've got to work this out with my people. When you hear something about the hit, please let me know." He took one more look around the room at the men there. Men he knew he could count on as friends if he'd allow them to be. He didn't have friendships. He didn't know how to have them. Looking at the men, every single one a hard, tough, battle-scarred leopard, but a good man, he wanted to belong with them. He just — didn't.

Elijah Lospostos was probably the man who came the closest to being like him. He knew Elijah had killed his uncle to protect his sister, but he hadn't wiped out a lair. He hadn't killed his own father. He hadn't committed the unspeakable crimes Alonzo had committed. His soul wasn't so black that there was no redemption. Alonzo didn't want Evangeline to pay the price for his sins and he feared, in the darkest recesses of his mind, that was exactly what the Universe had in mind.

I don't expect redemption, he whispered to anyone listening. *I'll live with what I did. She's innocent. Don't take her away from me. Don't do that.* Because he wouldn't want to maintain anymore. He would be as crazy and as vicious as his leopard. He wasn't a good man. He didn't know how to be, but for her sake he would try. Without her, what was the use of trying?

He found himself making promises to the devil with every step he took back down the hall toward the waiting room just outside of the surgery. Just save her. That's all. Just save her. His soul was already gone, so what was the point in taking her?

Sevastyan and Gorya stepped through the doors of the waiting room before Alonzo, taking a quick but thorough scan of the room before moving aside and allowing him entrance. The moment he walked in, his male went insane, raging and clawing, bursting toward the surface so hard and fast, Alonzo could barely contain him. He inhaled and knew immediately why his leopard had gone so crazy. The three undercover cops were there in the waiting room. Brice Addler paced back and forth as if so distraught he couldn't contain his energy.

Crispin Phillips and Reeve Hawkins lounged against the wall, talking quietly. They straightened abruptly when he walked into the room. Brice spun around, glared at him and strode toward him, his fingers curled into two tight fists.

"You did this," he snapped. "You had no right being anywhere near her and you got her shot."

Timur, who had brought up the rear, guarding him carefully, made a move toward Brice. Sevastyan and Gorya shifted smoothly around to put their bodies between the three cops and Alonzo. Alonzo held up his hand and all of them halted, but none of them liked it. They wanted action. Their leopards demanded it. Their leopards were every bit as savage as his, and he knew what it took to fight the big temperamental cats daily. Now, when everything had gone to hell and there was no one to challenge, the cops were making it easy to view them as targets.

Silence stretched along with the tension. If the three wanted to blow the fact that they were undercover, they could demand permits for the weapons his bodyguards — as well as Alonzo — were all obviously carrying. Alonzo didn't speak. Didn't react. He merely stared at Brice with his glacier-cold eyes, freezing him out. He was good at that. He'd perfected the look by the time he was thirteen. He scared grown men with that look back when he'd been a teenager. Brice wasn't any different. He could see the killer in Alonzo and it brought him up short.

"Why couldn't you just leave her alone?"

There was genuine grief in the cop's voice. He hadn't been playing her to get at Alonzo. He'd actually wanted a chance with her.

"She's mine," Alonzo said quietly. "She's always been mine. She told you, but you couldn't hear her."

"She's lying on a damn surgery table because of you."

Alonzo didn't reply. What was there to say? It was the truth. He didn't have to like it, but it was still the truth. He didn't owe Brice Addler an explanation, nor was there an explanation good enough. He just turned his back on the man and walked over to the window to stare out over the city. Waiting. His heart beating. Frozen inside.

He could see the other two cops move in on either side of their buddy, afraid he'd do something crazy. His leopard still raged and clawed, but he was used to it, that continual fury that seemed endless without Evangeline. He was weary of it, weary of the cat wanting to kill.

You are not worthy of your mate if you continue. It was the first time he'd ever rebuked his cat. Ever. He'd always known the leopard was reacting to the things done to him. The violence surrounding them. The kills and the battles and the blood. He'd never blamed his leopard until that moment. If he could find the discipline to stay still and quiet waiting for word on his woman, the leopard should be able to as well.

I hate the smell of him.

He cares for her.

Not him. The other one. Deceit. Treachery. He smells like the men surrounding your father.

Everything in him went still. His heart

beat in his ears, thundered there. Of course. Why hadn't he even thought of it? Why hadn't Timur or Gorya? Elijah or Joshua? Drake should have considered the possibility. *All* of them should have. A cop. A dirty cop. One on the payroll of a mobster.

All three had been in and out of the bakery nearly every day. They had surveillance set up. It would be easy enough to interfere with the outside alarm. To tamper with the little bell over the door. To shave the lock so that it was no longer functional. Who else hung around watching Alonzo and his men? The undercover cops frequented the bakery more than he did, so much so that he hadn't thought much about it beyond that Brice was attracted and making a move on Evangeline.

"Damn you anyway," Brice raged at him, taking another step toward him, his fists balled tight. "You stand there like she doesn't matter. Like none of this touches you."

The male leopard switched his attention from the dirty cop to the man who cared for Evangeline. His two friends caught at his arms, pulling him away from Alonzo and toward the door.

Just then the double doors opened and a woman came out, her scrubs stained with

284

blood. She looked tired. "Who is here for Evangeline Tregre?"

"She's my fiancée," Alonzo said before Brice or anyone else could interfere. The doctor beckoned to him and he followed her over to a corner of the room, his bodyguards behind him.

"She's doing fine," the surgeon hastened to say. "She lost a lot of blood, but her wounds were surprisingly not life threatening. One bullet skimmed her head, took a chunk of skin. Head wounds bleed but that one only required a few stitches. She'll have a headache for a few days."

His belly knotted. She was giving him the good news first, he was fairly certain of it. He braced himself. For the first time in a very long while, not since he was a boy, he felt the soothing stroke of his leopard, trying to ease his fear. On the outside, he was as cold as ice. On the inside, he was as terrified as he'd been when he'd held the gun in his hand and pointed it at a man's head for the very first time at age six.

"The bullet in her arm didn't hit anything major, so we lucked out there. Her muscle will take a little time to heal, but no bones, no major arteries hit, so it was the best case under the circumstances." She wiped at the beads of sweat on her face and looked around carefully, lowering her voice even more. "The other bullet nicked an artery in her leg. I was able to go in and repair it, but she lost a lot of blood. She must have angled her body to protect her leopard. The female wasn't hit, but Evangeline's thigh was mangled. The bullet was a through and through and it tore her up, although, again, it didn't hit bone."

"Bottom line, Doctor." He still felt as though he couldn't breathe. The doctor was giving him the best scenario possible. She'd been hit by or nicked by three bullets and she was alive with no permanent major damage thanks to Mitya, but he couldn't make his mind believe.

"Rest. More rest. She'll need care. I don't know if you can arrange that . . ."

"Of course. When she's released, she will come home with me. I can hire nurses if she needs them, otherwise I can see to whatever she needs. When can I see her?"

"They've taken her to recovery . . ."

"Then that's where I need to be."

She shook her head. "She won't be out from under the . . ."

"That's where I need to be." He pinned her with his ice-cold gaze. Deliberately letting her see the killer in him. See the vicious leopard he lived with. The one tamed by his woman, but now restless and moody.

"I'm leopard," she said softly, "and not intimidated easily."

He continued to stare silently. She was intimidated whether she wanted to admit it or not. He knew because he'd been intimidating people since before he was in his teens and he could read them easily. She was uneasy in his presence. He didn't blame her. Most people were. Even leopards.

She sighed. "I'll take you to her."

"I need information on Mitya as well. He was brought in at the same time." He could be nice now that he was getting his way.

"He's much, much worse, but he has the finest surgeon I've ever known. He's one of us and his skills are without rival. If it's possible to save your friend, he'll save him." She stood up. "Follow me."

Timur fell into step behind Alonzo. She turned, annoyed. "I'm already breaking the rules for one, definitely not two."

Timur didn't protest, nor did he break stride. He just followed Alonzo, ignoring all commands. Alonzo was fairly certain he wouldn't respond to Alonzo ordering him to stay in the waiting room either. Timur believed in taking security seriously. Now that someone had put out a hit on his brother, Timur wasn't taking any chances.

"I want to know the moment Mitya is out of surgery and I can talk to the doctor," Alonzo addressed Gorya. "Make certain the doctor doesn't leave without talking to me."

"You got it."

The doctor pulled open the door to the recovery room. Alonzo could see Evangeline lying very still beneath a thin sheet. She looked pale, her long lashes lying on her white skin like two dark crescents. Her dark hair was pulled back and braided, but like he had come to expect, wild tendrils had escaped and fell around her face and across the pillow.

Machines measured her heartbeat and blood pressure. There was a bandage high on her temple on her left side, one wrapped around her arm, and her left leg had a thick bandage covering the wound. IVs dripped into her arm and a male nurse stood by her bed, bent over her, a needle in one hand and the IV line in the other.

"What are you doing?" the doctor demanded, her voice total authority.

Alonzo shoved the woman out of the way and Timur shouldered him aside simultaneously. The nurse spun and fired his gun rapidly, first at them and then turned it on Evangeline. Alonzo went down on top of the doctor, his body covering hers, his gun out. He shot the nurse four times, each bullet precise, hitting him in the right eye, the throat, the heart and the middle of his forehead. Timur also fired, hitting the man as he went down. Gorya faced the hallway, looking for an accomplice.

"You all right?" Alonzo asked grimly, rolling smoothly to his feet and dragging the doctor up with him. At her nod, he indicated Evangeline. "Check her. Make certain he didn't inject her or the line with anything."

The sound of running footsteps heralded the arrival of security guards and the undercover policemen. Crispin Phillips was in the lead, his gun out, his gaze on Alonzo and the doctor checking Evangeline. Brice was behind him. Reeve Hawkins flanked him, his weapon drawn as well. All three undercover cops wore their badges around their necks in plain sight.

Timur spun, a smooth, fluid move that put him between the police and Alonzo. Crispin and one of the security guards seemed to collide, both tripped on the raised curved tile just outside the door. Both weapons went off.

One bullet hit the side of Evangeline's hospital bed, the other buried itself in the mattress perilously close to her body. Sevastyan and Gorya were on them in seconds, stripping the weapons from their hands and sending them skittering across the floor.

"What the hell are you doing?" Hawkins demanded of his partner.

Crispin shoved the guard. "You did that deliberately. You grabbed my gun."

"I didn't," the guard shouted back.

Brice shoved both of them to the side and dropped down beside the body to check for a pulse. It seemed silly, given the bullet holes in him, but it was ingrained in the man and he did it automatically.

"I want more guards on Mitya," Alonzo snapped. "Get it done." His gaze moved over Crispin and the guard and then went to Timur's face in a silent command. One or all of the cops were involved in the conspiracy to kill Alonzo. They'd put Evangeline in the line of fire twice now. He was done playing nice. He was done abiding by Elijah and Drake's rules. He wasn't waiting for them to figure out who was behind the hit, he was going to fall back on his training — and he had a lot of training.

Timur handed his weapon over to Brice, as did Alonzo. Neither said a word. That was what attorneys were for. The doctor gave her rendition of what had happened while she bent protectively over Evangeline and checked her carefully. She spoke calmly and concisely, an eyewitness, clearing both Timur and Alonzo of anything but self-defense and saving Evangeline.

"He wasn't able to get the shot into the IV. We walked in on him just in time," she pronounced. She pointed to the syringe on the floor.

Brice was careful when he picked it up, marking where it lay before lifting it to his nose. He jerked it away from his face fast. "Smells like almonds." He looked from Alonzo to the body on the floor. "That's twice now you've nearly gotten her killed."

Alonzo pinned him with a cold stare. "You want to tell me why the police response was so slow getting to the bakery? The helicopter got there before the cops did. You have that place on your radar. The minute shots were fired the police should have been all over it."

Brice opened his mouth, closed it and shook his head.

"I'm having my patient moved," the doctor declared. "And I want tight security around her at all times."

"I'll provide the security for her," Alonzo said. "She's my fiancée. My responsibility. I don't trust anyone at this point." Deliberately he swept his cold gaze to include the guard involved in the collision with Crispin.

Crispin flushed. "What the hell are you implying?"

"Crispin." Brice's tone was warning. Every time a police officer fired a weapon, there was a review. No doubt because this shooting involved suspected mobsters, it would require an extensive internal investigation. Brice was warning his fellow cop not to say a word.

That was fine by Alonzo. He didn't want to hear a word. He'd let Jake probe away to try to find money in Crispin Phillips's account or the security guard's, but it didn't matter what he found. There were other ways of getting at the truth fast. Alonzo wanted fast. He wanted the threat shut down so he could ensure that Evangeline was safe to go back to her beloved bakery.

He waited with Evangeline for the forensic team, refusing to leave her. Strangely, Brice didn't make it mandatory to go to the police station for questioning. Jake's lawyer showed up. Vince Petron was considered to be one of the top attorneys in Texas.

First Timur spent time alone with their attorney, telling him what happened, and then Alonzo did. All the while Alonzo was aware of time passing and Mitya still in surgery. Hours passed. Hours. With no word. When he left Evangeline to go into a private room with his attorney, Elijah and Drake took over her security.

Both men were grim faced and all business. They deployed teams around her and around the operating room where Doc worked on Mitya. All security personnel were leopard. No one was taking chances. This had been an aggressive hit. That meant money, big money, had exchanged hands. It also meant the contract called for the hit to be carried out until it was done. Alonzo understood that. He was familiar with that world and he knew exactly what to expect. He knew what the police would do and what they would find. He knew that if he didn't take action immediately, sooner or later gunmen would get to him, Evangeline, his brother, his cousins or one of his men. To him, that was unacceptable.

He lived in a hard, brutal world. He understood what Drake and Elijah were trying to do. He understood Jake Bannaconni's part in it. They all balanced precariously on the edge of a sword. He *was* a sword. He'd been shaped into a sword from nearly the moment he could walk. He'd tried to fit in. He'd tried to become what they needed, but no one, *no one*, threatened the life of his woman, put his brother and cousins in jeopardy, and walked around free.

He let the cops question him. He stated what happened clearly and concisely, just as the doctor had. Just as he was certain Timur had. Then he fell silent and let his attorney earn his money. He thought about Evangeline and what he had to offer her. Blood. Death. A life of suspicion. A life of danger. Everyone would look down on her — other than the women of the men in his immediate circle.

He supposed her bakery would become even more popular. People would go because they would want to catch a glimpse of a suspected mobster. That was simply human nature. His activities would be good for her business, but it would also mean increased security, which would make her even more upset than she already was with what they'd done.

She hadn't liked the cameras, not in her shop and certainly not in her home. They were necessary for her safety. When they had children, their children would need bodyguards and cameras. He doubted if she'd like that either. He pushed both hands through his hair in agitation.

She is strong. She tried to save your life. Again, for the second time since he'd been a young child, his leopard reached out to reassure him.

Alonzo had forgotten that feeling of comfort. Of camaraderie when he had no one else. What had made his leopard settle so much, even when his woman was sleeping off the anesthesia? With everything that had happened, normally he would have been snarling and snapping, raging to be free to wreak vengeance on anyone near.

I think just knowing you have a mate has mellowed you.

There was a silence. *Your woman is calm. Inside. She is calm. Always.*

What did that mean? Alonzo didn't care as long as it meant his leopard was easier to live with. Right now, he needed a little respite to think. To plan. He was bringing Evangeline to the Arnotto estate to recuperate. He could take care of her there, and the security was tighter. He wouldn't have much time to find out who had ordered the hit. The moment she felt better, she would want to go back to work. He had to have taken care of the problem by that time.

He was allowed to go into her room and sit beside her bed. A nurse was with her at all times and that nurse was also leopard, part of the surgical team Jake had brought in. Drake prowled the corridors, a roving guard, while Elijah's men stayed in the hallway outside of her room. Timur and

Gorya were just inside the double doors.

No one spoke. They didn't want to be overheard, or caught on camera. Alonzo knew Timur, Gorya and Sevastyan would know what was uppermost in his mind. Another hour went by. Mitya had been in surgery for eight hours. At least he wasn't dead. Jake had told Alonzo that Doc was the best. Evangeline's surgeon had reiterated that fact. He glanced at his watch. Evangeline was showing signs of waking. Twice she'd lifted her long lashes and turned her head toward him. Both times he saw her leopard staring at him and then she closed her eyes again.

Relief swept through him. At least the female leopard was alive and well. That would help to keep his male mellow. He'd never thought that he'd ever use the word *mellow* in the same breath with his leopard.

Evangeline made a soft sound, somewhere between a moan and a groan. He stared coldly at the nurse. "Is she in pain?"

The nurse shook her head. "We're giving her morphine. She's just coming out from under the anesthesia, that's all. Sometimes they talk."

Alonzo knew she wouldn't talk. She was too quiet. Too private. That spoke of long training, of a way of life. She would remain silent, and if she couldn't, her leopard would aid her in doing so. He was fine with that. He wanted Evangeline to choose to share her past with him when she was alert and focused solely on him.

He knew some facts about her, but very little. He knew which lair she was from. That she had a father and a brother. An uncle and a cousin who acted more like a brother than a cousin. Her brother was more like a distant cousin than a brother. She hadn't been raised with any of them. He had no idea where she'd been raised or with whom.

He knew her best friend was Drake Donovan's wife, but she rarely reached out to her, even when Saria texted. He knew Pauline Lafont Jeanmard had taught her to cook and bake. She stayed in contact with one other woman, although very, very rarely. That was a woman by the name of Charisse Mercier. Charisse was at the helm of a perfume empire. Very wealthy. Her perfumes were expensive and sought after. Otherwise, his woman kept strictly to herself. He was looking forward to learning about her past. What shaped her. What drove her. He wanted to know every single thing about her.

Alonzo tucked her hand under his chin,

holding her to him, watching her face. Drinking her in. She was awake behind those eyelids, her brain working, assessing, her leopard feeding her information. The next time she opened her eyes, she looked right into his.

"Hello, *malyutka*," he whispered. "You're back with us."

She moistened her lips and nodded. "Mitya?"

"Not out of surgery. At this point, I think not hearing anything is a good sign. He's still alive."

11

Evangeline wandered through the huge house for the first time. She limped, so she wasn't graceful, but at least she was up, on her feet. Mitya had been in surgery twelve hours, but he had lived through the terrible wounds he'd sustained. After hearing Alonzo and his bodyguards talking in hushed tones, she knew his surgeon had all but performed a miracle. He wouldn't be up and walking for some time, so she counted herself very lucky.

This was her first time exploring the entire house. It was very large. The kitchen was bigger than her living room and dining room combined. It was beautiful, no doubt about it, but the sheer size of it made her feel exposed. More, it didn't look or feel lived in. She saw no real signs of Alonzo anywhere. Each room looked pristine, as if it was staged and kept that way.

She loved the kitchen. It had everything

she could possibly want. Counter space, wide, with two convection ovens. The stove was a commercial one, as was the refrigerator. Both the bake and cookware were top of the line. A bank of windows let in the sun and gave her a view of the landscaping and trees in the distance. The vineyards started to the north and a lush grove of trees was to her west.

She wandered through the enormous great room. It had a fireplace, and beautiful furniture that looked brand new, as if no one had ever sat on it. It was comfortable furniture so it didn't make sense that this room was never used. She could imagine children laughing and running around, up and down the staircase that wound around the room and up in a curved circle to the next floor.

The sitting room was her favorite room. The floors were hardwood, a pattern ingrained deep into the polished, gleaming wood. It looked like a starburst, the darker wood glowing against the lighter strips. Another fireplace made the room seem cozy. The walls were immaculate, as if freshly painted, and again, the furniture looked comfortable but brand new.

The bedrooms upstairs were large and inviting. Walk-in closets. Soft, warm carpets.

All immaculate. All without use. Each bathroom in the house was the same way, large and pristine. Clearly Alonzo had someone come in to clean because there was no evidence of dust anywhere. The house felt as if it were frozen, cold and sad, waiting for someone to come along and love it. Live in it. Laugh and bring it to life.

She remembered Alonzo folding his clothes carefully and placing his shoes. He would want his house perfect. He would need it that way. She had the urge to bring warmth to this cold, cold place. She found it sad that Alonzo lived in such a place. He needed beauty in his life. Laughter. Warmth. He needed the same things this house did, to come alive and live.

She continued her exploring. There was a huge gym. It had everything from workout equipment to boxing and martial art gear. There was a shooting range. Both looked as if they had frequent use. She kept looking. The master bedroom was enormous, but Alonzo didn't sleep there. No one did. That was obvious and sad to her.

Her leg throbbed and burned, reminding her that the doctor told her to take it easy. She rubbed her thigh and kept exploring, needing to find Alonzo's secret lair. He lived in this house, or at least existed here, but there was no trace of him. Was that how he lived? She found a small apartment off the sunny verandah. It was attached to the house, but not really a part of it. She knew immediately it was created for someone working on the estate.

The moment she stepped inside, his scent enveloped her. This was where Alonzo lived. She took two steps inside and then stopped abruptly, her heart accelerating. There were steel bars on the inside of every window. A plate of steel covered the door to the apartment and every single door inside.

"Oh. My. God." She whispered the words aloud, her hand going defensively to her throat. This was a prison. Not to keep out his enemies, but to keep him inside.

She found herself moving into the center of the room, holding her breath. He had a sound system, and it was an expensive one. Wide leather chairs. Everything in the small apartment was top quality and it was neat. Lived in, but neat. Still. She was forced to take a breath before she passed out.

The heavy metal bars made the apartment look like a prison. The steel on the doors was just plain scary. She could see the deep scratches and knew the leopard had tried to get out, time and time again.

His leopard was terrifying. For Alonzo to

live with that. The knowledge that he had to barricade himself inside his home in order to sleep or his leopard could slip out from under his control and kill someone. She pressed fingers to her trembling lips. How could he live with such a monster? How had Fyodor survived his childhood, teenage years, his life, with such a monster slashing at him day and night?

"Now you know."

She looked up to see Alonzo filling the doorway with his wide shoulders and tall frame. He took up the space, cutting off her retreat. A blue flame burned hot beneath the glacier ice of his eyes. She couldn't tell what he was thinking. For a moment she was ashamed of ferreting out his secret before he was ready to tell her, but he'd said to go exploring.

He moved first, gliding across the floor in silence, his hand closing over her wrist, fingers wrapping around bone so that he effectively shackled her to him. "I didn't want you to see this until you got used to me."

"Used to you?" she echoed. What was he talking about?

He tugged, taking her from the apartment and the evidence of his killer leopard. "Used to me. Committed to me."

She scowled at him. "Throwin' myself in

front of a gun isn't enough of a commitment for you?"

"This is not the time to remind me of that particular moment."

He took her into the great room of the main house and indicated a chair. "You need to get off that leg. The limp is more pronounced than ever."

He had a point. Her leg was on fire. The doctor had definitely told her not to overdo it. The house was very large and it had taken her a long time to explore. She hadn't even gone into the conservatory or the atrium. Without a protest she sank into the chair he'd indicated.

"Don' tower over me. Sit down too."

His gaze drifted over her face. Brooding. Moody. He prowled away from her and then began to pace the length of the room and back.

"I'm not going to let you go, Evangeline. I know you came from a fucked-up lair and you're afraid of my cat being violent. He is. He's dangerous. I've handled him my entire life and now, with you, he's calmer. It will be easier. I'm not keeping you for my leopard, or because for the first time in my life, I don't have to fight him for control. I'm keeping you because I can't conceive of my life without you."

She kept her eyes on his face as he paced. No expression. He looked — alone. She rubbed at her thigh, around the wound that was healing. She was leopard and that meant she healed faster than most people. It was uncomfortable, but the pain was manageable. She knew she was lucky. Mitya had taken the brunt of the attack.

"I know what you saw — the bars on the windows, the metal plate on the door — was scary. I can't tell you it isn't needed, because you saw the way he tries to break free. You have to learn to live with him. He'd never harm you. Never. You hold his female. You're one and the same to him. Ours. He . . ."

"Stop, Fyodor." She kept her voice low because that was her way. "You don' need to dictate to me, and in fact, over time, you're goin' to find out it isn't goin' to work. I make up my own mind about things. I get that you're a big, bad, scary man. You've spent a lifetime intimidatin' people into doing what you say."

"You try to leave me and you'll find out just how bad I can be."

She rolled her eyes, she couldn't help it. She knew him. She'd watched him carefully for over a year. Alonzo wouldn't raise his hand to a woman. In fact, if his enemies really wanted to kill him, they should have sent a woman after him. She would have had a much better chance at ending his life. Now it was too late for that. Now he had her.

"Are you listenin' to me? You're goin' to have to start payin' attention to what I say, honey, because in spite of the fact that I appear to be sweet, I have a nasty temper. I am leopard, after all."

That brought him up short. He stopped pacing abruptly and turned to face her. Her heart fluttered at the sudden surge of hope in his eyes. It quickly faded to be replaced by ice, but she'd seen it. It was too late for him to cover up his feelings. He had intense emotions and those feelings were all for her.

"I'm listening."

She could see him bracing himself for condemnation. "I didn't say I was leavin', you just jumped to that conclusion. I'm not made of porcelain. You're — amazin'. An amazin', incredible man. I looked at those steel bars and wanted to weep for you. I can't imagine how difficult it's been with your leopard so vicious with the need to spill blood."

He didn't blink. Didn't take his gaze from hers. He looked as if he were holding his breath. "I don't understand."

She wanted to smile, but she didn't. She just kept looking up at him, letting him see how she felt inside. She had made that commitment to him months earlier, she just hadn't known. Even taking the leopards out of the equation, she knew Fyodor was hers. Born for her. And she'd been born for him.

"Evangeline? You called me 'honey.' I like that. I like hearing you say that. You don't call anyone else that."

"No, I don'."

"Damn it, woman." He raked his hand through his hair with a jerky motion. He was always so smooth. That little telltale sign of nerves endeared him to her even more.

"You need to just say it straight up. What the hell are you thinking?"

"I'm thinkin' my man might just be a little slow on the uptake. Why would you think I would run now?"

"The bars on the windows. The fact that my male is vicious. I don't expect you to understand what he's been through and I'm not going to defend him, but I'll protect him. From himself and from others."

"You don' have to do that with me. If I accept you as my man, then I have to accept your leopard. My female is part of me. We might be separate entities, but we're still one. I love her. I'll protect her with every-thin' in me. I imagine it's the same for you. Acceptin' you means every part of you, and that's your leopard too. My female will help me. She's a bit enamored with him at the moment, but she's slowly risin'. Once she gets through her first heat, she won't tolerate any nonsense from him."

He just stared at her as if he couldn't comprehend what she was saying.

"So no more dictatin' nonsense, Fyodor. And you might tell me your real last name. I'd like to know what my name will really be even if I'm never called by it."

"There's going to be dictating."

She shrugged. "Then prepare for rebellion."

He took a deep breath. "You aren't going to fight me on this? You're going to stay with me?"

"That's the plan. I'm warnin' you ahead of time, I don' have the first clue about relationships. I've always been on my own and I've made my own decisions. If we butt heads, it's goin' to be when you try to tell me what to do, so try to go easy on that."

He nodded. "I'll warn you, I don't have the first clue about relationships either, so I guess we'll make up our own rules." His eyes continued to watch her. Focused. His cat watching her closely as well. He held himself very still.

"Just say it, honey. If we're doin' this, we have to be able to communicate. It isn't any easier for me than it is for you."

"I'm the man."

"I get that."

"I don't think you understand what I mean."

"I'd have to be deliberately obtuse not to understand what you mean, Fyodor. You want to take the lead. You want the control. You think I'm goin' to run because you're very, very bossy."

"That's about it."

"I've seen your bossy. I get it. The thing is, you'd better get me as well. I don' roll over because you tell me to do somethin'. It isn't goin' to work that way. If you want me, it has to be *me* you want. That means you're not gettin' everythin' your way."

"You were angry about the cameras."

"Of course I was. Seriously, Fyodor, if I put cameras all over your house and place of business without your knowledge, even for the right reasons, even to protect you, wouldn't that make you just a little bit upset? You could have talked to me about it."

"You would have protested."

"That's my right."

"What is the point of arguing when I know I'm going to do it regardless of what you say? When it comes to your safety and the safety of our children, our home and business, it's my field of expertise and my job to keep you protected. Why argue?"

She blew out her breath, understanding where he was coming from, but he wasn't getting it. "I have to be your partner."

"No, you don't. You have to be my woman. My beloved woman. The center of my universe."

She liked that — and she didn't. She knew he meant what he said. She was his woman, beloved at that. She didn't question that. He was different with her than he was with any other, but she wasn't a woman to rely on someone else. She was independent. She liked making her own decisions. Truthfully, she wasn't certain how their relationship could work because clearly he was exactly what he was trying to get across to her: the man, a throwback to days gone by.

"I feel like we're in negotiations."

He shook his head. "Not that. We're a done deal. We're together."

"We still have to find our way together. If you mean what you say, and I'm that important to you, then who I am has to be important. I'm that girl from the swamp without a family, without a parent, or anyone at all. I made my own rules. I can't be anyone else, not even for you."

He dragged a chair close to hers and sank into it, reaching for her hand. "I'm going to drive you crazy, but I'll listen to what's important to you and we'll find a way to make it work. Timur and Gorya head the security team, and I won't mind you making them a little crazy."

She leaned back, liking the feel of his fingers curled around hers. "I won't mind makin' them crazy either, especially Timur. He's not entirely sold on the idea of you keepin' me."

"He is now. You proved yourself when you leapt over that counter. He's always suspicious of everything and everyone so it took a little while for him to warm up to the idea of having a sister-in-law."

"I love my bakery." She made it a statement.

He brought her fingers to his mouth and brushed a kiss across her knuckles. "I know you do. We already have security set up. Timur has one or two ideas to tighten security. We have a cleaning crew to make it easier for you, and I would like you to hire a couple of people to help you. We can talk about that, but one or two would make your life easier. Business is picking up and you can afford it."

She had thought to keep her business small because she wasn't certain what kind of boss she'd make. She was very picky about how her bakery was run. Still, if she hired someone to help her, she could get more baking done and customers wouldn't have to wait. He was nibbling on the tips of her fingers, his teeth scraping over the pads with exquisite gentleness, a sensual experience that sent heat curling through her veins and had her very core tightening with anticipation.

"I might be amenable to that. If I still have a business when I'm allowed to go back to work."

"You'll have business. Probably far more than you can handle."

He didn't sound like he was happy about it, but she decided to ignore that.

"I'm taking you up on your offer of an office in that back room. It would make it easier for me if I wasn't traveling back and forth so much. It will be easier on the security team as well. They can concentrate on the bakery and cars there during the day. This place is set up for security. Antonio Arnotto made certain of that."

"Is this your home?"

"It belongs to Siena Arnotto. She married Elijah Lospostos. She's offered the estate to me several times. She's happy where she is and doesn't want to come back here. The vineyards and winery she'd like to keep. Everything else she wants to deed over to me."

"She wants you to buy it? This place has to be worth millions. Can you afford it?" And did he even want it? He'd been there for some time but he'd never actually lived there.

"She wants to deed it over to me," he corrected.

She drew back and leveled a look at him, instant suspicion gripping her. Maybe, if she was honest with herself, jealousy as well. Alonzo had told her he hadn't been with another woman in years. Had he lied to her?

"Why would she do that?" What kind of relationship did he have with Siena Arnotto Lospostos? Why would the woman want to deed over an estate worth millions to him? It didn't make sense. She knew about Siena Arnotto. She'd been the only heir of Antonio Arnotto.

Her family had a violent history in spite of the fact that her grandfather had spent his life as a winemaker. His wine was famous, his vineyards legendary. From the countless magazine articles written about the Arnotto family, Evangeline knew that Siena was beautiful and very well educated. She didn't come from a poor family of criminals in the swamp.

"Stop it." Alonzo growled the words and bit down on the tips of her fingers, holding them between his teeth when she yelped and tried to jerk them away. "Siena was fifteen when Antonio assigned her to me. I was her bodyguard. That's all. She was a sweet, innocent girl living with a monster, but she didn't know that. She had no friends. Antonio made certain of it. He arranged for her to be married to a man who would have beaten her. He did beat her, and her grandfather did nothing."

"You care for her." She made it a statement. She hated that her voice had gone even lower, a total giveaway to him. She ducked her head, unable to meet his frozen gaze. It was difficult to feel stripped raw in front of him when he was so completely in control. She'd practically thrown herself at him, and now she felt uncertain.

"Yes. I do." When she tried to pull her hand back, he clamped down harder on it, refusing to relinquish his hold. "She was a young, innocent girl. My leopard didn't care. He was still as savage as ever. I care for Siena as a younger sister, not as a woman I would ever be interested in. In any case, *solnyshko moyo,* there is only one woman I'm interested in, and it isn't Siena."

She felt a little ashamed that she'd been jealous. Alonzo had a past. He'd been with other women. She didn't want to know their names or how many there were. She had to be secure in the knowledge that he'd chosen her. That he wanted her. Truthfully, she found that very hard to believe.

"Evangeline. *Malyutka,* look at me."

His voice was so gentle, her complete undoing. She jerked her chin up and glared at him. "Why me? Really, Alonzo, why would a man like you want to be with a woman like me?"

He frowned. "You need to tell me what that means."

"My grandfather was Buford Tregre." She paused, waiting for a reaction, but he just looked at her with his expressionless eyes. Just saying her grandfather's name sent fingers of ice creeping down her spine. "He was cruel and he liked to hurt everyone around him, especially women. He murdered his own son to keep him on the property. That was Uncle Renard, Joshua's father. Renard fought him in order to give his wife and child time to get off the property — which they did."

Alonzo didn't move. Didn't blink. He listened intently, fully focused on her. She took a deep breath. "My father wasn't like Renard. He knew what his father did to women — even his own wife — but he stayed. When I was born, he and my mother took me to a camp in the swamp, and he told my grandfather I was dead. I was female and sooner or later Buford would have done horrible things to me or killed me."

Alonzo stirred as if he might say something, but all he did was press his lips to her fingertips, his gaze never leaving hers.

She moistened her lower lip with the tip of her tongue. Talking about her father often made her throat close so she felt as if she were strangling. "They took me into the swamp. I was an infant. They wrapped me up and left me in one of the camps. Alone. My mother left. They said she died, but I know that isn't true. She left me. Just the way they left me."

Gold flecks began to appear in Alonzo's eyes, turning the glacier from pure blue ice to a greenish ice. There was no expression on his face, but he took her hand and pressed it open, finger by finger, until he could hold her palm over his mouth. She felt his breath on her skin, as if he breathed for both of them — and maybe he did.

She didn't look back. Not ever. That always reduced her to that child in the swamp. The toddler huddled alone with only her leopard to keep her company. The alligators bellowed and she could hear the rustle of the animals sniffing around the outside of her little sanctuary. She jammed her fist in her mouth to prevent any sound escaping. Sound meant death. Even her leopard told her that.

"I learned to become part of the swamp. Sometimes it flooded and I couldn't leave my home. It was cold or very, very hot. There were snakes. I was bitten a couple of times." She showed him her arm and the scar there. Her leg, down low near her ankle. "I was very sick, but my leopard refused to allow me to die."

His eyes went all gold and a snarl escaped. "You want to tell me where your father was? Where the head of your lair was?"

"He said he left me there to protect me. That's what he chose rather than escape his father. He brought me groceries, but if I wanted hot food I had to learn to cook. He brought books and workbooks so I could learn."

Alonzo erupted into Russian, spewing phrases she was certain were very bad ones. She winced, but she didn't pull away from him. She knew he wasn't angry with her. He was angry because her father hadn't protected her the way he should have. He *left* her alone in the swamp. Night after night. It had been terrifying.

"I'm tellin' you this because you have to understand me. That bakery represents me risin' out of the swamp. Taking control of my life. I learned to live with the alligators and the other animals. I know the swamp, its rhythm, its heartbeat. I know how to take care of myself, but I don' know how to have a relationship. I've never had one. Never, Fyodor. You had your brother and cousin. I had my leopard." She ducked her head, unable to meet his eyes. Ashamed. "My own father and mother didn't care enough about me to fight for me. They threw me away instead."

She hated telling him. She didn't want to think about her parents and how Joshua's father had fought valiantly to save his wife and child, but her father just pretended she was dead and left her alone. So alone. She shivered at the memories and tried to pull her hand away from Alonzo.

"Don't." He said it softly. "Look at me,

devochka moya."

She chewed at her lower lip. If she looked at him she would be lost. Unable to think clearly. That was what he did to her. He had to realize she was no bargain. She wasn't Siena Arnotto. She never would be. She would make mistakes, and she was independent. He was a dictator. A man used to others obeying him. She hadn't obeyed anyone in a long, long time.

"I need you to look at me."

For some reason, that low voice, so velvet soft, brushed over her skin like fingers. The commanding tone found its way inside of her. Deep. She felt herself go damp. She didn't understand how he could do that, make her entire body come alive. Be aware of him. She didn't want to feel so much for him, but she did. There was no hiding from it, not and be true to herself. She was a woman who faced the truth.

Evangeline lifted her gaze to his. At once she felt herself drowning. Caught. Captive. There was no looking away from either the man or the leopard. Both stared back at her, wholly focused on her. A shiver went down her spine. In that moment she couldn't decide if she was prey or under his protection. Maybe both. She wanted to be both.

"You're mine, Evangeline. For you, that's

both good and bad. You never have to worry again about anyone leaving you. That's never going to happen. I'll stand in front of you every time. You won't be alone and you won't ever have to face anything alone. Sometimes you won't like that trait in me, but I can't help who I am. I want you to remember that just as I'll remember you can only be who you are."

She wasn't certain she could get to the point that she believed he'd stay with her. That was the terrible part. She had committed to him. She had chosen him. She was here in his home with his steel doors and bars. She didn't even know if he'd let her walk out or if she was his prisoner. She only knew she had to be with him. She was obsessed with him. She thought about him night and day. And no one was going to take his life. Not without a fight from her.

He leaned into her, cupping her face with his hands. His fingertips bit into her scalp. "Your bakery is safe, *solnyshko moyo. You* are safe in my hands. You have to learn to trust me."

"I do trust you." She took a breath, knowing she couldn't be anything but honest. "Some of the time. You scare me. What you do. Who you are. What you are."

He bent his head until his forehead rested

against hers. "I can't change my past. I can't be anything but what they made me."

"That's not true." She glared at him. "Don' say that. Don' even think it. You aren't a natural-born killer. You're not a sociopath, no matter that they tried to shape you into one."

He sighed and straightened. "I don't want you to live with me and not know who I am. What I'm capable of. I've killed. Many times. I've hurt people. Beat them. I was an enforcer for my father. I followed orders. I can put all emotion aside and do whatever is necessary."

"Do you like it?" Her voice trembled. She needed his answer. She needed to know if he was what he said, or what she saw in him.

"Killing? No. Fighting. Yes."

Her heart jumped. He was telling her the truth. "You like to fight?"

He brushed back her hair with gentle fingers. "I'm not civilized, woman. I made that clear to you. I've inflicted pain on others nearly my entire life. I've had pain inflicted on me until I rose up and put a stop to it."

"When you killed your father and the others."

He shook his head. "Long before that. I beat the crap out of him when he was trying to beat me with a whip. I'd had enough. I grabbed the tails of his whip and yanked him into me hard. Then I let him know what it felt like being on the receiving end. I'm a big man and I'm strong. I trained every single day to fight. To kill. He didn't stand a chance."

She heard the satisfaction in his voice, and she didn't blame him. "If I make out a grocery list, will someone get the groceries for me? I get tired walkin' around too much. I'm so much better, I can't really complain, but walkin' around in a grocery store is out for now." She was secretly a little bit glad about that.

His eyes widened at the abrupt switch in subject, but he only nodded. "Anything you want, *malyutka,* write down and I'll make certain you get it."

"Is my car here?"

He went very still. Those golden eyes moved broodingly over her face. "It's here." His voice was noncommittal. "Locked in the garage with the other cars."

She ignored the obvious warning. "Good. I was worried that if I left it at my house or the bakery, some crazy person would decide to put a bomb in it. I can't really afford another car, and I like the one I've got."

"I'm going to kiss you and you're going to let me."

She had no problem with him kissing her. The moment she laid eyes on him, she wanted to kiss him. She loved kissing him. That was a bit intriguing in itself. She wasn't someone to give her body to another, yet she definitely fantasized, over the last year, about having wild, uninhibited sex with Alonzo.

She swallowed her trepidation. "Okay." Softly. A whisper. An invitation.

He took her mouth. Hot. Hard. Not at all like he'd kissed before. This was all about a leopard shifter showing his mate whom she belonged to. His hand bunched in her hair and held her still for him while he consumed her. While he poured domination down her throat. She couldn't help the shiver of excitement, or the way her body reacted to his possession. Her nipples peaked, rubbed against his chest, her breasts felt swollen and achy, her channel grew hot and clenched in need.

She melted under his mouth, holding nothing back because he demanded everything. He made it clear he would take nothing less, and she gave herself up to him. When he lifted his head, his eyes glowing, his face stamped with possession, she tilted her head and leaned close, in spite of the tight hold he had on her hair, in spite of the bite of pain at her scalp.

She brushed her lips over his. "Okay," she said again. This time she was agreeing to more than a kiss. This time she was saying, yes, she was his and she liked it that way.

He regarded her for a long time. "Okay," he agreed. "You need to rest."

"I need to make a grocery list. I'm goin' to make you dinner tonight."

"Not tonight. Tonight I have to go out, and I want you resting. I've already arranged for your dinner. Sevastyan and one of the new men, Kyanite Boston. We call him Kye. They have orders to lock up the house and to keep everyone out. You'll be safe."

She shook her head. "If you aren't goin' to be here tonight, then I think I should go back home."

"No." His voice was implacable.

"I'm uncomfortable around men. I don' want to be alone with them." She made her confession softly, one hand fisting in and then running up and down the front of his immaculate shirt. "I'll just come back when you're home."

"I said no. I nearly lost you, I'm not taking chances with your life again." He caught her hand, dragged it to his mouth and bit down hard on the pad. "Absolutely no."

"Did you hear anythin' I said to you?"

"The answer is still no. I'm sorry you don't like it but I'm not willing to compromise or lose this argument, not when it comes to matters of your safety."

"I wasn't aware we were arguin'," she said. "I was tryin' to express the fact that I'm uncomfortable with other people. Men especially."

He stood up and reached down for her, drawing her up by her hand. "We aren't arguing. That was me telling you what you were going to do, which is wait here in this house for me to return. You're going back to bed in the master suite and you'll rest like the doctor told you."

"You're gettin' bossy."

"I have to be bossy while I can. Once you're at full strength, I doubt too many things are going to go my way. But this one . . ." He trailed off and tugged so that she followed him.

"I like this house, Fyodor, but you don' actually live in it. Are you goin' to keep it, or what?"

"Depends on where you want to live."

Her breath caught in her throat. "What does that mean?"

"You committed to me."

"Yes." She was cautious.

"I want you living with me."

"That's a little fast."

"A year isn't fast. You've been mine since the day I walked into the bakery and you know it. I'm not wasting any more time. You want to keep your house, then we can live there. We can go back and forth. We can accept Siena's generous offer and live here. You tell me what you want and that's what we'll do."

He might not think it was fast, but moving in with him was the last thing she'd expected.

"We haven't even . . ." She trailed off. "I'm not experienced, honey. You don' know if we suit in bed."

"We suit."

She tipped her head back to look at him. He was staring down at her with golden eyes. Just the way his gaze moved possessively over her sent heat rushing through her veins. He was probably right. At least he suited her. She wasn't going to argue. In any case, they'd know soon enough.

12

"This place can't be traced back to us?"
Alonzo asked Gorya as they moved together
down the narrow corridor, avoiding tripping on the old bricks scattered everywhere.

"No. It belongs to the Dean estate and
has been empty for years. He was a slum
lord and his children aren't much better.
The best part of it is, it's right smack in the
middle of Deadmen territory. Our undercover officer infiltrated them a couple of
years back and took down key members of
the gang. They hate him with a passion. If
his blood and/or body are discovered here,
the gang will be prime suspects. They made
enough threats and two attempts."

"You found the money trail? On all three
of them?"

Gorya nodded, hurrying to keep up with
his cousin's long stride. "The dispatcher
and cop were easy. Both are greedy sons of
bitches. The security guard's name is Aaron

Alderman. He's out of Chicago. We caught him at the airport, and he's no security guard." Gorya sent him a grim smirk. "I think he thought we were soft out here."

"Wait until he meets my leopard." Alonzo yanked open the heavy door to the old kitchen. The building had once been a mental hospital, the patients gone for over two decades. The intention had been to tear it down and put up apartment buildings, but the owner had never bothered. The sprawling building had been condemned. Ceilings sagged and mold grew. Graffiti and used needles were everywhere. More than one dead body had been found on the premises over the years, and the notorious Deadmen, one of the bloodiest gangs in all of Texas, were known to claim the property, which might have been the reason the family did nothing with it.

The scent of blood and urine hit Alonzo as he strode into the room. The smells were familiar to him. He'd been raised on them. His mind instantly shut down the way it always did so that he felt absolutely nothing. Not anger. Not compassion. There was a job to be done, and he was very, very good at his job.

"Good evening, gentlemen," he greeted, his voice low. He never raised it. His father had liked to intimidate by shouting. Alonzo had learned that kind of energy could be dangerous and there was no need to expend it. If he showed rage, his leopard felt it tenfold and his leopard was dangerous most times, let alone when he felt Alonzo was angry or hurt. "I trust my brother has taken good care of you."

He walked right up to Crispin Phillips, caught him by his hair and yanked his head up. Phillips squealed, blinking rapidly over and over, his breath coming in ragged bleating gasps, mouth open wide.

"I really hate dirty cops, especially stupid ones. You didn't even try to hide the money." He dropped the undercover cop's head and turned to the hit man. "And you. Taking a contract on me, that wasn't your best decision."

Aaron Alderman managed a shake of his head. "Not you. The woman."

Everything in Alonzo stilled. *The woman.* He heard it, but it took a moment to process because he totally rejected the idea. *A hit on Evangeline?* Who would put out a hit on his woman? Had his uncles found him? It would be like the bastards to go after Evangeline instead of him.

He peeled off his gloves, closed his fingers one by one into a tight fist. He pushed his knuckles close to Alderman. "You see that? You know that symbol?"

Alderman's face paled. His eyes went wide. He'd seen that symbol before, the one tattooed on Alonzo's fingers, just below his knuckles. His brother and cousins had that same tattoo, the one that took all four fingers to create the Amur leopard crouched and waiting for a kill. That and a symbol of brotherhood. Their territory in Russia was fiercely guarded, undeniably wealthy and successful. Mostly, it had a reputation for being bloody, cruel and brutal. That symbol, while not known to be representative of an actual shifter, was known throughout the world and feared as being *Bratya.*

"What?" Crispin screamed. "What do you see?"

Alonzo pulled on his gloves. "This woman you tried to kill, she belongs to me," he informed the hit man in a low, almost casual tone.

Alderman shook his head. "It was a job. Business. I didn't know who she was."

"I'm going to make you an offer. Just once. You know who I am. You know my reputation. I want to know who put out the contract. No negotiations. You're going to die. You know that. But how you're going to die is up to you. You can take a long time and suffer, or it can be fast with no pain. Choose now."

Crispin's bleating noises began again in earnest. He wept, the sounds loud. The dispatcher's bladder let go. He struggled against the chains he was hooked to, his toes barely touching the floor. Alonzo didn't look at him. All of his attention was on the hit man.

Alderman nodded. "Amodeo. The bastard had a real hard-on for her. Wanted it done immediately and to keep going until it was finished."

"You the only one? Exclusive?"

"As far as I know, but he's got a rep for dirty dealing. My boss owed him a favor and I drew the short straw. I hope you get the son of a bitch."

"I'll get him," Alonzo said. He drew his gun, keeping his body between the hit man and his weapon so Alderman would never see it coming. He turned and fired in one motion, putting a bullet squarely between the eyes. He died instantly.

Alonzo turned his attention to the dispatcher. "You kept the 911 calls about the shooting at the bakery from going through, didn't you?"

The man moaned and rocked, his eyes bouncing all over the place in stark fear.

There was no mercy in Alonzo, not one ounce. Not since he'd learned the target had been Evangeline and not him. *Fucking dirtbags.*

"You're supposed to be the good guys," he reminded softly. "Are you on Amodeo's payroll?"

The dispatcher shook his head. "You made a mistake. A terrible mistake."

"I can hear lies," Alonzo said. "I can smell them. You're lying. Even now, when it might give you an easy death, you're lying to me." He turned to the cop. "What about you? Do you want to lie too?"

"You don't understand," Phillips said, tears streaming down his face. "He threatened me. Threatened to kill me. I had no choice."

"So all that money we found in your account is just a coincidence."

"He planted it."

Alonzo shook his head. Patrizio Amodeo might force cooperation by threatening to kill someone as well as their entire family, but he would never part with money unnecessarily.

"Have you ever heard of shifters?" He pulled his gloves off. Flexed his fingers. Carefully he shrugged out of his jacket, handed it to Gorya and began to unbutton his shirt. "Specifically, leopard shifters?"

Both men stared at him. Timur reached out and took the shirt, folding it with meticulous care. The prisoners' eyes widened in shock. Alonzo had almost forgotten the scars crisscrossing his chest and sinking low into his trousers. His hands dropped to his belt.

"In Russia, we have a rare leopard called the Amur leopard. There are very, very few of them left. The fur on these leopards is thick and long to adapt to the snow. The rosettes are wider spaced and larger than other leopards'. What's important for you to know, what I think you'll find the most interesting, is that they have denticles on their tongues." His hands paused on his belt buckle. "Timur, perhaps you would like to explain to these uneducated men just what denticles are and what they're used for."

Timur pulled off his gloves slowly and nodded. "Denticles are hooks or tiny rasps on the Amur leopard's tongue. They are used to scrape the meat right off the bones of their prey."

Both men stared at Alonzo and Timur with rapt attention. Timur looked at his hands and thrust them out toward the prisoners. "The Amur leopard has fur growing on the bottom of its paws to keep them warm. Claws are retractable." As he spoke his hand distorted. The knuckles cracked audibly. Fingers bent. Stiletto-sharp hooked claws sprang out, each attached by a ligament to the bone at the tip of toes.

Crispin screamed. The dispatcher's eyes rolled back in his head and he clearly fainted.

Alonzo leaned into the undercover cop. "You tried to kill my woman *twice,* you bastard. And all leopards can hear lies." With that he shifted, his upper torso and head along with both arms and hands. Hot breath blasted the cop's face as the leopard opened his mouth to show his teeth. All four canines were large and curved, with a space behind each to allow the leopard to sink his teeth as deep as possible during a killing bite. Leopard canines were stronger and longer as well as more cylindrical than those of dogs. They had to be when teeth hit bone. Molars could shear through skin and muscle like the blade of a knife.

Alonzo made certain his leopard showed every tooth to advantage, but he kept a firm grip on his cat. He never allowed the animal to eat human flesh and now was no different. Hot breath hit Crispin's face as his eyes went wide with shock. His mouth formed a perfect *O* in a soundless scream.

"I think you should rethink what you just said," Timur said softly, inspecting his claws. He suddenly ripped the hooked nails down Phillips's chest as if he couldn't quite contain his rage, or his leopard.

Alonzo's leopard snarled. Huffed out another blast of hot air onto the dirty cop's face. Crispin Phillips squeezed his eyes shut tight. "I've been taking his money for years. Since I first was in the academy. He wants her dead. He blames her for all of you not accepting him into the alliance and ruining all his plans."

Alonzo shifted back into his human form and slowly, without taking his eyes from the cop's face, closed his belt buckle and then held out his hand for his shirt. "He didn't know she was mine?"

"No. He thought the old man wanted her. I can help you. I know everything about his business. Everything."

Alonzo just stared at him with ice-cold eyes. "He won't live out this night, so it doesn't really matter what you know."

"I didn't know she was yours." Phillips tried another lie.

"She's an innocent woman, and you knew that." Alonzo lifted his gun. "You also knew she was mine." He shot him between the eyes and then turned and shot the dispatcher. "You left leopard DNA in his chest, Timur," he snapped at his brother. "What the hell were you thinking?"

Timur ducked his head. Shook it. Took a deep breath to breathe away his leopard. "I was thinking he was no different than Patva Amurov. Or Lazar or Rolan Amurov." He shook his head again. "Sometimes I can't take it, Fyodor. Not one more second."

Alonzo went very still. Timur was no different than he was. They had the same upbringing. The same father. Patva was a cruel man who beat his sons daily, humiliated them, insisted they be tough, brutal killing machines before they were in their teens. He fed their leopards pure rage. Now Alonzo was putting him in that same position.

"Don't," Timur warned him in a low, hostile voice. "You're my brother. I *choose* to follow you. To protect you. You protected me. My leopard won't accept any other way of life, any more than yours will. I had a moment of weakness. Of anger. It's under control now."

Alonzo knew he couldn't apologize or his brother would explode into violence. He was that close. He merely nodded, but deep inside, he felt the burden of another sin. So many. He shook his head. "We can't leave his body here. It has to go out with the guns, down to Louisiana and the swamp."

"I'll take care of it," Timur snarled. "It's my mistake."

Alonzo turned his cold eyes on his brother. "I need you with me. We have a cleanup crew for a reason. They can handle it. We're visiting Amodeo tonight."

"He's going to be armed to the teeth. Guards everywhere," Gorya cautioned. "He'll be expecting retaliation since they missed their target. No one can miss the fact that you were at the hospital every day until they released her and that she's in your home under your protection. Not to mention, Mitya was hurt and is still in the hospital. Amodeo might not give a damn if someone shoots one of his soldiers, but most *vors* would retaliate immediately."

"Leopards can get through his guards," Alonzo decreed mercilessly. He wanted to be like Elijah Lospostos and Drake Donovan. He'd thought he could be different, leave his past behind and maybe actually do some good, making up a little for his past, but no way was he going to let Patrizio Amodeo live. Not for another day. Not when he knew the bastard had put out a contract on Evangeline.

"Let's do it then," Timur said, already using the burner phone to call in the cleanup crew. He snapped the phone shut and followed his brother and cousin out.

Alonzo waited to call Sevastyan until he was in the car. He used the same phone Timur had, rather than his personal one. They'd learned, over the years, to be meticulous about their work. They couldn't afford one mistake.

"She okay?" he asked abruptly.

"She's a pain in the ass," Sevastyan said, although Alonzo could hear the affection in his voice. "She's got a list as long as my arm and wants me to go to the store for her. She's insisting tomorrow she's cooking for everyone."

"She's supposed to be in bed."

"Yeah, well, let me just say, that's not happening unless I put her ass in bed."

Alonzo remained silent.

Sevastyan blew out air in the way a leopard might. "Really? She'll take my head off."

"Better your head than your dick," Alonzo snapped.

Sevastyan sighed. "Consider it done, but I'm going to make certain she knows where the order came from. Then it will be *your* dick in danger."

"Lock that place down. She's got a price on her head. If anything happens, you can protect her from my room. There's a passage in the wall just to the left of the door. Find it in case you need it before we get back. You have any inkling of trouble, get her out of there and into the safe room. The passageway leads to one."

"Price on *her* head?" Sevastyan repeated.

"That's right." Alonzo snapped the phone closed and handed it back to his brother. Sevastyan would get rid of his burner the moment they returned. No one ever used their personal phone for business. Not. Ever.

Alonzo remained silent during the long ride to Amodeo's personal home. He lived on the edge of San Antonio, in a quiet neighborhood reserved for the wealthy. His house was a one-story, lengthy sprawling brick mansion shaped like a *U.* The courtyard had a swimming pool and a garden, with inviting decks and cool shade trees. The entire estate was surrounded by a high wrought-iron fence, very decorative looking, but perfectly functional.

To get to the house, one had to maneuver up a long, private drive to the gate, where a guardhouse sat, preventing entry. Two guards, both heavily armed, manned the guardhouse. Two dogs patrolled with their handlers on the grounds. No one stood around whispering and laughing. No one smoked cigarettes and looked bored. This was a camp prepared to do battle.

"Just the way I like it," Alonzo murmured as he, Timur and Gorya leapt from the car three blocks from the house. The town car drove off, barely slowing down to allow them out. The three leopards padded silently through the neighborhood, staying close to the bushes and trees lining the streets that led to the larger estates. Each wore a small knapsack around their neck containing clothes.

It wasn't difficult for the leopards to move parallel to the driveway, keeping out of sight of the cameras directed at the long drive. Their long fur camouflaged them easily in the heavier bushes lining the drive. They barely disturbed plants as they made their way to the fence.

All three cats were up and over the fence as if it didn't exist. It wasn't that difficult. Leopards could run up to forty miles per hour in a short burst. They could cover twenty feet with one leap. The fence was eight feet high. Leopards could easily jump it and all three did, landing on padded paws in the foliage, facing the house.

A dog whined close by and they went to the ground, flattening their ears as they crouched low. As the dog passed around the side of the house, they moved forward, slinking stealthily through the brush and the landscaping to gain the shadow of the porch. Alonzo took the lead. He'd spotted a curtain fluttering in the window just off the wing of the house on the left side. Positioning himself under the window, he stood on his hind legs and peered through the window. The room was empty.

He went in, the slide of fur making no noise. It was close to midnight and the house was dark, with only a faint light coming from under the door of one room. Patrizio Amodeo wasn't married, but word was, he always had a woman before he went to bed. He kicked her out the moment he was finished with her.

The big Amur leopards could hear the murmur of voices, a female and male. The hated male voice had all three cats grimacing, lips drawn back, teeth showing, ears flat, ready for combat.

A door slammed off to their right and they heard the heavy tread of footsteps. All three leopards slipped behind furniture and waited as a man strode into the room, all purpose. He knocked on the door where the voices and light came from and then twisted the door handle, opening the bedroom door.

Amodeo wore a silk robe and nothing else. He thrust a woman at his bodyguard. Her clothes were in her arms, but she was stark naked. "Get rid of her. She's not that good, but enjoy her if you want before you send her on her way."

The bodyguard grasped the woman's arm and yanked her from the bedroom. She struggled for a minute, and Patrizio laughed. He slammed the door closed. The bodyguard slapped the woman when she kept struggling.

"Shut up and be still or you're going to have a really bad night, honey," he snapped. He dragged her out of the room and back down the hall.

Timur's leopard followed silently. Alonzo indicated to Gorya to follow his cousin. He didn't need help killing Amodeo. He didn't want help and he wanted Timur protected.

Silence settled on the house. Behind the door drifted the scent of a cigar. Whiskey. The creak of the bed sounded. Amodeo turned down his light until only the glow of a nightlight slid under the door. Alonzo padded to the door, shifted just one paw and turned the doorknob stealthily. He'd noticed when the bodyguard had opened the door there was no sound, no telltale squeak of the hinges.

The big leopard slid into the room, staying low, moving in stops and starts using the freeze-frame stalk of the large cat. He took his time, his belly sliding along the hardwood floor. Patrizio's eyes were riveted to the screen across the room from his bed where the local nightly news played. Clearly he was hoping for something in particular to be shown. Ordinarily the midnight news was a repeat of the earlier news. Once in a while they gave coverage of an event happening at that time, but rarely.

Unease stirred in Alonzo's gut. He didn't like the smug look on the crime lord's face. Once he lifted his glass toward the news anchor and then took a deep swig. Alonzo waited until the glass was on the nightstand and the cigar was in the ashtray. Once the man put both down, the leopard rushed in a classic blitz attack. He was on Amodeo before the man had an inkling of danger.

The heavy body of the leopard pinned his prey down, his mouth clamping down on the vulnerable throat. The cat stared malevolently down at Amodeo and then backed off with a warning snarl. The man froze, although his bladder let go and he wet his bed. Alonzo shifted just his head, keeping the body and huge hooked claws on his prey.

"I just wanted you to know who killed you."

Amodeo's face twisted into a mask of hatred and he lunged for the gun sitting in the open drawer of his nightstand. The leopard shifted that fast, mouth clamping down around the arm, breaking through skin and bone, twisting as it did so, cutting the bone in two as if it were nothing. The leopard whipped its head around and drove for the throat as Amodeo opened his mouth to scream. The cat delivered a suffocating bite, breaking the neck at the same time.

Alonzo left him there, blood running down the bedsheets and pooling in the mattress and on the floor. He forced his leopard out of the room and down the hall, following his brother and cousin. He came across the first body just outside what appeared to be the kitchen. The man was dead with a look of stark horror on his face. His eyes were open and he stared up at the ceiling with glassy, shocked eyes. There was blood on his throat.

Two more bodies lay on the floor. The bodyguard was partially nude. His pants were down around his ankles and he had every indication that he'd died hard. Alonzo knew he was looking at Timur's leopard's kill. The cat had ripped apart the body below the waist, broken the neck and killed with a suffocating bite before the man had time to bleed out.

Gorya had shifted to his human form, hadn't bothered with clothes and was rigging the gas to blow. Timur had also shifted. He was dressed and carrying an unconscious woman out of the house straight into the garage. He placed her into the backseat of a car.

Alonzo quickly aided Gorya in rigging the house, utilizing every gas fireplace, including the one in Patrizio's bedroom. They wanted the explosion to be spectacular and the fire to burn hot, fast and wild. They needed to destroy all evidence of leopard DNA, which was never easy.

Gorya poured accelerant over each of the bodies and then indicated to Alonzo to leave. He would start the fire and then join Timur in the car. They'd drive out with the woman the moment the explosion brought all the outside guards to the house. Alonzo would kill any guard trying to stop them. It wasn't the best idea, but they couldn't leave the woman behind to be killed by one of Amodeo's men or die in the fire.

"Being one of the good guys has definite drawbacks," Gorya pointed out with a small grin.

Alonzo shook his head. "Fuckin' Timur. Just has to be the white knight." He wasn't about to admit he would have done the same thing. They had vowed they were never going to be like their father, no matter what their leopards — or circumstances — demanded. They didn't beat up or kill women, nor did they allow others to do it, not in their territory. Alonzo had made that clear to his soldiers when he took over. Any wife coming to him with a black eye meant swift and brutal punishment. Still, now they were in this mess. Gorya was right — being the good guys definitely had drawbacks.

It wasn't difficult to make his way back toward the fence. He was leopard and leopards could go right into a room full of people watching a movie, kill one quietly, drag him outside and feast. They were that stealthy.

He waited for the explosion. When it came, it was spectacular, better than anything he could have hoped for. The house had four gas fireplaces, the central heater was gas and so was the kitchen stove. The building went up fast, flames shooting orange and red through windows, breaking glass, eating the structure from the inside out. Guards came running from every direction. Some raced to the garage, hoping to get in that way or at least save the vehicles from going up in flames.

The moment one hopped in a car and drove it out, Timur raced after him. In the dark with the entire house on fire, no one paid attention. He drove straight through the gates without slowing down. Once down the road, he parked the car, pulled the woman out, set her a distance away from the car and the estate and walked away.

Their driver picked them up three blocks away. Sirens wailed. Police and fire trucks raced past them. Alonzo ignored the chaos and leaned toward Timur. "I've got this bad feeling, Timur. Right before I attacked, Amodeo smirked. I keep thinking about that expression."

"Smirked?" Timur repeated, frowning. He exchanged a long look with Gorya.

"You certain that's what you saw?" Gorya asked. "A smirk?"

Alonzo nodded. The knots in his gut tightened. Something was wrong. "There's only one reason that son of a bitch would smirk."

"Evangeline."

Timur and Gorya said her name simultaneously, confirming what Alonzo was desperately trying to deny. Timur reached for the phone, yanking it free of his pack.

Alonzo reached for it, snapped it open in one quick jerk and punched in the number for Sevastyan. It rang and rang. Went to voice mail.

"Step on it, Borya," he commanded the driver.

"We don't know anything is wrong," Timur tempered, the voice of reason, although it was strained. "We don't want to call attention to ourselves. Not with three men missing and Amodeo attacked. Even if the car is caught on cameras, we won't be seen inside of it. Borya is going to dump the car at the wrecking yard once we're home. It will be crushed. There won't be any trace of us anywhere — unless we get stopped by a traffic cop."

Alonzo swore over and over, trying not to think about what was happening at his home. How many guards had he put on the grounds? How many leopards were there to protect Evangeline? He tried to keep his mind blank, but the closer they got to the Arnotto estate, the more ice poured into his veins.

"Let us out here," he snapped, before Borya could turn onto the private drive leading to the huge property. He had the door open before Borya could fully stop. "Get rid of this thing and get back here," he snapped.

Borya nodded as Timur and Gorya followed Alonzo from the vehicle. Alonzo barely managed to take the time to shed his clothes. He shifted fast and allowed his leopard to leap the fence and move quickly and stealthily through the thick brush. The Arnotto property was massive and the terrain included slightly rolling hills. Acres of vineyards, groves of trees and beautifully kept gardens made the leopards feel right at home.

Antonio Arnotto had been leopard and he'd designed his home with the comfort and protection of the leopards in mind. Trees were abundant, their branches thick and wide, often touching or very close from one tree to the other, so the leopards could use the limbs of the trees as a kind of arboreal highway above ground.

Alonzo's male lifted his head to scent the air. His whiskers flared out, a sensitive guidance system, enabling him to read air currents. He could feel his way as he moved. The whiskers provided the exact location of obstacles and vegetation. He moved silently through the brush and flower beds until he reached the house.

Already, he knew that Amodeo's men had been here. He scented blood and his leopard grimaced, drawing back his lips to show his teeth. They found the first body just inside the flower beds closest to the house. He was a complete stranger, a man dressed in a suit and reeking of Patrizio Amodeo. This had to be one of his soldiers. The man had died fast, probably without even realizing he was in danger until it was too late, a leopard attacking and bringing him down before he could get a shot off. His weapon lay on the ground inches from his hand. He recognized Sevastyan's big male's scent.

The second body was around the corner of the house, on the large patio surrounding the pool. The man lay just in the shadow of the overhead roof. His gun was still in his hand, finger on the trigger. His suit jacket was shredded into tatters in places. The puncture wounds on his throat testified to the fact that a leopard had killed him. Again it was Sevastyan's male who had made the kill.

Alonzo didn't spare the body a glance. It wasn't one of his men on the ground, so he stepped over the carcass and hurried to the door. The heavy wooden door was open partway, as if in silent invitation. He wasn't buying it. Sevastyan had a way about him. He was fast and deadly. Alonzo wasn't taking any chances. Sevastyan would know anyone coming at him was an enemy and he'd kill fast without waiting to see first.

Alonzo, Gorya and Timur chuffed softly, letting Sevastyan know they were coming in. The third body was just at the entrance. He'd taken the invitation of that unlocked, partially open door. A classic mistake. What idiot would believe a guarded house would have one unlocked door?

Timur's big male tried to nudge his leopard out of the way, but Alonzo refused to let his younger brother go ahead of him into danger. Mitya had taken bullets for him. So had Evangeline. He didn't want anyone else he loved hurt because of him. Not again. And yeah, he could finally admit he loved his brother and cousin. Because of her. Evangeline. She'd melted some of that ice inside of him, enough that there was no doubt his family was everything to him and he wasn't going to lose another member that he loved.

His father had beaten him if he'd showed affection to his brother or cousins. He remembered that very clearly. Every beating. Every lesson. He knew it was so his father could kill anyone he felt was weak. Love was a weakness. It made one vulnerable. He understood that. He understood that love had a price tag. He was willing to pay it. Timur, Gorya, Sevastyan and Mitya were also willing to pay that price. His father hadn't won after all.

The big male leopard thrust his head inside the door and scented the air. His whiskers reached out like antennae, his radar system fully working as he nosed through the door. He chuffed again, letting Sevastyan know he was coming in.

At once he sensed the other cat. He smelled blood and inwardly cursed the devil for his continual interference and then sent up a small prayer that his cousin hadn't been shot. He pushed farther into the room, Timur and Gorya pacing close to either side of him the moment he fully entered.

Another one of Amodeo's soldiers was down. This one had seen death coming. The leopard had leapt from a higher position, most likely the top of the heavy sideboard. There were bullet holes in the ceiling. The cat had hit him hard in the chest, probably breaking bones, his teeth clamping on the windpipe for the suffocating bite of death.

Alonzo moved quickly past the dead body, heading deeper into the room. Sevastyan's male, a big leopard with thick, long fur and huge paws came out to greet him. Sevastyan shifted, reaching for the pack around his neck to drag on his jeans.

"She's safe, Fyodor," he said immediately, cutting straight to the heart of the matter. "They came at us from every point of entry. I had us locked down tight. Had a bad feeling and acted on it. Tucked Evangeline into the safe room and went hunting. I had to send the human soldiers on a wild-goose chase, but we took out all of them. Seven. The man I questioned said they were sent to kill Evangeline. Amodeo is serious about killing her."

Alonzo and the others shifted as well, pulling on clothes and fitting the weapons from the pack easily back onto their bodies. Weapons were part of them and they felt naked without them, whereas they didn't feel naked without clothes. It had been drilled into them from birth to always be prepared for any situation.

"Thanks for keeping her safe." Alonzo said. "Timur, call Elijah. He can deal with this mess. If they'd just gone after the son of a bitch right after he left the bakery, he wouldn't have had time to do all this damage. Have him find out about the contract. Does it end with Amodeo's death? I need to have the information. Also, I want an update on Mitya. He needs around-the-clock guards. I want him protected at all times."

Timur nodded, already on the burner

phone. Getting rid of seven bodies wasn't going to be easy. Because they'd been killed by a leopard they had to be disposed of so no one would find them, a task much harder than most people thought.

Alonzo took a deep breath and clapped one hand on Sevastyan's shoulder, relieved that he was safe and grateful he'd watched over Evangeline. "Thanks," he reiterated, unable to articulate just what he felt.

Sevastyan grinned at him. "You think she's only for you, Fyodor, but she's for all of us. You really feel something for her. She calms your leopard. If that can happen for you, maybe it can happen for the rest of us. If not, we see what she does for you, and she matters."

Alonzo hadn't thought of it that way. He looked at Timur, who had one ear to the phone but was obviously listening because he nodded. Gorya did as well. His heart clenched and he set his jaw and turned away from them before he could allow himself to feel the depths of his emotions. And they were deep. He knew that but he'd spent a lifetime not feeling and he didn't know what to do with emotions.

Barefoot, he moved through the house silently, heading for his bedroom. She was there, inside the safe room, behind the walls where hopefully no enemy would detect her. Still, she'd had so many bad experiences already because of him and the life he led. Every step closer filled him with dread that when he looked into her eyes he'd see everything she felt for him gone. He wouldn't blame her, but he had no idea what he'd do.

The idea of losing her was terrifying. He tried to tell himself that it was his leopard he worried about, but he knew that wasn't the strict truth. *He* needed her. Fyodor Amurov, that frozen block of ice, a man who never needed anyone or anything, needed her. He kept walking, putting one foot in front of the other, but he felt as if he were walking to his doom.

13

Evangeline curled into the fetal position, drawing up her knees to her chest, trying to make herself as small as possible. So many times in the swamp, night after night, the big male leopard had prowled around her camp, scratching and biting at the door, trying to get in. She knew he was a shifter because he often tried the door with his hands. Once he broke the lock, but she had already gone out the window at the urging of her female.

The leopard tried to track them in the swamp, but she knew her way around by that time and she'd gone to the very center of a heavy grove of cypress trees, climbed very high into the thinner branches where the cat couldn't follow. The next morning she'd found his paw prints circling the grove of trees, but he hadn't followed her all the way through the thicker brush. She'd been so scared. She'd moved camps after that.

She'd been eight years old.

He didn't get us. Her female brushed a caressing stroke along the inside of her skin as she'd done when Evangeline was a child. *We're older now. Even if they got past the male leopard guarding us and broke into this room, we would kill them.*

"You haven't emerged," Evangeline whispered. "You mean I'd have to kill them."

I would come to your aid.

She was being a baby, allowing the circumstances to throw her back to her childhood. It happened. Just not often anymore. Evangeline forced herself up into a sitting position. "I'm happy you think you could come to my aid, but it doesn't work that way. You can't just come out whenever you feel like it. The circumstances have to be right. We both have to be fertile at the same time. Saria told me all about it."

That's happened already. Twice.

Evangeline's breath caught in her throat. She couldn't stay still and had to get to her feet and pace. "What do you mean? That's impossible. I would have known." She'd been told that the emergence was extremely uncomfortable sexually.

The first time you were very young. Fourteen. I tried to keep from making it difficult on you. We hid in the deepest part of the swamp

357

for days.

Evangeline's hand crept to her throat. She remembered that. She thought she had some kind of infection. She was hot all the time. She burned between her legs and her skin hurt. Her breasts ached. She was certain she was ill. At her female's urging she had sought the little mini-camp secreted in the middle of the swamp where few ever traveled. Saw grass around the island kept most people out. The ground of the island was boggy, unstable for anyone very heavy.

"You protected me." She made it a statement. "But at what cost to you? I'm supposed to take care of you. You should have told me."

You were fourteen. Her female was pragmatic about it. Casual, even.

"This is *terrible.* I've been neglectful of you." Evangeline wanted to cry. Her leopard had been fiercely protective of her. Always there for her. Always. In the worst moments of her life she'd been able to count on her female, when she'd never been able to count on a single human being. "It must have been awful for you. You should have told me." She kept pacing, because she desperately needed movement. Her leopard was close to the surface. She felt the familiar itch under her skin. A burning, as if her internal temperature was soaring. Her mind felt chaotic and no matter how she tried, she couldn't rein it in.

You were too young. The leopard sent in images rather than actual words. They'd perfected their communication skills over the years until they were both adept at it.

"What about the second time. You said twice." But she already knew. She couldn't help but remember that time. It was right after she'd left the swamp. She'd gone into the mountains, searching the high country for something, but she hadn't known what it was and she never found it. She'd been driven though. Again, her body felt hot beyond all compare. Worse than before when she'd been a teenager.

"It was your idea to leave." She remembered that as well. Vividly. Her female had pushed and pushed to get her to leave the swamp.

No decent males. I didn't know if I had enough control. Wasn't strong enough to protect you from a male leopard during the heat cycle.

Evangeline couldn't help but wince when her leopard reminded her of the way they would be when both females became fertile at the same time. "Why did you accept this male? He's far worse than the ones back home in the swamp. You've seen his human. That man is dangerous to both of us."

Her female gave the mental equivalent of a shrug. *He is your choice. His male is strong and that pleases me. He can help me protect you.*

Does he scare you?

Evangeline received the impression of her female trying to answer without upsetting her. Searching for the right images. *He is strong. But I am strong. Your mate is very strong because he can control mine. He scares me more, but I know you, and you can handle him.*

That answer set her heart pounding. If her female believed that she could handle Alonzo's male but was a little concerned about Alonzo, what did that say about him? Had she made a mistake? She chewed at her lower lip as she paced.

You're strong.

"Ten minutes ago I was curled up in the fetal position like I did when I was two."

She got the distinct feeling her leopard was laughing at her. *You always do that. And then you get up and take care of the problem. You did when you were two.*

That was true. Evangeline couldn't deny it. Her first reaction was to want to hide and pull the covers over her head, but there was never anyone else around to figure things out or aid her if there was danger. She'd learned to do it herself if she wanted it done.

You have no intention of giving him up. You're just doing that thing you do.

Evangeline stopped pacing. "What thing? I don' do a thing."

You do. He makes you nervous because he's unpredictable and you think you want normal and steady. You always think that in your head. But you don't. You want him. You always go after what you want.

She did. She *so* did. And her female was right. She was locked in a safe room, had been shot, her bakery had been taken over and still she found herself arguing, trying to think of reasons to stay. It was ludicrous to want him, not to run as far and as fast as she could. It wasn't logical to be with him.

"I can change. I don' have to give in to this because I find him . . ." She trailed off. What did she find him? Overwhelming. Gorgeous, certainly. But was her attraction to him all physical? If that was the case, she could have sex with him and move on. She knew that wouldn't happen. If she actually had sex with him, there would never be any moving on. She had to make up her mind. Right. Now.

His male is my mate.

Evangeline's heart jerked. She loved her leopard but could she stay in a dangerous situation, one that she'd sworn she would never be in, for her cat? "What about children? You saw what happened to me. Do you want that for our child? I've been thinkin' with my body, not my head."

But it hadn't been just her body. She'd been drawn to Alonzo in so many ways and now, knowing his past, knowing what happened to him as a child, she wanted more than ever to be the one in his life showing him love did exist. But how could she? She didn't know the first thing about love. Or family. Or relationships. She'd never had love. No one had ever loved her. She was a throwaway. A female not worth fighting for.

Joshua's father had fought for him. His mother had taken him away from the depraved, vile, despicable man who had been their grandfather. Her father had chosen to abandon her to the swamp. He'd left an infant alone in a camp, at the mercy of the swamp, so he wouldn't have to face the insane man who ruled their household with an iron fist. He'd pretended she was dead. He'd kept his son, but he had all but abandoned her to survive a nightmare alone.

Not alone. I am always with you.

"But he didn't know that." Any time she thought about her father and brother, her chest hurt so bad she was afraid she was having a heart attack. She'd promised herself she would never live that life. Never live in a lair surrounded by male leopards. They were bad-tempered, dangerous, moody creatures, sometimes amorous, sometimes cruel. She'd seen them at their worst, never their best. She had known her grandfather's leopard, a terrible, vicious cat that had hunted her once he'd found her scent. He was dangerous, but not anything like Alonzo.

"This is my fault. I want him with every single cell in my body, but I should never have let him anywhere near you." So stupid of her when she'd spent her life learning to be smart. "I got us into the situation because when I'm with him I can't resist him, but I'll find a way to get us out."

Shifters mate for life.

"Exactly. If somethin' goes wrong, it isn't just us. It's our children. We have to think about that. You know what he is. A person can't just overcome all that conditionin'. He didn't start out a killer, but that's where he'll go every time somethin' goes wrong. He's a criminal. I let that into our lives. We have to go, and we have to go now."

For the first time ever, her leopard disagreed with her, not just disagreed, but was adamant about it. She sent an impression of great danger. Of her mate raging. Of Alonzo coming after her, every bit as ferocious and intensely powerful as his leopard. More so.

We can't leave them. My mate will not accept such a thing. I rose to the surface when he gave the claiming bite. We're sealed together.

"Then we'll have to find a way to unseal you. I was wrong. Do you see where we are? A safe room. How is this different from the camps?"

He's protecting us. No one ever protected us before.

That was true, but this would be her life. Alonzo was a criminal. He wasn't Italian, he was Russian. He'd lived his entire life being a criminal. She'd been mesmerized by him from the very start. Maybe she was drawn to him because of his leopard and she belonged in that world. Maybe it was because he was a criminal. Joshua's mother had gotten him out, and yet he was back in the bayou. Rumor had it that when Rafe Cordeau disappeared, he'd taken over that territory, and it looked to her as if the rumors were right.

"I don' have to follow my family's legacy

of greed and violence. I refuse to give that to our children. Be angry with me, I deserve it, but I'm gettin' us out of here."

Not angry. Afraid.

That made Evangeline all the more determined. If her leopard, who had always exuded complete confidence, was afraid of what Alonzo and his male might do because they went against them, then she was right to get out of the situation. And she had to do it fast. Really fast. Whatever was going on, she couldn't be a part of it. More, she didn't want to face Alonzo. He made her weak. She lost herself when she was around him. They had to go, and they had to do it while their guards were otherwise occupied.

She went to the security screens. Sevastyan had told her to leave them off. She knew it was so she wouldn't see his leopard hunting. They were under attack and it stood to reason he would allow his leopard out to defend them. She had to see where everyone was so she could avoid them.

The moment the cameras went online, her breath caught in her throat. Alonzo had just shifted. He was in the house. Naked. She tried not to look as he caught a pair of trousers and casually pulled them up. He listened to what the others were saying. She didn't turn on the audio. She didn't dare because she'd fall under his spell all over again. His voice hypnotized her. She started to turn away from the screen when he suddenly looked up, straight at the camera.

Her breath caught in her throat. Felt trapped in her lungs. He knew. He looked — desolated. Destroyed. His eyes were pure cat, his leopard still prowling close to the surface. Before she could stop herself her hand went to the screen and touched his face. So alone. So frozen. Her Russian. The Iceman. Her heart contracted. She ran her finger down the lines of his face in a small caress.

He began walking down the wide hallway toward the back where his room was located. He was coming for her. She should run while she had the chance. It would be her only chance to save herself. A small sound escaped. A soft moan of protest. If she saved herself, who would save him? Because if ever there was a man who needed saving, it was Alonzo.

She knew she couldn't leave him, and there was despair. She was condemning herself to a life with a criminal. A life with a leopard. Not just any leopard, a crazy one. Still, she couldn't move. She could only watch him come for her. As he moved closer she could see the way he moved. Fluid. All leopard. Stalking. She couldn't help the little thrill that ran through her, or the frisson of fear that crept deliciously down her spine.

She'd lived in the swamp her entire life, surrounded by danger. She tried not to believe she craved it. Needed it. The rush. The adrenaline running through her veins as she pitted her intellect and skills against adversaries. She'd spent a lifetime outwitting male leopards; now she had one of her own, and he was the most dangerous of all. She had to come to terms with this side of herself. It wasn't her female choosing Alonzo's leopard. It was all about Evangeline choosing Alonzo.

The door swung open and he filled the space with his large body. The width of his shoulders took up the frame. He wasn't wearing a shirt and for the first time she saw the crisscross slashes embedded deep in his chest. The scars ran all the way down his heavy muscles, rib cage and narrow waist to disappear into his trousers. Instinctively she knew his father had put those scars there. His father had a lot to answer for.

Alonzo took a deep breath, his gaze never leaving hers. His eyes glowed, his cat right there, at the surface, waiting right along with him. "You were going to leave me."

"Yes. Self-preservation kicked in, and after an argument with myself, I decided to leave while I had the chance." There was no point in lying. Leopards heard lies.

His expression didn't change. He didn't blink, his gaze completely focused on her. "I would come after you."

That frisson of fear slid down her spine again. Delicious. Perfect. She was in her element. He was gorgeous standing there, looking all male with no soft edges.

"I would come after you and bring you back and no one, not Joshua, not Brice, not anyone could keep you from me."

"It isn't necessary to threaten me."

"Did you think that was a threat? I don't do threats, Evangeline. You're my woman. You made that commitment to me. I get that you're afraid. I get that I'm intense and my world is violent and scary, everything you don't want, but running isn't the answer because I would come after you and you'd be all the more frightened because of it. That's a fact, not a threat."

His voice was pitched low, like it always was. She loved the way he sounded so commanding. Mesmerizing. So completely in control. He wasn't. He just believed that he was. She tilted her head and studied his features. He was far too rugged and tough-looking to be called handsome, but she loved the way he looked. All man. All hers.

"I didn't leave for a reason, Fyodor."

"Your reason?"

"I couldn't." She stated the stark truth. Felt raw for revealing so much to him, but she couldn't help herself. Telling him made her feel vulnerable and exposed, but he looked so remote, as if she'd hurt him but he refused to acknowledge it.

"Just so you know," she continued, "I'm not so easy to find when I don' want to be found. I stayed because I can't leave you, not because I was afraid you'd come after me and find me."

"Come here."

Her heart jerked, nearly stopped and then began pounding. She knew he heard because she did. She studied him, taking her time. The room had gone from scary tension to sexual tension in one heartbeat. She moistened her lips with the tip of her tongue, suddenly aware of her body going liquid. Of her breasts swelling and aching. He did that without even trying. With one small command.

"Evangeline."

Her name. That was all he said. Just that. But it was a clear order. She was tempted to defy him just to see what would happen, but his will was like iron and she couldn't resist the way his gaze moved over her so possessively. Her female was curled up, still in a snit, unwilling to help her out. Evangeline had confidence in herself until it came to this. Sex. Alonzo was a man who clearly knew what he was doing. She didn't. She wasn't going to be his equal.

His eyes had gone nearly golden, the entire white disappearing. She took a step and then another, compelled forward by the sheer force of his personality. When she was close to him, he wrapped his palm around the nape of her neck and drew her against him. His skin was hot. At once her breasts pushed tight against his chest. Aching. In need. He tipped her chin up with one thumb. Her gaze met his. Caught there. Trapped.

"Tell me what you're afraid of."

She swallowed hard, unable to look away from his piercing gaze.

"What made you feel as if you had to run?" He waited. She squirmed. He refused to release her captive gaze. "I know they shot you because of me. I know they came after you —"

She shook her head. "It's the children," she blurted and then clamped her mouth closed tightly.

"Children?" he echoed. "Are you afraid for our children? That these monsters might come out of the woodwork and try to harm them? Because I can protect my own."

She shook her head again. "If you lose control of your leopard, he might react the way my grandfather's leopard did. He might hunt them. Try to kill them. Or hurt them in some other way."

He was silent for what seemed forever. He didn't wince, although he knew her fear was that *he* might harm them in some terrible loss of control.

"I'm not capable of harming one of our children, Evangeline. You'll just have to take my word for that."

She took a breath and tried to ignore the way his thumb brushed caresses back and forth over her jaw. Each touch sent a million little darts of fire racing through her body. The blood in her veins felt thick and hot.

"What if I don' meet your expectations and you need . . . more?"

His thumb stopped moving. "More?"

She tilted her chin at him. "Yes. More."

"I can't promise you easy, *solnyshko moyo*, but I can promise you there will never be another woman. I'll spend every day doing my best to make you happy. I know you're afraid, I know that, but I'll take care of you. There isn't ever going to be a need for more because you're all I want."

"Alonzo." She swallowed his name. "Fyodor. I might not be any good at sex. You clearly are." *Sex* was the last word she wanted to utter in that room. Not with the bed only a few feet away. Not with his bedroom just on the other side of the passage.

"*That's* your fear?" He looked amused. His golden eyes glinted at her, the blue flame flickering through the ice.

She tried to step away, but his hand tightened and his head bent toward hers. Not fast. Slowly. Infinitely slow. She stared into his eyes as his head descended. Anticipation was in her mouth. His taste. His touch. She craved his kisses. She stood very still, waiting, her heart pounding. Needing him. Needing the feel of his mouth on hers.

His arm locked around her back and he brought her up tight against his body, his lips brushing hers with exquisite gentleness. He looked hungry. His eyes darkened with a mixture of lust and something else, but his mouth was tender as he coaxed her lips to part for him. He held her with such strength she knew he could break her into pieces, yet she felt cherished. Protected. Maybe even loved. She didn't know what love felt like, so she couldn't really say, and then she couldn't think because his lips firmed and her mouth opened for him and he was inside. Melting her.

His taste. Addicting. She lost herself in his mouth. In his taste. In everything Alonzo. It was strange that for such a big man he could be so gentle. He moved her backward, holding her carefully so that even in motion, his mouth on hers, he made certain she was safe. She felt as if she were dancing with him, floating backward. He kicked the door closed. The lock snicked automatically.

He kept her moving until she was in the center of the room. He lifted his head, his gaze moving over her face with stark possession. "Take off your shirt."

She smiled tentatively at him even though a thousand butterflies took wing in her stomach. "You say that a lot."

"I'll be saying it even more. Off."

She was wearing a button-down shirt and, because she couldn't look away, she stared into his eyes as she slowly released each button from its respective hole. The shirt gaped open. He didn't drop his gaze.

"Off. All the way off." He clearly glimpsed the lacy bra, and he shook his head, his eyes reprimanding her. "Why in the world are you wearing a bra?"

"You weren't home, remember? I was uncomfortable without you." She admitted it even as she complied, slipping out of the shirt, almost letting it drop, but his hand closed over hers.

"Fold it. Neatly. Place it on the chair over there."

His voice alone could make her go damp. Her breasts strained toward him, needing his touch. She felt sexy and *his* following his low orders. She very carefully folded her shirt, remembering how meticulous he'd been. She had to move around him to get to the chair and she felt his eyes following her as she placed her shirt in the center of the seat.

He crooked his finger at her and pointed to the spot in front of him. She went, heart beating in her throat. Blood roaring in her ears. She stood in front of him, trying not to fidget, forcing her hands to remain at her sides when she had an insane desire to cover up the fact that her nipples were hard and aching for his mouth.

His index finger slid under her bra strap and brushed along her shoulder from front to back, causing serious trembling. "Now your bra."

She wasn't altogether certain she was that brave. She stood a moment, looking up at him, trying to decide if she could stand there in front of him half naked or not.

"Evangeline. When I ask you to do something in our bedroom, I expect you to do it. I know you're nervous, but you have to trust me to take care of you in all things — especially here." His fingers caught her chin, slowly forcing her head up until once again her gaze was held captive by his. "Do you trust me with your body? That's what I want from you. Your trust. Your full surrender. You give me that and in return, I'll give you pleasure like you've never known."

Considering she wasn't experienced in the pleasure department, she figured she had the better end of the bargain. She found herself still hesitating. Shy, when she'd never considered herself shy. Nervous, when she knew she wasn't about nerves.

"I'm leopard, *malyutka.* That means I'm dominant. You know that. You respond to that in me. Your body is flushed. Your nipples are hard. Your breath is ragged, and I know you're damp for me. I can scent you. You like me in control."

"I'm not submissive," she denied.

He bent his head and brushed his mouth across hers. The pad of his finger traced the swell of her breast and moved lower to find her nipple through the lace. "No, you're not, not outside this room. And I'm quite certain you'll make a few demands of your own in it, but you like this. You even need it."

She did. It made it easier for her not to think about what she should do next. He told her. He took that uncertainty away from her.

"Your bra, Evangeline."

She reached behind her and unhooked the lace. It wasn't covering all that much of her anyway. She had full breasts and the moment the bra was gone the soft curves jutted toward Alonzo as if belonging solely to him. And maybe they did. She did. Her body did. Her body knew she belonged to him almost more than her brain knew it.

"On the chair. And take off your shoes as well. Put them under the chair."

Shades of his childhood. She knew he needed order and control. She gave him both. A gift. She knew he recognized it as a gift. He wanted her trust. Her surrender. She was determined to give him that as well, although she was very nervous. She placed the bra precisely in the middle of her folded shirt and her shoes beneath the chair, perfectly lined up, and then she went back to him to stand directly in front of him.

"Your skirt." She'd put on the skirt because her leg had been aching and when she'd jumped out of bed at Sevastyan's insistence, she'd dragged on the long, flowing skirt to keep from having to find a pair of jeans. She liked skirts. She'd never worn them in the swamp, and she liked the feel of them. She slipped the material off her hips and down her thighs, over her calves and then stepped out of it. She folded it carefully, all the while standing in her lacy little boy shorts.

She'd never felt sexier. She hadn't known she could feel sexy, but his gaze had grown so hot she thought she might go up in flames. Strangely, his eyes had gone back to glacier blue, but that flame was there, leaping beneath the ice to show her even ice could burn. She walked over to the chair, conscious of his gaze on her. She bent to put her skirt on top of the bra and shirt.

"Take off your panties right there. No, don't turn around. Just like that."

Her breath nearly stopped, strangling there inside her lungs. Could she do that? Shimmy out of them with her back turned? With him looking at her butt? She'd always thought her butt was too big. He was staring at it, she knew he was.

"Evangeline. Do you want me to help you?"

His voice had dropped even lower. A warning. She had the feeling whatever help he gave her would send her crashing right over the edge. Her body was coiled tight. Her clit throbbed and pulsed. She felt her feminine sheath spasm at his tone. She hooked her thumbs into the lace and drew the material down. Once again she folded the panties and put them on top of her pile of clothes.

"Come here and don't cover up, I want to look at you."

That was the hardest thing to do. Walk over to him. The moment she did, forcing herself to keep her hands at her sides, she knew why he had asked her to remove her clothing the way he had. She felt sensual. Feminine. A temptation to him. Her body moved with every step, her breasts swaying enticingly. Her hair fell around her back, sliding over her skin sensuously. Her nipples were hard pebbles, and deep inside she *craved* him. So much so that, even though she was nervous, she wanted him with every cell in her body.

She stood in front of him. He stood for a long time staring down at her, his gaze moving over her body, ratcheting up her tension, her sexual awareness. He began to move in a small circle around her, as if inspecting her from every angle.

"You are so beautiful, Evangeline. So incredibly beautiful."

Leopards could hear lies, and she knew he believed what he was saying. She let her breath out. He made her feel beautiful and sexy. He came back to stand in front of her and he reached for her hands, placing them on his chest.

"I belong to you, *devochka moya.* Everything I am and will ever be. My heart. My body. I belong to you and I want you to be familiar with what is yours. To know every inch of me. What I like. What brings me pleasure. That's what I intend to do with what's mine." He brought her hands to the waistband of his trousers. "Take them off."

His palms cupped the soft weight of her breasts, thumbs sliding over her nipples. Instantly white lightning streaked through her body straight to her clit. She heard a soft moan escape before she could stop it. He'd barely touched her and she was so ready for him. She knew this was all about getting her over her shyness. He wanted her to feel confident, and truthfully she was growing more so with every passing moment. Well, it was about giving her confidence and bringing them both pleasure. He was thick and long and hard beneath his trousers.

"You like lookin' at me," she said.

"So much," he agreed. "And I like telling you what to do and have you do it," he added. "That's a huge turn-on for me."

"Because you're all about control." She slipped his trousers open and slowly unzipped them. He wasn't wearing any underwear and his heavy erection sprang free. She couldn't help the shocked gasp. His cock matched the rest of him. She should have known. He was leopard.

"I'm all about control," he agreed. He caught her nipples in between his thumbs and fingers, tugging gently, making her gasp again, this time as more fire sizzled through her body. "Take the trousers off me and fold them, Evangeline."

She nodded and hooked her fingers in the waistband so she could pull them down over his hips. She had to bend to bring them to his ankles so he could step out of them. The action brought her mouth in line with his impressive cock. The leopard in her wanted to taste him. To see if he tasted as good there as he did when he kissed her. Before she thought, she licked along the hard shaft as she crouched low.

His body shuddered, and he dropped a hand on her shoulder as he stepped out of the trousers. She hid a little smirk as she straightened again, indulging in another tongue swipe up his shaft, this time flicking under the crown as she stood. Without looking at him, she folded the pants and walked over to the chair.

She never heard him behind her, but then he had her in his arms, cradling her against his chest as he walked back to the bed.

"When your leopard really begins to rise, and my male says she's close, what we do together is going to be intense and maybe a little scary and shocking. I'm going to take you every way a man can take his woman. I'll be rough sometimes, most of the time, because I'm a rough man, but I'll make certain you love it, *solnyshko moyo,* every single time, no matter what we do. You have to learn to be comfortable with me and to trust me." He laid her in the center of the bed, so gently she felt the burn of tears. She had no idea he could be so gentle.

He moved over the top of her, so that his much larger body blanketed hers, although he kept his hands on either side of her head, so he supported his weight. Very slowly, he bent his head and kissed her with such tenderness she could barely conceive of him being that way when he truly was a scary man.

He shifted just a bit to one side of her, although his thigh remained over hers, pinning her down while his hand swept from her neck down the center of her body. "I want to play with your body for hours. I never had that luxury ever with a woman. I never had the inclination, but with you, because you're mine, I can indulge every fantasy."

She liked that idea.

His hand stroked another caress between her breasts down to her navel and farther to the tiny curls at the junction between her legs. "I'm going to shave you so when I eat you like candy, there's not going to be anything between my mouth and your body."

She shivered. His touch was very possessive, his words even more so. She couldn't look away from his face, although he was looking down at her body.

"I love that you're mine. I've never had anything for myself. Not one fucking thing, Evangeline. I love that when I finally have something, it's you. Your body. Your mind. Your heart. I'm going after that you know. Your heart. I want complete surrender from you. Nothing less will do."

He kissed her again, over and over until she was squirming with need, her hips bucking and her breath coming in ragged gasps. "Are you going to give that to me, woman? Everything I ask for?" He kissed his way down her throat, stopping to suckle gently and then shockingly, use the edge of his teeth.

She heard her own broken cry. The little bite sent waves of heat crashing through her. Sent liquid heat coating her lips and the tiny curls guarding her entrance.

"See? You were made for me. My woman. My everything. I hope you're not too tired, because I intend to indulge myself tonight."

14

"I mean every word I say," Alonzo whispered against the sweet curve of her breast. "You're mine. Your body belongs to me. I intend to make love to you slow and easy. Fast and hard. I'm going to drive you up as high as I can and watch you shatter for me. While you rest, I'm going to play with your body." He slid his hand between her legs while his mouth closed over her nipple and sucked hard, taking her breast deep into his mouth, flattening the nipple against the roof with his tongue.

She cried out and liquid heat spilled into his hand. He rubbed a slow, lazy circle and kept suckling. Gentle. Hard. Laving with his tongue. Biting down with his teeth and tugging until he felt that answer spilling into his palm. "Feel that? That's your body loving what I do to it. There's never a need to be afraid. I'm loving you no matter what we do, even when I'm using you as my little fuck toy. And I will use you like that, *sol-nyshko moyo,* because I can and you'll let me. I've dreamt so many times of taking my time with you and doing whatever I want." Another wave of hot liquid spilled into his hand at his rough, dirty words.

He licked his way over the creamy swell of her breast and suckled again, leaving behind his mark. Then he bit down carefully, watching her face, feeling her reaction. He was being very gentle with her. He wanted her to know what he liked. What he needed, and he wanted to know what she liked and needed. This was her first time and he wanted to initiate her as gently as he was capable of. Still, he wouldn't lie to her. He wanted her to know what to expect, and so far, she hadn't shied away from his language or his teeth.

"Once when I was in the bakery and you were wearing that tight skirt with the big bow in the back, right under your ass, all I could think about was ripping that off of you, pushing you down to your hands and knees and fucking you so hard neither of us could breathe. Where is that skirt? Do you still have it? Because you didn't wear it after that."

His mouth was on her other breast, pulling strongly. Her back arched, pressing her soft flesh deeper into his mouth. He loved the taste of her. Her skin was like satin. Her silky hair was everywhere, across the pillow, all over the mattress, so sexy he could barely stand it. Her breath came in a ragged gasp.

"Your skirt, *malyutka*. Why didn't you ever wear it again?"

She swallowed hard as he lifted his head. He waited for an answer, demanding one silently. He wanted her to know that when he asked a question, he wanted an answer.

"I felt you. Looking at me. It was intense."

He kept his gaze on hers as he leaned down to lap at her nipples with his tongue, rewarding her for her bravery. "How was it intense?"

Her skin was flushed, but he could still see the blush stealing up her neck into her face. Her eyes slid from his. He bit down and pulled her nipple toward him with his teeth. Still gentle, but she definitely could feel the bite. She cried out, her gaze jumping back to his.

"It was the first time I ever had a reaction."

"What kind of reaction?" His finger stroked her clit, drew circles around it and then stroked again.

"It's embarrassin'."

"Nothing is embarrassing with me. Do

you know how many times I went home and jerked off thinking about you? Fantasizing about you? Wishing your mouth was on me? Or I was in you? I'm not ashamed of wanting you. Are you really ashamed of wanting me?"

She shook her head. "No. It's just that I never talked like this with anyone."

"I'm not anyone. I'm your man. I was born for you. I belong to you. Your body is mine. *You* are mine. Tell me." He stroked her clit again, feeling her shudder. Feeling the wave of slick cream coating his finger. It was hot. So hot his cock jerked and pulsed, wept with need, but all that mattered to him was Evangeline and her pleasure.

He chose a spot on the curve of her breast to leave another strawberry. Right in the center of it, he used his teeth, biting down. At the same time he pushed into her with one finger. She nearly came apart, so scorching hot and so tight he felt she was strangling his finger. He couldn't imagine what she would feel like surrounding his cock with all that silken heat. "Tell me, Evangeline."

"My panties got damp and my breasts ached. It wasn't my female, it was all me," she confessed in a little rush. "I couldn't get you out of my head or the way your gaze felt on me and that night I stopped by a store and bought a toy."

His cock jerked hard at the thought of her being so brave as to walk into an adult store and purchase a toy and then use it on herself. "I fucking love that, *malyutka,* I want to watch. Better yet, I want to use it on you. Something else to look forward to."

His mouth traveled down her body, tongue sliding along every rib. He dipped into her belly button. "I'm going to drink vodka off you. Pour it over your breasts, let it run down your body and lap it off of you." His tongue showed her how and then his teeth teased her abdomen. He shifted his weight, sliding down her body so he could grasp her thighs and pull them apart.

"So beautiful, Evangeline." He stared at her, that beautiful flower waiting for him. All his. Not once had his leopard protested. He was quiet. Calm. Giving Alonzo his freedom to enjoy his woman, to indulge himself like he'd never been able to. This time was all about accustoming her to him. Initiating her. Loving her. Exploring her body. Seeing her reactions to everything he did to her. Bringing her the most pleasure possible for her first time.

"I love to hear you make noise, *malyutka,* so don't hold back. I need to know what you're feeling." That was important to him. It never had been. He got off to get release, and he did his best in the limited time he had to make it work for a woman, but he never kissed her, was never intimate with her. Intimacy was for her. Evangeline.

She was spread out for him like a feast, the cool air whispering over all that heat. She moved restlessly, and then attempted to bring her thighs closer together. His fingers clamped down tighter, holding her thighs apart, spreading her even more for him. "Stay still. I want to look at what's mine." He bent his head and nuzzled between her legs, allowing the rough shadow on his jaw to rub along her inner thighs like sandpaper.

"What if I can't do the things you want me to do? What if I'm too afraid?"

He heard the first real fearful note in her voice. Not at the things he had told her so blatantly he intended to do, more to test her reaction. Leopard sex was brutal at times. Raw and violent. Passionate beyond imagining. His leopard was so ready, so crazy for his mate. Alonzo never wanted Evangeline to be afraid. Not the reality of real fear. He wanted her trust, that no matter what he asked, or what their leopards drove them to do, she knew without a doubt that he would take care of her. A shiver of trepidation could add to the pleasure, but not if she didn't trust him to watch over her.

He lifted his head just enough to meet her eyes. He could see that same fear building there. She was worried about being good enough for him. That humbled him as nothing else could have. His woman. She was amazing. Perfect.

"*Solnyshko moyo,* that would be impossible. You are the most fearless woman I've ever met. You stand when you shouldn't, even in the face of bullets. You had an opportunity to run, but you didn't take it, even knowing I might be angry. You have more passion in your little finger than most people do in their entire bodies. Everything I've said or done so far has shown me you're exactly who I need most. The last thing you're going to do is run from pleasure, and I'll always, always bring you pleasure."

She kept her eyes steady on his. "What if I don' want to do something?"

"Then it isn't done." He bent his head and kissed the inside of her left thigh and then proceeded to suckle there to leave his own personal brand. When the strawberry was satisfactory, he pressed his finger to her slick entrance, bit down in the center of the mark and pushed his finger deep into her.

Her hips bucked and she arched her back, crying out. A flood of scorching liquid heat gripped him like a velvet fist. His cock raged at him. He brought his head up so he could survey his handiwork. "Did you feel your response? You can't fake that, *solnyshko moyo.* You like what I do to you."

"What if it's something you really, really want and I can't do it?" she pressed.

He had to clamp his arm tightly on her hips to keep her still. "Then we talk about it, find out what you fear, and it is up to me to alleviate those fears. I would never do anything without your consent. Even tonight, telling you I would find you. I would, Evangeline." He kissed his way up her other thigh, his heart contracting. "But I would persuade you to come back with me. Leaving me after my leopard claimed yours is tantamount to putting a gun to my head and pulling the trigger. After you gave yourself to me. You know that. That's why you stayed."

"It's not. I stayed for you. Because I need to be with you."

His heart nearly exploded at her whispered admission. "If I haven't told you enough, or you don't get this, *Ya tebya lyublyu.* I've never said that to another soul, man or woman, and I know it is the stark, naked truth." His voice wasn't his own. His body wasn't his own. He belonged to her. Every part of him. The bad could protect her, the good, what little there was, he would use to make her as happy as possible.

Ducking his head so he wouldn't have to meet her eyes, he rubbed his jaw along her inner thigh, kissed her again and then suckled. Her leg was satin soft. Warm. He loved running his hands over her perfectly shaped ass. He'd looked at it enough. Now it was his. He bit down on the center of the strawberry, felt the surge of heat. Her moan was low and sexy. In her throat. He felt that sound right through his cock.

"Fyodor. Honey, I need you to . . ." She broke off, her face flushed and her lips parting on a gasp as he curled his long thick finger into her, finding that perfect little spot. His thumb brushed her clit.

"I know what you need, Evangeline. I'm going to give you everything. I'm big, though, and you have to be ready for me." She was nowhere near ready, but she thought she was. He wanted her out of her mind. Begging. All fear gone, because this experience was all about loving her, and she had to feel it. She had to know and always be confident that he loved her.

His hands gripped her thighs and he

lowered his head slowly. Feeling his leopard. Feeling his heart pound. His woman. All his. For him. For the first time he allowed himself to taste her. It was a miracle he had this moment when he never thought it possible. It hadn't been possible until . . . her. Evangeline. She changed his world. Gave him everything. He knew he would never forget that moment or his first taste.

Cinnamon and spice. Honey and cream. He took his time, holding her hips still while her head thrashed on the sheets. Her gasping cries played like a symphony, accompanying the thunderous roar in his ears and the sound of his heartbeat drumming hard. His cock reacted, so full and hard he thought he might burst. The ache was primal and satisfying. He took his time worshiping her, telling her without words what he felt, wanting her to see that yes, he was all those things she feared, but he was also this, paradise, and he would always be this for her. Only her.

She tasted like heaven and he indulged his craving for her. His woman. So perfect. Her ragged breathing punctuated by his name — *his* name; Fyodor, not Alonzo — added to the surreal perfection of the moment for him. He wanted it to last forever, but his painful cock was making demands and she was so close to shattering. He wanted that. To make her come apart.

He kept his eyes on her face, watching that dazed expression come into her eyes. The thread of fear of the unknown. Her hands went to his hair, anchored there, using him, trusting him. She gave that gift to him, heightening his pleasure, his love for her.

"All the way, *malen'kaya lyublyu moyo*, come to me all the way. Give yourself to me." He stabbed deep, his tongue lashing, driving her up higher, he suckled and drew out more of her citrus spice, all the while watching her eyes. He knew the moment she gave herself into his keeping. He saw it on her face. That sweet surrender to him.

Her gaze clung to his face, eyes wide and shocked. Her mouth formed a perfect little *O* and she cried out, a strangled sound somewhere between a moan and keening his name. He watched her come apart. Felt the ripples deep inside her with his mouth, his finger. Saw it in her belly muscles, the sway of her breasts. So beautiful. That was his. That was all for him. He'd given that to her, but it was his.

He rose above her on his knees, keeping her thighs wide apart, dragging her legs tight against him. His cock was thick and hot in his hand as he positioned himself, pushing into that slick heat just enough to get the broad head into scorching heaven. She was tight. So tight. A scalding tunnel surrounding him with fiery silk. His breath hissed out of his lungs and he wanted desperately to plunge into her, drive himself deep to feel that sensation along his shaft. His balls actually ached, boiled in urgent need.

He made himself go slow, watching her face for any signs of discomfort. The walls of her sheath still pulsed and rippled from her first orgasm, and every inch he slid in her body gripped and squeezed his cock like a tight fist. He hit that barrier and he knew she was his as well. Evangeline. Such an unexpected gift.

He slowly leaned over her, blanketing her body, all the while holding her gaze with his. "A bite of pain, Evangeline. A small one. You understand. And then I give you plea-sure. Only that."

Her gaze clung to his, and he loved that even more. The way she looked at him as if he were the only man in her world. Her white knight when he was anything but. She'd looked at him that way before and a small part of that frozen block inside of him had melted a little.

He flexed his fingers on her hips and took

a deep breath to keep from slamming home. "You're so hot, *solnyshko moyo,* so tight. I could get lost in you." Not remember his childhood for a few moments. The deaths on his soul. She did that, took it all away. Brought him solace. Peace when he didn't deserve it.

He nuzzled her neck, keeping her pinned when she thrashed and tried to force him to go deeper. Still in that heightened state, needing him urgently. Exactly where he needed her to be. Every time she moved and he slid just a little deeper, her channel tight and scorching, he lost his breath and almost his resolve. He bumped that thin barrier over and over, but he refused to give in to her bucking hips or her gasping pleas.

He took her mouth. Demanding her response, centering her attention there. Kissing her over and over and then leaving a trail of kisses down her neck to her shoulder. He bit her, catching her soft skin in his teeth and biting down as he surged forward, pushing through, feeling that barrier give way and his cock slide deep, deep into her channel until he was surrounded by a fist of pure fire. So good. So beautiful.

She cried out, the sound strangled in her throat. He kissed the bite and then suckled gently, wanting to leave his signature mark on her. His woman. His. He licked over the spot and gently eased back, his cock still buried balls deep in her. Not moving when his body screamed at him. He waited for her body to adjust. To find pleasure even in pain.

"Open your eyes for me, Evangeline." It was a command, delivered in his low tone, but a command nevertheless.

Her lashes fluttered. Her small white teeth tugged at her bottom lip, but she did as he'd asked. All that emerald green looked melted and liquid. Need was there. A little bit of fear. Trust.

"I need to know you're good."

"You have to move."

"Say it for me. I need to know you're good," he reiterated, easing back more so he was once again on his knees, her legs tight against him and her bottom off the bed. He was in complete control of her body that way.

He loved looking down at her. Her hair spilled on the pillow and all around her, a wild mass of silk. Her breasts were perfect, jutting up at him, swaying with every movement. Her skin flushed a beautiful rose. *Ya tebya lyublyu.* He whispered it, more in his mind than aloud. He did love her. If his heart had been frozen, and he was certain it had been, that had been the first thing she'd melted.

"Please move, Fyodor. I need you to move. I'm good. I really am."

He didn't wait for more. He pulled back, feeling the delicious bite of her sheath strangling him, the hot friction that built anticipation. He slammed deep into her. Pounded. Used the strength in his hips to take her hard and fast. Every stroke jolted her body and he held her still so she couldn't move, her legs clamped to him, straight up against his shoulders, spread wide. All for him. His.

He lost himself for a little while, shattering her twice more so that she clamped down on him, trying to take him with her. Each time, before she went over, he commanded her to go. Whispering his demand. Holding her gaze captive, wanting her to respond to his voice. Her pleas grew louder, her breath hitching in her throat, her eyes wide with shock. He kept going. He needed to stay there, buried in her, allowing her to take it all away, every horrible moment of his life, and fill it with her. Streaks of fire rushed from his cock to spread throughout his groin and belly, down to his thighs, up to his chest. Consuming him. Giving him new life. Melting the ice inside of him until there was only Evangeline and their bodies coming together in a wild frenzy.

Lust was sharp. Love was terrible. Passion was bliss. He lost himself in that paradise, in the knowledge that she belonged to him. That she gave him that gift. Her body. Her trust that he'd take the greatest care of her and give her everything. He poured himself into her — wanted to drive so deep he branded her inside with him — where she'd feel him every moment of the day. Where she'd crave him when he wasn't inside her.

Her nails bit into his arms, and he let his gaze move over her face. Seeing her. Knowing he'd driven her up as high as she could go right then. Pushed past her comfort zone. He tightened his hold, moving her body so that he hit her most sensitive spot with every stroke, so that his shaft blazed directly over her clit, the friction wild and perfect.

"Again. Now, Evangeline. Give me you. All of you. Right now."

She let go. Surrendered to him completely. Her body clamped down on his like a vicious vise. The scorching heat surrounding him. The silken fist gripping and milking him. There was no way to hold on and he growled out her name hoarsely, his seed boiling up and rocketing into her, jet after jet, filling her body with him. His. All his.

He collapsed over top of her, his body still pumping hard, and then slowing to an easier glide. It felt so good. Him. Her. The mixture of the two of them. He buried his face in her neck, his lips on her skin. Inhaling her. Inhaling them. He'd never thought he could be happy. He didn't know what that was. He hadn't experienced it. Never happiness or joy yet now, he recognized both emotions for what they were. Both were simply Evangeline.

He knew he was too heavy. Crushing her. But he had to stay there for a few long moments, her body under his. Small. Fragile. All woman. Soft skin and beautiful curves. His. He nuzzled again and was surprised when she didn't tell him to move. Her breathing was shortened, ragged, raspy even, due to his weight crushing her, but she held him, her arms around him, cradling him to her. She gave him that, knowing instinctively he needed it.

No one held him. When he was a baby, a toddler, his mother didn't dare hold him even if she was so inclined. His father didn't believe in coddling an infant. He knew Evangeline had never been held either. Maybe she needed it as much as he did.

Eventually he knew he couldn't stay. He

was just too heavy. He eased out of her reluctantly, still semi-hard at the knowledge that he could have her again and again whenever he wanted or needed. His. It was still sinking in. He was still trying to absorb the knowledge that she'd really given herself to him.

Alonzo slipped to her side, keeping her pinned with one leg thrown over her thigh. He lifted his head up to look down at her body. Looking at his marks of possession with satisfaction. She hadn't once protested. She got off on his lovemaking — and he had made love to her with every stroke. Every touch.

She started to move her legs, to close them. He had her spread fairly wide to accommodate him. His hand stopped her. "I like to look at you. To see what's mine. I especially want to see us together." He reveled in the sight of his seed seeping down her thighs along with evidence of her innocence. The gift she'd given him.

She appeared to be drifting a little, still floating from the crashing orgasm. Her body had rippled with aftershocks all the while he'd lain over top of her, blanketing her thoroughly and possessively. When he drew circles with the pad of his finger over her breasts, stroking her nipples, he saw her stomach muscles bunch and knew more ripples teased her sheath.

Her eyes suddenly went wide again. "Fyodor. We didn't use protection. I forgot. You forgot. My female is gettin' close. This could be a bad time."

"I don't forget to use protection, Evangeline." He was amused at the thought. He was gloved all the time. His hands and his cock. He was bare for her. Only his woman. She could see the tattoos on his fingers proclaiming him a killer for his lair. She could have his cock bare and hot and hard just for her. "It doesn't work so good on leopards anyway."

She closed her eyes and turned her face away.

He caught her chin and turned her head back toward him. "Don't do that, *malen'kaya lyublyu moyo.* If we have children, I will love and care for them with the same passion and intensity I do you. You're a strong woman. You said yourself you're no submissive and you aren't. You'd kick me hard if you thought I'd harm our children."

Her eyes opened and he saw resolve there. Determination and truth. "If you tried to harm our children, Fyodor, I would find a way to kill you. Understand that. Know I mean what I say. No one will ever do to our children what your father did to you, or mine did to me. When I have children, they will be loved and they'll know it. They'll be cherished and protected fiercely. I'll guard them with everything I am."

"No, Evangeline, *we'll* guard them. I feel exactly the same way. My children will get to be children, and they'll know they're loved. I want that as much as you." He loved that she thought she could kill him if necessary — and maybe she could. He would never harm her, not for any reason, and that would give her a huge advantage if it ever came down to a real fight between them.

He leaned down and kissed her mouth. Instantly she forgot all about everything else and gave herself up to him like she always did when he kissed her. Her body was so warm and soft he couldn't help sliding his hand under her breast and just letting it rest in his palm. When he lifted his head she looked a little bemused.

"You need to go to sleep, *malyutka*." He brushed another kiss on her temple, his thumb sliding lazily over her nipple. He couldn't help enjoying the shiver that went through her body. It was visible and she didn't in any way try to hide it from him. "You're sensitive."

"Very."

"I like that. Someday I'm going to get you off by just lavishing attention on your breasts." The idea excited him. To see if he could do that for her. "When I do this . . ." He brushed her nipple again lightly and then bit down with his thumb and finger briefly. One more brush as she arched her back and gasped. "Do you get damp for me? Tell me what this does to you."

She touched her tongue to her lip, drew in breath and settled on the bed again. "I can feel it inside. Deep. It's like there's a straight line leading from my breast to my vagina. I not only go damp but my muscles clench."

He liked that. He liked that she hadn't hesitated to answer him. He wanted her comfortable, talking to him about every-thing so if she was worried, he'd know about it.

"You won't be alone, Evangeline," he said. "Never again. You'll have my brother and cousins and me. Especially me. But also friends. I want you to meet Siena and the other wives."

She lowered her lashes. He was coming to know that was rejection of whatever it was he was telling her.

"I don' need friends. I have Saria and Pau-line and I suppose if I wanted, Charisse.

I'm not good at relationships, Fyodor. I never had them so I don' really miss them."

That was a lie. He could hear it in her voice. She wanted those things, she just didn't think she could have them. He picked up her hand and brought it to his mouth, first kissing her fingers and then turning her hand over to place a kiss in the center of her palm. "I want you to have the best possible life, Evangeline. There are things I can't change. What I am. Who I am. I made a commitment and there's no way out now. But the rest of it, I can do for you and I will."

She turned her head and looked at him again. Straight in his eyes, the way she always did when she meant something. "I'm happy, Fyodor. I take responsibility for my own happiness. I always have. I don' want you to think you have to do anythin' special for me to be happy. You make me happy. My leopard. The bakery. Even the boys, as weird and crazy as they all are, I sort of consider them family. They've been comin' in the bakery for so long, especially Timur and Gorya."

He suckled at the center of her palm, drawing her skin into his mouth. Her hand was small and soft. Her voice was drowsy. He'd worn her out, and he liked that too.

"Did I hurt you?"

"You know you didn't."

"In a minute I'll get a washcloth and clean you so you can go to sleep."

"Not before you tell me what happened tonight. Who keeps tryin' to kill you?"

He was silent. Leopards didn't lie to each other. He couldn't give her everything, because he didn't want her to have any part of his business, but on the other hand she deserved the truth. He sighed. "Not me, Evangeline. You. They came after you. In the bakery. At the hospital and here."

Her eyes widened. She frowned. "Why in the world would someone want to kill me? Who? Who wants me dead?"

"It was Patrizio Amodeo. Evidently he blamed you that the meeting he was counting on didn't go so well."

"That's insane. I'll talk to him . . ."

"You won't." He said it abruptly. "No one talks sense into a man who takes a contract out on them. We'll be careful. At the bakery and here. I want you to move in with me here. Your house is nice, but it's small and I can't protect us as well there."

She opened her mouth to protest so he leaned in and kissed her again. When he lifted his head his gaze moved over her face, drinking her in. "She's so close to rising,

Evangeline. I can feel her every time I kiss you. My male gets close to the surface. Can you feel her?"

She nodded. "She makes me itch. It comes in waves, although while you were . . ." She trailed off.

"Making love to you." He wasn't about to say *fucking.* He hadn't fucked her. Even when he did, when he made it all about wild, he knew he would touch her with love, that it would always be about making love to her.

She nodded. "She left me alone with you. I appreciated that. I wanted it to be just us the first time."

"It was. My male left us alone as well."

"And it was perfect. Really, Fyodor, I loved every single thin' you did." That flush slid up her neck and into her face, turning her skin a rose color. "And the things you said to me. It was hot. Dirty maybe, but hot."

"I intend to do dirty things to you. I thought you might want to know what you were getting into." He brought her palm back to his mouth, teeth scraping gently.

"Where did you go tonight?"

"I had to take care of business. It didn't take long. I was anxious to get back to you."

"I don' know about movin' in yet, Fyodor. When you aren't here, I get nervous. I could spend a few nights here but then when you have business I can head home."

"Not. Going. To. Happen." He punctuated each word with a scrape of his teeth and then he bit down harder in the center of the mark he'd put on her palm. He ignored her yelp as she jerked her hand away from him and glared at him.

"If you insist on being at your house, I'll be staying there as well. I want you in my bed. I want to wake up to you. Go to sleep to you. Wake up in the middle of the night and take you however I want. I was serious about your body belonging to me. Mine belongs to you. When you want something, anything, I want to be there. And, *malyutka*, the next time you reach for your little toy, I'd better be with you. When you pack your things, make certain you pack that as well."

"You have a thing about bitin'."

"I'm leopard. I like to use my teeth and you're very . . . bitable."

She blushed again and squirmed a little, her hips shifting restlessly. He smiled at her, although he felt like smirking. She liked his teeth and the way he talked to her. He rolled off the bed and padded on bare feet to the small bathroom in the safe room. He washed himself thoroughly and then got a washcloth wet with warm water. He went back to her, watching her face. She had her eyes on his cock. The desire made him go from semihard to hard instantly.

"Spread your legs wider for me," he instructed.

She complied immediately, reaching for his belly, trailing her fingertips there, just above the head of his now pulsing cock. He washed her carefully, looking for signs of damage. He was as gentle as possible, taking his time, enjoying the look on her face and the way her fingers drifted down his belly to outline his cock.

"Are you shy about touching me?"

She shook her head but then nodded. "Maybe a little."

"Remember when I said my body belonged to you? I meant it. Whatever you want to do, I'm here for you."

"What if I don't know what to do?"

He leaned down and pressed a kiss to the tiny curls covering her mound. "Then I'll give you instructions. I'm going to shave you. Right now."

She squirmed again. "You are?"

He slid off the bed, went back to the bathroom and returned with shaving cream, towels, a razor and water. "While you tell me what you'd like to do to me."

She swallowed hard. "Fyodor. I don' know if I can do that."

"It's just me here with you, *malyutka,* your man. If we're going to have the best sex life possible, we have to be able to talk."

He placed a thick pillow under her bottom to raise her hips, rubbed his palm over her mound and then pressed a kiss over the short curls again. "I might miss these, but I want you to feel every single sensation I can give you with my mouth." He spread the shaving cream over her mound lavishly. "Keep still while I do this and keep your legs wide apart for me."

She did so, her eyes on his face. "I want you to feel every sensation I can give you with *my* mouth," she said, her voice no more than a whisper.

His gaze jumped to hers, his heart beating right through his cock, and then he looked down at what he was doing. He found it sexy, sitting on the bed with her, taking a razor to her most private area, with her talking about her mouth on him. He rinsed the blade in the water and returned to his project.

"What will you do with your mouth?" he prompted her.

There was a small silence. He willed her to talk to him. The easier she could talk about the subject, the more he knew he would be safe trying anything he wanted. He would trust her to object if she didn't like it or tell him if she was nervous.

"I want to learn to please you, Fyodor, to bring you the kind of pleasure you bring me." Her voice got a little stronger. "That's important to me."

His heart clenched at her admission. He moved her leg to get her lips clear. Already she looked smooth and bare so that he wanted his mouth there all over again.

"Tell me what you want to do first?"

"Explore. Take my time. Kiss every single scar on your chest and back. The ones on your belly and that single line across your . . ."

"Cock. And it's your cock so you can kiss it, suck it, fist it, deep throat it, do whatever the hell you want to do. Trust me when I say it's going to love being inside that sweet mouth of yours."

He was looking right between her legs, and every word elicited fresh citrus-cinnamon-spice cream. She liked the images in his head. Clearly the things he said turned her on. He was careful to get every hair and not cut or give her razor burn. As in all things, he was meticulous in his detail. That had been drilled into him from an early age and there was no changing it.

"I definitely want to do every single one of those things," she assured in a low tone. "All of them."

The intercom buzzed. "Boss, we've got company. Elijah and Joshua are here."

He sighed as he cleaned off every bit of shaving cream remaining, feeling her gaze on him. "I'm sorry, *malyutka,* you can rest, or take a bath and then rest. This might take a little while." Elijah was going to be angry. He had to have heard about the fire at the Amodeo estate. There were dead bodies scattered all over his house and sooner or later he'd hear of the missing cop, security guard and dispatcher. Honestly, he didn't give a fuck how angry Elijah was, but he still had to deal with it.

"It's the middle of the night, Fyodor," she protested, clearly not wanting to give him up. "Why would they come this late?"

"We're leopard. Leopards like the night. They aren't aware I've finally coaxed my woman into my bed. I'll be as fast as I can. Go into my room, use the large bathtub and climb into my bed after." She wouldn't have access to the audio and security screens in his room. He ran his finger from her chin down her throat, between her breasts, to her belly button and right to the vee between her now bare lips, feeling her shiver. "Go to sleep, *angel moya,* and I'll wake you when I send them on their way."

She nodded.

He kissed her because he couldn't resist kissing her and because of that little nod. She might not be in the least submissive, but she did like to please him. He was fairly certain there wasn't a luckier man on earth.

15

"Damn it all to hell, Alonzo," Elijah snapped. "You've got dead bodies from one end of the city to the other. What were you thinking?"

Alonzo studied the man's face for a long time, keeping his features expressionless. For years Elijah had been an enforcer in his father's territory. He'd become the same for Antonio Arnotto. He had been a soldier. He'd wanted to stay a soldier. Elijah had talked him into becoming a boss. That hadn't felt right until now. This moment. He knew what he'd done was necessary to keep his woman safe. Not just his woman, his family. Timur. Gorya. Mitya and Sevastyan. The other members of his crew. His soldiers. They needed someone strong or they'd all get eaten alive.

He'd made his decision and he'd carried it out, showing the other bosses no one messed with his people. Elijah didn't have to like it, but then, he didn't need Elijah's permission or his approval. He wasn't about to defend his decision or argue. It was done. He merely stared at the man who had recommended him for his position.

Elijah shook his head slowly, taking a deep breath and letting it out. Beside him, Joshua stirred. There was no doubt his leopard was very, very close.

"My cousin got out of this world," Joshua said. "You brought her back into it. I want her out." There was iron in his voice. His eyes glittered dangerously. "She deserves better than dead bodies in her home."

Alonzo felt the stirring of his leopard. A snarl. A rake of his claws in warning. He kept his expression frozen. His gaze cool. He shrugged. "She's my leopard's mate and she's my woman. We'll be married very soon. If you really want to challenge me, that's up to you, but you won't win. No matter how fast, no matter how experienced, you don't have that killer's edge to you. I do."

Elijah shook his head. "Joshua, you know once a female leopard accepts a mate, it's too late to interfere."

"She deserves a good life."

"I'll give that to her." Alonzo made the concession of reassurance because he genuinely liked Joshua. He didn't want the man for an enemy. He knew Joshua and Evangeline weren't close, but the man was still her family and clearly Joshua felt responsible for her.

Joshua paced across the floor trying to calm his leopard. Elijah ignored him, spreading his hands out in front of him. "We have to do damage control immediately. You have dead bodies here."

"We're taking care of it."

"Then speed it up. You'll need the cleaners to do their job a hell of a lot faster than they're doing it, because I can guarantee you're going to get a visit from the cops in the next few hours. Is there anything else you need to tell me?"

"I took care of business."

"Yeah, the fire is on every news channel. What else did you take care of?" Elijah asked suspiciously.

"No one threatens my woman, Elijah. What would you do if someone threatened Siena?"

"I'd take care of business," Elijah conceded. "I need to know if there's any chance of blowback."

Alonzo shook his head. "None. The cops can come and search and they won't find a thing here or anywhere else. I've been home all night. My men can testify to that."

Joshua spun around. "What about your woman? Because they sure as fuck are going to ask her without you in a room."

Alonzo remained silent. He simply stared at the man. He understood why Joshua didn't want him for Evangeline. If he was in Tregre's shoes he wouldn't want anyone like Alonzo near her. The fact remained that her female had accepted his male. She had made her commitment to him.

Joshua swore again and shook his head. "She had a shit life, Alonzo. You have no idea what our grandfather was like. He raped women, even his own daughters-in-law. He beat them to death. He beat my father to death. He searched for Evangeline, and her father and uncle were too chicken-shit to go against him so they left her out in the swamp to fend for herself. She deserves . . ." He swore in Cajun and paced across the room again. "Not dead bodies in her fucking sitting room."

"Amodeo put out a contract on her. Not on me. On her. That hit in the bakery was supposed to take her out. The security guard at the hospital was a hit man, and one of the cops was in on it. He was on Amodeo's payroll, as was a dispatcher who prevented the police from answering any

911 calls from the bakery. The hit might still be open."

Joshua turned back toward him, clearly shocked. "That son of a bitch. We should have killed the bastard while we had the chance."

Elijah studied Alonzo's face, clearly seeing far too much. "I've never asked about your past because I didn't think it mattered. You're surrounded by Russians. They're obviously related in some way, and you never take off your gloves. Leopards don't like gloves because it's one more thing to take off when shifting. So I guess you're covering tattoos. It's common in Russia for the brotherhood to tattoo their fingers, especially if they've served any time."

Alonzo remained silent. There wasn't a question in there. Elijah was fishing.

Elijah sighed. "Joshua, would you mind stepping out of the room? Just for a few minutes?" He looked at his bodyguards.

Alonzo shook his head. "That isn't necessary."

Elijah took him at his word. "You swore allegiance to me. You gave your word that you were on board with what we're doing. No one thought you'd find your mate, least of all me. I sure as hell didn't think I'd find mine, and I'd never have asked you if I didn't think you could handle the position."

"You want the territory back, I'll be more than glad to hand it over."

"Don't be an ass. The point I'm making is you learned far too fast how to be in charge of a territory. You know exactly what you're doing and the role fits you perfectly."

"I was never a *vor,* if that is what you're implying."

"No, but you were born into this world. You learned the ropes from the time you were a child, just as I did."

"Where is this conversation going, Elijah?" He'd given his past to Evangeline, and he'd whitewashed it. Living in a nightmare world such as he had with Timur, Gorya, Sevastyan and Mitya was unconceivable by outsiders. There was no describing the kind of hell they lived and witnessed every single hour of their existence. There was no reprieve. No safe place to catch a minute of normal. The cruelty and depravity of leopards deliberately mating with women not their own so they could later dispose of them after they provided sons was unimaginable. He'd give that to his woman but not anyone else, and only what he had to reveal so she'd know who he really was.

"I'm asking if there's going to be blow-back from your past. We have to be prepared for anything."

It was possible. They were getting too much publicity, something he'd worried about when he'd agreed to take over Antonio Arnotto's territory. He nodded slowly. "I didn't think so at first, but now . . ." He shrugged. "It's possible."

"Will we have trouble with the Russians?" Elijah was blunt, voicing his biggest concern aloud. "We don't want to go to war unless there's no other choice."

Alonzo shook his head. "As a last resort our enemies might reach out to them but only for a hit. No, they'll want to come after us themselves. They're leopards, particularly vicious, and they enjoy not only killing but torturing as well. They live to see others in pain." He looked up at his brother. "I didn't want that for them. They've been through enough, but if we keep making the news, if they keep putting our pictures everywhere, they'll come."

"We aren't so young anymore," Timur murmured.

Unexpectedly, Alonzo's heart jerked in his chest. It was rare for his brother to speak in front of the others. He was ferociously protective of Alonzo, but around the others outside of their family, he played the role of a bodyguard to perfection. He was deadly serious about keeping Alonzo safe, so it wasn't that difficult to fade into the background and watch for trouble. Timur had come out of the shadows to reassure him that what he was doing wasn't a mistake and they could handle it when their uncles showed up. And they'd come the moment they found out where Alonzo was.

"Will they go after Evangeline?" Joshua asked.

"We'll protect her in the way we protect my brother," Timur said, acknowledging their relationship aloud. His voice was firm. Resolute. Very, very dangerous.

"No doubt," Elijah said, with a hint of amusement. "So we'll schedule a meeting and talk about this issue with the others." He held up his hand when Alonzo would have protested. "We're in this together. What affects you, affects the rest of us. We have a mission. A plan. We have to carry it out together. You knew that going into this. We have to be together on everything."

"It was my problem long before I ever met you, and I'll deal with it if it comes here." Alonzo kept his voice low, as always. Ice was back the way it always was anytime he had to think about his father or walking in on him beating Timur and Gorya, savaging them to death, so they lay broken and bleeding and hopeless on the floor beside their dead mother. She'd been torn apart and she'd seen death coming to her. It was there in her eyes, wide open with horror, fixed that way for all time. Frozen. Like he was inside.

"*We'll* deal with it together," Elijah corrected. "You're no longer alone. We're all bound together. I get it, Alonzo. It was a difficult concept for me as well. I lived a life similar to yours. Not the same, but close. I didn't trust at first. Not anyone. But Drake is . . . Drake. You can count on him. He's exactly what he seems to be. Your leopard can hear lies. I don't think Drake is capable of lying to one of us even if we weren't leopard. Believe in him, all of us and what we do. That's how you can live a double life. That's how you can hold on to your woman through it."

Alonzo had listened to them pitch their plan to get the criminal world under some semblance of control. There was always going to be that world. Nothing, no amount of policing would ever stop it, but they could be on the inside and stop the worst of it. If they knew all the players, there were ways to stop them, just not lawfully.

Working one's way to the top to be acknowledged as a crime boss was a double-edged sword. A finite balance with a terrible price. All of them had been willing to pay that price in the hopes that in the end something good would come of it. *He'd* been willing, he'd been all in. He'd grown up seeing the worst that could be done to innocent people and he wanted to be part of what stopped it, but now there was Evangeline.

Elijah shook his head, leaning toward him. "Do you think, when I found Siena, that I didn't want to take her and run? I want her safe in the way you want your woman safe. Siena is carrying triplets. I'm going to have three children in a few months to protect as well. Do you think I want them in this life for one moment? I know other people will whisper about them behind their backs. I grew up with my grandfather and father committing crimes in countries all over the world, destroying lives. I know what they'll have to go through. Just as you know what's in the future for Evangeline."

"Joshua's right about one thing. She deserves better."

Elijah nodded. "She does. There's no question about that. None of us thought we would ever find the right woman before we made our decisions, but we have them and all we can do is go forward. If we try to run, to disappear, we'll never be safe. You know yourself you can't stay on the run forever and have any kind of life."

That much was true. Alonzo knew that. He lived in a room with bars on the windows and steel plates covering his doors. He didn't have friends. He didn't spend money. He barely interacted with others until Elijah had brought him into his world of redemption. Alonzo had wanted to make some kind of a difference before he died. He'd accepted the territory because he had so many sins on his soul he knew he had to balance them out in some way. He suspected Elijah felt the same.

He glanced at his brother. He should never have brought Timur and Gorya there, but he'd needed someone he could trust. Arnotto had soldiers, and they all knew him. They'd worked with him. He just wasn't certain whom he could trust to have his back. Still, now Timur was mired in as deep as he was.

Alonzo knew he'd been pulling away ever since Evangeline had come into his life. He'd been looking for a way out. He needed a way out. Elijah was right, the other bosses would want him dead, figuring he knew too much about their business.

He took a breath and let it out. There was

no way out. If there were, Elijah would have been gone. He loved Siena and he would have left everything behind in order to protect her. Alonzo was trapped in the life and that meant he'd trapped Evangeline and his brother and cousins right along with him. More sins on his soul.

"Set up the meeting with Drake," he capitulated.

"Cleaners are almost finished," Gorya announced. "Bill said another ten minutes. Two trucks are already gone. We sent them out with the freight trucks. We have another ten minutes before the next scheduled departure."

"Good," Alonzo said automatically. Antonio Arnotto had a good system in place. He'd managed to stay under the radar of law enforcement for his entire criminal career. His vineyards had a reputation and his wines were sought after. Alonzo had stepped into his shoes easily, already knowing most of the ins and outs of the various businesses and how Antonio had set things up to run so efficiently, incorporating his criminal activities so smoothly with his legitimate businesses.

"What else do I need to know about tonight?"

"Three men disappeared tonight. One of

425

them was a cop, and they'll look at me very closely for that," Alonzo said.

"You're absolutely certain nothing can tie you to anything that happened tonight?" Elijah pushed.

"I'm certain."

Evangeline touched the security screen with her finger, brushing a little caress over Alonzo's face, trying to smooth those rough, frozen lines. He was back to being the Iceman. His eyes were as glacier blue as they could get. There was no sign of the passionate man who had lain with her, his body hot and hard inside hers. She could barely equate the two men as being one and the same.

She'd been smart enough to lock the door and run a bath in the small bathroom provided. She wanted the scent of cinnamon and spice to permeate the room so her man wouldn't be suspicious. He was very used to intimidation and his icy dictatorship getting him whatever he wanted. He gave an order and it was carried out.

When he'd suggested so sweetly that she return to his room, take a bath and go to sleep and wait for him, she knew he wanted her out of the safe room, away from the security cameras. She had found the audio, turned it on and listened unashamedly to every word Elijah, Joshua and Alonzo had said. Most of it she didn't fully understand. Only that there was far more to his criminal activity than she had at first understood. She knew Saria would never be involved with a criminal. Her husband, Drake Donovan, ran a security team, and more, those men rescued kidnap victims around the world. They were considered elite and they had the reputation of being incorruptible.

Why would Alonzo allow her to believe he was a crime lord if he was something altogether different? She knew just from the little he'd told her about his family that his background hadn't been good, but the small snippets he'd told Elijah scared her. If his uncles found out where he was, they would definitely come after him. She wasn't in the least worried for herself, but for him.

A slow flush spread over her body, heating her from the inside out. Her temperature soared and for a moment she had to hang her head and breathe deep to try to still the inferno that suddenly began to rage between her legs. "Stop it," she told her female. "Seriously? Right now? I'm tryin' to learn a few things."

I'm burning for him. Burning up.

The moment she heard the distress in her

female, Evangeline was ashamed of herself. "It's okay, Bebe, we've got this. Do you need me to call him to us?" She hoped so. She wanted Alonzo with every breath she took. She needed him inside her, his mouth on her, his teeth. The itch was horrible, rising in waves under her skin until she thought she might scream. Her hands hurt, knuckles aching, fingers curling into claws so she couldn't quite straighten them.

Not yet. Close though. It's happening faster than I thought it would.

"Maybe havin' sex with Fyodor triggered this," Evangeline surmised. Her clothes actually hurt her skin. She couldn't take the way the material rubbed against her nipples. She'd dragged on her shirt but left it unbuttoned with the idea that she'd jump in the bathtub if Alonzo returned sooner than she thought he would. Now, she pushed the two sides open and off her breasts hoping for a respite. The material slid across her nipples like the brush of his thumb. Her sex spasmed. Clenched. Wept for him.

She tried to breathe the need away, but it was like a wildfire sweeping through her. She knew if Alonzo were in the room, she'd be all over him. "Is it this bad for you?"

Yes. I want my mate close to me, but the time isn't right yet. It will pass soon.

Evangeline wasn't certain she would survive if it didn't pass soon. She could call Alonzo to her, but she needed to know what was happening in her new world. He would try to shut her out, keep the worst from her, but she was self-sufficient and independent. She wasn't the type of woman to have a man make all her decisions for her.

She lifted her head determinedly and stared at his face on the screen. Listened to his voice. So low. So mesmerizing. She could see the men in the room were as affected by his voice as she was, although not in the same way. Her hand slid up her rib cage, her fingers trailing fire. She gasped when she cupped her breasts and her thumbs brushed her nipples just as he did. All the while she kept her eyes glued to his face.

He was frozen again. Inside. Outside. Her Iceman. She realized that only she really thawed him, melted that ice inside of him. She gasped again as her fingers tugged and rolled her nipples. Lightning streaked from her breasts to her core. Her sex clenched again, clenched and burned in desperation.

She tried to concentrate on what the men were saying, but there was no letup. She had no idea the Han Vol Dan would be so intense. She found herself on her hands and knees, her hips bucking. Her fingers slid deep and her thumb found her clit. She needed Alonzo, or at least her toy. It was brutal. The worst thing she'd ever felt. She *needed.* It was all-consuming. Frightening in its intensity. The burn couldn't be assuaged, and she found herself sobbing.

She could barely see straight. Her vision was banded, as if she were seeing through waves of heat. Colors were different. Dull. She was acutely aware of her body. Every cell in need. Her skull too tight for her head, pushing outward. Her teeth ached. At the same time, she became aware of her leopard. The fear. Discomfort. The pushing outward when she wanted to retreat.

Evangeline hadn't thought it was possible to force her brain to work when blood thundered in her ears, roared through her veins and chaos reigned in her mind, but the moment she realized her leopard was afraid and in the same kind of agony she was, she began to breathe through the brutal hunger.

"I'm with you," she whispered softly. "We're doin' this together. If Saria can go through it, we can. We're strong."

At first her leopard didn't respond, the heat pouring through her, forcing her body to writhe and burn for her mate. Evangeline put her head down and breathed. "If you need to come out, Bebe, do it. I've waited for you. I want you to run free. To have your mate. You deserve that."

Her voice barely worked. She sounded husky, so sensual she barely recognized herself. The invitation was answered by another wave of itching skin. Something rose beneath the surface so that she could see it moving on her arms and legs, something alive and desperate to come out.

"That's right, Bebe, let's do this. We don' need anyone else to get us through this. We've always done things ourselves. We're good." They weren't. They weren't good at all. They both needed their men. Their mates.

Even as she breathed deep and tried to reassure her leopard, she felt the burn ease. Her cat subsided just enough that both could get a handle on the vicious hunger raging through their bodies. Her bones ached and her skin was still on fire, but she could think better.

"That's it. We're fine. We're fine," she chanted. Sweat dripped from her body. She really needed that bath now. Whatever the men were up to, she didn't care. She had to think about this. "Can you imagine what would happen if I was at the bakery and this came over us?" She tried for humor. "I'd rip all my clothes off and become an instant porn star. Of course business might really pick up fast." It hurt to even smile. Her jaw ached beyond belief.

She took another deep breath and managed to sit back on her heels. "Bebe, I need to know you're all right. Talk to me."

I hurt you.

"No, you didn't," Evangeline hastily assured her. "This is just what happens to shifters. To both of us. Luckily we've got Fyodor and your mate. They'll help get us through. In the meantime, I'm goin' to jump in the bath, rinse off fast and then we can go for a walk around the grounds. The more we explore and know the property, the better we'll be able to handle this."

They knew the swamp inside and out. First the Tregre property, and then the surrounding swamplands, until they were familiar with all of it. They could run through the swamp with a heavier male after them and they knew every safe step through the boggy ground. She wanted to be able to do the same on the Arnotto estate. It was vast and had everything from groves of trees to flower gardens, koi ponds and vineyards. She would feel safer knowing every inch of the property, where there were places to hide and what was safe and what wasn't, if she was going to be staying there.

The hot water stung her skin, but she forced herself to stay in the water long enough to rinse the sweat from her body. "Wouldn't you know women have to go through this hormonal thing and men don'?" she whispered to her leopard as she released the water in the tub and toweled off.

She was a little worried about her female. Always, the cat had looked out for her. She was upset now and very quiet. There was no trace of amusement no matter what Evangeline said to her.

She unlocked the door and pushed her way into the passageway inside the wall. The bathwater hadn't helped calm her body down at all. If anything, it had heightened her needs. She was still sensitive and flushed from her leopard rising so close to the surface. She was still on fire, a fierce throbbing in her clit, her sex clenching and slick with need.

She dressed in soft yoga pants and a clingy T-shirt. She didn't put on underwear because her skin was too sensitive. And she itched all over. She sighed and put on her running shoes. There was no running without a bra, but she could explore the property. She zipped a light jacket on, hastily scribbled a note, telling Alonzo she went exploring, and she left his room, looking for the nearest exit that would avoid the men gathered in the great room.

The conservatory was just down the hall from Alonzo's small apartment. She ducked into that, knowing he wouldn't be happy with her going outside without a guard, especially after she heard the hit was on her, not Alonzo. Still, she was used to being on her own and taking care of herself. She started to open the door when her leopard stirred.

It is armed. Do you not hear the hum?

Rookie mistake and Evangeline was no rookie, not when it came to escaping and evading. She'd been doing it since she was a toddler. She let go of the doorknob and examined the doorjamb. "I hear it. I was too busy thinkin' about getting out into the fresh air. Thanks, Bebe." She liked that her female had stopped her. That told her they were in sync once again. She needed that. Her cat always steadied her.

Her female gave a little inelegant snort of derision. *It's the other way around and has been since you were about sixteen.*

Evangeline was certain that wasn't the truth, but at least her leopard was back to

434

her usual self. "Are you all right?" She found the sensor over the door. It was just that little bit too visible. Hidden, but not. That meant a backup.

Yes. The female gave the impression of stretching languidly.

Evangeline found herself smiling in spite of the fact that her body hadn't quite settled, her injured leg was on fire and her arm hurt like hell. She moved her fingers along the sides of the doorjamb where the wood was intricately patterned. The house had hidden passageways built into the walls. There were all kinds of hidden devices within the wood. Alonzo had told her all about the history of the house and how Antonio Arnotto had it built for leopards and with an eye to escape trouble.

Her fingers found the little hidden button in the middle of a swirl of golden wood. It was no more than a depression but she pushed down and instantly the hum stopped. She yanked open the door and went through. At once the night air hit her. There was little moon and a lot of clouds and it was cold, but she inhaled deeply, drawing the night into her lungs.

"Just what we need," she told her female and began to hurry across the open yard to the heavier brush. As she jogged across grass she scented the male. He was off to her left, a slight breeze warning her.

Evangeline angled away from him, put on a burst of speed and gained the maze of thick bushes and shrubs. Her leopard gave the impression of laughing. She was happy. They were in their element. She dropped low to the ground, winding in and out of the shrubs, turning sideways to slip through narrow openings. She moved fast, but avoided shaking branches.

The male came close to where she'd entered the brush. He stopped moving, inhaling sharply. He was in human form, but Evangeline could scent the wild in him. "Timur." The guard spoke into his radio. "We've got trouble out here. I think the female's loose. My male's going crazy. She's throwing off enough pheromones to call in every male for a hundred miles."

That didn't sound good. At. All. Evangeline swore, using every Cajun cuss word and phrase she'd heard over the years. She just was very quiet about it. *Stop, Bebe. They'll track us for sure and I wanted some outside alone time.*

It's not like I can control it, her female pointed out.

"Boss says track her but don't get close. His male is a fuckin' killer, Vitaly. I kid you

436

not. That's his woman and you get near her, his male will tear you to pieces," Timur said, his voice tight.

The guard swore out loud in Russian, and Evangeline was fairly certain he said far worse than she had. She kept moving, a little slower, a little lower to the ground, trying to move with the wind instead of against it. She didn't want her female broadcasting to every male in the vicinity.

Not all me. You're fertile as well.

Great. She'd had unprotected sex like a complete idiot and she was fertile. She came to the edge of the shrubbery and found herself right at the very tip of the grove of trees. They were tall and thick and formed a dark, intriguing forest with the canopy high and the branches intertwined, forming a highway for leopards.

She knew exactly what she was looking at. Arnotto had deliberately cultivated the trees to grow for an emergency escape route. The dark was inviting, but there were a number of male leopards on the property. More than she'd realized just staying in the house. Alonzo was well protected, with a security force of leopards and soldiers that were human but loyal.

She was going to have to do her thinking on the run, not the best of circumstances, but sooner or later the leopards would corner her. Once they shed their human form, they could track her very easily. Without broadcasting pheromones, she would have stood a chance, even bet she had even odds, she knew she was that good, but not dousing everything she touched with "come hither" scent.

She wanted time with Alonzo. That's what it boiled down to. Time without men trying to kill her or going into heat and having their leopards take over. She needed a foundation with him, and she needed it to be solid if this thing between them was going to work. She had to trust him with more than her body. She had to want to be with him for more of a reason than wanting to be the one to give him something he'd never had before.

She melted the moment he was around. No, it was worse than that. Hearing his voice. Seeing his face on the screen. She had no idea how other women felt, but she always wanted to hold him close in her arms and offer him — everything. Was that even normal? She didn't know. She'd never witnessed a relationship between a man and a woman. She'd heard about it from Saria, but only in brief terms, and most were simply that Saria was crazy in love with Drake.

She found the wall surrounding the huge maple garden. It was well over six feet high and along the top of the winding wall a dragon curled his long body and tail as if guarding the interior. She crouched low, called on her leopard and made the jump over the wall. Landing easily on her feet she stood still to admire the breathtaking garden.

It was huge, with hundreds of maples, all different varieties, from dwarfs to rare to larger shade maples. The leaves were in all shapes and colors, and the bark on the various trees ranged from bright red and pink to a peculiar green. There were a few trees with the bark peeled off. She loved that look as well. Someone had created bonsai trees out of three of the dwarf trees near the pond and they looked spectacular. A long stream wound its way down several tiers to flow into the large koi pond.

Evangeline wandered down each stone path, admiring the layout of the garden and how tranquil it was. Whoever had designed it had placed a barrier in the form of the artistic wall to block any real wind. Trees wept into the pond. Cherry blossoms on several dwarf trees lit up the night with their beauty. By far, this was going to be her favorite place. She was in love with it already.

She could think here. She curled up in large body-sized pillows on the floor of the gazebo overlooking the koi pond. The pillows were made of a thick weave, were comfortable and invited contemplation. She listened to the sound of the water running over the stones as it fell to the pool below it. It was steady. Like Alonzo. Like his heartbeat and his incredible gift of a voice. She wanted steady.

"I don' need him, Bebe," she murmured softly to her leopard. "When the heat isn't on me, I don' need him. But I want him. Very, very much. From the moment he walked into the bakery and didn't smile at me. Snuck looks, as if I wouldn't notice him starin' at me from behind the magazine. He's so gorgeous of course I noticed. And I wanted him."

He had been so remote. So aloof in the beginning. Those ice-cold eyes staring at her. Even then she wanted to melt all that ice. He was the thing of fantasies, and she didn't want a fantasy, she wanted the real man in the real world.

Even if he's a criminal? Her female always took the opposite side of the argument.

God help her, yes, even then. There was something about Alonzo that drew her right from the start and being around him only made that so much more. She liked everything about him.

Other than that he's a criminal.

Evangeline's breath hissed out of her lungs. "You're bein' deliberately annoyin' tonight. Goin' into heat hasn't improved your disposition one little bit." Her leopard brought up a good point, and that was even more irritating. What exactly was she doing, and what did she want?

Fyodor and really good sex.

Evangeline burst out laughing. She *loved* her female. Loved her so very much. Her leopard's amusement slipped through her mind. Warm. Comforting. Familiar. The smile faded and her heart began to pound. "I have to let him in all the way," she whispered. "He could hurt us."

You've already let him in. If he's not who he says he is, we're both going to get hurt. That's just life. Her female was pragmatic as always.

"Or dead."

Not that. They will always underestimate us. Her female suddenly went on alert.

Evangeline scented the big male, although she didn't hear him. She hadn't heard him clear the wall or pad toward her on silent paws. She turned her head and watched him come. He was huge. The biggest leopard she'd ever seen. He was also beautiful, but battle scarred. His fur was long and thick, the rosettes larger than usual. She would know him anywhere by the ice blue of his eyes. Even if the gold spread through, letting her know what mood he was in, she would always know him.

She smiled. She couldn't help it. She knew he'd come and she was happy that he had.

16

Deep inside the male, Alonzo crept up on Evangeline. He didn't know what to think or feel. Whether to be angry with her or just let terror take over that she might be running from him. Or fear that Amodeo had another hit man waiting for a moment just like she'd given him, presenting a target without a bodyguard.

She should never have taken such a risk. There are males everywhere. She's close to emerging and any of them could have been stupid enough to try to claim her.

His leopard was angry. He couldn't blame his cat. Neither ever expected to find a mate. Not. Ever. Evangeline had risked so much more than she realized. The men he surrounded himself with were good men. Loyal. The scent of her would send them all into a mating frenzy. His cat would have fought them to the death. More, so would the man.

The leopard was within striking distance of her. One rush and he would teach her a lesson she'd never forget.

Don't you dare. Alonzo took control of his beast. *She's mine and you won't hurt her, no matter what she's done.*

She's ours, his leopard corrected him. *We are not going to lose either of them.*

Evangeline turned her head toward the leopard and smiled. That smile. *His* smile. The one she reserved for him alone. She looked right into the eyes of his leopard and saw him. She wasn't afraid of his leopard because she trusted him. Alonzo felt that trust as an arrow straight to his heart. She had every reason to fear male leopards, and his was one of the worst. She knew that and she still remained calm.

Do you understand the gift she's giving us? She was terrorized as a child by a male leopard.

Show him to me and I will kill him.

"I knew you'd come as soon as you were finished with your business. I was waitin' for you." She patted the large pillow next to her. "I wanted to talk to you about my female, so it's good you're here in this form."

The leopard hesitated, one paw in the air, freezing in position as if he didn't quite know what to do. Alonzo had been in the act of shifting to human form. He'd come out looking for her immediately and hadn't brought a pack with clothes. He remained as a leopard, giving her the opportunity to see that his male would protect her as well as her female.

Be gentle. Earn her trust, he cautioned.

The big male moved slowly to Evangeline's side. The pheromones she was throwing off were so potent, Alonzo knew the female was rising very fast. She could emerge that night, early morning or the next afternoon, but it would be soon. It had to be soon because the soldiers closest to him were all male leopards. Evangeline in such close proximity was dangerous to all of them.

"Sometimes I can't stand being inside," she confessed softly. "I go runnin' when that happens. Or I sit on my porch. Sometimes I sleep outside."

He knew that much. He'd had bodyguards on her for the last few months and they'd told him about her penchant for running or sitting outside at midnight. He had never asked her about it because he hadn't wanted her to know he was watching her. That would lead to questions, such as why. And the why of it had been complicated then.

445

He didn't want her to know about his life, or that by continually going to the bakery after he'd been named Arnotto's successor he was possibly bringing danger to her — and he'd been right.

Evangeline looked him in the eye again and Alonzo realized he'd been wrong. She was afraid of his male. Afraid, but resolute and determined to trust that Alonzo would make certain she was safe. This was her female's mate and she was determined to get over her fears. His heart contracted and the glacier, so thick inside of him, melted even more.

"I spent most of my life being hunted. Runnin' free in the swamp. Alone with just my female. She came to me when I was an infant. She got me through those toddler years. We had to hide over and over and be so quiet while he prowled around our little room deep in the swamp. We knew he searched for us and that he would kill us if he found us."

Her soft admission broke Alonzo's heart, but it enraged his male. The thought of his mate helpless with a male leopard hunting her infuriated the cat. The amber eyes glowed with wrath and the big leopard abruptly moved away from Evangeline, pacing across the stone path to maple trees, where he smashed his giant paw through the leaves to send them up in a swirling tower.

Evangeline fell silent. Alonzo hoped that she realized his male was letting off steam and wouldn't harm her.

We won't allow anything like that to happen again, Alonzo assured. *We took care of the threats to her.*

You're still worried.

His leopard knew him too well for Alonzo to lie to him. He *was* worried. He wanted to keep Evangeline close to him until he knew for certain that Amodeo's contract had died with him. The man had been bold enough to send a crew to wipe them all out right on his home turf. That was insanity and Amodeo knew it. He would have had to have given orders to kill all of them, otherwise Elijah and Joshua would have retaliated if they knew for certain who had been behind the killings.

We'll keep her safe. Go reassure her.

The male swung back around and prowled right up to Evangeline. He rubbed his body along hers, scent marking her, making certain the other males in the area knew she was his. He wasn't taking any chances with her either. She held herself very still, not trying to move away from the big male. Her eyes widened and he realized she was in communication with her female. The animal was probably explaining what his male was doing.

When the male leopard settled, lying down, wrapping his body around her so that his thick fur kept her warm in the cool of the night, she let out her breath and relaxed again. "I didn't mean to upset you." Tentatively she sank her fingers into his fur and then leaned back against the leopard with a little sigh. "I think what I'm tryin' to tell you is that I lived almost my entire life outdoors in the swamp surrounded by danger. More than anyone else, you should know what it feels like to live that way. I want you to know that my female got me through that. She's beautiful and strong and she deserves a mate who will care for her and see her for what she is."

His male rubbed his large head along her shoulder and then looked her straight in the eye. Like Alonzo, he knew what she was conveying to him. She wanted him to know that her leopard was extraordinary. He knew that already. She'd revealed herself immediately when her human counterpart had been a baby and needed her. That alone made her special.

"The other thing I think it's important for

you to know —" Evangeline said. She stopped abruptly and swept a hand through her hair. "Aside from the fact that I wanted time with you, Fyodor, so much more time before Bebe emerged, I needed to know you wanted me for me. Not just for her. I still need that. I've never been wanted. Not by my family. Not by anyone. I'm not tellin' you this so you'll be sympathetic. I want you to know how important it is to me to feel as if I am the one you want. Me. I foresee, in a long-term relationship, my self-esteem issues when it comes to you and me comin' up and givin' us problems."

Alonzo wanted to shift, to hold her close, but he would have been stark naked and she wanted to talk. There was no getting close to her while he was naked and not taking her, so he remained in his leopard form. The male nudged her gently with his muzzle and then rubbed along her shoulder as if offering comfort or reassurance.

Alonzo knew he had a few of those issues of his own. He wanted her to be as obsessed with him as he was with her. He needed her to want him, to want to make a home with him. He'd never had that and he desired it — with her.

"I also think it's important to tell you, because I spent so many years outsmartin' that big male and livin' in a dangerous situation, I know, no matter how much I tell myself that I want a normal, quiet life with a nice man, that just isn't true. No matter how much I try to be someone else, I'm still me. I'll always be me. And always want you and whatever life we have together."

Alonzo couldn't stop himself from shifting. That revelation had to be hard for her to admit to him. She'd come outside not to run from him or to be defiant, but because she needed it. She felt most comfortable outside, and he understood a comfort zone. He also understood needing that adrenaline rush.

He found himself curled protectively around her back. He caught her face, turned her so she looked over her shoulder at him and then his mouth was on hers. Heat rushed through his veins, a fireball spreading hunger as he kissed her. He loved her mouth. Her soft, full lips, how velvet soft her mouth was, moist and hot and tasting like cinnamon and honeyed spice. He didn't give her time to breathe. To protest. He simply poured everything he was into her. Demanding she give him everything.

"Everything," he whispered against her lips. "I want it all from you."

"You have it," she reassured, reaching with

one arm to circle his neck, holding him to her.

He kissed her again and again, losing himself in her taste. Despite the cool of the night, her body felt warm to him. Hot even, as if her skin were on fire. He closed his eyes for a moment, knowing her time was close. Too close. They weren't going to get what she so desperately wanted.

He lifted his head and very gently turned her toward him. He could see the knowledge in her eyes. The fear. She was trying to be brave, not to panic. He couldn't imagine what it must feel like for her. He reached around her and unzipped her jacket, tugging her arms out of the sleeves.

So terrible. She burns. Inside. Outside. Both of them. His leopard pushed closer to the surface. Desperate to get at his mate. The heat rose in the male leopard as well, answering the fire in the female.

Alonzo knew that was true because he was already burning for her. His cock was a steel spike, so hard and thick he felt his heartbeat pounding right through it. He cupped Evangeline's face between his palms. "She's close. Timur will warn the other leopards away. It's going to be rough, *malen'kaya lyublyu moyo,* but I'll get you through this."

Evangeline curled her fingers around his

451

arm, almost convulsively. "It happened earlier. When you were busy. I tried to get through it alone but it was horrible." She made her confession in a low, frightened voice. This was worse. So much worse than before. Every single cell in her body was on fire. She could barely breathe with the need burning so hot. Her heart pounded and the roar of her blood was like thunder in her ears.

Alonzo brushed kisses over her eyes. Trailed them down her cheek to the corner of her mouth.

She pulled away from him, her eyes going wide with the shock of how much she craved him. She couldn't stop moving, writhing, her hips bucking. "My skin hurts, Fyodor." She began tearing at her shirt, desperation causing her to rip at the material. Her nails were longer, curved and very hard. One tore a strip of skin from her ribs. It hurt, but not nearly as much as the fire building between her legs did.

"Stop." He made it a command. "Evangeline. Let me. Just breathe for me." He dragged the shirt from her and flung it onto the pillow.

A part of her realized what a sacrilege that was for him, but she could barely breathe with wanting him. Her hands dropped to her pants, but he pushed them away and tugged the material from her hips. When he had her naked, she rolled away from him, coming up on her hands and knees, a low keening sound escaping as her body undulated and rocked.

"Let me help you, Evangeline," Alonzo said. "I'm right here. You aren't doing this alone."

This was a million times worse than what happened earlier. Every single cell in Evangeline's body felt raw and inflamed. Her bones ached. Her breasts were on fire. Between her legs that burning need built and built until she thought she might go a little insane.

I'm sorry. I can't control it. It's so much worse than the other times. So strong. Heat. Fire. Burning. I don't know what to do.

Evangeline took a deep breath and let it out. Her leopard was in distress. So much more than she was. When she touched her cat, she found fear. Chaos. Guilt. The guilt was overwhelming. She shook her head and forced herself to think past the terrible roaring in her head. The hunger, the need for sex was so strong, she feared she might go insane, but her leopard needed her to be strong.

Her leopard had always, always been there

for her. Twice she'd gone through the Han Vol Dan. Both times her leopard had deemed Evangeline too young and she somehow had managed to hold on and not emerge. She didn't want to force Evangeline to accept a man not worthy of her. She'd *suffered*. Her leopard had suffered for her.

No, Bebe, this is your time. Something beautiful. We can do this. Alonzo is right here. He's a good man. I know he is. He'll take care of me and then your mate will take care of you. I want you to emerge. I want you to run free. This time is your time. Don't try to hold back.

You're afraid.

Only because the need is so strong. I'm not afraid of Alonzo. I want you to emerge. We'll do this, Bebe.

She soothed her leopard even as her body grew hotter and more demanding.

"Evangeline." There it was. Just her name. Alonzo's voice, soft and compelling.

She had to get past humiliation and embarrassment that she couldn't control herself. This was her man. Her choice. He would always be her choice, and he was a shifter. He understood. She needed him in every way. Not just her body crying out for his, but his guidance and understanding. His caring. She'd put herself in his care.

454

That meant that now, in her scariest hour, she had to trust him. Rely on him. That single whispered sound of her name told her she could.

She raised her eyes to his. He hadn't moved. He was on the pillows, his large body naked, bare to her. All muscle and magnificent cock. Hers. She needed him. Was desperate for him. Her man. The one person in the world she trusted. She needed him, and he had made it clear that he belonged to her.

Keeping her gaze on his, loving the glacier blue of his eyes and the way he looked at her as if he could devour her, she began to crawl toward him on her hands and knees, deliberately seductive. One slow hand and knee at a time, much like a large cat. She felt sexy, beautiful even, because when Alonzo looked at her, there was no other way to feel. Her breasts swayed with every movement, aching, swollen, her nipples hard peaks that burned in the cool night air. Whereas before, the intensity of her body's needs frightened her, now, with her gaze on her man, she felt a temptress, demanding what she needed.

Alonzo, his gaze still captured by hers, dropped his hand to his cock, fisting the thick shaft, almost as if he didn't realize what he was doing. She loved that reaction. Loved that his gaze was filled with a dark passion, with lust, with a burning hunger to match her own. She needed that from him. She needed to know that he wanted her every bit as much as she wanted him, and he told her so without saying a word.

She made her way to him slowly, drawing the moment out, feeling sensual and knowing stretching out the tension just got him hotter. She loved that she could put that look on his face, the sensual lines carved deep so he looked the epitome of sin. He widened his legs, opening his thighs so she could crawl between them. She did, feeling the heat pouring off of him, as his skin brushed along hers.

She'd melted all the ice fast. Keeping her eyes on his, she lowered her body by just bending her elbows. Her breasts swayed against his thighs as she opened her mouth and deliberately lapped at the broad head of his cock. Velvet soft. Scorching hot. His taste addictive. His fist was still wrapped around the base of his shaft and she took advantage of that, engulfing him in the heat of her mouth.

The moment she took him deep, her body shuddered with pleasure. Her sheath clenched and spasmed, went slick with need. He was all man and she loved that about him. He tasted like man, like hers. She took her time, absorbing the way her body caught flame just from what she was doing. She loved pleasuring him to the point where he nearly lost control. She loved the way his hips bucked, pushing him deeper into her mouth, yet his fist was there to make certain she felt safe. His other fist wrapped in her hair, guiding her as she took him deep and suckled strongly.

Each lash of her tongue, each strong pull of her mouth, sent shudders through him. She reveled in her ability to do that to such a strong man. She loved hearing his breath turn ragged. Labored. His eyes glittered at her, lids lowering to half-mast, so that he looked sexy beyond words.

Fire spread through her, another wave of unbearable heat, and she pulled back, gasping at the sheer intensity of the need consuming her. Her hips wouldn't stop moving, so restless, the terrible hunger overcoming her. She backed up, panting, trying to keep from pleading with him to do something. Anything.

He leaned his head down to hers and took possession of her mouth. Kissing her. Hard. Urgent. Demanding her response. She gave it to him willingly. Savoring his taste. Savoring the way he kissed her. Over and over. With lust. With that dark passion, so much of it, she could taste it. Mostly, she savored the taste of love. It was there, something she barely recognized, but it made her feel stronger. More courageous. Beautiful. Wanted.

"Turn around for me, Evangeline," he said softly, his lips a whisper from hers. In that voice. Velvet soft. So smooth. All commanding.

She would do anything for him, and not just because her body was in total meltdown. Because he was her choice. Hers. Fyodor. A man from another country. A man lost without her, because he was. She knew that. She knew she would always be the most important person in his life.

She turned, deliberately taking her time when her body was shouting at her, screaming with need. She wanted him to see her, full breasts flushed and swollen for him. Nipples twin hard points. Her body on full display. His. All for him. She turned until her back was to him. At once he was on her with the speed and strength of a leopard. A shifter. His hand caught the nape of her neck and pushed her head down even as his arm circled her hips and pulled them higher.

"Like that, *devochka moya,* stay just like

that for me."

She heard that note in his voice, the one that said he expected her to do exactly as he said. The one that got her hot but made her want to defy him just to see what he'd do. Not now. Now she was in desperate need. She bit down on her lip to keep from pleading with him to take her right then because her greedy body refused to wait one more second.

She expected him to plunge into her, but for a moment there was only the cool night air, his hand firmly on her nape and the scent of him in her lungs. She felt exposed, her butt in the air, knowing she was slick, moisture seeping helplessly and her female pheromones declaring she was impatient and eager for his cock.

His fingers danced up the inside of her thigh, brushing streaks of fire over her skin. He pushed at her legs, forcing them wider and then his hand dropped away. Her breath caught in her throat.

"Fyodor."

He leaned into her, caught her left cheek in his mouth, suckled right in the center. He took his time while she squirmed, her hips bucking back against him. "Yes, Evangeline?" His tongue lapped at the strawberry circle. Then his teeth were there, scraping back and forth seductively. He bit down and she gasped, his name a panting cry, and pushed back hard to get him to hurry.

His mouth was gone instantly. She looked at him over her shoulder with narrowed eyes. "Fyodor," she warned.

"Yes, Evangeline?" He gripped her hips in strong hands, stopping all movement on her part, his voice deceptively mild.

"Get on with it now."

"You want my cock buried inside you?"

She snapped her teeth at him. "Yes."

"You just had to say so."

There was a teasing note in his voice that warmed her, that made her heart contract. He made it clear his possession wasn't just about wild leopard sex, it was about the two of them. Fyodor and Evangeline. She loved that. More, she needed it. She was burning up, her body temperature soaring. The burning in her sex was so intense it was actually painful, but with just that little bit of playfulness, he made her feel human. His. That everything was all right and would be.

He surged into her, all heat and fire, a steel sword, spreading lightning through fire. She cried out, pushing back, needing to impale herself on that wonderful weapon. He wasn't gentle. It was rough. Brutal even. But the hands at her hips steadied her, and his voice, so velvet smooth, murmured to her.

"You're so beautiful, Evangeline. So perfect. You feel like heaven. Scorching hot. Tight. So tight, *malyutka,* like a vise made of the hottest silk."

He kept moving in her and all she could do was try to breathe through the fire consuming her. Her breath came in ragged pants. She wept, but knew it was for joy. Joy for her leopard and for herself. Because she had this man.

"Ya tebya lyublyu."

She knew he'd told her he loved her. He'd done that more than once. She'd never said it back, not a single time, but she knew she did. She hadn't wanted to give that much of herself away, to be so vulnerable to a shifter male. She hadn't been nearly as courageous as she wanted to be. Love was something she hadn't believed in until Alonzo. Until he'd walked into her bakery and taken over her heart.

She tried. "I . . ." A streak of fire burst through her and deep inside she coiled tighter and tighter, the fiery friction taking her higher than she'd ever been. "Love." She got that out. It came out on a sob.

His fingers flexed. He paused, his cock buried deep. So deep. So thick, swelling more, expanding in her until he was pushing at the walls of her sheath, so she could feel his heart beating inside of her.

"You," she managed.

She knew he heard her. That it mattered to him. That her ragged admission was truly from her heart and that it had been difficult for her. He understood her, and it mattered, those three little words.

For a moment he laid his body over hers, so his heart beat deep inside her feminine channel and she could feel that same heartbeat against her back as his lips brushed the nape of her neck and then her shoulder. "No one in my life has ever said that to me. Mean it, Evangeline. Mean it or don't say it."

The terrible fire of the Han Vol Dan was everywhere, in every one of the cells of her body, burning out of control, a raging firestorm, and yet in that moment, there was utter calm, as if the eye of the storm were over them. She felt his every breath. The need in him. The fear to believe. She realized he was far more vulnerable than she could ever be. Holding himself still. Surrounding himself with ice. Inside and out, her man was totally a fortress but for her. To her he made himself completely and utterly vulnerable.

Love for him welled up, every bit as sharp and terrible as the fire of the Han Vol Dan. She turned her head so he could take her mouth. His possession was every bit as savage as a leopard could get, but his kiss was so beautiful it brought tears to her eyes.

"I've never meant anything more," she managed to get out between the ragged, labored breathing made worse by his kisses. "Get. On. With. It."

There was another moment of absolute silence, as if he needed to fully absorb what she'd given him and then he laughed softly and rubbed her left cheek, just where he'd left his mark. Then he was moving again and her world narrowed to feeling. Sensation. The exquisite, terrible fire that burned through her, forced her body to push back hard against his, driving him deeper into her, always wanting more. She needed more.

He pounded into her, a thick, harsh piston that never stopped taking her higher and higher. Her bones ached. Her skin was on fire. Every brush against her sensitive skin hurt, yet deep inside she needed more. It was frightening. It was exhilarating. More, it was the sexiest thing she could imagine.

Still, the more he took her, the more she needed and the tighter that brutal tension inside her coiled until she was sobbing for release.

"I've got you, Evangeline. Now, *solnyshko moyo,* fly for me. Give me everything."

She did because it was Alonzo. Because it was the only man she loved or would ever love. She did because he told her to and she trusted him implicitly. She came apart for him, her body fragmenting, the ripples like an earthquake, building and building and then roaring through her. She screamed his name, halfway between sobbing and laughing. Happy. Shocked. Coming apart at the seams until she was certain she could never be put back together.

His release triggered another large quake, until she thought she would just die right there. She collapsed, Alonzo over top of her, still holding her hips, still inside her.

The fire hadn't gone away. It burned hotter and brighter than ever. Terrified she couldn't go through it again, she turned her head to the side and looked over her shoulder at the man she knew she could count on. "Fyodor?" She couldn't keep the note of fear out of her voice.

"I know, *malyutka,* let's catch our breath and then we'll do this. Together."

That made her feel a little better. At least he knew what was going on. She couldn't keep her hips still, and he didn't stop her from bucking against him. That didn't put out the fire, it only built it higher, as if she were burning from the inside out.

"Oh my God." Of course. *Bebe, I'm here with you. It's happening right now. My bones ache. My joints. Every part of me is making way for you. It's your time and you're going to love the freedom. You'll love your mate the way I love mine.* She poured reassurance into her mind, swamping her cat with her confidence.

So hot. Can't stand it. I have to stretch. I have to rise closer. I don't want to hurt you.

It won't hurt me, silly. This is what we are together. You're supposed to emerge.

Her leopard had protected her for so long, she feared that appalling, ferocious burn would consume Evangeline if she tried to emerge. Evangeline understood now why females didn't show themselves until that moment. The fire was too hot and the fear too great. She reached for her leopard, soothing her in spite of the way her own body hurt and felt as if it would never be sated.

Her man was moving in her again, and she didn't have far to go before she was coming again and again, that wonderful, frightening high that threw her soaring and fragmenting. She needed to fragment. Her skull ached. Her jaw. The hands under her couldn't lay flat, her fingers curling and her joints making terrible popping sounds.

Deep inside she felt Alonzo's hot release, his seed pouring into her, triggering an even bigger orgasm. This one took her by surprise. She didn't think it was possible to let go again, to have the sensations consume her. She collapsed completely onto the stone walkway. Alonzo immediately pulled out of her and crawled up beside her.

"I'm going to shift, Evangeline. She'll rise faster for him. Don't be afraid of it, just let go. You'll still be there, I promise. The freedom as a leopard is unbelievable."

She nodded, unable to speak, still gasping for breath, still on fire. She wasn't a frightened little girl. She was a strong woman, and she knew about shifters almost from the day she was born. She wanted her leopard to emerge. She wanted that for her. The female deserved every moment of happiness she could have.

Alonzo leaned into her and took her mouth. Gently. Tenderly. So lovingly tears burned behind her eyelids. Then he was gone so fast she hadn't even blinked. In his place was his massive leopard. So beautiful. All roped muscle and long, amazing fur.

The male rubbed his face all over her back and sides. Along her shoulders, down her buttocks to her thighs and then her calves. Everywhere his fur touched, her skin burned, but she could feel her female rising faster and faster toward the male scent marking her.

The tips of her fingers and toes burned. Ached. Became painful. Nails burst through, curved and thick and very scary-looking. Her wrists curved, her mouth felt too small for her teeth.

Now, Bebe. Come to him now. She let go. Joyously. Embracing that moment. Letting her female know she was overjoyed.

Bebe rose fast without hesitation, her small body falling to the ground, legs under her, her fur golden with black rosettes. She lifted her face and scented her male close to her. Too close. She gave him a look that told him to back off. She wasn't ready yet. Not by a long shot.

The male moved against her, his fur sliding along hers, his heavier body warning her to be cautious. She snarled and swiped one paw at him, leapt the wall and bounded away. The male leopard followed at a distance, careful to keep her in sight at all times, scenting the night for other males, watching to see his mate came to no harm.

He allowed her to run free, to experience the wonder of the outside, the freedom of sprinting, of finding every new smell, every pond and rodent, the downed tree trunks, the arboreal highway Antonio Arnotto had planned so many years earlier. The estate was large, and he had built and planted every single acre with leopards in mind. It was perfect.

Deep in Bebe's body, Evangeline rejoiced. Seeing the estate through her leopard's eyes, knowing the joy her female was experiencing, she decided she was going to have to revisit the fact that Siena Arnotto Lospostos was willing to give or sell the estate to Alonzo.

I love this, Bebe told her.

I love this for you. Your mate is gettin' closer. She couldn't help teasing her female. Her leopard was beautiful. Gorgeous. *He's gettin' vocal and amorous.*

I hear him. Bebe gave a little sniff of disdain.

She was close though. Even inside her, without her own body, Evangeline could feel the ferocious need building stronger and stronger. She retreated more to give her little leopard privacy with her mate.

Bebe raced through the woods, playfully pawing at rotting vegetation just to see what emerged. All the while she was conscious of the male following her. He was very large and a little intimidating, but she had the upper hand and she knew it. She teased him, showing off, rubbing along tree trunks to spread her alluring scent, making certain he caught it.

He made little chuffing sounds. In truth, she loved the way he called to her, but she wasn't ready to give up her freedom. She wanted to see everything she could before the night was over. The burning sensation deep inside her wouldn't let her alone. She found herself calling back to the male until he ran beside her. He wasn't playful in the least, but he didn't try to stop her.

She rubbed along another tree and then dropped down, panting, crouching. At once the heavy male was on her. Before he could bite down on her nape to hold her in place, she sprang away, swiping leaves at him, snarling to tell him to back off. He simply followed her. Now, she could see, he was all business and purpose. That was a little thrilling, and scary.

She couldn't stop herself from crouching again, and he was on her, his teeth sinking in to hold her. The bite of pain gave way to something altogether different as the male took possession of her.

From that moment on, all through the night and most of the dawn, the two leopards were side by side when he wasn't claiming her. He showed her the outside world, every water source, every bit of cover. They ran together, lay together, but mostly the male took her, claiming her for his own over and over.

Light streaked across the sky when he turned her back to the house. They moved together to the side entrance leading to Alonzo's room. Timur was there to open the door for them, letting them into the sleeping chamber. The male leopard leapt onto the bed and she followed suit. He curled protectively around her, and exhausted, she fell asleep.

17

Pounding on the door penetrated Evangeline's sleep. She moved, trying to pry open her eyelids. It was impossible. A stone lay across her. She couldn't move at all and she was way too tired to care. She managed to get her eyes open partially and the light nearly blinded her. She groaned in protest.

"Go away," Alonzo snarled.

"Cops are here," Sevastyan informed them. "Timur might shoot them if you don't get out here."

"Let him," Alonzo muttered and buried his face in the hollow between her neck and shoulder.

Evangeline had to agree with Alonzo. She wasn't moving. Even the smallest of movements sent an ache spiraling through every muscle and bone in her body. Her leg, where she'd been shot, burned as if she'd run for miles on it — and maybe she had.

There was more pounding. Alonzo threw

a pillow at the door. Evangeline hissed and then tried to pull the covers over her head. "Go away, Sevastyan." The covers were under her. Under both of them. With Alonzo on top of her, she could barely breathe.

"You're heavy." She wasn't certain it was a complaint. She didn't want to move and breathing hurt anyway. He was warm and all muscle. He felt — nice.

"Spread your legs." He nuzzled her throat.

"No. I can't move. Not one single muscle."

He bit down gently on her chin and then suckled at the side of her neck, right over the spot where her pulse was beginning to accelerate.

"Yes." His knee slid between her legs and nudged.

"You have to do all the work. I'm not movin'."

His teeth scraped over her pulse. "You'll move. You like to move even when I tell you not to." He bit down. "Spread." The order was muffled against her neck.

At first she felt only the lazy brush of his tongue and then the bite. Her body responded with damp liquid, already hot and welcoming for him. Then he was inside her, filling her. There was always that moment when she thought it was too much, he wouldn't fit, but then her tight muscles gave way for his invasion and she surrounded his thick cock with a fist of hot silk. He felt hot. Hard. He stretched her so that she could feel his blood pulsing to his heartbeat right through his cock.

He was right. She had to move. She couldn't help herself. It was a beautiful way to wake up, regardless of whether her leopard had been out all night having wild leopard sex. She was happy. Alonzo made love to her, slowly and leisurely, but it was every bit and more satisfying and sexy than his wild, aggressive sex. She found her body coiling tighter and tighter, the pressure almost unbearable. And then he was taking them both over the edge. He kissed her when they both could breathe again, ignoring the pounding on the door until she found herself hiding her face on his chest and laughing.

"I might have to kill him," Alonzo said.

"Well don'. At least not while the cops are here. I don' want to have to visit my man in prison." She pressed kisses over his chest, following the whip marks there.

"Are you all right? It was brutal last night." He rolled off of her to inspect her body for bruises.

"It actually was wonderful thanks to you."

473

"Alonzo!" Sevastyan's voice was persistent.

"We'll shower and be right there. Tell them they'll have to wait," Alonzo called back. He kissed several bruises on her body, two low down close to her hip, and then lapped at the marks of possession he'd deliberately put on her.

"I'm good. Really. Let's shower and see what the cops want."

"They may ask you if I was here all night."

"Weren't you?" She raised an eyebrow. "I thought you were. I went to our room to take a bath so you could play cards or whatever you were doin', but you came in later."

He nodded, a slight smile softening his mouth for just a moment. "That's my girl. Keep it simple."

She shrugged. "I don' know anythin', so I can't very well do anythin' else."

The tiled shower was large and spacious with two shower heads. They took advantage of them, although Alonzo clearly wasn't playing fair and kept sliding soapy hands over her body, just to help her out. She was laughing even more when she stepped out to wrap her hair with a towel.

"I've got to get back to work." She pulled on a long flowing skirt and a matching peasant blouse. Alonzo had bought both for her. She loved feeling girlie after all the years in the swamp. She didn't bother with shoes. He hadn't either.

"Not until Doc gives you the okay. Don't worry, we're watching over it. Nothing is going to happen. Besides, I have a surprise for you."

She raised an eyebrow at him. "I've had enough surprises, Fyodor. You're too generous. Half the clothes in my drawers you bought for me."

"We're going to move everything to the master bedroom. I've decided to negotiate with Siena for the estate. I've got a good amount of money saved and I think I can swing it. I'm not just going to take it from her."

"Really?" She couldn't help slipping her arm around his waist and hugging him. "I love this place. My leopard does too. It's perfect for her. For the both of them to run free and not get into trouble."

He nodded. "My male let me know your female was crazy about the grounds. It's defensible and I've lived here for years. I know the place inside and out. With you here, it feels like a home."

"I'll admit, that's a good surprise."

"That's not the surprise." He dropped a

kiss on the top of her head. "We're getting married. That's not the surprise either."

"Whoa. Back up, Fyodor. You're movin' too fast for me. I just said I'd move in with you, and now you want to get married."

"Immediately. I'm not taking any chances with you running off."

"I don' run off."

"You did last night."

She rolled her eyes at him. "If I ran off, baby, you wouldn't ever be able to catch up with me. You just think you could."

"I like that you're so confident. Keep believing that, *malyutka.*"

Alonzo swept his arm around her and they went out of his room together. Evangeline wasn't surprised to see Brice and his friend Reeve in the sitting room along with two uniformed cops. She smiled at them. Alonzo didn't remove his arm. If anything, he pressed her front to his side, keeping her under the protection of his shoulder.

"How unexpected to see you here, Brice," she greeted. "Alonzo told me you were a cop working undercover. Where's Crispin? I've never seen one without the other."

Alonzo could have smirked over the complete honesty in her voice. No way could either of the undercover detectives believe she was anything but innocent. "What can we do for you?" he asked.

His marks were all over Evangeline. She made no attempt to hide them. The neckline of her blouse was low, revealing the creamy swell of her breasts. Right at the top of the curve on her left was another strawberry with his bite in the center. He fucking loved that.

"Please sit down," Evangeline said, indicating the comfortable armchairs and couch. "Can I get you anythin'? Coffee? I haven't done any bakin', I'm still recuperatin', but I make a mean cup of coffee."

"No, thank you, Evangeline," Brice said. "We're here on business."

She frowned and looked up at Alonzo. "Okay. Sure." She looked and sounded puzzled.

Perfect. He loved that too. Alonzo sank into a chair and pulled her down beside him. It was a snug fit, but she didn't seem to mind.

Evangeline leaned toward Brice, her gaze steady on his face. "What can we help you with?"

We. He loved that too. She was sitting there in the chair with him, relaxed, looking as if they belonged and talking as natural as could be. Brice winced. He couldn't hide that from Alonzo, but Alonzo didn't gloat.

He kept his features expressionless. Pure ice.

"Evangeline, were Alonzo and his crew home last night?"

She frowned. Looked up at Alonzo and over into the corner where Timur lounged against the wall. "Yes. I mean, I wasn't with them every single minute, but they were here when I went back to the bedroom to take a bath and they were here when I got out. So unless they raced out during my bath, then yes, they were home." She raised one eyebrow. "Why?"

"How long was your bath?"

Her frown deepened. "Is somethin' wrong, Brice?"

"Just answer the question."

"When you talk to her, you can be respectful," Alonzo said. "Or you can leave our home. I don't much like your tone."

"It's all right, honey," she said softly, looking up at him. She brushed her cheek along his shoulder. "He's obviously upset about somethin'. I don' know exactly, but usually about forty-five minutes. Maybe an hour."

"I can help with that," Sevastyan stirred from where he was in the shadows, directly across from the five policemen.

Brice scowled at him. So did Alonzo.

"You know how long she was in the bathtub?" Alonzo's voice said he'd better not know.

"It was forty-eight minutes," Sevastyan said helpfully, ignoring his boss's warning. "We were waiting for her to come back and make coffee. She makes a hell of a cup of coffee."

That much was true. No one could possibly dispute that. Alonzo pinned Brice with his ice-cold stare. "What is this about? I'm not into game playing. You made your bid for my woman and you lost. She's mine. She was always mine. Coming to my home on some bullshit pretense is beneath you."

"Crispin has disappeared." Brice watched him closely and then flicked his gaze to take in Evangeline.

Alonzo didn't dare look down at her. She didn't have a poker face. That was one of the things he loved most about Evangeline. She was exactly who you saw. No subterfuge. For a man like him, one who spent his entire life one way or another in a crime family, her innocence was like a breath of fresh air.

"I don' understand, Brice." She spoke very softly, genuinely concerned. "Why would he disappear? How long has he been gone?"

"He didn't show up for work this morning and we went to check on him. He was gone. He doesn't answer his cell. He's vanished. We can't even raise him by calling or trying to track his cell."

"Just this mornin'?" There was relief in Evangeline's voice. "He could be anywhere, Brice."

The cop shook his head. "No. Someone took him. His security camera was offline. His house was armed as if he'd left himself. No signs of a struggle."

"I'm more confused than ever. It sounds like he just is runnin' a little late," she said. She frowned, looking from Brice to Reeve. "Brice, are you accusin' Alonzo of somethin'? Of kidnappin' Crispin? Because if you are, that's just ludicrous."

Now there was a little bite to her voice, and Alonzo loved that as well. He didn't have to say a thing. He kept his gaze glued to Brice, who looked more uncomfortable by the moment. The detective didn't want to disclose the fact that Crispin's cell phone had mysteriously shown up on his captain's desk along with a file showing the payoffs the undercover officer had been taking. The phone had countless pictures on it, ones Crispin had taken showing he had participated in shakedowns, sex with unwilling prostitutes and one particularly damning picture showing him doing cocaine with Patrizio Amodeo. How he'd taken that picture without Amodeo knowing, Alonzo would never know.

"Alonzo and Crispin weren't friends."

"So?" Now she looked outraged. "I'm not friends with lots of people, but that doesn't mean I'm goin' to harm them in some way. And he'd have to do the kidnappin' while I was takin' my bath because we weren't exactly sleepin' last night."

Alonzo could have kissed her. He raised his eyes and caught the smirk in Timur's eyes. Yeah, his woman was truly magnificent. He was glad his brother could witness her defense of him.

"Do you know a man by the name of Patrizio Amodeo?" Brice changed tactics, his gaze pinning Evangeline's.

She nodded. "He's a horrible man. He came into my bakery a couple of days before I was shot and made a pass at me. Well . . ." she hedged. "Not exactly a pass. He was insultin' and thought he could put his hands on me. I wanted to smash him over the head with a fryin' pan."

She gave a genuine shudder and slid her hand into Alonzo's larger one. He closed his fingers around hers immediately and brought her knuckles to his mouth. She just was too honest not to be believed. No one could mistake the expressions on her face or fail to hear the truth in her voice. She was better than any lawyer Alonzo had, although he wondered where his lawyer was. Timur had to have called him. He would have to stop her from answering if Brice pulled any bullshit.

"He's dead," Brice said abruptly. "He died conveniently in a fire last night."

Evangeline gasped and her fingers curled inside of Alonzo's. "I don' understand, Brice. First it's Crispin disappearin', although there's no sign that he actually was harmed in any way, and now Amodeo's fire. Do you think Alonzo or one of the boys had somethin' to do with either of those two things? Because even if my bath took an hour, that's a little preposterous to believe."

The way she said it made it sound as if Brice had lost his mind and was on some personal vendetta, because no way could Alonzo and his crew be responsible for Crispin's disappearance and a fire as well. Alonzo just happened to know that the two men lived on opposite ends of San Antonio. San Antonio was the third largest city in Texas and the Arnotto estate was nestled in the hill country outside of San Antonio.

"Are they tryin' to pin somethin' on you

that you didn't do, Alonzo?" She sounded a little afraid.

"They have cameras all over the city, *devochka moya*. They can track any vehicle and most of the time tell who is in the car, isn't that right, Brice?" He kept his voice gentle. Soft. Loving, even. She needed that. She'd been delivered a blow whether Brice could see it or not. She knew he'd been gone. Now Crispin had disappeared and Amodeo was dead. They both deserved death. He should have killed Amodeo long before the man had a chance to put a contract out on her.

He had wanted to believe he could live by Elijah's rules. They were putting their own men in place of crime lords, taking over territory to control the underworld. There was no stopping corruption. No matter how many cops, how many people doing their best to prevent crime, someone would always break the law. Greed and power were huge motivators. When one head was chopped off, another grew, sometimes someone far worse than whomever had been stopped. They hoped to take the worst out and minimize the crimes in their streets.

He rubbed her hand along his jaw. He hadn't shaved and he had a shadow. That stubble provided the same kind of radar as his leopard's whiskers did. When she touched him, he felt that touch driving straight to his cock. He wanted to push her hand down to cover the thick erection building in his groin — he would have if the cops hadn't been there. His men were leopard and they could just leave. It was his home, now that she was in it. *Home.* He savored the word. He'd never had a home. He'd never thought he'd have one. That he could sit in a room and want his woman to wrap her fist around his cock and bring him pleasure beyond belief.

Her eyes jumped to his face and for one moment there was only the two of them in the room. He saw very, very clearly that she had exactly the same idea, that she wanted to wrap her fist around his cock. Her tongue touched her lips. Moistened top and bottom. He nearly groaned. She wanted more than her fist around his cock. His erection went from semi-hard to just plain aching, throbbing, pulsing hard. *Holy hell.* He was in trouble with her. He could find control when it was only him, but it would be impossible if she didn't help him.

He leaned down, one hand going to her hair, bunching there, his thumb sliding along her cheek as he raised her head and lowered his even more so his lips were against her ear. "You're going to pay for that."

Her eyes darkened. Burned for him. Were lost in him, just the way he wanted when the room was full of tension and suspicion was on him. She'd said she loved him. She'd *said* it. But they had been in the midst of the Han Vol Dan and who knew what a woman might say when her body was on fire and desperately needed her man? He needed her to love him. He needed it to be true. The way she looked at him, he could almost make himself believe it was the truth.

She reached for his hand, the back of hers sliding into his palm. Automatically his fingers closed around it. Her hand was so small, she felt fragile in his large one. Delicate. Who knew that a woman could be made of steel when her skin was softer than satin and her mouth was heaven? She exerted a little pressure as if she wanted her hand to drop, her gaze steady on his. He knew the cop was talking, asking more bullshit questions. He heard every one. He kept his eyes locked with Evangeline's as he relaxed his arm and allowed her to guide them where she wanted to go.

She shifted a little in the chair, shivering as if cold. Automatically, with his free hand, he reached for the nearest throw always kept on the back of the chair. He knew immediately what it was for. He tossed it over them and she smiled innocently up at him.

"Thank you, honey. With no fire in here, it can get cold."

It was about to get hot. She didn't settle her hand on his groin right away. She laid her palm very gently just above his growing, lengthening cock so that it reached for her from beneath his now very uncomfortable trousers.

Her fingertips brushed the sensitive crown of his cock. Back and forth. Right through his trousers. His breath caught in his throat as blood surged hotly and he thickened even more. He hadn't thought that possible. For the first time in his life, with an enemy near, his attention was centered somewhere else. He could barely think with the roaring in his ears.

Her gaze shifted to Brice, who scowled at her. "Is your name even Brice?"

He had the grace to look uncomfortable. "I was working." Immediately he realized just how bad that sounded. He'd been flirting with her for weeks. He'd asked her out repeatedly.

"I see." She drew the word out.

Her hand moved over Alonzo's cock, rubbing gently, persistently, sliding lower to find his balls and massage them as well. A little jackhammer began tripping in his head. His blood pooled. Her hand felt like sin to him.

"You don't see. I didn't want to give you a false name, but I was working undercover."

"Who were you investigatin' in my bakery?" She lifted her chin, her voice very quiet. "Me? Were you comin' in every day to investigate me?"

Alonzo stirred beside her. He didn't like where the conversation was going. He hadn't wanted to be questioned in front of her about the fire or the dirty cop, but she seemed satisfied with his answers. She knew Amodeo had put a contract out on her. She knew a hit squad had come to their home. Now the topic had shifted to something much more personal, and Alonzo didn't want anything personal between his woman and another man.

Her fingers moved again, this time to the front of his trousers. His breath hissed out of his throat as she grasped the zipper with her thumb and index finger, opening the front of his trousers. He'd dressed hastily, pulling on clothes without bothering with underwear, and his cock, already hard and ferocious, sprang free. Her palm covered him, fingers wrapping around his thick shaft.

His breath caught in his throat and he held himself very still, grateful for the years of discipline that taught him control.

"I'd like to talk to you in private, Evangeline," Brice pleaded.

"No." Alonzo made that clear, his voice a soft whip.

Timur and Sevastyan both moved very subtly, just enough to draw attention to their very silent presence.

Brice bit back a curse. "I was working on something that had nothing to do with Alonzo Massi, although the moment I saw him in there, I knew you were in danger. Do you have any idea who this man is?"

"Brice," Reeve, his partner, cautioned.

"No." Brice shook off the warning hand on his shoulder. "She needs to know who she's in bed with."

Alonzo's leopard roared with rage. *What if she listens to him?* It was the same question Alonzo asked himself. He had tried to tell her about his past. He'd never shared that with anyone.

Her thumb moved to the broad head of his cock, smearing the drops of anticipation all over the crown. She sighed and abruptly pulled her hand out from under the blanket, shifted toward him and brought her knees up.

"Who Alonzo is, is my man." She brought her open hand up to cover her mouth.

"Antonio Arnotto owned this estate," Brice snapped. "He was as dirty as he could get. One of the big bosses. I'm talking mafia, Evangeline. Running guns. Prostitution. Drugs. Not a good man. He had people murdered. Your man worked for him as one of his soldiers. Probably an enforcer. In case you didn't know, that's a man who makes someone the boss points at die."

Her hand slipped back under the blanket, palm wrapping tightly around him. Her palm was wet and she pumped her fist in a slow glide up his shaft and then back down. She was killing him. Pleasure burst through him, radiating out from his cock to his belly and down his thighs. Her touch could do that, but it was so much more than her hand on him. It was the fact that she would give him pleasure secretly in a room filled with cops. Cops telling her things that should make her run. She wasn't running, she was snuggled into him, her hand working him slowly.

"Arnotto was murdered right here in this room, Evangeline," Brice continued. "One of his own men shot him. His granddaughter is now married to the boss of one of the worst crime families in the mafia. They originated in South America and spread their filth throughout several countries. Elijah Lospostos is your man's friend."

Her fingers danced and slid, her fist squeezing even tighter. "I've met Elijah. He seems very nice."

Brice glared at her. "Are you listening to me at all? Alonzo Massi took over Antonio Arnotto's territory. That's who you're in bed with. A man running those same things. Drugs. Prostitution. Guns. Murder. Murder, as in taking out a crime boss such as Amodeo and a cop like Crispin."

"Oh, for heaven's sake, Brice," she snapped. "I've had enough of this. If there isn't anythin' else, and there shouldn't be, I'd like you to leave. You've insulted Alonzo and my boys and you came on what is clearly a fishin' expedition."

Her hand slid right down Alonzo's shaft to cup his balls. She worked them gently, rolling and massaging until his entire body was on fire and lightning streaked through his body. His cock jerked, and she pushed one knee higher so that the blanket tented more, preventing anyone from seeing what was going on.

The leopards knew. They could scent his

heightened state. The smell of sex and sin right there in the room. He caught Timur and Sevastyan exchanging smirks of approval. They didn't want her listening to the cops any more than he did.

"The thing with Crispin is silly," she continued. "It sounds as if you made it up just for an excuse to come to our home."

"So now it's your home?" Brice snapped belligerently.

Her chin lifted and her eyes blazed at him, her leopard close. "Yes. I've asked you to leave."

Reeve stood up immediately, as did the uniformed officers. Brice hesitated. "Evangeline, I'd really like to speak to you privately. I could explain . . ."

"That's not going to happen," Alonzo answered decisively. "We've given you our time. We didn't ask for a lawyer, although we probably should have since you were clearly accusing me of having something to do with the disappearance of your partner and perhaps the fire at Amodeo's. Either way, you have your answers and we'd like you to leave." He was shocked that he even had a voice with her hand working him. "Timur will show you out." Because he couldn't move.

Brice stood reluctantly. Neither Evangeline nor Alonzo moved. Timur started for the door, clearly indicating that they all leave. Alonzo allowed his gaze to sweep the room and the two archways leading to other rooms. The cleaners had done a good job. The cops had no idea that Amodeo had sent a hit squad to his house at the same time Amodeo's residence had gone up in flames.

"Clear the house, Timur," Alonzo managed to get out. "Evangeline has something she wants to say to me."

Brice glanced back to see Alonzo bunch Evangeline's hair in his fist, pulling her head back so he could fasten his mouth on hers possessively. The cop swore as he was shown out.

Alonzo couldn't think about anything but his throbbing cock. "Woman, you are a fucking menace."

"I know." She smiled complacently against his mouth.

He threw off the blanket and all but yanked her to the floor between his thighs. "Take off your clothes." Even as he bit out the command, he was shimmying out of his trousers. The relief was tremendous.

"In here?" She looked around her. The sitting room had open archways on either end leading to other rooms. They'd slept most of the morning away, so light spilled in from all directions.

"*Now*, Evangeline. You don't take them off, they'll be in shreds in under a minute."

She laughed softly, kneeling between his legs. "Such a savage. It's a wonder what a little thing like pettin' does to your disposition." She pulled her peasant blouse over her head and folded it just as he'd folded his trousers, her eyes on his the entire time. Her bra followed, spilling her breasts out into the open for him.

Her hands cupped both creamy mounds, her thumbs sliding over her nipples. "I ache, honey. So hot and swollen just thinking about your mouth on me."

"You tortured me in a room full of men. You don't get my mouth on you." He pointed to her skirt.

"I did, didn't I?" she teased, unrepentant. "Quite brilliantly, I might add."

"Get rid of that skirt. I swear to God, if there weren't so many men around here I'd just have you walk around naked all day. You're beautiful, Evangeline. I could look at you forever and never tire of the sight."

"They might walk in now and find me naked," she pointed out with a little shiver, but she stepped out of the skirt and panties, adding them neatly folded to her blouse and bra.

"If they do, they'll find you with your mouth busy. You need to finish what you started."

Her eyes laughed at him. "Did I start somethin'?" Her gaze dropped to his cock and she reached out and smeared the pearly drops across the head, sending darts of fire streaking through his shaft. "I'm burnin' for you. So damp. Just thinkin' about your cock so hard for me under that blanket with those idiots questionin' you. It was so sexy, knowin' what I was doin' to you while they sat there all self-righteous. If they stayed any longer actin' like you weren't worth my being with you, I might have gotten on my knees right in front of them and showed them I practically worship you."

His cock jerked. He clenched his teeth. "Woman." His only warning. The fist in her hair pulled her head forward and down, right over the top of him. "Open your mouth." Because she couldn't say things like that to him and not have his heart explode.

Her laughter teased at the crown. She blew warm air over him. He swore at her in Russian and pushed her head down over him, giving her no choice. Her mouth engulfed him. Took him deep. Nearly swallowed him. Her hands came up to massage his balls. She didn't grasp the base of his shaft to limit how deep he went; she worked him, hollowing her cheeks and suckling strongly.

He thought the top of his head might blow off. She had him so ready. He was leopard and they weren't modest by any means, stripping easily in front of one another in order to shift, so the fact that she had taken out his cock in a room full of men had been extremely hot to him. He loved that she wasn't shy about their sex life either. She wanted him and she made it known.

She gave herself up to pleasuring him. Enjoying herself. Loving what she was doing. She watched him, watched his face, his eyes. He watched her. The sight of his cock swallowed by her, her lips wrapped so tightly around the thick girth of his shaft nearly sent him over the edge. Her body was beautiful, her breasts swaying, her legs parted enough that he could see liquid gleaming on her bare mound for him. Her body loved what she was doing as well.

He placed both hands on her shoulders and stood, forcing her to tip her head back. He fisted her hair again and held her head while he began to move his hips. "That's it, *malyutka,* take all of me. Suck harder. Use your tongue." He gave her orders and watched the heat in her eyes darken to pure passion.

She followed his every instruction, relaxing her mouth as he picked up the pace, his fist tightening on her scalp. The pleasure was exquisite. Torture. Moist heat surrounded him. Her tongue was velvet, her cheeks soft, her throat tight.

"Can you take more? This is paradise, Evangeline. I need to know if you can take more."

She slid her arms up his thighs and around, to grip his buttocks, pulling him into her. Her mouth suckled hard. Her tongue lashed at him and stroked the underside of his rim. He took that as a yes and surged into her, nearly out of control. He'd never had a woman work his cock like she did, his leopard would never have allowed it. His body belonged to her alone, and she made certain he knew it.

He heard himself swearing over and over in Russian. His shaft swelled. Went deep. "I can't hold back, Evangeline," he warned.

He didn't want to stop. Not now. Not when it felt so fucking good. So perfect. She didn't pull back and he couldn't help his hips bucking, thrusting deep while he held her head in place. Her eyes never left his and she deliberately took him deeper. So deep. Her muscles massaged and squeezed.

He swelled more as fire streaked through his body, rushed through his veins. Deep in his balls, his seed boiled and churned and then rocketed, jet after jet pulsing into her. She didn't fight for air, but swallowed, massaging him even more.

She held his cock in her mouth, her tongue gentle. When he could finally breathe enough to withdraw, she followed after him, lapping at him. He closed his eyes, savoring the sensation and holding the vision of her on her knees, taking his cock down her throat, so that he could burn the image into his brain forever.

When he could, he reached down and lifted her, tossing her into the chair. The chair was wide enough for both of them to sit in. He caught both of her legs and placed them over the arms so she was spread very wide, completely open to him. He sank to the floor, lifted her butt into his hands, brought her to his mouth and without preamble, began to devour her.

Her cries had to be heard throughout the house. He loved the sound. He loved how there was no inhibition. She thrashed in the chair, but he clamped his hands on her, and his hands were large. His shoulders wedged between her thighs so she couldn't move her legs from off the arms of the chair. He indulged himself in the taste of her. She tasted like she baked, all honey and cinnamon spice. He could eat her for breakfast. Or lunch. Even dinner. He definitely liked her for his midnight snack.

He nuzzled her, inhaling the scent of her arousal. He made certain to rub his shadowed jaw over her bare mound and lips. She writhed and gasped when his teeth tugged first one lip and then the other. He devoured her again, sucking her clit, using his teeth to bring her to the edge, stabbing with his tongue, and then collecting more honey and spice.

Her body was flushed a beautiful rose all over. He loved that. He slid one hand free, making certain to keep her pinned with his shoulders so he could slip one thick finger into her, massaging her sensitive walls and especially that one spot that made her hips buck and her mouth form that perfect *O* in shock. He took her up again and again, but refused to allow her to soar. "You're so fucking hot, *malyutka.* I love looking at you. Feeling you. Just watching you come apart for me."

"I don' care how hot you think I am," she snapped between her clenched teeth. "Less playin'. Stop teasin'. Get to the comin' apart part."

"You did a lot of teasing," he mused, all thoughtful. He bent to her again, lapping at the honey and spice, tugging with his teeth, pushing deep with his finger to massage that hot little spot. "I need something from you."

"What?" she demanded through her ragged breathing.

"You want a reward, figure it out."

"You're such a baby, Fyodor. *Such* a baby. I told you with my hand and my mouth. Strippin' for you. Sheesh. Get on with it."

All the while he nuzzled her. Teased her. Smiled inside because Evangeline was pure happiness. The one thing he didn't do was let her come apart.

"Al*right.* I'm madly in love with you."

There it was. All his. "Now, Evangeline. Give it to me now." He sent her soaring because those six words had done it for him.

18

Evangeline was nervous. She didn't have many friends. She'd read a lot of books, and she'd done well in the bakery because she could keep a distance between herself and the customers. The counter was always there. She liked people, she just wasn't comfortable interacting closely with them.

Alonzo curled his palm around the nape of her neck and pulled her a little closer to him. "You aren't going to your doom, *malen'kaya lyublyu moyo.*"

She shot him a glance from under her lashes. He had no idea. "Why does it feel like it?" She narrowed her eyes at Timur, who had exchanged an amused glance with Gorya. "It's not funny."

"Yeah, it is. You take on my brother, his crazy-ass leopard and the cops, but you're afraid of a few women. That's hysterical."

"No more desserts for you." She poured hostility into her voice.

Timur grinned at her. "I've got news for you, *mladshaya sestra,* you don't have a mean bone in your body. Your threats are empty."

She rolled her eyes at him and gripped the two carriers she'd brought with her, desserts for the women she was meeting for the first time. "Maybe I shouldn't have brought anythin'. They might think I'm tryin' to show off."

"Anytime you bake, Evangeline, you're showing off," Timur said. "You're that good. They don't like it, they don't deserve your friendship."

She wanted to wrap herself in that compliment. More, in the genuine fact that she'd somehow gotten past his reserve and wariness that she might be out to harm his brother. "Thanks, Timur."

Alonzo pressed the doorbell firmly, not giving her any more time to rethink her decision to come. Elijah's home was a very large, sprawling house. Like the Arnotto estate, the Lospostos property had been landscaped and the mansion constructed with leopards in mind. Lots of secluded acreage for the cats to run, hidden passageways in the house as well as groves of trees for an arboreal highway. The property backed up to Jake Bannaconni's.

Alonzo had told her Jake and his wife, Emma, would be there. Also, Eli and Catarina Perez would be present. She would be meeting Siena for the first time. Siena was pregnant with triplets and, although it was early in the pregnancy, they were taking precautions, so everyone thought it best to meet at the Lospostos home.

She glanced back at the men surrounding them — the men she thought of as her "boys." Timur, Gorya, Sevastyan and Mitya. Mitya had no business being there, but for some reason Alonzo had insisted he come. He hadn't been out of the hospital that long, or for that matter, up. He was pale and still walked as though something hurt, but he would never admit it, at least not in front of her. He'd told her to quit fussing over him, but she ignored his order and just did it anyway. Timur, Gorya and Sevastyan laughed at him and told him he'd just have to live with it. They'd called her *little sister* in Russian and she hugged that to her as she stood there on the wide verandah wanting to run.

Alonzo bent down toward her, shifting his body slightly to put himself between her and the bodyguards. "You don't have to do this, Evangeline. If you're doing it for me, don't. You don't ever have to do anything you prefer not to."

She heard the ring of sincerity in his voice and her heart turned over. Just like that her nerves settled. If she could slip through the swamp, hunted by a dangerous male leopard and survive, she could do this. These women were extending the hand of friendship toward her, just as Saria had all those years ago when she was just a child. She'd been equally as afraid, but she'd let Saria into her life and it had proven to be one of the best things she'd ever done. She'd let Alonzo into her life, and it *was* the best thing she'd ever done.

"I'm doin' this for me, honey," she assured.

Timur snorted. "She calls him *honey,*" he whispered overly loud to Gorya.

Alonzo turned and cuffed his brother hard, all in one motion, his leopard leaping to the foreground to reprimand his sibling. Timur tried to get out of the way, but Alonzo was too fast. The huge paw hit him on the side of his head. Claws were sheathed, but the strike was a hard blow, making Timur stagger back.

Gorya, Sevastyan and Mitya snickered. Timur grinned even as he got his legs under him and shook his head to clear it. "Fuckin' maniac," he said.

Evangeline kicked Alonzo in the shins hard just as Elijah Lospostos opened his door. "I see you two are getting along," he greeted. He opened the door wider and waved them through, his gaze on Mitya.

The humor receded from Timur's face and he stepped through the door in front of his brother and Evangeline, on high alert, making certain it was safe before he allowed them inside.

Elijah shook his head, ignoring the fact that Timur insisted on inspecting the room before he allowed the couple in. "Evangeline, so good to see you again. Are you fully recovered?"

She nodded. "The doctor gave his okay for me to be workin' and I've been back for the last two weeks. Business has doubled, so I'm grateful for the cleanin' crew Alonzo hired. I've got a new employee, Jeremiah Wheating. I believe you recommended him." She kept the sarcasm out of her voice. Jeremiah Wheating was no baker or barista. He was leopard and already chafing a little at his assignment. She felt a little sorry for the boy. He wanted to be where the action was, not working behind a counter in a bakery.

"Jeremiah needs to learn patience," Elijah said. "He's young and he's had a few bad experiences. He's eager to prove himself. He'll be a good man if he can learn patience."

"Lovely that I'm the one teachin' him." The sarcasm slipped right out in spite of her determination to behave.

"Who better? You learned patience as a child. That trait is invaluable, especially in a shifter. The women are going to be in the far wing of the house, and we'd prefer you stay there because there's a meeting here today and not everyone coming is part of our alliance. It would be best, Evangeline, if you stay with my wife."

It was a subtle order. Something big was going on. She sent her man a look that told him she wasn't very happy with his subterfuge. He could have just told her. Her gaze fell on Mitya speculatively. Why had they brought him when he really needed to be resting? She was fairly certain it had something to do with their meeting.

"I thought this was a family get-together," she said, staring Alonzo straight in the eye. If the men were having some big secretive meeting, that meant she'd be alone with the other wives. It was silly to think she had to have him with her, but on the other hand, he'd implied that they were going to a barbecue. She'd brought dessert with her.

"The meeting won't be long," Alonzo assured. "Let's introduce you. I want you to meet Siena."

"She thinks she's as big as a house. Catarina is a little further along than she is and she's way smaller. I keep telling her that she's got three inside of her, but she doesn't listen." Elijah shook his head in exasperation.

He indicated for them to follow him down the wide hall to the opposite end of the house. There were three women in the large room and all three went silent and turned as they entered. Evangeline recognized both Emma Bannaconni and Siena Lospostos from pictures in magazines. She thought they were both beautiful. Emma held her baby, a boy a little over a month old. Siena was clearly very pregnant. She looked as if she might have swallowed a small beach ball. Catarina barely showed.

Siena smiled immediately. "Alonzo, you brought her. I didn't think you ever would and I threatened Elijah. If you didn't show up today, I was going to come to your house."

Evangeline had been living for just over four weeks on the Arnotto property and already she thought of it as her home. In that moment she realized the house, the entire estate, actually belonged to Siena. She'd known, but she'd thought of it as her home.

"I brought her," Alonzo assured, taking Evangeline's hand and walking her forward. "*Solnyshko moyo,* this is Siena. She is family to me. Siena, my Evangeline."

It was his voice that was nearly her undoing. The way he said *my Evangeline.* She would have done anything for him to hear that tone. To hear him say her name that way and claim her for his own.

"Evangeline, Siena. And that's Emma Bannaconni and Catarina Perez."

Evangeline forced a smile. Her belly was tied up in tight little knots. Emma Bannaconni was a gorgeous woman. Her hair was flaming red and very thick. She had enormous almond-shaped aquamarine eyes. She was very small, which surprised Evangeline because she didn't look that petite in her photographs.

Emma smiled sweetly at Evangeline all the while holding her sleeping son with expert hands. "So good to meet you. I wondered who would be melting Alonzo's heart."

Evangeline glanced up at her man. He didn't change expression, but she felt him wince. He didn't want anyone to know she'd melted his heart. She stepped a little

507

away from him, trying not to feel abandoned.

Elijah took the two dessert carriers out of her hands and put them on the table. "Looks good, Evangeline. You women can't eat all this. How about letting me have one of these for our meeting? I can serve them with coffee." He lifted one of the cases and peered through the transparent plastic.

"It's good to finally meet you as well," Evangeline said, ignoring Elijah. "Alonzo told me you were in the hospital the same time I was."

Emma nodded. "Yes. I had a little trouble with this one, but it all came out right in the end. I have two more, a daughter and another son, but I left them with the nanny at home. I thought it would be nice to have a little time with friends."

"I'm so glad you agreed to come visit us," Catarina said. Her dark hair was long and wavy, falling in a waterfall of shimmering silk down her back. She had very unusual cobalt blue eyes surrounded by long dark lashes. Her full lips turned up at the corners just slightly. She was very curvy and had a little pouch where her baby hid. "I love to bake or cook and I'm so happy to have another person to share recipes with. Emma loves cooking as well. We're always comparing recipes."

"Did you notice the absence of a name when they're talking about cooking abilities?" Siena said, laughing softly. "I can't cook or bake. Elijah does most of it for us." She smiled up at him with her generous mouth. She had perfect Italian skin, large cat-shaped brilliant green eyes with lush, thick black lashes. If that wasn't enough, she had a straight nose, high cheekbones, beautiful teeth and rich dark hair, very thick.

Elijah instantly was beside her, reaching down for her hand and threading his fingers through hers. "I like to cook. It relaxes me. I also like you sitting in that chair in the kitchen talking to me while I cook. That relaxes me too."

Siena laughed. "He means the lounge chair he paid a fortune for. It's super comfortable and is supposed to have back support and all kinds of other benefits. Elijah researched for weeks and then tested it out so it would be perfect, and it is."

Evangeline found she liked Elijah Lospostos just for buying his pregnant wife a comfortable chair to sit in while he cooked. That was sweet. She also liked that he didn't mind showing them all how much he loved her.

"I am not a good cook," Alonzo said. "I'm

very thankful Evangeline is."

"Did your mother love cooking?" Emma asked.

Evangeline's heart accelerated. She hadn't considered that the women would be curious about her and ask questions. They weren't prying so much as being friendly, trying to get to know her. She was so closed off to others that it hadn't occurred to her exactly what would transpire.

Alonzo moved closer to her again, close enough that she could feel his body heat. She shook her head, her chin going up a fraction. "No, I didn't know my mother, but a friend of mine, Saria Donovan, introduced me to Pauline Lafont. She owned the inn Saria has now. Pauline taught me to cook and to bake. I didn't talk a lot and it was somethin' we could do together that didn't require a lot of talkin'."

"Saria is married to Drake Donovan," Emma said. "Drake is a dear friend of ours. You'll meet Jake in just a few minutes. He's around here somewhere, talking to Eli and Joshua. I haven't met Saria yet, but I heard she was planning to visit soon. She's expecting as well."

Catarina nodded. "Look out, Evangeline, shifters don' fool around when it comes to gettin' their woman in the family way."

Evangeline could hear the bayou in her voice and immediately identified with her. The accent was strong, as was hers. She couldn't help smiling. "He knows better." Deliberately she put a threat into her voice and glared up at him.

He held up both hands in surrender. "It isn't my fault if you can't resist me. I peel you off of me every night, but you don't stay on your side of the bed." Even teasing, there was little inflection in his voice, as if he had forgotten how to talk with any kind of expression. His voice was always low and compelling, but without a single teasing note.

The women laughed anyway, Siena especially. "That's the most I've ever heard you say, Alonzo," she said. "*Ever.* I didn't know you knew how to talk."

Evangeline liked knowing she got Alonzo's words. That she got his real past and therefore his real name.

He swept his arm around her and took her with him to the door. Bending down, he cupped her face in his hands. "I've got to go, *malyutka,* but I'm assured this won't take very long. Jake and Eli will be in here with you. There will be two of my men just outside the door. If you need me for anything at all, you tell them and one will come get me."

His blue eyes moved over her face, and her heart clenched. He was certainly giving away the fact that he cared about her now. He kept his voice very low, but there was no mistaking body language.

"I mean what I say, Evangeline. Any reason at all. You're uncomfortable, you need to send for me. Understand?"

She knew she would be all right. Just knowing he was leaving two men behind in case she needed him meant the world. She'd wondered why he'd brought along Kirill and Matvei. She was getting to know them. She knew Kirill and Sevastyan had been childhood friends. Matvei was also from the same lair. He'd followed Kirill and Sevastyan to the United States and then to San Antonio.

"I will," she agreed.

"Kiss me."

His order shocked her. If he was trying to play it cool, he wasn't succeeding. She didn't hesitate. Her arms went around his neck, she leaned her body into his and brought his head down even as she went up on her toes. He tasted like love to her. Like everything sensual. Dark, dangerous and wholly wonderful. Her tongue tangled and danced with his, and then he took over, the way he often did when he was kissing her, sweeping every sane thought away until there was only feeling. Only Alonzo.

"I'll hurry," he said, lifting his head slowly, taking his time in the same way he had with his kisses. "Enjoy yourself."

"I will." She watched him leave with Elijah. He was so beautiful, that fluid, easy way he moved in silence. When she turned back, all three women were staring at her.

"Oh. My. God." Siena immediately was out of her chair and coming across the room toward Evangeline. "That was so beautiful. The way he looked at you. The way he touched you. I wanted that for him." She kept coming until she had Evangeline enveloped in her arms. "I think of him like my brother. I never had any siblings, so I've claimed Alonzo. Thank you. Thank you for giving him that."

Evangeline was terrified Siena would get hurt just walking around. "Are you supposed to be up?"

Siena laughed and held her at arm's length. "Of course I can be up. Just not for long periods of time. Doc doesn't want me to take any chances. I'm not exactly running races. He said I can be in the swimming pool lazing around. And I can go for short walks. No shifting. My poor girl can't go running at night, but she understands we have to protect the babies. I haven't told Elijah yet, but she says they're females."

Emma burst out laughing. "Jake is going to have a field day giving him a bad time. He thinks one daughter is bad enough."

Evangeline wanted to help Siena back to her chair but didn't know how to make her go without acting bossy. "Do you know what you're having yet, Catarina?" She tried not to sound desperate for conversation, and in any case she genuinely wanted to know.

"We're havin' a boy. Eli's all happy about that because he says a girl should have an older brother to look out for her. He's not exactly hip to this century."

"None of them are," Emma said. "Come sit down, Evangeline. Really, it's so nice to have another woman to join us. We're in our own little world here, and we have to be. Having friends and knowing our children will have friends is such a bonus. I wouldn't trade Jake or our life for anything, but it did get lonely before Catarina and Siena came along."

Siena put her arm around Evangeline's waist and walked her back to the others. The couches and chairs looked very comfortable. Evangeline took the chair between where Siena had been sitting and Catarina.

"Elijah said you and Joshua are first cousins. Joshua doesn't say much. Emma knows him better than Catarina and I," Siena said. "He worked for Jake for a long time before he took over Rafe Cordeau's territory."

Evangeline tried not to think about that too much. She knew there was far more to Alonzo's business than met the eye but she didn't know the entire story and she didn't want the other women to know that.

"Joshua was raised in Borneo. I was raised in Louisiana. We actually don' really know each other."

"He's always been really quiet. Not like Alonzo," Emma said. "I never heard Alonzo talk until he did here in this room."

Siena laughed. "He was my bodyguard ever since I was fifteen, and I don't think I heard him say more than three sentences. But if he looked at one of the men they did exactly what he wanted them to do. I guess he didn't need to actually talk."

Jake and Eli walked in and closed the door behind them. Both men went straight to their respective wives and kissed them before turning to Evangeline. Siena made the introductions.

Jake Bannaconni was an imposing man. It

wasn't just about his looks. He clearly was leopard and had the added advantage of muscle and power clinging to him. He was highly intelligent and that showed in the burn of his golden eyes. He owned several oil fields and was renowned for discovering new pockets of oil. More, he acquired companies and often took them apart.

Eli Perez was a very scary-looking man. Like Alonzo, danger clung to him, but he looked rough and scarred. He had tattoos everywhere and his muscles were the roped, powerful muscles of a leopard. He moved with fluid grace and had eyes for one person — Catarina. He smiled at Evangeline and devoured the baked goods along with Jake, but mostly he watched his wife and saw to her every need. It was a little shocking to see the man wait on her. He didn't seem the type, but then neither did Alonzo. When she'd been laid up in bed, he'd been the one to bring her everything she could possibly want.

"Why did Alonzo bring Mitya?" The question slipped out before she could stop herself.

Jake smiled at her. "Your man will no doubt tell you that, and you won't be happy with him." He took another bite of her cannoli. "This is heaven. You know how to bake. I thought our Catarina was the number-one baker but you just might give her a run for her money."

"What are they up to?" She wasn't going to be distracted by compliments.

"You'll know soon enough," Jake said, making it clear he wasn't about to give her information if Alonzo didn't want her to have it.

She made a mental note to tell Alonzo she wanted to be informed of everything that had to do with her family, and that included her boys. If he didn't like it, he would have to learn to live with it. He knew when he'd chosen her that she wasn't a woman to be pushed aside easily.

Alonzo and Joshua were seated at the table to Elijah's right. Elijah's bodyguard, Joaquin, brought in Emilio and two other men Alonzo had never met. One was introduced as Fredo Lombardi and the other was Ulisse Mancini. Alonzo had heard of both.

Ulisse ran a counterfeiting ring that was very successful. Mitya's father had wanted in on it in a bad way. Ulisse was a shark, always hungry for more territory and power. From what Elijah had said, the other bosses were leery of Ulisse.

Fredo Lombardi was clearly an ally of

Elijah's. He was younger than Ulisse and a bit older than Elijah. He'd taken over the reins of his father's business a few years earlier, and was someone who was considered very steady. He had few enemies, because he didn't appear greedy. He conducted his business quietly and seemed a company player, although Elijah had told Alonzo that the man was no one to mess with. He was genial because he could afford to be.

Emilio was all smiles, but his smile didn't quite reach his eyes when he looked at Alonzo. "I hear congratulations are in order," he said without preamble once introductions were made.

Alonzo inclined his head. "Thank you."

Emilio turned his gaze on Joshua. "I thought you said she was unavailable. Was I mistaken?"

Joshua smiled easily. "I'm sorry, Emilio. I knew that Alonzo was courting my cousin, but they were keeping it under the radar. I didn't want there to be any bad feelings between you two should a misunderstanding have occurred."

Emilio nodded, still hanging on to his smile. "Let's get down to business."

Elijah stood up and went to the large screen, bringing up a conference table with seven men seated at it. "Gentlemen, can you hear us clearly?"

"Yes, Elijah. We're ready." The man at the head of the table tapped his palm several times as an indicator that all talk should cease. "We've come together to discuss what should be done with Patrizio Amodeo's territory. Several suggestions have been made and three people's names have been put up to take over. We need to vote. Emilio has put in a request. The two territories are next to each other and it would make some sense. Elijah has put in the name of a man wronged by Amodeo. It is unexpected and highly unusual to say the least, but he has backing in this. Two others have put in Alonzo Massi's name as he was also wronged by Amodeo."

Emilio's smile faded. Before he could say anything, Alonzo did. "I appreciate the vote of confidence, but my territory is already quite large and still new to me. With the advice of the men here at this table, I've been slowly working to understand the scope of Antonio's businesses. They are vast and complex. To take on Amodeo's territory at this time would be spreading myself thin. I prefer to keep the Arnotto legacy strong."

Several of the bosses at the conference

table nodded their heads in approval, as did Emilio. He was smiling again.

"Emilio, you have the floor," Mario Esposito said.

Emilio nodded and stood up. "I have been in this business now many years. My father was in this business of ours. Patrizio wronged Alonzo, it is true, and he should never have betrayed our alliances that way. He was a man with little regard for others. His soldiers are without guidance and his businesses left in chaos. I believe I can provide that guidance quickly as I was privy to quite a few of Patrizio's dealings." He sat down.

"Ulisse?" Mario prompted.

Ulisse nodded. "I will cast my vote for Emilio."

"Elijah, you have another candidate in mind?" Mario said.

Elijah stood. He made an imposing figure. He was far younger than Emilio and looked as tough as nails. He'd been born into the life and he'd worked his way up. His territory was international. "Patrizio Amodeo harmed more than one man. Mitya Amurov is the man his hit squad shot."

There was instant silence. The name Amurov was known throughout the world as one of the most brutal and powerful names in the business. "Mitya is the son of Lazar Amurov, although he is no longer affiliated with his father's businesses. He was nearly killed. He grew up in this business of ours. He would come in under the alliance here with Alonzo, Joshua, Fredo, Emilio and Ulisse."

"No. No." Emilio jumped to his feet. "He's Russian. We can't get in bed with the Russian mob. They are never satisfied with their territories. They always seek more. Always. No, this man cannot possibly join us."

"Emilio." Mario's voice held warning. "The man sitting across from you, the one you know as Alonzo Massi, is in fact Russian. He is Fyodor Amurov, son of the late Patva Amurov. Fyodor joined Antonio's soldiers many years ago, and Antonio thought it best that he become Italian."

That was the story Elijah had sold to the other bosses and they believed him. They weren't all Italian American. Two were just plain American. It made sense to them that Antonio would want to keep the origins of his soldier, a valued enforcer, from the others, especially that he was Russian. They had a loose alliance with the *bratya,* but they didn't necessarily want them in their ranks. Now one was a boss and another was put

521

before them as a potential boss.

"No." Emilio shook his head again. "Absolutely not. These men operate separately from the organization. They don't recognize one collective group or head. Mario, listen to me. I have had dealings with them and they . . ."

Mario lifted his head. "Dealings with them? In what capacity? You said nothing of dealing with the Russians."

There was a sudden silence. Emilio subsided, settling himself at the table with great dignity. Alonzo could see he was very careful not to look at Ulisse, and the other man stared down at the table with a small frown on his face.

"It was nothing more than an inquiry but it didn't go anywhere," Emilio said. "I'm just pointing out that they think differently than we do."

Alonzo lifted his hand. "Emilio is right. The brotherhood in my country is run very differently. It is for that very reason that I decided to come here and work for Antonio Arnotto. He taught me a better way. The way of a family."

Ulisse sighed and shook his head. "Antonio was a great man. He spoke highly of you at all times. He put his granddaughter in your hands, and more than once you kept her safe in spite of impossible odds. Everyone knows your reputation. But what do we know of Mitya Amurov? His father, Lazar, is one of the cruelest and bloodiest men known to us. He's a shark. He eats people and territories alive. Your father was . . ."

"Patva Amurov. Lazar is my uncle. Mitya is my cousin. My entire family was wiped out when our territory was attacked. Only Timur and Gorya survived. I came to the United States to work for Antonio Arnotto when he reached out to me. I realized had we been structured differently, that wouldn't have happened. I would still have my family. Although their families and territories were still intact, I knew Mitya and Sevastyan felt the same as I did. There had to be a better way. They followed me here."

"Alonzo" — Ulisse leaned forward — "what of your uncles? What happens when they find out their nephews and sons are working for us? What happens when they demand we do business with them? And they will."

Alonzo shrugged. "Any problem with my uncles will stay my problem. If they wish to go to war, it is with Mitya and me. They are businessmen above all else. It would be a disaster for them to go to war with all of you. You and I both know it is a symbiotic relationship. If they ask for favors, Elijah will be told immediately."

He'd just cut the legs out from under Emilio, but he did it in such a way that he seemed to be backing him up. He couldn't be faulted on his logic. Antonio Arnotto had been considered one of their best businessmen. He was well respected by everyone, as was Elijah Lospostos. Alonzo had the endorsement of both men. He had offered to take on any problems with the *bratya*.

"Mitya grew up in this business. He understands what is needed to lead. He was groomed for leadership, but he came up from the bottom so he appreciates his soldiers. He understands loyalty and family."

Emilio snorted. "The *bratya* does not hold family sacred. There are rumors that Lazar Amurov murdered his own wife to prove his loyalty."

"Lazar Amurov murdered his wife because he likes to kill," Alonzo explained in that same low tone devoid of all expression. "As did my father and Sevastyan's father. My father killed my *mother.* Some things should be sacred. Antonio Arnotto cherished his granddaughter. I saw that every day. I want a family. That is important to me. This . . ."

He swept his arm around to take in the

conference table and the men sitting there. "This is a family. This is where I belong."

Fredo nodded. "I knew Mitya Amurov when he was attending the university with my son. He is a good man and very intelligent. He is also extremely loyal and has connections we all could use once he is established."

There was a small silence. Mario nodded slowly. "If no one else has anything to say . . ."

Ulisse stood up. "I respect all that *Fyodor* has to say, but the fact remains that he acquired his territory under false pretenses. He acquired it as Alonzo Massi, not Fyodor Amurov. I know this man's reputation, and he is one of the worst of the Amurovs. How do we know he's telling us the truth? Excuse me, Fyodor, but we need to make absolutely certain of what we're doing here. Loyalty is needed in our business, and you were not raised that way."

Elijah stood up, facing Ulisse. "This man is known to me. He used that fierceness to protect Siena, my wife. He stood for her when every other one of her grandfather's soldiers stood solidly behind the man who beat, kidnapped and tried to rape her. He risked his life for her over and over, even to the point of coming to my home when she was with me. Alone. Knowing I would kill him if he made one slipup. He still came to make certain she was safe. That is loyalty. He wasn't getting paid. Antonio was dead. He'd opposed Paolo Riso and there was a price on his head. Still, he didn't run. He didn't throw in with Riso; he protected Siena. That's loyalty. That's a sense of family. I knew who he was and so did Siena. I asked him to take over the Arnotto territory for Siena. He didn't want to do it, said he was a soldier, Siena's soldier. That's loyalty, Ulisse. I don't think you ever have to question his loyalty or his desire for a family. He's already that much a part of this thing of ours."

Elijah sank back into his chair, leaving Ulisse still standing. The man stood for another few moments while the seconds ticked by. Alonzo saw Emilio's hand come up to subtly tap Ulisse's wrist. Only then did the man nod as if he understood and agreed with everything Elijah had said.

"We vote. Everyone in favor of allowing Mitya Amurov the Amodeo territory raise their hand."

The vote was overwhelming in favor of Mitya. Elijah had already done the preliminary work for Mitya. Emilio had made a few enemies stepping on others to get what he wanted. Now, when he was weakened by several of his companies being swallowed up and taken apart, he appeared too weak to hold on to Patrizio Amodeo's territory. More, even though the territory was small, it would have put Emilio in a stronger position, and his enemies within the organization didn't want that.

Emilio accepted the vote graciously, hanging on to his smile while Mario asked that Mitya be brought into the room. Elijah went to get him. Alonzo studied Ulisse and Emilio. They appeared to have regained their genial smiles, but Alonzo was leopard and he smelled the anger under the surface. More, he scented conspiracy.

Ulisse had come prepared to back Emilio's bid for the territory. Ulisse never did anything without getting something out of it. Alonzo just had to figure out what it was that Ulisse wanted from Emilio. Whatever it was had to be extremely important to him. He had aligned himself with a man everyone considered a toothless shark. That made him look weak, but he'd done it in front of the council. Why? The question nagged at Alonzo.

Mitya followed Elijah into the room. He stood absolutely straight, although his skin was nearly gray and beads of sweat stood out on his forehead. He inclined his head and refused to so much as grip the back of a chair for support.

"Sit," Mario commanded. "I see you have not fully recovered."

Elijah pulled out the chair next to him and indicated for Mitya to take the seat. He did so slowly.

"I'm alive, that's what counts," Mitya said.

The next hour was spent with the various bosses asking Mitya questions. Alonzo paid attention to their voices more than their expressions. All the while he watched both Emilio and Ulisse. They both asked questions, but they were no longer confrontational, as if they both had accepted the council's decision.

No way had Emilio accepted it. Anger and the need for revenge came off of him in waves. He sat there smiling, and all the while, Alonzo was certain he was plotting retaliation. But against whom? Mitya? Elijah? Him? Where would his rage be directed, and what form would his retaliation take? Why was Ulisse aligning himself with Emilio? Good questions with no answer.

In the end, Mitya was brought wholly into the organization. He now was boss of Patrizio Amodeo's territory. That meant the alliance was really spread thin. Timur had been approached by Elijah first, but he'd steadfastly and adamantly refused to leave his brother without adequate protection. Timur had no desire to be a boss in any way. He was determined to stay close to Alonzo and Evangeline. Alonzo was secretly pleased, although he wasn't about to let his brother know.

"I believe we're done here, gentlemen," Mario said. "I trust you'll take care of things there, Elijah."

Elijah nodded. Good-byes were said. Coffee and Evangeline's desserts were served. Throughout it all, Emilio and Ulisse entered the conversations and laughed with the others as if they were all good friends. Alonzo didn't believe it for one minute.

19

Evangeline woke, every nerve ending alert and on fire. She didn't have a stitch on, something that happened often. Her night-clothes often ended up in shreds on the floor beside the bed. When she woke, her clothes were gone as if they'd never been. Alonzo was always neat once the sun came up.

Right now, he was devouring her, one of his all-time favorite things to do. She caught his hair in both fists and shifted her head on the pillow to get a better look at him. The moon spilled through the open window. They had made the master bedroom their own and even the covered porch outside their sliding glass door couldn't block that bright ball from illuminating Alonzo's harsh features.

His face was carved in sensual lines. He concentrated on using tongue and teeth to get what he wanted. Her body responded to his growls to be still with more honey and cinnamon spice spilling into his mouth.

"Baby," she whispered. Nothing could make her feel the way Alonzo could. So alive. So loved. No matter what he did to her, she felt thoroughly loved. He enjoyed going down on her. He stayed focused and was in absolute control of her body when he held her still and completely open to him.

She tried not to squirm, but it was impossible, her hips bucking, trying to get closer to his mouth. She knew she was already close. Her body wound tighter and tighter until she wanted to scream for release. He pulled back abruptly, and rubbed his shadowed jaw on both inner thighs. She always found that incredibly sexy when he did that, sending heat ratcheting up another notch.

"Fyodor," she protested. "Stop playing around." But she knew that was exactly what he was doing, playing around. He liked to play — and he was really, really good at it.

He growled but didn't lift his head. One arm clamped tight around her hips, leaving him one free hand — and he was wicked with that hand. His mouth roamed up her inner thigh and then he bit down. At the same time his thumb brushed little caresses over her inflamed clit. She yanked on his hair in retaliation, even as her body spilled more honey for him. It was a vicious circle. He knew every way to bring her body pleasure. His mouth, his teeth, his fingers. He drove her up again and again, right to that precipice, but he never relented, despite her pleading, and let her fall over.

"Fyodor, *please.*" Now she didn't want anything but him. Her mind had gone to complete chaos, a roaring in her ears, blood thundering through her veins.

Alonzo could barely breathe with wanting his woman. Every time he touched her, no matter how often, how long, the addiction to her grew, not lessened. He knew it had nothing to do with sex and everything to do with emotion. He'd had plenty of sex and never once had it been like this. So perfect.

He loved that she never ever stopped him playing. He took her every way he could think of, and he was inventive. Sometimes he was rough. Really rough. She went up in flames for him every time. He loved that she went wild for him. That she was noisy about it. Pleading. Demanding. He loved to hear both.

Her legs were draped over his shoulders and her exotic, spicy scent called to him. He waited another heartbeat while she squirmed and yanked at his hair. He stabbed his tongue deep. She screamed his name, half sobbing, half commanding. She was hotter than hell, burning like a firestorm out of control. He craved the taste of her, and he couldn't get enough of her. Ravenous, he held her still while he took as much as her body would give him. He knew every way to have her spilling more for him.

He was ruthless, using his mouth to drive her higher and higher until she was gasping, pleading, and sounded close to tears. He took her over immediately, loving the hard earthquake tearing through her body. It was brutal. Perfect. The aftershocks providing more of what he wanted.

He didn't wait for the ripples to stop but pushed her right back up. He stroked with his thumb, small caresses designed to make her body his. He sucked on her clit and then used his tongue to draw out the hot liquid spilling out of her just for him. She went wild. He felt feral. Primitive. He growled at her as he took what was his.

She detonated again, a fierce quake that raced up her belly and down her thighs. He rubbed his face along her thighs again and then rose above her, dragging her to him. Her eyes were dazed, that wonderful look she got when she was gone. When he'd sent her to bliss and she couldn't think straight.

"You're mine, Evangeline," he said. A jackhammer drilled over and over in his head. He felt savage. Possessive. He knew she could see the brutality stamped deep, those ruthless lines betraying the fact that his leopard was close. His blood pounded with a terrible need beyond anything he could imagine.

"Yours. Absolutely." Truth rang in her voice. Honesty.

He didn't wait. He couldn't. He pushed into her, inch by slow inch. Her folds were scorching hot, and his breath left his lungs in a hissing rush. She was a fiery inferno, her muscles gripping him so tightly he could barely catch a breath. All the while he watched her face.

Bog. He loved her. *Loved* her. Lust drove him. His leopard nature drove him. Most of all, it was this. Loving her. Watching the beauty of her. That helpless need that took her over. He loved that her gaze clung to his. Her lips parted for her ragged breathing and her hips rose to meet his. Her eyes held love, but also trust. That gift not only of love but of trust. She gave it so willingly.

He couldn't wait another minute. He buried himself deep, slamming home. There was one moment when he savored the feeling of her muscles milking him and then he moved. Hard. Fast. Over and over until she was chanting his name and her nails bit deep into his shoulders. He kept driving deep, taking her with him on the wild, insane ride.

So perfect. So absolutely perfect. "Say it." He bit out the demand between his clenched teeth. He couldn't hold out, not with her scorching heat strangling him, not when she was so close he could feel her body coiling tighter and tighter.

"I love you, Iceman. *My* Iceman."

She could never say it enough. He drove into her again and again so that her body, already scorching hot and tight, clamped down on his cock, a vise like a silken fist wrapped around him, nearly to the point of strangulation. He kept driving into her, a deadly piston that wouldn't stop, the friction pure fire.

She screamed his name, her fists tightening in his hair. The bite of pain added to the wild savage nature inside of him. The orgasm hit like a tidal wave, ripping through her. Powerful. Hard. Vicious. His body nearly seized, the orgasm tearing through him, his balls burning, the rush as his seed jetted into her, again and again. So many times. His body was out of control. Dying. Living. Reborn.

He collapsed over top of her, burying his face in her neck, letting her take his weight. She was soft, her breasts pushing into his chest. He kissed the skin right over her wildly beating pulse. She never complained about his weight or the fact that her ability to breathe was limited, she simply held him tight and waited.

It was times like this, knowing he was heading out into something dangerous, that he realized how much she'd changed his life. How much he loved her and couldn't live without her. He always went to the bakery with her, not so much to do his work but to make certain she was safe. He had existed before her. He'd lived without hope. Now, his life was full and he looked forward to every morning, to every minute of the day. The nights were especially beautiful.

"Honey?" She made the inquiry softly. "What's wrong?"

She knew him so well. To distract her, he nibbled his way across her chin and down her throat to the sweet curve of her breasts, adding several new marks to the fading ones. He loved marking her. One hand slipped down to the junction between her legs, his thumb gliding over her clit while his finger curled inside, pressing against that sweet spot, sweeping back and forth while his teeth and tongue tugged at the nipple of her right breast and his hand was at her left.

She came apart again for him, breathing deep and ragged. He felt every ripple and watched the beauty come over her, flushing her skin, her eyes wide and filled with that glazed look he loved. He held her a long time, kissing her over and over until he knew they both had to get up and shower, to get ready for the day.

He took her in the shower, against the wall, another hard but fast tango, his hands and mouth possessive. It wasn't unusual, but still, she regarded him with suspicion. He had to make certain he told his brother and cousins, if they found a woman, to make certain she wasn't extremely intelligent.

"I won't be coming to the bakery this morning with you. I'll have to meet you later, but I'll take care of things and get there as fast as I can." He dressed in clothes he could remove fast, clothes made specifically for shifters. One of Drake's friends manufactured them. They added needed seconds onto their speed.

Evangeline looked him over with a slight frown. "What are you doin', Fyodor? And don' try to pretend it's nothin'."

"I've got a little business thing this morning."

"It's three in the mornin'."

It never boded well for him when she put her hands on her hips and gave him that look, the one he always wanted to kiss off her face. *Bog,* but she was adorable. He pulled on his shoes. Those were just as special, easily removed when needed. She followed him down the hall to where his brother and cousins waited.

"*All* of my boys are goin'? This doesn't look good. At least tell me you're goin' to be safe."

"I'll keep him safe," Timur promised.

She raised her chin, and Alonzo could have told his brother that wasn't a good sign. "Who will keep you and Gorya and Sevastyan safe, Timur? You count. All of you do. I'm not willin' to lose any of you. Do you have to do this, Fyodor?"

Love for her nearly overwhelmed him. She could bring him to his knees. She didn't ask him again what he was doing, nor did she protest. Clearly she was worried for them and knew it was something big. She also had to assume it was something illegal.

"*Solnyshko moyo,* I can tell you this much. Emilio Bassini is shipping guns overseas disguised as furniture. If we don't stop that shipment, those guns could be in the hands of terrorists. He's a major player in gunrunning. We haven't figured out where his source is yet, but we will." He gave her that much. The truth. She needed to know what she was facing living with him.

She took a breath, comprehension on her face. "All of you are in on this. Now Jake and Drake make sense. They didn't before."

"I'll never be entirely clean, Evangeline. Never. We'll have to go to our graves with others believing we're dirty, and they'll be right. We'll never be out of danger from either side. That's what I've dragged you into."

She didn't hesitate, but then she never did. "I love you, Fyodor. All of you. Your crazy brother and cousins as well. I'm with you one hundred percent. Just be safe. All of you come home. Every single one of you."

He hooked his palm at the nape of her neck, dragged her to him and kissed her hard. It would have to be enough to sustain him until he got back safely.

"Are you ready to go, Evangeline?" Ted Freemont called. "Get a move on."

"Warm up the car, it's freezin'," she called back. "I'm lookin' for my gloves. I'll be right out." She wasn't about to tell him she'd misplaced the keys to the bakery again. It was something she'd done more than once, and they had warned her over and over to hang them up on the key rack.

"You're nuts, woman. It isn't freezing. It's warm this morning," Ted called back. "I'll have Max bring the car around to the front."

"You know I could drive my own car. It's goin' to have problems sittin' in that garage."

"Boss got rid of that death trap a while ago."

Evangeline's head snapped around as she caught up the keys to the bakery. "He did what?" It would be just like him to get rid of her car and not say a word to her. "He'd better not have."

"Got rid of it myself. Had it crushed. He said it was at my discretion, and having been around you, I knew you'd go looking for that piece of junk just out of some misplaced feminine crap independence."

She was *so* going to kick him for that. Evangeline stomped out of the bedroom and down the hall toward the front door. Ted just stood there, his hand wrapped around the doorknob, a grin on his face.

"Don' you pretend you didn't get rid of my car just so I won't kick you, because you did." She'd heard the ring of truth in his voice.

"I'm with the boss on this one. That car wasn't safe." He opened the door. "We've got to get moving if you're going to bake. The kid is meeting us there. He took his motorcycle."

They all called Jeremiah "the kid." Once Alonzo and Elijah were aware she knew Jeremiah was a shifter, he had moved into one of the small rooms over the garage. He liked being around Timur and Gorya, although she wasn't certain why that was. Not when every time she turned around they were boxing with him and beating the crap out of him. Still, he was a male and a shifter, so maybe that was her answer.

Ted opened the door to the backseat and slid in beside her. Ralph opened the door on the other side. Max turned in his seat. "Ralph, would you check the garage? The boss doesn't like it if it isn't locked at all times and I was in such a hurry I think I forgot."

"It's that kind of morning," Ralph said good-naturedly. He closed the door and turned away.

Afterward, she would never know exactly what it was, the scent of Emilio, a note in Max's voice, or the quiet snick of the locks, but she flung herself at the driver just as he turned, gun in hand pointed right at Ted. He pulled the trigger as she hit him. The bullet tore through the back of the seat beside Ted's head, burning his cheek as it flew past.

Evangeline was strong, using her leopard's strength. Gunfire erupted outside the car and she caught a glimpse of Ralph sinking into a crouch, firing his weapon toward the double gates. She twisted the gun from Max's hand and hit him on the side of his head very hard with the barrel. Max slumped down in the seat, blood pouring from his temple.

"I'm going to cover you, Evangeline," Ted said grimly. He had his weapon out as well as his cell phone. "Get into the safe room and don't come out until Alonzo gets back." He punched in numbers and frowned as it went straight to voice mail. He texted frantically with one hand as he looked up at her. "Are you ready?"

"Ted," she hedged.

"Do it." Cars poured into the entrance. "This is a large force. I can only hold them for so long."

She didn't argue. What was the point? Ted and Ralph couldn't possibly stop these men. They weren't shifters, and they were only two men against what looked like an army. She opened the door on Ralph's side and leapt out, ignoring Ted's cursing. Ralph was down, still firing, but he'd been hit at least once. She got an arm around him and began pulling him up.

"Can you walk?" Bullets spat around them. Deliberately she stepped in front of him. She'd noted that none of the bullets came near her. That meant they wanted her alive. Whoever these people were, they weren't going to kill her outright. She began dragging Ralph before he could answer, back toward the house.

Ted stepped around the side of the car to give them cover fire. She propelled Ralph forward, running toward Ted. Just as she reached him, he went down, rolled over and continued firing. "Go. Get the fuck out of here."

She all but shoved Ralph through the front door and raced back for Ted. He sent her a mean look as she wrapped his arm around her.

"Are you out of your fucking mind?" he demanded, trying to limp and run while keeping most of his weight off of her and firing at the advancing wall of men.

"Considerin' that I'm savin' your life, you might be nicer," she informed him snottily as she shoved him inside and slammed the front door. She dropped the bar in place and helped both through the house into the safe room.

"They're jamming the phone lines or something. I can't even get 911," Ted snapped.

She flung the medical kit at him. "I've got to warn Fyodor. I think Emilio sent these men. If I'm right, they're running into a trap."

"Damn it, stay in here," Ted shouted.

She ignored him and slammed the door closed, praying he would lock it on his side. He had cameras and audio. If he couldn't get a message to the cops, at least he could hold out for a few days if she didn't make it back. By that time whatever they were doing to the phone service would be long gone.

Running fast, she moved through the secret panel leading into the wall, closed it, raced for her bedroom and pulled out the small pack she had prepared for just such an emergency. Putting it around her neck she headed for the stairs. There were three safe rooms built into the walls. If she didn't make it out of the house, she could use one of the other rooms, but right now, all that mattered to her was getting to Alonzo.

The intruders would succeed in breaching

the house. The good news was she knew the grounds now. She stealthily opened a window in the guest bedroom and peered out. There were men moving in silence around the house, surrounding it. She didn't wait to see if one of them might be looking up.

Shift. I can slip past them easier than you can.

She'd always done this in human form. She'd played hide-and-seek with a male leopard for years in the swamp. She knew how to cover her tracks, to change her scent, to slip through humans hunting or fishing. Evangeline hesitated.

I learned from you and my mate. He has been teaching me, and I don't get to make many mistakes without his anger.

That much was true. Alonzo's leopard was bad tempered and mean when crossed. He wanted his female to be every bit as good a fighter as he was and he worked nightly with her. Sometimes when she shifted back to human form, Evangeline could barely move, feeling as if she'd been beaten with a baseball bat.

"Be careful. Don't get shot."

She stripped fast and shifted. Bebe slipped out the window onto the long, thick branch that was the beginning of the arboreal highway. She looked down and snarled at the intruders and then back at the house, clearly worried about the two humans they'd left behind.

Don't think about them. We have to get to Fyodor and the others. They're all that matter right now.

Evangeline couldn't think about Emilio's men doing anything crazy like burning down her house, especially with Ted and Ralph needing medical assistance. They had the security screens, even if they cut the electricity. There was a built-in generator.

Her leopard ran along the branches easily, heading toward the highway. *Another leopard. Right there, coming onto the property,* Bebe warned.

Evangeline recognized the rosettes and the way the cat moved. It was Jeremiah. *Let him know we're here.*

Bebe immediately let out a soft chuffing noise. The leopard below them froze and then looked up. Bebe didn't need her human counterpart to tell her what to do. She leapt through the branches until she could land safely on the ground beside the bigger male. Both leopards ran for the safety of the brush just inside of the fence.

Evangeline shifted, reaching for the pack. "Turn around." The men showed no modesty, but she wasn't there yet. She dressed hastily. Jeremiah pulled on a pair of jeans and a jacket.

"I have to warn Fyodor that he's walkin' into a trap. Ted and Ralph are in the safe room off of Fyodor's old bedroom. You'll have to . . ."

"I'm going with you. They'll have to just wait. I tried using my phone before I left and couldn't. Then as I was going down the road, several blocks from here, there were trucks and cars unloading men. I continued up the road until I could get service. It was much farther away than I wanted to go but we needed help. I called Elijah. They'll be coming, and they can get Ted and Ralph aid. I couldn't raise Fyodor and Timur."

She didn't argue with him. He had a motorcycle and she needed a ride. They both looked up at the fence and went over it at the same time. She landed in a crouch. Jeremiah was already on the run. She made a note to herself that she was going to learn to do that. Land running. She followed him as he jogged down the road. Just like Emilio's men, he'd parked away from the property.

"Do you know where they went?" She swung her leg over the bike and wrapped her arms around him, holding tight as the motorcycle roared to life.

"Yes. If I didn't hear from them or they didn't come back, I needed a place to start. As soon as we get service, we'll keep trying to call."

"Did you tell Elijah?"

"Yes. I figured it was too much of a coincidence that they were hitting the house on the very morning the trucks were heading out toward Houston."

Elijah would send help to Alonzo. She knew he would. That made her feel a little better. "If you know the route the trucks are taking, get ahead of them," she shouted.

He nodded, and they tore down the highway. If they could just find them before Alonzo and the others made their move, she knew she could find a way to warn him. Time seemed to inch by as they hurried to catch up.

"How many guards did you pull off of Evangeline?" Alonzo snapped at his brother. "I wanted leopards on her, Timur, not regular soldiers."

"We're stretched thin right now. We need to pull in our best people if we're going to take these guns without killing anyone. You want trigger-happy soldiers who might see some of us moving faster than normal, then fine, we'll switch people around."

"Who's. On. Evangeline?" Alonzo snarled. The car ran with no lights, trailing behind the car guarding the freight trucks Emilio had sent out.

"Lighten up, *brat.*" Timur leaned toward his brother. "Do you think for one moment I would take a chance with her life? Not. Likely. I put two of our most experienced soldiers on her. Ted Freemont and Ralph Hurley. You know them. You've used them multiple times for all kinds of jobs. You even like them, and you don't like anyone."

"I don't like you right now. I wanted shifters on her."

"The moment I heard you were coming with us, I had to put the shifters on you. You didn't give me much choice, Fyodor. The boss shouldn't be doing a ride-along. You stay at home and direct from there."

"I have a bad feeling." He never ignored his gut. The last thing he wanted was for his brother and cousins to walk into a trap or be outmanned. He couldn't really be angry with Timur when his brother was doing his job, protecting him.

"All the more reason for you to stay home."

Alonzo ignored his brother's terse statement. They had eliminated the threat to Evangeline. He'd kept digging until he turned up the fact that the hit on her life didn't outlive Patrizio. With him dead, no other threats were even uttered in whispers. Mitya was safe, recuperating at Elijah's in order to learn more about what they were trying to accomplish and how they had to go about it from Elijah and Drake.

Some of the knots in his gut eased just a bit. Evangeline had insisted she go back to work a week earlier than he'd wanted her to go, but Doc had given her the okay as long as she had help. She'd agreed to that. They had a young man working for her, a plant of course, but she'd figured that out the moment he walked through the door. Alonzo loved that she was so smart. On the other hand, it made it impossible to fool her.

Jeremiah Wheating was leopard. He was young, but he'd been trained by some of the best. Elijah trusted him, and that went a long way to ease Alonzo's mind. Jeremiah had been with Evangeline at the bakery for a couple of weeks and that had given Alonzo time to observe him. He didn't want the work there, he'd prefer to be a bodyguard for Elijah, but after Timur had talked to him, he'd settled down. Alonzo was fairly certain his brother had threatened to kill him slowly, inch by inch, if Evangeline so much as got a burn on her little finger.

"She calls us her boys," Timur said.

Alonzo shot his brother a quick glance. There was no inflection in the voice at all, but just the absence told Alonzo that mattered to Timur. Evangeline had gotten to him. He was protecting her, not just for Alonzo.

"She does," he agreed.

Timur shook his head. "I hope you know how lucky you are."

"I know." And he did. Every single morning he woke up to her. He went to bed at night with her after running their leopards. He knew. He'd had nothing before Evangeline; with her, he had it all.

He'd woken her early knowing he had to get on the road. He knew he'd taken her a little roughly. He sometimes felt desperate for her. Insane for her. Like a wild, feral beast that had to ensure she knew she belonged to him. He had to hear her say it. He had to taste her, all that wild honey that drove him crazy. He had to see the helpless pleasure on her face. Mostly, he had to see that love for him shining in her eyes.

He'd set up an office in the back room of the bakery. Timur hadn't objected, and now he knew why. His brother had come to look upon Evangeline as a younger sister. She had known instantly that Alonzo was going to do something dangerous. Timur objected strenuously to his telling her anything, but she deserved to know. He *wanted* her to know, to go into their life together with her eyes wide open. It was important to him that Evangeline love the man — the real one. To his astonishment, she did.

"With Mitya taking over Amodeo's territory, we're spread very thin, Fyodor. I've put in a call to the others from our lairs that we know left after we did. I've kept a loose connection with them. If they had planned to turn me over to Lazar or Rolan, they would have done it. I heard through the grapevine that they have prices on their heads as well."

"You and I both know that can be manufactured."

"I'll vet them first with Gorya and Sevastyan. No leopard can tell us a lie without our knowing. With the three of us there it will be all the easier to know if any one of them is a plant and a danger to us."

"We need to recruit humans as well, Timur. Joshua and Elijah both have a mixture. They are just as valuable. Ted Freemont and Ralph Hurley are two men I trust. They're good soldiers and it's lucky you assigned them to Evangeline." He might have turned the car around had it been anyone else.

"We still have Arnotto's network. Most of his soldiers remained loyal once they were aware they'd been duped. There were only a few that left and maybe one or two I keep my eye on." Timur eyed his brother. "We need more leopards, Fyodor. Half will be going off with Mitya. Even if Drake pulls in others from Borneo, we'll still need to recruit those we can trust."

Alonzo sighed. "Interview them, Timur. And then keep a close watch. I don't trust anyone we aren't absolutely certain of with Evangeline."

The traffic was particularly light this time of the morning. The moon shone on the strips of foliage on either side of the highway. Alonzo and Timur both scanned with the eyes of a leopard, seeing in the dark, looking for anything unusual.

Alonzo's eyebrow went up. "You're keeping an eye on one or two of our soldiers? You didn't tell me you were worried we might have a mole."

"I always worry we might have a mole. If we have them, it stands to reason someone else does as well," Timur pointed out. "I'm responsible for your security. It's my job to worry."

As they approached an overpass, movement above caught their eyes simultaneously. Two leopards prowled along the walkway where people could cross on foot. Alonzo sat up straight, his heart in his throat. He'd recognize his woman anywhere, anytime, no matter what form she took. Jeremiah had to be with her.

"What the hell?" Timur snapped. He swore in Russian. "I'm going to kill that cub. He's supposed to protect her, not bring her out here because she's worried."

"The two trucks are slowing down, Fyodor, pulling off the highway to the access road," Gorya reported. "Looks as if the lead truck has a flat. Good for us, bad for them. Sevastyan took out their tires like a pro."

The knots in Alonzo's gut were back, tighter than ever. "Hang back, Kirill," he told their driver. "It's a trap, Gorya. That's why Evangeline and Jeremiah took a chance being seen as leopards. Pull ahead of the access road and when you get to a spot where we can't be seen by anyone in the trucks, pull off the road. We'll go on foot, but all of you know, this is going to be kill or be killed."

"That's why we brought all shifters," Timur noted.

The two cars pulled over to the edge of

the freeway and let the passengers out before the drivers took off to race up to the next exit. They would come back on the access road. With the cars moving on, those in the trucks wouldn't know for certain if they'd been followed or not.

Timur slipped from the car and ran, in a crouch, ridding himself of clothes and shifting with blinding speed. Alonzo remained fully dressed, his weapons out. He wasn't going to allow his leopards to get shot. Someone had to return fire. If Emilio's men saw him there, they would concentrate on him, giving the leopards time to start tearing through the soldiers.

He heard the back door of one of the trucks raise and then snippets of conversation. The men didn't like the wait. They especially didn't like that they couldn't see where the cars that had been following in the distance had gone.

"What the hell is that?" someone called out and then screamed.

At once there was gunfire. Bright flashes of red and orange in the night. Alonzo ran straight up to the first truck, the one with the flat tire. The driver and the guard occupying the passenger seat were crouched by the tire pretending they were examining it. They turned toward him, the guard lifting his gun. Something struck him between the eyes with deadly force, throwing him backward. Alonzo shot the driver and kept going.

Jeremiah must have brought his rifle with him. Elijah had told Alonzo that the boy was a marksman, and now he believed it. It was a hell of a shot to make in the dark. Men poured from the backs of both trucks, so many he wasn't certain the few leopards they'd brought could handle them all, especially since they were armed to the teeth and firing indiscriminately at every movement. Jeremiah's rifle sounded off steadily, and men went down.

Alonzo chose his targets as carefully as the boy, trying to make each one count, making certain to protect his men. Two men loomed up behind his brother's leopard. Timur was taking down a man with a semiautomatic as the other two rounded the truck and spotted him. Both weapons went up. Alonzo had just fired his last bullet and hadn't yet slammed a new magazine in. He shifted as they brought up their guns, rushing them as he did. He had speed — incredible speed — and the surprise and shock of seeing a man shifting in midair was on his side. He hit both men with the force of a freight train, taking them both to the ground, hearing bones break as he did so.

He killed them both with a vicious swipe of his paws, taking out the jugulars and moving on to the next one. More leopards poured in from all sides, taking down the men while two more rifles were added to Jeremiah's as Elijah's men joined in. The battle was won quickly and decisively.

Elijah's men checked the dead while Elijah and Alonzo broke open the furniture. Guns spilled out but with them were stashes of cash. Hundreds of thousands of dollars. They exchanged a long look.

"Ulisse is moving his counterfeit money along with Emilio's weapons. He wanted the international transport and buyers Emilio has," Elijah said.

"There is no way we can take care of these bodies," Alonzo pointed out.

"No, this is going to be one of those mysteries the M.E. lives for. Death by leopards and bullets. What in the world? The tabloids will have a field day. We walk away from this. Let the police have the guns and money. Emilio will answer to them."

Alonzo looked at him. "Tell me."

Elijah sighed. "Emilio and probably Ulisse sent a team to your house. Two of your men were shot. They're at the hospital. Evangeline saved them and then she went tearing off to warn you."

Alonzo closed his eyes briefly. For a moment he could barely breathe. He let Elijah and Timur push him away from the scene of the battle. The other leopards were melting into the night as well. "I'm going to tie that woman to my bed and just let her live there. I'll have to put a thousand guards around the house, and even then I won't be satisfied that she's safe."

"Welcome to my world," Elijah said.

"Let's get out of here. I need to have a few words with my woman before she goes to work."

"Not that it will do you any good, but I wish you luck," Elijah said and then trotted off with a wave of his hand.

Gorya opened the door for him to slide into the passenger side, Timur right behind him.

"I've got a few words for her as well," Timur muttered.

For some reason, that made Alonzo smile.

20

"When did you learn to do hair?" Catarina asked Emma. "That's beautiful and so perfect for her dress."

Evangeline looked at herself in the mirror. Emma had woven magic with her hair. Half was up in an elaborate twist of curls while the rest fell in waves and curls down her back. Catarina had done her makeup. It was very subtle and light, but a little smokier on the eyes than she'd ever worn. She loved it.

Emma laughed. "I didn't go to school for hair, but I watch videos all the time and do Andraya's hair as well as my own. I knew what her dress looked like and searched for the perfect hairdo."

"You found it," Siena said. She hadn't been able to go wedding dress shopping with Evangeline. Both Emma and Catarina had, as well as Saria Donovan. Drake had brought his wife out for the wedding. She had insisted on coming early for the preparations.

Evangeline was grateful to the women. She might have run for the hills if she'd been alone.

"Just so you're warned," Siena said. "Fyodor will get bossier once you're married."

Evangeline shook her head. "That's just not possible. He can't get any worse."

The women laughed. "He will," Saria confirmed while Emma and Catarina nodded. "Just ignore him, that's what I do. Drake is really bad now that I'm pregnant. I mean really, unless there's a problem with the pregnancy, women can do everythin' they did before, right?"

"I've always had a problem with pregnancies," Emma disclosed, "so I wouldn't know."

"Look at me," Siena said. "I think Elijah has X-ray vision and can see through walls. Even if he's at the other end of the house, if I move, he knows it and saunters in to give me a lecture."

"We're not even going to talk about Jake. I lived in his house before I married him and thought it would be impossible for him to get any bossier," Emma said. "Then I married him. He got worse. Then I got pregnant. The man just escaped getting shot several times. It's only because he's great in bed and really hot that he still lives."

Evangeline sighed. "Great. I don' just have Fyodor trying to boss me around, but Timur, Sevastyan, Gorya and Mitya are every bit as impossible as well. I might have to rethink this gettin' married idea."

"Um, it's a little too late," Siena pointed out. "You have about five minutes."

"It's never too late. I'm a shifter. I can go out the window."

"Actually," Siena said. "It wouldn't do you any good. Fyodor told Elijah you'd probably try to be a runaway bride. He has guards on every door and window we have. There isn't going to be any running."

The women burst out laughing. Evangeline smoothed her hand down her dress. She loved it. They'd found it in a boutique Emma knew of. The dress fit like a glove after the seamstress had worked her magic. In white with a sweetheart neckline, the dress seemed timeless. The lace appliqué was romantic and lovely, flowing over tulle, creating a beautiful sheath that looked elegant and bohemian. Buttons were covered over the zipper and corset closure.

"Well, the dress is beautiful," she hedged. "I guess I'll go through with it and he'll just have to learn I don' get bossed so easily."

"It is gorgeous," Saria said. "You're beautiful, Evangeline."

"I'm going to go get seated," Siena said.

Evangeline watched her go. "Is she really all right? Elijah seems genuinely worried about her. How much danger is she in?"

Emma sighed. "Carrying triplets is tricky for anyone. The babies share the same placenta. That's a rare condition and can be difficult for the babies. They're taking extra precautions and following Doc's advice to the letter. They're both worried about the babies, but Elijah worries about her. In the beginning he considered terminating the pregnancy so she wouldn't be at risk. Don't get me wrong, he wants them, but he's terrified of losing Siena."

"Is that a possibility? I mean, a *real* threat to her?"

Emma shrugged. "She says no more than anyone else. I have to believe her. In any case, Elijah conceded and allowed her to carry, so she's compromising by following every single thing Doc says and trying to make Elijah a little less worried."

"Wow. I hope she's all right. Do you know what she did? For our weddin' present she gifted the Arnotto estate over to us. Signed it over just like that. We had planned to buy it, but she refused. She said Fyodor was the closest thing she had to a brother and she wanted us to have it. She kept the vineyards and winery but the entire rest of the estate is ours."

Catarina nodded. "She's like that. So sweet."

"We can't take it of course, but wow."

"You have to take it, Evangeline. It would mean the world to her," Emma said. "We talked about it. Her memories aren't the best there and she wants someone to raise a family and be happy there. Obviously you and Fyodor love the place. She wants it to be you."

Evangeline bit down on her lower lip and Catarina immediately shook her head. "Don't ruin your makeup."

"I'll tell Fyodor, but it's worth a fortune."

"It's what she wants," Emma persisted. "She hopes you have lots of children and they're all very, very happy there."

"Having children means gettin' pregnant," Evangeline pointed out. "That means bossy man gets ever bossier. I don' think I could handle that without throwin' somethin' at him."

"Shifter males are a pain sometimes," Saria said. "I'm as healthy as a woman can get. It isn't a multiple pregnancy and the doctor says I can do anythin' I want to do.

Drake doesn't take that same attitude, and he's pretty mellow most of the time."

"Mellow?" Catarina's eyebrows shot up. "Eli wouldn't know mellow if it bit him on the butt."

A knock on the door had Evangeline's heart racing. Catarina leaned over and kissed her cheek. "I'm up first."

Emma squeezed Evangeline's hand. "Be brave. You look beautiful. Fyodor won't be able to take his eyes off of you."

Saria hugged her hard. "I'm so happy for you. You deserve this. Pauline and Amos have come, and so has Charisse. I didn't want you to be so shocked you fainted or something when you saw them out there."

Evangeline caught her hand before she could step out the door. "I'm so in love with him, Saria. I had no idea it could be like this."

Saria nodded in understanding. "That's exactly how I feel every day still."

Music began to play, and then Bijou Breaux — or rather Bijou Boudreux — began to sing. Bijou had grown up in the bayou with Saria and had recently married Saria's brother Remy. Her voice filled the house, and Catarina, Emma and then Saria went down the hall to the room where everyone was seated.

Elijah waited by the door and offered Evangeline his arm. "You look beautiful."

"Thank you."

"Nervous?" He walked her up the hall to the doorway where the ceremony would take place.

He had to hear her heart tripping so fast she was afraid she might have a heart attack. "Yes."

"Don't be. He's the right man for you. This is a good thing."

She nodded her head and then they stepped into the doorway and everyone stood up. She saw Fyodor. He was in a suit, that inevitable suit that looked so good on him. His eyes were on her, only her, and the room fell away until there was only him. The man born for her. The man she was born for. She loved belonging to him. She loved even more that he belonged to her.

"You ready?" Elijah asked.

She nodded. She was more than ready. She walked straight up the aisle to the man she loved. Elijah put her hand in Fyodor's and his fingers closed around hers. Tight. Protective. Deep inside, her leopard yawned and stretched.

I told you so. Bebe always wanted to have the last word.